CAPTAIN TO THE BRIDGE!
 RED ALERT!
  ALL HANDS TO BATTLE STATIONS!
  THIS IS NOT A DRILL!
  CAPTAIN TO THE BRI—

The first impact was felt more than heard, a booming, shaking roar that knocked them off their feet. The lights died, and, through the bulkhead that led to Hangar One, they heard the horrible sound of air whistling away into space, of screams and cries and alarm bells dying off when the air that carried them had vanished into space.

"Oh my God, they've hulled Hangar One," Sir George said, his voice deep with shock. "They're all dead in there. My God."

Joslyn climbed to her feet. The gloomy red of the emergency lighting system flickered on, and she saw Sir George striding purposefully across the deck, toward the airlock at the aft end and the nearest way to the bridge.

ROGER MACBRIDE ALLEN

ROGUE POWERS

BAEN SCIENCE FICTION BOOKS

ROGUE POWERS

This is a work of fiction. All the characters and events portrayed in this book are fictional, and any resemblance to real people or incidents is purely coincidental.

A Baen Books Original

Baen Publishing Enterprises
260 Fifth Avenue
New York, N.Y. 10001

First printing, September 1986

ISBN: 0-671-65584-1

Cover art by Alan Gutierrez

Printed in the United States of America

Distributed by
SIMON & SCHUSTER
TRADE PUBLISHING GROUP
1230 Avenue of the Americas
New York, N.Y. 10020

Dedication

For Mom, who shared her love,
taught me self-confidence, and
gave me the world's greatest middle name.

CHAPTER ONE

January, 2115

Aboard LPS *Venera*

The ship stank.

The *Venera*'s ventilation system had been shot up two days after the hijacking, when the Survey Service students had tried to get the ship back. The students had failed, of course: They were armed with only a few side arms the Guardians hadn't found, and the Guards controlled the ship, had all the heavy guns, had all the advantages. The Guards had killed a few more Survey personnel, taken the side arms, spaced the bodies, confined the survivors to their cabins, and that was that.

But the Guards were stupid enough to fire heavy ammo through life-support equipment. Now, twenty-one days after the hijacking, the air pumps wheezed and shuddered instead of humming. The scrubbers weren't working properly and the whole ship was rich with the smell of bodies and fear and burned-out machinery. Everyone had a headache, which probably meant that the carbon dioxide count was going up. And the water was starting to smell like the bottom of a pond. The few members of *Venera*'s crew who were still alive could probably have patched things up, but they were confined to quarters, two to a cabin, like everyone else. Either the Guards couldn't do the repairs or they didn't care how bad things got.

1

The Guardians were human and spoke English. But no one in the League had ever heard of them. Somewhere, somehow, out among the uncharted stars, the Guardians must have gone off to settle their own world and hide from the rest of humanity. At least that was one theory that made sense. The Guards themselves didn't explain anything.

Lieutenant Lucille Calder, Royal Australian Navy, was locked up in her cabin, but she was a good enough pilot to *feel* the clumsiness in the way the Guards handled the *Venera*'s controls. She knew how much fuel the *Venera* had carried. She carefully timed the burns the Guards made and estimated how many gravities of thrust they used. She kept a rough running account in her head of how much fuel this thumb-fingered crowd of barbarians was wasting as they corrected and over-corrected and re-corrected their errors. Bad piloting wouldn't kill them just yet—there was still a fair amount of fuel left. On the other hand, the fouled air and water might be enough to do them in very soon. For the sake of Guardian and prisoner alike, *Venera* had to get somewhere fast.

But Lucy and the other survivors of the hijacking had no idea where *Venera* was being taken. The viewscreens were shut off, so there were no stars to look at—whatever good that would have done—and there was no real way of telling if they had remained in normal space or made one or more jumps into C^2 space, where the ship's velocity was kicked up to the square of the speed of light. Lucy knew nothing, could do nothing, could see nothing. She didn't like it.

She stared across the tiny cabin at her bunkmate, Cynthia Wu. Ensign Wu was from High Singapore's tiny Defense Force, an outfit with little more to do than track the endless stream of cargo ships that called on the huge Earth-orbiting city. She was used to waiting, to dull patches. Lucy wasn't so lucky. The deep-space fleet of the Royal Australian Navy had trained her for command, for quick decisions and independent action. She needed to be in control, to have some effect on what happened to her. She needed a viewport to see out of, an idea of where they were going, an idea of why they were being taken there. She wanted to know who these surly men were who called themselves the Guardians. She had to know what they wanted with the *Venera*—and whether or not she would live through this.

And she wanted a shower. Lucy's mother was an Australian aborigine, and her father the descendant of British stock. They had raised her on a huge range station, a sheep ranch, at the edge of the desert, where the Sun baked down and made a person sweat and smell. Both Mom and Dad had come from families where you weren't allowed to bring that odor inside. That's why there was a showerbath outside. And now Lucy had been indoors with the smell of many unwashed bodies—including her own—for the better part of a month.

Lucille Calder was a short, stocky woman, dark-complexioned with short-cropped, brownish-blond hair. With a pug nose and a hint of a double chin, she would never be called pretty, but she didn't much care about that. Pretty wasn't her job.

For the thousandth time, Lucy looked across the cabin and watched Wu calmly turn over the page of her book and continue reading. For the thousandth time, Lucy overcame the urge to grab the book out of Wu's hand and heave it at the bulkhead. But even at the moment she was ready to commit mayhem against her cabinmate, Lucy knew Cynthia Wu was probably the best person she could have been locked up with. Wu had patience, and faith in the power of logic and the careful examination of possibilities. Those were things Lucy had to learn from somewhere.

Lucy wished the ship was under spin so she could at least pace the deck. It was hard to expend nervous energy in zero-gee without literally bouncing off the walls. She undid the restraint line that held her to her bunk and pushed herself toward the hatch. There was a peephole in it that let you see out into the corridor. Not that anything was ever out there but another gray bulkhead. Floating in mid-air, she sighed and peered out the hole. Nothing there—

Quite suddenly, she found herself pasted to the deck, a roaring noise filling the cabin. The goddamned Guards had fired the main engines without any warning again. Lucy swore to herself and got up off the deck. She hit the stopwatch function on her wrist-aid and began timing the burn. It felt like a shade under a standard gee and a half this time.

Wu didn't even look up from her book. Lucy wondered which of the two of them was being more foolish: Wu, for doing nothing at all, or she, for fussing over thrusts and burn times that wouldn't really tell her anything useful.

But *this* burn went on a long time. By Lucy's timing, the engines fired for twenty minutes and a few seconds. In the ringing silence after the roar of the engines, she worked out the resulting acceleration in her head—about eighteen kilometers a second. *That* meant something. No reasonable flight between two points in a star system would require such a big change in velocity. On the other hand, eighteen klicks a second was a fairly modest relative motion between two stars.

It had to mean that the *Venera* had indeed made a C^2 jump. *Venera* must be matching velocity in a new star system.

"Cynthia," she said quietly. "We're here."

Wu looked at her sharply. "How do you know?"

"That was a burn to match velocity between two star systems, and if you're trying to hide where you're going, you do that after you get to the new star. Besides, that burn must have just about emptied the tanks. They wouldn't risk running out of fuel unless they were in range of their own people."

Wu closed her book. "God, Luce, I think you're right."

The two of them waited in silence, listening, attentive, for an hour or more. Then, suddenly, there was a series of bumps and jumps as the Guardian pilot used the trim thrusters to fine-tune his course. For a long time, there was no sound but the complaints of the overstrained ventilation system. Finally, more bumps and stutters from the trim thrusters and then, far-off and faint, a series of dull thunks and clanks.

"Docking collar," Lucy said.

There was a series of sharper clacking noises. "And there go the capture latches," Wu said.

They could hear voices now, bellowing, yelling, the sounds of every gangway crew that had ever brought a ship into port and secured her in a berth. The air changed, became cleaner, sweeter, as the ship's air mingled with the atmosphere of whatever it was they had docked to.

They heard the rattle of keys and the sound of angry, urgent voices. Finally, the hatch to their cabin slammed open, and a man in battle armor hung in the hatchway. "Get your stuff and move," he barked, his voice made deep and booming by the suit's speaker system. "Head to the main sternward hatch and through the airlock into the station. Do what any Guard tells you to do and you might not get hurt." He turned, grabbed at a handhold, and pulled himself down to the next cabin without looking to see what Lucy and Cynthia did.

Lucy had a mad impulse to race after him, to smash the faceplate on his suit, to demand an explanation, to run like hell, to do something, anything—and then she turned to see Wu calmly packing up her few belonging into her duffle bag. Lucy pulled herself to her locker and did the same. She would have to learn patience, if she wanted to live.

The stern airlock was a knot of chaos. Guardians in battle-armor took no nonsense, answered no questions, did nothing but grab at their prisoners and heave them through the hatch and down a connecting tunnel. There was a viewport by the airlock, and Lucy managed to get a quick peek through it. She caught a quick glimpse of a fair-sized orbital station of some sort. The Guards were still grabbing anyone who didn't move fast enough to please them. Lucy decided that she didn't need some metal-clad goon groping her, and got through the tunnel unassisted.

She emerged in a large hemispherical loading bay, surrounded by baffled, angry, frightened classmates. Her fellow prisoners were still coming through the hatch, which was set in the base of the hemisphere, and led to the *Venera*. Lucy tried to count the people in the bay, to see how many of her classmates had stayed alive and made it this far, but they were still in zero-gee and it was impossible to keep track of all the men and women hovering or drifting in the air long enough to tote them up.

Prisoners were still struggling through the airlock tunnel. A scuffle of some sort broke out across the loading bay. Lucy couldn't see much through the tangle of floating bodies, but she could hear shouting and meaty thuds. Then three small, perfect, globes of bright red blood sailed quietly past her and splattered onto the bulkhead in slow motion.

"AW RIGHT, SHUT UP!" An overamplified voice boomed through the bay. "SHUT UP! Make your way down a bulkhead and set your feet on the flat deck of the bay. There are handholds all around the edge of the dome at waist height and I want you to grab one and stay put. I'm gonna get a head count, and nobody is going anywhere until I do, so clear the center of this bay, get off of the dome wall, and get down to the flat deck. Line up around the edge of the dome. Move it!"

Slowly, with a lot of muttering and grumbling, the prisoners did as they were told. Lucy spotted Cynthia Wu at the base of the dome and headed over toward her, towing her duffle bag.

"Hey, Luce. There you are. Now maybe we get some answers," Cynthia said.

"At least we're out of that cabin. And into some cleaner air," Lucy said.

"Give thanks for small favors. We won't see any big ones."

"PIPE DOWN!" The bay was just about clear, and now

they could see the speaker, a heavy-set man in his forties, standing on the flat deck of the bay. He was in full battle-armor, his faceplate open. He wore magnetic boots and clomped to the center of the deck, holding a clipboard. What looked like sergeants' stripes were painted on the arms of his suit. "Awright. Now, I'm gonna do a roll call, and you'd better cooperate, because nobody's going anywhere until everyone is accounted for. Call out when you hear your name. And say whether you were crew or passenger on the *Venera*. I gotta split this out into two lists later. Ackerman, Daniel."

"Yo!"

"Passenger or crew, Ackerman?"

"Passenger."

"Right. Akomo, Dwight."

"Present. As the senior surviving member of *Venera*'s crew, I demand—"

"Shuddup, boy. You ain't where you can demand anything. Calder, Lucille."

"Present. Passenger."

"Danvers, Joseph."

"Present. Passenger."

"Desk- Desk—"

"Deskophsky, Dmitiri. Present. Passenger."

"Okay. Right. Entin, Robert. . . ."

Lucy waited out the roll call with the rest of them, keeping count herself. Two men turned up missing, and there was a twenty-minute delay until it was discovered they were still locked in their cabin aboard the *Venera*. Finally, it was over. Five crew and fifty-three passengers were in the bay, still alive. Twelve crew and sixty Survey Service personnel had set off from Bandwidth.

"That does it. Now stay put and keep it down." The sergeant hit a stud on the arm of his suit and spoke into a helmet mike. "Captain? All present, accounted for, and ready for you in Bay Three, sir."

*   *   *

Captain Lewis Romero pressed the mike key on his desk intercom. "Thank you, Sergeant. I'll be there directly." Romero's office was in the spin-section of the station, under the 1.13 gees of his home world, Capital. As befitted the commander, it was the largest and most luxurious office in the orbital station. As befitted the commander of a small post located in a backwater rear area of an over-extended military, Romero was an ignoramus. Competent officers were too much in demand to waste one on what amounted to garrison duty.

But Romero's back was straight, his uniform was pressed and cleaned at all times, his jackboots (which were more than slightly incongruous on a space station) were gleaming, and his black hair and moustache were neatly trimmed, and that was all that was required of him. At the moment, his sallow face bore its usual expression—a patently synthetic look of friendly interest. He spent a lot of time in front of a mirror, rehearsing facial expressions. Romero saw himself as a reasonable fellow, ready to listen, who led by gentle persuasion and example. He was proud of the effort he put into appearances. After all, if one didn't look the part, how were the troops to know who the boss-man was?

He pressed the call button on his desk, and within a minute an answering *beep* came from the console. His escort was ready. He stepped out of his office to find the four surly-looking troopers in their full dress uniforms, two on either side of the doorway. They formed up, two ahead and two behind him. "To Bay Three," Romero said. They escorted him to the lift. Romero, so concerned with appearances, would have been horrified to know how foolish his men thought the whole idea of an escort squad.

The lift car arrived and the five of them squeezed into it. Without waiting for instruction, the two troopers on either side of him knelt down, a bit awkwardly in the tight space, and each pushed a small stud set into the heel of Romero's boots. That powered up the electromagnets in the boots, making them suitable for walking the corridors in the zero-gee section of the station. Romero had had them made up specially. They looked a great deal better than standard mag work shoes, which clashed horribly with his jet-black uniform. The elevator door opened, and there was a slight pause while the escorts changed into standard mag boots. Finally they made their way to Bay Three. The head of the escort detail opened the hatch and they ventured out into the center of the large deck, stepping most carefully.

The first thing that struck Romero was the stench. Well, these poor devils couldn't help that. Lieutenant Higgins had taken their ship quite a while ago, and a ship under guard had little time for sanitary questions. Still, perhaps he ought to have a word with Higgins about keeping CIs cleaner in future. The smell was quite ghastly. Romero did not allow any reaction to the odor to cross his face, but held to a stern-but-fair expression that seemed quite suited to the occasion. He took a good look at what was going to be the replacement technical staff. Damn shame that *Ariadne*'s whole tech crew had been shipped out with the main fleet, but such were the needs of the times.

But what of their replacements? A motley bunch. Every color of the rainbow, but then that was true of practically every gang of CIs ever taken. They seemed to have no idea about the foolishness of mixing the races. And their women! Women not only in the military, but outranking men, if he followed the insignia. Lieutenant Higgins had reported that a woman—and a black one at that—had been *Venera*'s skipper, before he shot her. He stared hard at one or two of the white men they had bagged in this haul. How could they bring themselves to take orders from some blackamoor female? Blackamoor. That was a good word. Much more refined than "nigger" or "darkie," and yet clearly indicating an opinion. Suited to use by an officer. He must remember it.

Finally, Romero completed his inspection and spoke. "Good day to all of you, and welcome to Guardian Orbital Station *Ariadne*. My name is Captain Lewis Romero, commander of G.O.S. *Ariadne*. Let me start straight off by clarifying your status. You are not prisoners of war, or technically prisoners of any sort. You are under the jurisdiction of the Guardians of the Planetary Commonwealth of Capital. Under Guardian law, you are Conscripted Immigrants—CIs—and have the rights and obligations of any other sort of immigrant." Romero didn't mention that there *were* no other sorts of immigrants. They'd find that out soon enough.

"Now, you were brought here to work. Work well, pay attention to your duties, and many of you may well prove eligible for Guardian citizenship. Sloth, inefficiency, or refusal to obey orders will gain you nothing and could cost you dearly." He paused meaningfully, then went on in a more cheerful tone. "But, I'm sure there won't be any such difficulties. You are here to work. Work hard, and you will be treated well. I think that about covers it. Sergeant Mosgrove here will arrange for you to be escorted to quarters and—ah—cleaned up. Then we can see about explaining your duties to you." Romero turned as if to go when a high, clear voice called out.

It was Cynthia Wu. "Excuse me, Captain, but just so I've got this straight. It sounds like you've prettied it up, but we've been kidnapped and brought here as skilled slave labor. Is that about right?"

Romero flushed angrily. The insolence! And from a tiny little doll of a Chinaman's girl. He chose to ignore her. No response at all seemed best to him. He calmed himself and said "Sergeant Mosgrove. You may commence with the processing of the priso—of the immigrants, Sergeant."

"Yessir." Mosgrove saluted Captain Romero and watched as his commanding officer and escort turned to leave the bay. The sergeant glared at Romero's back with undisguised contempt. He didn't do a damned thing to her! This captain was all spit and polish and no backbone. In a real outfit the little Chink slut would be a dead and bloody pulp by now. That was the way to set an example. But if the captain wanted to ignore it, the captain could deal with the results. "Aw right. Now I'm gonna take you in groups of six for cabin assignments. The sooner we're done, the sooner you can wash and eat."

Exhausted by their nerve-wracking journey and glad for the chance at showers and hot food, the *Venera* survivors settled in without much argument. The Survey Service prisoners began to learn about their new home.

Ariadne Station was a fairly standard design. It was made up of three cylinders linked together through their common axis, like three fat tin cans stacked end to end. The three were simply called *A* Drum, *B* Drum, and *C* Drum. *B* Drum, the center cylinder, was spun up to simulate one Capital gee, 1.13 Earth gravities, at its outermost deck. The two outer cylinders, *A* and *C*, were zero-gee work areas.

Ariadne was a communications center and a space traffic control station, tracking the orbital tugs and other craft, assigning orbits to spacecraft moving in orbit of the planet below.

The station was a gloomy, uncomfortable place—or at least those parts of the station the Survey Service prisoners could get to were. As with all such spun-for-gravity systems, the closer to the axis a deck was, the weaker the force of simulated gravity. Lucy and Cynthia found themselves assigned to a small, bare, austere cabin with four other women on Deck Three, the living area nearest to zero-spin. All the "Conscripted Immigrants" were on Three and Four. Decks One and Two were nearer zero-gee, but housed the command and communications centers. Deck Six was furthest from the spin axis. That was split between officers' country, sick bay, the commissary, and some engineering and exercise areas.

The CIs' barracks decks were painted a uniform gunmetal gray, and the lighting was kept dim to save power. The cabins were tiny, cramped, and stuffy. Nothing folded up into the walls to make more room. The beds were welded in place, and the one chair, which was bolted to the deck, was bare aluminum and usually too cold to sit

on. There was no storage space, and keeping the place at
all tidy meant stuffing everything back into the single
duffle bag each of them had. The duffles themselves took
up a large part of the cabin. The six women settled on the
convention of keeping them on the bunks during the day
and stacking them in the corner to sleep.

The Guards wasted no time in getting some work out of
their new "immigrants." It seemed the CIs were to replace a Guardian crew that was being shipped out to other
duties. The Survey Service prisoners were hurriedly trained
to do the technical work of the station, often literally with
guns to their heads.

Cynthia might have gotten away with speaking up in
Bay Three, but the CIs quickly learned that was an exception. Several of the Survey students protested their treatment and were beaten severely. That, at least, the Guards
didn't try to make mysterious. They were quite happy to
let the CIs know what would happen if they didn't cooperate. There were further protests and further punishments,
but nothing changed the situation. The Survey Service
CIs were on *Ariadne* Station whether they liked it or not.
Escape was clearly impossible, and Guards controlled the
guns, the food, the water.

The CIs were expected to run the station's communications
center, operate the space traffic control system, manage the
station computer system, and generally do routine technical
work. Failure to cooperate got them nothing but another
beating. The Guards made that simple to understand.

The League of Planets Survey Service had chosen the
brightest young people from the military services of every
League member and trained them to be skilled pilots,
ready to adapt to new situations. The CIs—they were
already calling themselves that—mastered their new jobs
quickly. It helped that the equipment was more or less
familiar, as if the Guardians had begged, borrowed, and
stolen whatever old and new designs they could get their
hands on, and copied them.

The CIs tried to protest, to sabotage, to avoid work.

Until Wilkie was shot. Wilkie hadn't done anything. They shot him because Leventhal had refused work, wouldn't cooperate. Romero had strutted out to talk with them all the next day and announced that Wilkie's death was not an accident—it was policy. "Shirk your responsibilities, and it isn't your life you risk—it is your friend's, your cabinmate's, your comrade-in-arm's. I was reluctant to take extreme measures, but you have left me no choice. Each of you is hostage to the behavior of the others."

Leventhal tried to kill himself by slashing his wrists the next day. They got him to sick bay in time.

But that settled it. They did the work. They cooperated. "Bide our time, wait and see," Wu had said, and they did.

Lucy drew a regular shift in front of a communications console. It took her only a day or two to confirm her vague impressions of what was going on. Most of the signals were encrypted, but enough was in clear for her to find things out. She compared notes with the other CIs, and they quickly came to some conclusions. *Ariadne* wasn't in orbit of Capital, but circling another planet, called Outpost.

Much of Lucy's job was in relaying data and voice communications between at least two dozen ships in different orbits. *Ariadne* relayed any traffic for ships that didn't have line-of-sight on each other.

Lucy's console, and nine others, were in a large compartment on B Deck. As she and the other CIs worked, two well-armed Guardians watched them, sullen-faced and bored. Slave labor, Cynthia had called it, and that was close enough. And Lucy told herself that no half-abo Aussie from the Outback was going to be a slave. Not for long, and not without revenge.

Another signal was coming in from the big ship in high orbit. *Leviathan*. The *Lev* was using the same code as the planetside stations, and Lucy wanted to know that code for her own reasons. She hit a few keys on her console and a copy of *Leviathan*'s signal went into a very private computer file she had set up. Lucy was learning.

CHAPTER TWO

Aboard G.O.S. *Ariadne*

First Lieutenant Johnson Gustav, Guardian Navy, knew he was lucky not to be dead already, shot for treason. Being transferred out of Headquarters Intelligence to be the executive officer of some unimportant orbital station wasn't much, but being alive was something. And Gustav had all his off-duty hours to reflect on the concept of the truth being treason.

His report had been erased, shredded, burned, purged, eliminated in whatever form it had existed but one. It was still in his mind. Gustav had the feeling that Captain Phillips had arranged to keep Gustav alive so that one last copy of the report, up there in his brain cells, wouldn't be "erased" as well. Which meant the Phillips knew Gustav was right, and Phillips was a good man—so why didn't Phillips forward the report instead of wiping it out of existence and shipping its author to some tin can orbiting Outpost?

Because Captain Phillips knows that doing that would get us both shot without accomplishing anything, Gustav thought. Phillips was like that. All the good officers in Intelligence were. They had to balance the necessary against the possible. Odd phrases like that cropped up in Intelligence a lot. Phillips had sent Gustav off with another one:

"Pay more attention to politics and less to reality. Until the times change."

Well, the times were about to change all right, but not to anyone's benefit. It was all there in the report.

The trouble was that Intelligence trained its men to be objective in analysis, and it was the only branch of the Navy that sent its men out of the Nova Sol star system to other settled worlds.

It had been easier before he had been trained to go out. He had heard what every kid heard growing up, from the school books and the Political Orientation lecturers: that the Guards had threatened the established order on Earth and had been driven off the mother planet by the plutocrats, cleverly leaving misleading clues as to that part of the sky for which they were bound. That the League of Planets had been formed with the sole purpose of tracking the Guardians down and smashing them, that the League would never stop searching for Capital, the one world that threatened the League's utter domination of human space, and that Capital must be prepared, well armed, disciplined, ready to fight.

Then Gustav had been approved for Navy Intelligence, started his training, and learned a whole new story, one he hadn't really believed until he had shipped out in a tiny one-man ship with a phony Liberian High Free Port registration to wander the League worlds gathering information for Capital.

He had gone out and come back in a score of times. He had stolen designs and collected technical journals that would end up in Guardian labs. He had fingered likely ships for the CI "recruiters." He had read news services and passed back political reports. He had travelled. He had seen.

Gustav had been to Kennedy, to New Asia, to New Finland, even to Earth. He had seen Capital's "enemies" and discovered that the plutocrats and hedonists and demagogues and bloodsuckers of grade school P.O. were just—people. Worse, they were people who had never even *heard* of the Guardians, and it took a day of digging in the New York Public Library datafiles to find more than a passing mention—and the truth—about the Guardians.

The Guards had indeed left Earth a hundred years before, but only after attempting a hopeless and pointless double coup against the American and British governments. In both nations, local police had mopped up the Guards without so much as bothering to call up the military. The schoolbooks' hundreds of thousands of heroic Guardians of the Atlantic Front turned out to be a few hundred rowdies scraped up from the LaRouchists, the Birchists, the Afrikaaners in Exile, the National Front, something called the Ku Klux Klan, and a few other groups. The near-victory over the forces of plutocracy turned out to be little more than a busy afternoon for the police in Washington and London. And the *Oswald Mosley* hadn't narrowly escaped destruction by the space fleets of Earth's criminal nations. Earth's nations didn't even *have* space fleets at that time. The *Mosley* would have been permitted to leave peacefully, and good riddance, except Thurston Woolridge and some of the other Guardian leaders had been sprung from jail in raids that had killed some people and freed a number of dangerous criminals. As it was, the *Mosley* got away only because the British and the Americans didn't have ships available to chase her. Once she had left the solar system, no trace of the *Mosley* was ever found—but then, no one had ever looked very hard. She was missing and thankfully presumed lost with all hands. The Guardians weren't a heroic page in history; they were a grubby little footnote. No one remembered or cared about a nut group from a century past.

To discover one's hated enemies to be civilized, decent people was disquieting. To discover them to be completely unaware of one's existence was galling. To discover the legends of one's people to be the glorification of a seedy little bunch of political thugs was humiliating. But to discover those hated enemies had a combined military potential a thousand times, ten thousand times, greater

than one's own planet was bone-chilling. Earth certainly
had space fleets now. So did Britannica, and Europa, and
Kennedy and Bandwidth. The League was big.

And Supreme General Officer Jules Jacquet, Tenth
Leader of the Combined Will of the Guardians of the
Planetary Commonwealth of Capital, and head of a rather
shaky government, needed some sort of external crisis to
divert attention from other problems. And it couldn't hurt
to grab some technology and skilled laborers at the same
time. Jules Jacquet was planning to attack the League.

When Johnson Gustav heard that through the back channel gossip at Headquarters Intelligence, he had decided
then and there he was a Settler, not a Guardian.

Then-Commander Gustav had done what he had seen
as his duty and filed that damned report, and had ended
up busted in rank and posted to a pesthole named *Ariadne*.

Now he had other duties, the day-to-day jobs of running
a space station. Among those was watching the CIs. The
Survey students were smart enough to assume their cabins
and work stations were bugged—and they got better and
better at finding the mikes. They "accidentally" sabotaged
a tap now and then, and Gustav usually let it go, simply
repairing the damage after a day or two. The CIs were
prisoners in fact, whatever they were in name. They could
never escape, they could never contact the outside universe. Gustav allowed them their secret meetings, their
conspiracies to collect information. After all, another of his
duties was keeping them sane enough to work, and they
needed the chance to grouse and complain and talk their
situation out with each other. Everyone needed a way to
let off steam.

Gustav never forgot that his CIs were soldiers. If he had
ruthlessly crushed every attempt to circumvent the authority of the Guardians with an iron discipline, his CIs
would probably have rebelled violently—and died point-
lessly, wrecking *Ariadne* and thereby hurting the war
effort in the process. Gustav stopped the train of thought

right there, before he could ask himself if hurting the war effort was such a bad idea.

So he didn't erase the CI's many "secret" databanks. If he had, it would simply cause them to start over, hiding things better the next time, perhaps in some memory section he couldn't find. Gustav didn't stop Schiller from using the station telescope and spectrograph to try and identify the brighter stars. Even if Schiller succeeded (which was most unlikely) the twin star system of Nova Sol was 150 light years from the nearest League world. What was Schiller going to do? Walk home? Use a message laser to send an SOS that would arrive in the middle of the next century?

Gustav sighed and glared at the desk he was stuck behind. Paperwork and playing footsie with the slave labor.

The damn fools around Jacquet! They put a joke like Romero in command of a station and used kidnapped spaceship pilots to run the place. Why the devil couldn't the Central Guardians *see* that meant they were in trouble?

Cynthia Wu had rigged her "bug-sniffer" out of parts stolen from an old pressure suit radio and from some other odds and ends. She moved carefully around the storage compartment, checking the deck, the bulkheads, the storage racks.

Finally she shoved the device back in her pocket. "Clean, as best I can tell. Unless Gustav is playing the game a new way. But none of the standard-issue bugs are in here."

Lucy and a half dozen other CIs relaxed slightly. Lucy pointed at Dmitiri and nodded toward the door. Dmitiri nodded back and headed out into the corridor to watch for Guards. "So maybe it's safe to talk," Lucy said. "So we talk. Schiller, any luck?"

"Yes and no." Sam Schiller was a tall, dark, clear-eyed farm boy from Iowa, USA, with a thick mop of deep brown hair and a quiet, serious manner. As a kid in the corn fields, he had loved to look at the stars, and had joined the Navy and signed up for the Survey just for the chance to see them up close. He had been in the Navy Astrocartography Command, and was the obvious choice to look for home amid the points of light. "No really solid idea of where we are yet," he went on, "but I've got a program running right now: Every time the high-gain antenna is out of use, I've got it checking a different piece of sky for radio sources. I'm not just after artificial sources of course, most of the signals that transmitters and radars and so on put out are too weak at interstellar range. But there are pulsars, hot gas clouds, that sort of thing. I've got eight mapped now. None of them are strong enough for me to get a really good signature with our gear, but sooner or later we'll nail the galactic center. That'll give us a lot."

"What about visual?" someone asked.

"Not so great. I'm working with gear that's supposed to spot incoming ships, not read spectra of stars. Without spectra you can't really tell one star from another reliably—especially when you have no idea of the distances to the stars in question. All I can say for sure is that we're a long way from home: at least 100 light years from Earth. I need a star catalog. Has anyone found anything like that in the computers?"

"Not a thing," Wu said. "They've got what looks like a bootleg copy of a standard databank reference encyclopedia, but it's been edited or, I guess, censored. I cracked into it. Almost no history left, something on a few of the sciences, but everything on stars and astronomy and astrogation is gone. Nothing left but the titles of the articles."

"That makes sense," Lucy said. "If you were trying to keep your home world hidden, you'd make astronomy a state secret."

"But how could you keep it secret? All you have to do is look up at the sky!" Amoto objected.

"That's just it," Schiller said. "If all you've got is eyes, you'll never get anywhere. To tell one dot of light in the sky from another, you need to measure spectra and radial velocity and doppler shifts—and if you're doing what I'm trying to do, trying to find some signposts in the sky to point you home, you've got to plot the apparent positions of stars in the sky against their true positions in space, in three dimensions. That takes either a properly programmed computer or years of counting on your fingers. And I don't have a computer programmed for astrogation.

"But I *can* tell you a bit more about the star system we're in. I *think* it's a binary star system, but with a weird geometry I haven't worked out completely yet."

"How come you're not even sure about being in a binary system?" Cynthia asked. "No offense, but that seems so obvious."

"If it *is* a binary system, the other component—the other star—is pretty distant, and to the naked eye it doesn't show a disk. It just looks like a very bright star. I'd be more sure about things, except the geometry is so crazy. The planet we're in orbit of is called Outpost, we all know that. Well, the usual thing would be for all the stars and planets of a binary system to be moving in the same plane. Okay, there's one very bright star with an extremely high proper motion against the background of the sky— measurable over a period of days even with the equipment I've got. But it's way the hell out of the plane of Outpost's orbit. On the other hand, it's moving so fast across the starfield that it's *got* to be in a mutual orbit with *our* star. The evidence says a rare type of binary system. But everything I've ever learned about binaries says there shouldn't be planets in such a system. Which I guess means the theories are wrong. Wouldn't be the first time.

"One other thing: There's a very strong radio source associated with that star, all sorts of noise on all sorts of frequencies. I haven't checked with any of you in Signals, but I'll bet that radio source is Capital, circling the other star of whatever the hell this two-star system is called."

"I picked up some in-the-clear traffic that called Outpost's star Nova Sol B," Lucy put in.

"So presumably the other star is Nova Sol A. At least we've got a name," Schiller said.

"But Sam, will you ever find Earth?"

"I've had six weeks, and I've had to dodge the Guards and run the space traffic center at the same time. Give me six months, or a year, and I'll find it, well enough to navigate in the right direction and refine our course between C^2 jumps."

"Okay," Lucy said. "What about a ship?"

"No chance," Wu said, "at least in the short run. Nothing larger than a tug ever calls here, besides the atmosphere landers. Nothing with a C^2 unit aboard, you can bet that."

"What about the *Venera*?"

"They undocked her the day after we got here," Stana said. "My guess is she's already got a new name and that flame-and-delta Guardian flag painted over the Survey Service symbol."

"Any chance of building a C^2 unit ourselves?" Schiller asked.

"Out of what? With what tools? Anyone memorize the plans of one?" Wu said.

Somebody in this crowd must at least know the principles," Stana objected. "And there are parts and tools."

"With Guardians sitting on them," Danvers said. "And those are warships in orbit around us. With guns. Cynthia's right. And even if we did make a C^2 unit and plugged it into a ship, remember we're talking *light years*. The thing's got to move a ship with a minimum accuracy of one part in a million. What do we calibrate it with? And what about a power source?"

No one spoke for a long time.

"At least we know where we stand," Lucy said. "Sooner or later Sam will come barrelling down the corridor with the news that he knows where home is—and just as important, where *we* are. And then, somehow, we've got to grab a ship and launch it. Only one person has to be on it, or it could even be a drone. Just so long as it carries the message that we're here—"

"—And that we're not alone. Luce, I bet whatever you want that we're not the only CIs," Stana said.

"She's right," Amoto said. "They've got a bureaucracy set up for it. I saw a form that said 'Office of Conscripted Immigration' on it. And one of the troopers posted on duty in my section told me it wasn't so bad—one of his *grandparents* was a CI."

Everyone spoke at once. "My God. How long have they been grabbing ships?" "Why hasn't anyone ever caught them?" "Why do they want all these people?" "C'mon, Dwight, if that was true, why didn't the League find 'em years ago?"

Amoto ignored everyone but the last speaker. "When a ship is lost in interstellar space, you never *expect* to see it again. And given the choice between believing ships blow up now and again, and saying pirates from beyond the stars have been kidnapping people—"

"Yeah, I suppose," Schiller said.

"You realize what that means," Wu said. "When we were back on the League worlds, *we* never heard a hint about hijacked ships. The League doesn't know such things happen, or that these people, these Guards, exist. The League thinks we're dead, and that *Venera* was lost with all hands. They won't come looking for us. We're on our own."

"Not for long. Something's up," Lucy said. "That's why we're here. The immediate reason we were put on *Ariadne* was to allow them to transfer its crew elsewhere. And I've picked up a lot of traffic from the big ship, *Leviathan*, the one that arrived in orbit about twenty-five days ago. They're still having trouble filling billets even after 'recent transfers of comm personnel.' Which I figure means the men from here. And what does it suggest to you when a big ship rushes around to fill all billets? Plus, there's more general radio traffic everyday. They call the ships orbiting

Outpost the Main Strike Fleet. The Guards are going out on some sort of military mission."

"You're saying they're going to attack someone," Schiller said.

"And who is there to attack but the League worlds?" Lucy replied. "Unless there's another mystery planet, which I doubt. And if the Guards attack the League, the League will find out there are such things as Guards, and the League will come looking for 'em. Our job is to do our work, gather as much information as we can, be good little boys and girls, and watch for the chance to get the hell off this station and back to the League carrying a road map with Capital on it."

Two weeks later, there was a sudden increase in radio traffic. Ship orbits were changed more and more. The CIs were kept busier than they had ever been, patching calls and tracking ships. Then, one after another, the ships left orbit altogether, heading away from Outpost to deep space, to a point far enough distant from Nova Sol B to allow a safe C^2 jump. As Lucy watched her board, the realization sunk in: Main Strike was leaving. Lucy wanted to jam the calls, send bad messages, whatever she could to stop them, but it was too late. Clear of the planet, whose bulk had served to block signals most effectively, the ships had perfect line-of-sight on each other: Their messages bypassed the relay station altogether.

One ship was left behind. *Leviathan.* Lucy had never seen her, but the scuttlebutt from the Guards and the radio channels was that *Leviathan* was the biggest starship ever built, the first of her class.

Why the hell would they leave the big ship behind? Curious, Lucy glanced over her shoulder to see if the Guards on duty was watching carefully. No, thank God, they were talking with each other about last night's poker game. She tapped into the signal traffic from *Leviathan* command channel directly and listened on her earphones. With luck they'd be using one of the codes she had broken.

"—long, Carruthers. We'll see you in a few months."

Lucy's eyebrows shot up. They were talking in clear! No encryption. But it wasn't the first time. The signals crew on *Leviathan* seemed to be out to lunch half the time.

"I suppose, Johnny. You go and have your fun while I try and get those pinheads on Capital to send me some fighters. Or maybe even the rest of my crew. I'm still only half-manned."

Lucy got more interested. This sounds like two commanding officers talking, saying goodbye.

"Come on, now, they're only 6000 hours behind schedule."

" 'Only' he tells me. Listen, seriously, you guys be careful. Main Strike shouldn't be flying without *Leviathan*. We shouldn't divide our forces."

"Yeah, I know. Bollixed up the whole battle plan. But orders are orders. 'Main Fleet is to depart on schedule, and no debate on this point will be heard.' "

" 'Any ship not yet prepared will join the fleet later,' " the other voice said, completing the quote. "But look on the bright side. They were going to send us with you as we were."

"But *Leviathan*'s nowhere near ready!"

"I talked 'em out of it. Pounded my fist on the table at the admiralty and showed them what was what."

"Bloody fools."

"But it's going to be all ri—"

"Calder! Quit staring into space and get back to work!" One of the Guards had finally noticed that Lucy had stopped pushing buttons.

She came to herself and cut off her tap on *Leviathan*'s radio.

Whatever it was the Guardians were up to, had begun.

CHAPTER THREE

June, 2115

Ariadne

Two weeks after the fleet left, Gustav came out of his daily meeting with Romero covered in a cold sweat. Something new had come up. New information received, a big new job to do. The news was stunning. Incredible. And they had handed *Ariadne* the job of dealing with it. *Romero* in charge of it! That damn fool wasn't competent enough to tie his shoes without consulting the manual, and they handed this job to him because *Ariadne* was in charge of communications! Brilliant logic. Obviously no one had any idea how big this was. A check of the computer personnel files completed the chain of rotten luck. A CI, not a loyal Guardian, was the best qualified person to do the actual work. If anyone was qualified.

Lucy thought she was being arrested when the call came. Gustav *had* bugged the meetings, knew what was going on, knew that she was tapping the comm lines. But the Guard who came to her work station said nothing beyond ordering her to the executive officer's office. None of the CIs had dealt much with the XO yet, and Lucy had little idea of what to expect. She pushed the buzzer at the entrance to his office.

"Come in," a tinny voice said through a speaker. She

opened the hatch—why couldn't they call it a door?—and
entered. Gustav looked the way he always did: too young
for his job, dark-haired, with deep, intelligent eyes and a
face that would have been handsome smiling—if Gustav
ever did smile. He was of medium height, or slightly
above, in good shape, though his midriff seemed in the
first stages of going to fat. A good field officer recently
trapped behind a desk.

"Lieutenant Calder. Have a seat."

She took a chair and sat down. "Thank you."

"All right, let me clear the air of the easy part. I don't
know and I don't care about any and all of your conspiracies and plots and plans and meetings, and that's not why
you're here. Your people are prisoners—and I'll call you
that even if it's against policy—and you can never ever
escape. Period. You're too far from home and have too few
resources. I don't care about your plots because they can
never do you any good, or me any harm. You are here for
the rest of your life. So as long as you do your work, we
don't care. Or at least I don't, and as far as you're concerned, it's the same thing."

Lucy swallowed hard. "I see."

"That's all unimportant now. Something has happened
and you are a part of it. There's a group on Outpost, and
we need a linguist. The files on you we took off the *Venera*
say that you are one. Close enough?"

"I know some languages. French, Russian, a few Australian aboriginal dialects, Chinese, but I'm—"

"Then you're better qualified than anyone within fifty
light years. No one here has spoken anything but English
for a hundred years. One or two in Intelligence have been
taught a few Western languages, but that's it. We need
someone to learn a whole new language, and you know
how to do that."

"But what lang—"

"I don't know. Nobody knows. We found them four
weeks ago, and so far no one knows *anything* about them."

"But who is it I'm to talk to? Where are they from? And how is the language unknown?"

"They're from right here. Outpost. And it isn't a human language you'll be learning. Your teachers will have six legs."

On Approach to Outpost's Surface

The lander came down, a strictly routine sort of flight of a completely unremarkable craft. The lander was a fat, rounded cone shape, a standard design for a ballistic lander; she could have come off a production line anywhere in the League—and perhaps she had. Lucille didn't even know the lander's name. The Australian Navy's space fleet had always had a superstition about such things—if you didn't know the name of a ship, it was bad luck to fly in her. Lucille didn't have much truck with superstition, but it didn't make her any more comfortable.

Gustav had been assigned to the mission. A sergeant named McKenna piloted the lander, and there were two troopers along, Carlton and Mansfield. McKenna brought them in carefully, setting down in the center of a large clearing in a temperate-zone forest. The moment the landing engines shut off, Lucille heard an oddly familiar thrumming noise on the hull. It was raining out there, making the same noise on the hull that it had on the tin roof back home on Earth, in Australia, during the all-too-rare rainstorms of the arid Outback.

The lander had four viewports. Lucille cautiously unstrapped herself from her crash couch and stepped to the closest one. That was no desert out there, but a dark, dank wet field and forest. She could see two circular burned spots in the clearing, the signs of other landings here. Lucille carefully rocked back and forth on her feet, heel-to-toe and back. She felt rather light, say perhaps .8 Earth gravities.

Gustav rattled off a chain of statistics without looking up. "Before you can ask, I did my homework and converted the figures to scales you know. Surface gravity .83

Earth gees. Atmospheric pressure 110 percent Earth sea level value. By percentage, much more carbon dioxide and water vapor, much less nitrogen, slightly less oxygen than Earth. The carbon dioxide makes it unbreathable. Possibly, we can get by without full pressure suits, but right now I'm not taking any chances. Local environment in landing zone: dank, murky, cold, but somebody calls it home."

"Thanks for the travelogue. Now what?" Lucille asked.

Gustav joined Lucille at the port, then turned to one of the troopers. "Go below to the galley and get us some coffee, Mansfield. What we do now is wait, Lieutenant. We wait. Our friends will have heard and seen the ship coming down, of course. And we hope the rain lets up. Our friends don't seem to like it, though that's just a guess."

"How did you first find them?"

"It was a scientific mission. Someone was doing a survey of temperate-zone plant life on this planet. Anyway, the Outposters appeared and our people ran like hell, back into the ship. Thought they were just a herd of some sort of animal that was large enough to be dangerous. But they watched through the ports and the Outposters had *tools*. All the cameras and viewports were half-blinded by mist and fog, but the crew saw that much. They radioed that little tidbit back to HQ, and were ordered to withdraw. Get back to orbit. Smart move. It let both sides think things over for a while, gave us a chance to put together a team."

"And the second landing?"

"Oh, they launched direct from Capital. All the heaviest scientific brass. They had all the cameras and recorders and whatever along, everything waterproofed and hooded against rain and so on. A lander this size, and three times as many people on it. They landed, and then sat here for two weeks until their supplies ran out. And of course, since the second group was ready for rain, there wasn't any. They were just about ready to give up and try a search from orbit when the Outposters came out of the trees again. Our people got all excited, went out in their pressure suits for the First Contact—and the rains came down. Heavier than this, heavier than ever. Couldn't see three feet. Our people were suddenly up to their knees in mud, and the 'Posters vanished."

"Never to be seen again?"

"That's right. The powers-that-be decided they couldn't afford to keep all that scientific talent waiting around. I think they got nervous about putting all the big brains in such a dangerous situation. Anyway, the orders came down two days ago, and here we are, the smallest practical crew with the most supplies they could cram in a lander."

"And we sit here until hell freezes over, or until the natives show?"

"And then we put the one linguist in the star system in charge. We don't try anything else this time until we can talk. Our job is to make contact, or die of old age waiting to try."

"What you're telling me is that I'm going to do humankind's first contact with another intelligent species," Lucille said. "Me, a prisoner, a slave laborer."

The troopers and the pilot looked up sharply at that. "Relax, all of you," Gustav said warningly. "She's telling the truth. She is what she says she is, and we all know it, no matter what we're told. It's just us followers here without any leaders. No one to pretend in front of." He turned back to Lucille. "Yes, you're here to do the contact. You *are* the closest thing to a linguist we've got, and you're expendable. As are the rest of us. And let's not pretend about that, either."

The trooper came up from the lower deck, carrying a thermos and coffee cups. He poured for Gustav and Lucille. "Thanks, Mansfield. Get at ease and stay there. We could be cooped up for a while. Might as well take it easy or we'll be at each other's throats." Gustav handed Lucille a cup and the two of them returned to the viewport. "We don't know anything about them," he told her. "We don't

have any decent close-up photos of them, we don't know if
they're a high civilization or sitting around in mud huts.
There's no way to be certain they're really *intelligent*, in
our meaning of the word. Apes use tools, and some insects
organize well—but the photos we've got seem to show
them carrying things made of worked metal. Working ore
into metal sure as hell suggests intelligence. But we don't
know. We don't know if they are nomads or have vast
cities. No one has ever bothered to map the planet properly. You've seen the cloud cover from orbit—it hasn't
helped. Our charts are barely more than outlines of the
continents. We've never taken much interest in the planet
itself. The temperate zones are as you see them here—*this*
is as attractive as Outpost gets."

Lucille said nothing. First Contact. Very old words for
something new, something that had never happened. And
it was hers.

The raindrops drummed down on the hull.

They waited. The sun went down and Gustav gave up
watching at the port. He dug a book out of his kit and
began to read.

The pilot and the two troopers went belowdecks to their
bunks, but Lucille stayed at the porthole, too caught up in
it all to do anything but watch and wait. Never had she
seriously considered the possibility of making First Contact. Oh, she had dreamed of it, talked it up in the bull
sessions with the other Survey students, in a time that
seemed far removed from being a CI and a prisoner to the
Guardians. No one who ventured into unknown space
could help but think of the possibilities. But this was real.
The myriad possibilities had focused down onto one actu-
ality, and that was Lucille Calder, the half-abo rancher's
daughter, about to be the first human being to converse
with an alien race. Except humans were the aliens *here*.

She turned and looked at Gustav. He was leaning back
in his crash couch, reading a novel he had borrowed from
Cynthia Wu. Gustav was not simply one of the few Guard-

ians interested in the books the CIs had carried for pleasure reading, he was the only Guardian who would think of politely borrowing—and later actually returning—books, rather than simply taking them.

"You know, Gustav," she said, "try as I might, I can't make you look like the enemy."

Gustav looked up at her, lay down his book, and gave her a wry half-smile. "That was exactly the thought I had when I first saw your people on your worlds."

"I thought Guardians didn't travel outside the Nova Sol system."

"They don't, except for spies."

"Ah." Lucille didn't quite know how to answer that.

"Or, to use the more correct phrase, Intelligence operatives. And I guess I should thank the luck that got me kicked out of Intelligence to be XO on *Ariadne*—or else I'd have missed the chance to see whoever it is out there."

"What got you kicked out of Intelligence?"

"Telling the truth. I filed a report saying it would be a disaster to launch a war against the League."

"And has it been a disaster?"

"Too soon to tell. But numbers don't lie without help. Mine might have been the first un-jiggered statistics the big brass had seen in generations. And those honest numbers said we don't have a chance against you."

"Why are you telling me all this?"

"I suppose I don't really count on coming out of this alive. The Outposters could be hostile, or there could be misunderstandings. Too many variables, too many things to go wrong. I'll consider this mission a success if we can radio back a basic vocabulary for the next team to work with before we die of whatever this planet uses to kill people.

"I've been to Earth, I've been around the League, and I don't like the idea of attacking you. I feel as if I ought to apologize." Gustav paused for a moment. "And I suppose I don't want the woman who's going to talk to the aliens to think that all our people are barbarians and fools. We're not. There are good people on Capital. Honest and decent. But the situation is out of control."

And again, Lucille knew no way to answer him.

The hours and days slid past. On the third day, the rains ended. The sight of blue sky and fleecy white clouds perked everyone up. Carlton, Mansfield, and McKenna were watching out the portholes, enjoying the chance to at least see something besides rain.

"Sir, can't we at least take a little walk around the clearing?" Mansfield asked.

"No," Gustav said. "We stay here, we wait here. Passive. We play it safe and wait. It's hard on our patience, but we let them come to us. We don't want to seem threatening."

"*Are* you threatening?" Lucille asked.

Gustav sighed. "*I'm* not. And I doubt the Central Guardians want to be. If you want to know if we plan to conquer Outpost, no, we don't. Up until a year ago, when the Main Strike Fleet operation began, we didn't even bother landing on it. We could tell from orbit it wasn't much good for human use, not particularly habitable. It's not land we need, it's people and skills and manufactured goods. The 'Posters are safe from us. So look on the bright side, Mansfield. You've got a nice soft duty. You could be out with those poor bastards in the Main Strike Fleet. God knows where they are."

"Even you don't know the invasion target? Sir?" Mansfield asked.

"Nope. That one they kept very tight."

"Sir!" McKenna shouted. "They're out there!"

Lucille rushed to join the three enlisted men at the port. "Can we transmit to *Ariadne*?" she asked.

Gustav shook his head as he switched on the outside cameras and started all the recorders. "No. The station's below our horizon and there's nothing in line-of-sight with us at the moment. We'll tape it and transmit it all the first chance we get."

Lucille grabbed a hand recorder and started it. If something happened, if they got eaten or couldn't get back, she wanted a record, something besides video tapes to send back. Eyes saw things cameras didn't. "Contact. We see them! Four, five, six individuals crossing clearing from the treeline toward the lander. They are dark brown in color. They are bilaterally symmetrical, but they do not appear to be six-legged. No, they're centauroid. The main length of the body carried horizontally, like a horse, but the forward part is rotated up to carry the chest and head upright. Their heads are raised on long, flexible necks. Too far off to see many details of the head. Getting closer. They have two forelimbs, arms we should call them, set at the base of that long neck—the shoulders, I guess. They have two pairs of rather heavy, stocky legs, so they walk on four legs and have those two arms besides. Better compromise than ours, bipedalism for hands. Can't see the walking legs too well through the brush. They have long, thick, heavy tails that might be used for balancing somehow. Some have their tails raised to point straight out behind them. Two are just dragging their tails. They seem to be carrying various kinds of tools or weapons in their forelimbs, their hands. Still too far off to get a clear look at the hands or head."

Lucille kept talking, barely stopping for breath. Her heart was hammering against her ribs. This was *it*! "They seem closer to reptilian than to mammalian, but that doesn't mean anything. There won't be true reptiles or mammals here, of course. I say reptile, but I guess I say that because they don't have fur, their skin is naked—and by that standard, humans are reptiles.

"They aren't clothed, though some of them seem to have belts and wraps and bracelets on. I can't say why exactly, but none of it looks like decoration. All functional-looking stuff, tools and equipment. There's definitely worked metal there, a lot of it.

"Scale. Hard to say precisely, but I'd call their body length at about a meter and a half, plus another meter for the tail. And the head on those shoulders comes to about the height of a man. They're bigger than we are.

"Okay, they're maybe fifty meters away now. I've got the binoculars now. Can see the head better. The head is elongated, front to back, shaped sort of like an egg lying on its side. The neck attaches at about the center of the head, the balance point. I'd say the head is about 30 centimeters long, back to front, and maybe fifteen from top to bottom and side to side.

"I see eyes. All of them have dark eyes, black eyes, no white to be seen, just shiny round black spots. All of them look very much alike. It's a first impression, but it seems to me they would be very hard to tell apart except for the things they wear. But back to the heads. The eyes are set very far forward in the head. They probably have binocular vision like ours. I don't see anything we'd call a nose or ears, but there's something, some sort of low structure, on the top of the head, toward the rear. A mass of flesh with a complicated fold structure. It's moving with a breathing sort of motion, and as they get closer I can see what could be earholes on it.

"The mouth. Hard to see from this angle. It's small in proportion to the rest of the head. The jaw is hinged very far forward. Can't see any of the dentition, or ever if they have teeth in the first place.

"They've stopped. They are standing close to each other, clustered together, about twenty meters from here. One of the them, the one in front, is making some sort of gesture with his right arm. Those arms look very strong.

"They're waiting for us."

Lucille pulled herself away from the port and turned and look at Gustav. His face was pale, excited, and he seemed short of breath. "It's time for me to go out there," she said. "And I think the best way to do it is alone. You said we don't want to seem threatening."

Gustav opened his mouth as if to protest, but then nodded. "Dammit, you're right. McKenna, I want this ship at launch-ready. If we need to run, make sure we can do it. Mansfield. Carlton. Suit up. No weapons, period. We don't defend ourselves. You two and I will stand in the lock while Lieutenant Calder descends to the surface. Let the—the natives see you. We'll make sure they know Calder didn't come by herself, but we don't leave the ship unless she's in trouble. Don't you leave the ship *until I give the order*. Lieutenant Calder—you realize that I might be forced to leave you out there. The information we've got already is more valuable than any of us. If I have to leave you to get it home, I will. And if they kill you, all we dare do is stand and watch. I don't intend to start a war, or get them started hating humans, whatever the provocation."

Lucille nodded stiffly. "I know. It's the only way you could do it. I'd make the same call in your place. We've got no choice but to take the chances." *And I don't know if I'm doing this for Humanity with a capital H, or curiosity, or glory, or the thrill, or to show I'm not scared, or to score points with the goddamned Guards to get the CIs a better deal. It doesn't matter. This is bigger than all those things.*

"Then let's go," Gustav said. His voice nearly cracked.

There was more than being unfamiliar with Guardian suit design that slowed Lucille down. Her fingers shook, her mind wouldn't concentrate on the job of getting the clamps clamped and the seals sealed. Gustav and Mansfield finally had to help her after they were in their own pressure suits.

The four of them crowded into the lock. Gustav hit the buttons that ran it through the decontamination cycle. The inner hatch slammed to, and the air in the lock was pumped into a holding tank. Lucille could feel her suit swell up slightly as the lock's pressure reached a vacuum. The flash heaters came on, and the lock's interior was briefly above the boiling point of water. A poison gas was pumped in, held in the lock for 60 seconds, and then pumped back out. The procedure was intended to kill any bacteria or other microbes that might have been in the air or on the suits. No one was really sure it worked. Maybe cross-contamination was impossible between Earth and Outpost microbes. Maybe there wasn't a need for pressure suits either, and they could get by with breathing gear. Now wasn't the time to find out.

Their helmets misted briefly as the cold, wet air of Outpost was introduced into the lock. "Pressure balanced," Gustav announced. "I'm opening the outer hatch."

Sunlight flowed into the lock. Lucille shuffled forward cautiously. She saw the world through the thin glass of her bubble helmet.

Suddenly, a long-forgotten memory burst into her mind. This place, these colors, all looked familiar. As a child, Lucille had often visited a cousin's house on the verdant southern coast land of Australia. The deep blue skies and dark, wet greens of Outpost's forests and meadows brought back thoughts of long-ago cool spring mornings, the fresh-scrubbed moments when all things seemed possible. No hint of Outpost's air came through her suit, but she recalled the rich, clean odor of a new-mown lawn, the heady fragrance of fertile soil after a good rain. Lucille breathed deeply and found only the soulless scent of sterile, sanitary canned air. Try as her frightened subconscious might to convince her otherwise, this wasn't home.

"Okay, everyone move up a bit so we can be seen," Gustav said.

"Where are they?" Mansfield asked. "McKenna, can you see them through the ports?"

"Just a second." McKenna's voice came through the suit radios. "Yeah, they were waiting around the other side of the lander. They must have heard the lock opening—they're circling around to find you."

"There they are!" Carlton said, pointing.

"Everyone take it easy, move slowly, calmly," Gustav said. The Outposters came into view around the side of the lander. They saw the hatch and stopped, swung around to face it, and waited.

"Here I go," Lucille said. Her voice sounded weak, young, reedy, even to her own ears.

One of the landing legs was directly below the airlock's outer hatch. There was a small platform atop the leg, and a set of ladder rungs bolted to the leg. Lucille stepped out onto the platform and slowly, carefully, made her way down the ten meters of the ladder. She stared hard at the polished metal of the ladder, watched her own gloved hands moving from rung to rung with a fascinated stare. The details of the gloves' stitching, the wrinkling and un-wrinkling of their fabric, the movement of shadows in the bright morning sunlight as she moved her hands, all seemed incredibly complex and important. She grasped for every mundane detail, memorizing it, cherishing the known and accepted as she went to meet something that was neither. There was a meter-and-a-half drop between the last rung and the ground. Lucille got to the bottom of the ladder and let herself go.

She forgot to allow for the mass of the suit and hit the ground heavily, nearly stumbled. She flung her hand out and balanced herself against the solidity of the landing leg. She turned out away from the lander, faced the natives.

There they were, a few meters away, separated from her only by the tall grasses.

Something was wrong. It was too quiet. No outside noise reached her. She kicked in her helmet radio with the chin switch. "Gustav! I forgot something! Does this suit have external mikes and speakers?" Lucille's stomach knotted in needless panic as she imagined crossing to the aliens, standing close enough to touch them, but unable to speak or hear.

"Yes, damnit I meant to tell you. The switches are on the left arm of the suit, marked 'MIC' and 'SPK'. Hit the one marked 'REL' too. That will transmit the outside speakers to us. I'm starting the recorder. We've got cameras on you and the Outposters, and the lander's external mikes are running too. We'll get it all, sight and sound."

Lucille lifted her left arm and found the switches. She

carefully pressed the three buttons, her movements made
slightly awkward by the suit.

Suddenly the rustle of leaves, the small cries of far-off
animals, the thousand small sounds of a living world, were
in her ears.

She stepped forward toward her hosts. The grass was
taller than she had thought, over a meter high, and the
ground was wet and muddy. More and more, she felt
divided out from her surroundings by the suit and the
fragile glass bubble of her helmet. Would they think the
suit was her skin? Could they see her head through the
helmet, and know she was the living being instead of the
suit?

She walked slowly, deliberately, toward them, avoiding
any sudden motion. Fifteen meters, ten, five, three away
from them. She stopped.

The Outposters shifted their stance nervously and looked
at her through their black doll's eyes.

Lucille looked back at them. Their heads seemed huge
and faceless. The eyes seemed expressionless, the mouth
too small and unimportant. She noticed for the first time
that the skin around the eyes and atop the head seemed to
be moving, constantly and rhythmically. Perhaps it had to
do with breathing. That structure on top of their heads
seemed involved with the movement. It might be their
version of a nose.

They seemed huge. Lucille decided they were about
the size of a small horse or pony. Their skin was indeed
naked, and leathery.

The nearest one gestured with his right hand. The
fingers were strange. There were four of them, all mutually opposable, like four very flexible thumbs.

He—she, it, something else? Call them "he" and "him"
for the moment—"he" made sounds. Deep, booming sounds
that had odd timbres and tones. Lucille thought she heard
what sounded like vowels and consonants, but nothing
distinct enough to be noted as words. Was he shouting,

making a speech, singing, or yelling because someone had stepped on his tail? Was he welcoming or warning?

Lucille spread her own arms wide and opened her hands to show they were empty. She hesitated, searching for words, finally saying the best and simplest thing: "We come in peace." She stared hard at them and remembered the Guards and their fleets. *At least, I hope we do*, she thought.

The Outposter who had spoken came closer, and the work of meeting each other began.

CHAPTER FOUR

March, 2116

Navy Castle On The Planet Kennedy

Commander Terrance MacKenzie Larson, Republic of Kennedy Navy, turned the knob, opened the door, and stepped into the courtroom to face his court-martial. *I should have known it would come to this*, he thought. *But I did know, and it didn't make any difference.*

It was a high-ceilinged, old-fashioned, somber sort of room, the walls and floors of polished oak, cut from Kennedy-grown trees. The judges waited behind the massive judicial bench, heavy red drapes behind them, the flags of Kennedy and the Navy set to either side. The wall paneling was intricately carved into friezes, scenes of heroism on the seas and in the sky, the proud moments in the ROK Navy's history. The courtroom was a deadly serious place.

Pete Gesseti followed Mac Larson and his chief counsel, Captain Brown, into the chamber, and looked over the friezes. *They should be carving one for Mac*, Pete thought, *but instead they want to nail him to the wall in person.*

Mac Larson didn't like to hear it, but he *looked* like someone who belonged in a historic scene. Tall, blond, tanned, handsome, lantern-jawed, muscular, a very imposing figure in the jet-black ROK navy uniform.

Peter Gesseti, Republic of Kennedy State Department

Assistant Undersecretary for League Affairs, was short, had a few wisps of brown hair left, and was a round-faced sort of man on whom all suits looked rumpled. His profession and his own poor skills of deportment had taught him the importance of looks. Pete was certain that Mac's appearance would be a help in the case: Mac certainly didn't look like a traitor. Pete also believed in playing every card: He had urged Mac to wear all his decorations. It never hurt to remind the court of the defendant's reputation.

Stern-faced, walking with a firm, measured step, Mac approached the bench, saluted the court, removed his side-arm from its holster and laid it in front of Rear Admiral Louis Leventhal, the presiding judge.

"Commander Terrance Mackenzie Larson reporting as ordered, sir."

"Thank you, Commander. Sergeant-at-Arms, if you would be so good as to accept receipt of the defendant's weapon. Be seated, Commander." Leventhal straightened some papers on his desk and watched the sergeant bear the gun away. An ancient ritual, the surrender of the defendant's weapon. Putting that gun in the safe was a good way of asking: Was the accused worthy to bear arms in the name of the state? Was he guilty of a crime, or, of equal importance to a military tribunal, had he betrayed his trust? The gun itself was meaningless; was certainly unloaded, perhaps had never been fired. But it was a symbol of what the state put in the hands of its young men and women. Starships, for example, were powerful things, powerful weapons. Was Terrance MacKenzie Larson to be trusted with one?

Leventhal sighed. He was an old man, old enough to have been stuck on-planet for twenty years, and old enough to have served on dozens of courts-martial. He was almost entirely bald, and his face was worn and solemn. When he had had hair, it had hidden the fact that his ears stuck out. Now he was old enough, respected enough, known enough, that no one dared think his stuck-out ears looked funny. He had a wide, thin-lipped mouth that fell easily into a frown that was not of anger or sadness, but of concentrated thought. His eyes were as clear as ever, and of a deep, penetrating gray.

Pete Gesseti considered the chief judge. He knew that drawing Leventhal was a big plus. The admiral's kid had been on the *Venera*, had been a classmate and friend of Mac's. Mac and the admiral even knew each other slightly. Pete had dickered and dealt hard to snag Leventhal. He hoped it was worth it.

"Mr. Gesseti," Leventhal said.

Pete rose. "Admiral."

"Are you involved with this case? I was not aware that the State Department was taking an interest."

"It is not, your honor. I have requested and been granted a leave of absence to serve as assistant counsel to the defense. I hold a law degree and a reserve Navy commission." *And if State wasn't taking an interest, I wouldn't have been let within ten kilometers of this place, and you know it, Admiral.*

"I see. Might I ask what school and what rank?"

"I was law school class of '98 from New Amherst College, and hold the reserve rank of captain." *But don't ask to see the commission because the ink's still wet.* It had taken a few more deals to get the military rank, but Pete had wanted to be damn sure Mac had a friend in court.

"You are aware that these proceedings have been classified as secret?"

"I hold a higher clearance from State, Admiral." *And leaking this farce to the press would raise some merry hell indeed*, Pete thought: *"Navy Brass Puts Hero On Trial." Don't tempt me to use* that *weapon, Admiral.*

"Very well, Captain Gesseti. Thank you. The clerk will read the charge."

"Republic of Kennedy Navy Judge Advocate's Office proceeding in a general court-martial against Commander Terrance MacKenzie Larson, ROK Navy, this 9th day of Fifthmonth, year 97 Kennedy Calendar, March 19, 2116, Earth Standard Calendar. The Honorable Admiral Louis

Leventhal, presiding judge; the Honorable Captains Benjamin Stevens, Eric Embry, David White, and Sandra Tho, associate judges. The defendant, Commander Terrance MacKenzie Larson, is charged under Article VII section iii paragraph 3 of the Uniform Code of Military Justice: 'public utterances detrimental to an alliance to which the Republic of Kennedy is a signatory,' and paragraph 6, 'public utterances detrimental to the prosecution of Naval operations,' both charges raised from a Class IV to a Class III violation under the provisions of Article I section ii paragraph 4, 'the Republic being in a state of War, each charge shall be considered one Class higher than described in this Code of Justice.' Charges are brought in regards to the following allegations, to wit: numerous public oral statements by the defendant in opposition to the deployment of RKS *Eagle*, USS *Yorktown*, and HMS *Impervious*, the three large space-going carrier craft available to the League of Planets in the prosecution of the present war against the Guardians."

"Captain Brown, how does your client plead?"

"Not Guilty, your honor."

"Then let the record show a plea of Not Guilty. Captain Tsung, if you would proceed for the prosecution."

"Your honor, as the facts themselves are not in dispute, and by prior agreement of opposing counsel, I elect to forego my opening remarks and reserve my evidence until the defense has concluded its own case."

"To the defense, then. Captain Brown."

"Thank you, your honors. I will be as brief as possible in my opening remarks. As Captain Tsung has remarked, the defense will not dispute the facts of the case, which are well known. The defendant did indeed make statements and comments and allow himself to be interviewed at the times and dates and with the persons itemized in what will be the prosecution's exhibit A. Our case will instead turn upon an entirely different point of military law and tradition.

"It has been said that the sublimest word in the English language is 'duty.' Duty is service, and military service especially. Duty above self-preservation, duty above honor, duty above even the orders of a superior. Any sailor or soldier of this Republic would be liable to arrest, court-martial and punishment for obeying criminal orders—orders, for example, to massacre civilians. Under such circumstances it is the sworn duty of our military personnel to not only question, but refuse, their orders.

"The Navy of the Republic of Kennedy traces its traditions back hundreds of years, to the ocean-going navy of England that defeated the Spanish Armada and the American wet navy that held the sea lanes against Hitler. It looks back to Task Force One, the three U.S. Navy starships that made the first journey beyond Earth's sun a century ago. Since our race first left the solar system, we have come to be more and more spread out among the stars, and so communication has become more difficult, slower, less reliable. At the same time ships have become faster, more powerful—and thereby, potentially—more dangerous. For this reason, independent judgment, the ability to react to a changed or entirely new situation not covered by orders, has been a vitally needed skill in the Navy. Also for this reason, no Kennedy naval officer is trusted with a ship until and unless he or she is thoroughly indoctrinated into our traditions, until the events carved into these walls are etched as well into the psyche of the officer, until that naval officer has learned the many things a ship *can* do that it *must never* do. Our defense against the might of our own weapons is and always has been the quality and integrity of our people.

"Obviously, the refusal of orders is a serious thing. It cannot be done lightly, and in all but the most drastic of cases—such as the hypothetical one I have offered—the commanding officer must be allowed the benefit of the doubt. Obedience to orders is the due of a commander.

"A sailor or soldier must be prepared to obey orders that will result in his or her own death, in the destruction of his or her unit, in the loss of all that is held dear—just as an officer is expected to give orders, if need be, that will kill that officer and destroy that officer's own command. Clearly, such sacrifice must be made to a purpose. No person in our military is expected to die uselessly. He or she is expected to die and kill willingly *if it is needful*.

"It is an assumption inherent in all this that there is a higher good than survival. That higher good is the preservation of one's family, one's people, one's society, one's beliefs. Defense of these higher goods, perhaps at one's own expense, we call 'duty.' But when a sailor or a soldier or an officer knows, with certainty, that obedience to an order will accomplish the destruction of men and material sorely needed in the fight to come, and will accomplish no other thing, then duty lies with disobedience. Such, we will prove, is the present case. Terrance MacKenzie Larson was ordered to remain silent. With full knowledge of the consequences of his actions, he spoke. As he expected, this resulted in the present court-martial. As I have noted, duty is above honor, and Commander Larson has willingly risked the shame of imprisonment and conviction to do *his* duty. It is now the *duty* of this court to see that justice is done, and to see that Commander Larson is held blameless for his actions, released from custody fully vindicated, and returned to his unit with his reputation intact."

Pete leaned over and whispered to Mac. "Now *that's* some kind of speaking. You might get out of this yet."

"I didn't get in to get out, Pete," Mac whispered back. "That twenty bucks still says I lose."

Brown winked at Mac as he collected a sheaf of papers from the defendant's table. Then he turned to the bench and said, "The defense calls as its first witness Terrance MacKenzie Larson, Commander, Republic of Kennedy Navy."

The prosecutor rose and spoke. "For the record, I wish to insert a correction. The defendant's rank was conferred by brevet, and was not even conferred by a ROK Navy officer. His permanent rank is second lieutenant."

"Your honors, I object!" Brown shouted. "My client's brevet rank—conferred at the discretion of the U.S. Naval

officer under whose command he serves in the joint operation known at the Survey Service—is every bit as legal
and binding as a conventional promotion, and I defy the
prosecution to suggest that it was undeserved. The only
effect the brevet promotion has had upon my client has
been the denial of the pay and benefits of a commander.
He continues at the pay schedule of a second lieutenant. I
thank the prosecution for reminding us of yet another
injustice done my client."

The five judges conferred briefly and then Leventhal
spoke. "Objection sustained. Captain Tsung's remark will
be struck from the record. Commander Larson, you may
take your stand."

The clerk swore Mac in. Brown went through the usual
preliminaries of identification and then began to question
him.

"Commander. For the record, and for the information
and with the permission of the court, could you repeat the
opinions that got you into this situation?"

"Yes. As I have said publicly on many occasions, I
believe that the deployment of the *Eagle*, *Yorktown*, and
Impervious would be potentially disastrous to the Republic of Kennedy and to the alliance, the League of Planets."

"And why is that?"

"These carrier ships are the largest men-of-war ever
built by the League. Their function is analogous to that of
an ocean-going aircraft carrier: They carry fighter and
attack spacecraft, and deploy these fighters in battle. The
idea is simple: The carrier serves as a forward base. The
fighters and attack ships can return to the carrier rather
than to home base, and can thereby be shorter-range,
lighter, faster, and carry less fuel and more armament
then a fighter forced to travel from a distant base."

"But this sounds as if the carriers are ideal for space
war."

"In theory, they are. However, like the old ocean-going
carriers, including the namesakes of the *Yorktown* and the
Impervious, these carrier ships are extremely tempting

and vulnerable targets. Because they are so large, their fusion rocket engines must be very powerful, and of course a fusion engine emits a lot of energy across the electromagnetic spectrum. The *Yorktown*'s engines, for example, would be detectable at least a light year away. Beyond that, of course a large target is easier to pick up on radar than a small one. For these and other reasons, it's easy to find one of these ships. The enemy, having found it, will certainly try to destroy it, both because it is a great threat to him, and because destroying it will remove such a large fraction of our war-fighting capability.

"There is an additional problem with the three ships in question. They are old—of old design and old construction. They have been more or less mouthballed for decades. Upgrading a forty-year-old engine or attempting to retro-fit a modern system into these old hulls is far more difficult and expensive than starting from scratch on a new ship."

"We are all naval officers here, Commander, and all have no doubt heard these arguments before. What made you pursue your views so vigorously, so publicly, all but forcing a prosecution, risking damage to your career, or even a term in the brig?"

"My experiences in the New Finland star system soon after the League-Guardian War began."

"Could you elaborate?"

"Objection! The prosecution must object in the strongest terms." Captain Tsung had been waiting for this, and dreading it. He had to try to cut this line of questioning off. "The defense is attempting to bring in extraneous side issues. How the defendant came by his view is irrelevant. For that matter, the defendant's views are themselves irrelevant. The defense it attempting to build a case on the altar of duty. This, too, is beside the point. The only issue here is whether or not the defendant did indeed violate the Uniform Code of Military Justice by making certain statements. The defense admits he did indeed make such statements. As this is the only point on which the case turns, I respectfully request the bench to instruct defense to rest so we may proceed to the prosecution."

Pete looked on admiringly at Tsung. The old snow-'em-with-everything routine. Every possible argument for ignoring side issues. Not a bad gambit. If the judges bought just one bit of Tsung's argument, they'd have to buy the whole thing. If they did that, the defense was dead. Pete and Captain Brown had been expecting this, and Pete was ready to do his bit. It would require a little sarcasm, and better for assistant counsel to be snotty then let Brown himself get in trouble with Leventhal for being disrespectful.

Pete stood up slowly. "Your honors, I must raise a number of counter-objections. Captain Tsung knows damn well he's stuck with the unpleasant job of trying to throw an interstellar hero in the brig, and he's doing his best—doing *his* duty, if you will. Fine. But don't let him tell you how to do *your* job. If you wish to cut off the defense, you can decide that on your own without his help. Furthermore, five minutes ago my learned friend was foregoing his opening statement and reserving his case—and now he wants to shut down *our* key witness after five questions! Your honors, I submit that entertaining such a motion, permitting such a strategy, would deny our client's single chance to defend himself. As it is, he will be heard only in a secret proceeding. Allow him at least that."

"It seems to me, Captain Gesseti, that we now have the choice of being instructed by either the prosecution or the defense," Leventhal growled. "We shall confer." The five judges bent their heads together and whispered briefly. Finally, Leventhal addressed the court. "In this matter, we overrule the prosecution. We find that it is conceivable that reasons could exist that would compel the defendant to act as he has. Therefore, the search for such reasons in the experience of the defendant is not irrelevant. Defense may proceed with the current line of questioning."

"Thank you, your honor," Pete said as he sat down. It had *definitely* been worth all the trouble to get Leventhal on the court.

"Let me restate the question, Commander Larson," Brown went on. "What were the experiences in the New Finland system that led you to your views?"

"It began with the loss of the Survey Service transport *Venera*," Mac began. Pete and Captain Brown had rehearsed Mac very carefully, and Mac was a quick study. He gave his testimony calmly and carefully. "Many Survey personnel were lost with the *Venera*. The Survey's commanding officer, Captain Driscoll, decided to launch the Survey ships with undersized crews rather than have the program cancelled altogether."

And Driscoll had been looking at a court-martial herself for that decision, until things had broken the way they did, Pete thought. *Then she was suddenly a far-sighted hero.*

"As the court might know," Mac went on, "First Lieutenant Joslyn Marie Cooper Larson of the Britannic Navy and I were the entire ship's complement aboard the League of Planets Survey Ship Number 41, the *Joslyn Marie*. I was in command of the *J.M.* and named it for Lieutenant Larson, who is my wife.

"While on her first Survey mission, the *J.M.* was intercepted by a messenger drone with orders to proceed to New Finland. All anyone in the League really knew at that point was that contact with New Finland had been lost, and some group named the Guardians had attacked and conquered the planet. Up until the time of the attack, no one still alive, except a few historical specialists, had ever even *heard* of the Guards.

"The only other thing we knew was that the Guardians were rapidly setting up a system of interceptor missiles capable of detecting the burst of radiation peculiar to a starship reentering normal space from C^2 space. However, the system was designed for the sensors to look out into deep space. Once inside the New Finnish system, ships were safe from the missiles. The *J.M.* was the only ship in position to get to New Finland before the anti-ship missiles were all in place. If the *J.M.* hadn't been in the right place at the right time, there wouldn't have been a chance."

And that's what saved Driscoll, Pete thought.

In the steady voice of an officer reporting the results of a routine assignment, Mac talked on. "We launched for New Finland and arrived at that star system safely. The drone which intercepted us also carried a new device. It was the key components of a receiver unit for a matter transmitter. We were ordered to get that device to New Finland, assemble the complete receiver, and receive from deep space 5,000 League troops so as to counterattack the Guards. Obviously, using the matter transmitter got the League around the anti-ship missiles and gave us the element of surprise.

"The troops arrived safely—though I understand there was an accident on the ship that transmitted them toward us, the *Mayflower,* after the last of the troops got off, and it will be some time before they risk using the matter transmitter again.

"With a great deal of luck, courage, and sacrifice, the League troops and the Finns were winning. We would have driven the Guards off the planet and out of the star system. Then we discovered that a ship called *Leviathan* was on its way.

"*Leviathan* is—or rather was—basically similar to the *Eagle* and the other carriers, except for three major differences. One, she was much larger than our ships. Two, she was designed to enter an atmosphere; she could operate either in air or space. The third difference was that *Leviathan* was a lighter-than-air craft. *Leviathan* used a combination of aerodynamics and the lifting power of hydrogen gas to keep her in the air.

"The points central to this court-martial are these: *Leviathan* was by a factor of a thousand the most powerful ship in that system, but she could have been destroyed at any time by a single nuclear weapon. Our side did not do so because the controls operating the anti-ship missiles were aboard her. The missile system was designed so that it would fire at any ship entering the system unless it was told *not* to. A dead-man system. Destroy the control system, and there would be no way to tell the missiles to let a ship past. If we had blown *Leviathan*, the missile system would have kept the New Finnish system sealed to our forces for perhaps fifty years, during which time the Guards could have returned by controlling the anti-ship missiles from outside the star system, obviously, the League didn't have the missile control codes, so we couldn't do that."

"In other words," Brown put in, "had not circumstances made the League and Finn forces hostage to the continued existence of *Leviathan*, she could have been destroyed easily."

"Perhaps not easily, but there is no question that we could have blown her. As it was, we were forced to board *Leviathan* and take over the missile-control center long enough to send a self-destruct to all the missiles. That left the way open for League ships to enter the system."

"What happend to *Leviathan* then?"

"After the last of the boarding party had gotten off the ship, we used the fusion engines of a lander craft to melt through the hull. They had relied on that hull, made of an extremely tough material, woven metallic superwhiskers, to protect the lift cells, which were filled with hydrogen. When the flames finally burned through to the lift cells, *Leviathan* was destroyed by explosion and fire."

"You have touched lightly on your own part in all this. Did you not in fact take command of all the League and Finn space forces when all the more senior officers had been killed?"

"Yes I did."

"Did you not in fact plan and lead the boarding operation, and *personally* use the the missile-control system to send the self-destruct? Furthermore, was not your lander the last ship to leave *Leviathan*, remaining there at great risk and at your specific orders to pick up any survivors and ensure that the enemy ship was destroyed?"

Mac hesitated. "Yes, that is correct," he said.

Pete smiled. It was hard to be a modest hero under oath. Brown wanted to make sure the record showed what sort of man they were putting on trial.

Brown went on. "I have here a list of decorations awarded to you. Have you not in fact received the New Finnish Gold Lion, the U.S. Legion of Merit, the British Victoria Cross, the Britannica Order of Honor, The League High Cross, the Finnish Hero's Medal, the League of Planets Survey Service Stargrid, as well as the Republic of Kennedy's Purple Heart, Silver Star and Medal of Honor, as well as many other honors and citations?"

Mac shifted uncomfortably. "Yes, that is correct."

"Commander Larson, where is your wife? Have you seen her recently?"

"She was reassigned to the Navy Yards at Britannica. I haven't seen her in some months."

"Was she not in fact transferred away from the Survey Service base shortly after you first spoke out against deploying the three carriers?"

"She was ordered back home within thirty-six hours after my first statement."

"Has it ever occurred to you that the two of you were separated as a punishment for your statement, punishment without benefit of trial or appeal? Was this not indeed persecution and harassment of a heroic man and woman because of your—"

"Objection!" the prosecutor shouted. "Counsel is clearly not questioning the witness, but making a speech. I request that this leading and biased so-called 'question' be stricken from the record."

"I withdraw my last question," Brown said smoothly. Getting the judges to hear it was enough, on the record or not. And it didn't hurt to tweak the opposition before turning Mac Larson over to him. "Your witness, Captain."

Captain Tsung was clearly rattled enough for Brown's purposes. He rose uncertainly and approached the defendant. "Ah, ah, Commander. I'm certain that no one in this court questions your courage, or your contribution to the

war effort . . ." Tsung's voice trailed off for a moment.
"But that is not what is on trial here, Commander Larson.
You base your assumptions on the vulnerability of the
three carriers on the fact that you were present when the
Leviathan crashed."

"Yes, that is correct."

Pete bounced up. "I'd like to clarify the answer to that
question. Commander Larson did in actual fact command
the ship that wrecked *Leviathan*, and the larger ship was
destroyed by his command and according to his plan.
Excuse the interruption," he said brightly, and sat back
down.

Captain Brown leaned over toward his assistant counsel.
"*That* wasn't approved courtroom procedure," he whispered to Pete.

"No, but why let Tsung make Mac seem like he was
standing around watching the world go by when a giant
spaceship just happened to crash in front of him?" Pete
replied. "Mac came as close as anyone ever has to winning
a war single-handed."

"Except the was isn't over yet. No one's found the
Guardians' planet."

"Don't remind me."

Tsung seemed more and more unhappy about the job of
prosecuting Mac. "Ah, Commander. Conceding that you
did indeed destroy *Leviathan*, how does that bear on the
vulnerability of the League carrier ships? After all, *Leviathan*
was destroyed in large part by fire, in an atmosphere,
while flying as an aerodynamic vehicle, under circumstances wholly different from those the *Eagle* and the
other carrier will experiences. Our ships are, after all,
incapable of entering an atmosphere, and certainly do not
carry large lift cells filled with hydrogen gas."

Mac smiled slightly. "Forgive me, Captain, but I don't
think you've done your homework. I was debriefed very
carefully after the missile system was destroyed. In that
statement, which I can see on the prosecutor's table, I
reported that the *Joslyn Marie* at one point attacked the

Leviathan using space-to-space torpedoes." For the first time, Mac's voice and manner showed some emotion, some passion. Even talking about the carriers here, in court, got him visibly angry. "As I noted in the debriefing, the *Joslyn Marie*, although perhaps a thousandth the mass of the *Leviathan*, was able to make several direct hits on the big ship. As I have stated already, we could not risk the destruction of *Leviathan*, and so the torpedoes were armed with conventional explosives. The *J.M.'s* attack was a partially successful attempt to prevent the big ship from launching fighters against the League and Finn forces." He paused, then went on in a louder, almost threatening, tone. "As I reported to the debriefing team, if we had armed the *J.M.'s* torps with nuclear warheads—which we could have done easily—there is not the slightest doubt that the *J.M.* could have taken out *Leviathan*. Those hits made by conventionally armed torps prove that a ship the size of the *J.M.* could certainly destroy the *Eagle*, and the people and equipment aboard her. And I might add that the Guards know all this as well as we do. They have learned it the hard way. They foolishly put all their eggs in one basket. We must profit from the enemy's error instead of making the same fatal mistake ourselves. The secret we are trying to keep is no secret to the enemy—it is secret only to our own people and the men and women aboard those carriers."

Tsung knew when to quit. "Thank you, Commander. No further questions."

Pete popped up again. "The defense rest its case at this time, your honors. By prior agreement with opposing counsel, we will waive our concluding statement. The prosecution may now proceed with its case if it so chooses." *In other words, we're quitting while we're ahead.* Pete thought.

Tsung had the sense to request a recess for lunch after Mac's testimony. He needed time to collect his thoughts and get his notes in order, time to relax and plan, and he needed to give the judges time to forget a bit of Mac's impressive bearing. So far nothing had gone his way, and he was determined that would change.

After lunch, Tsung began his case by quoting Mac's statements and showing a recording of one of his interviews. The message was the same one, but put in far less respectful tones.

Mac and Pete watched the screen impassively as Mac's image spoke. "The carriers are deathtraps. They are sitting ducks. We are told that these ships were built 'to interpose powerful forces across the spacelanes in times of crisis.' Those ships were never needed for that, in all the years they were on active duty. They were mothballed because modern weapons and tactics—and the absence of a major war—made them useless.

"Their true purpose, the true reason that these ships were built, the true reason that they are now being re-commissioned, is that admirals like to have big impressive ships to fly around in. Every cost-effectiveness calculation, every war game, every strategic plan, has shown that these ships are as much liabilities and targets as they are advantages and weapons."

Tsung stopped the recording. "That, your honors, is what Commander Larson had to say to the public last week. That statement was carried on Kennedy's largest video network. It was widely quoted. Commander Larson has said the alleged peril these carriers face is a secret—but that peril is no secret, thanks to him. Fortunately, none of his statements have gotten into the off-planet press as yet, though that is but a matter of time. No doubt ships are carrying copies of our war hero's opinions to every major world in the League.

"And what effect will that have on the war effort? Commander Larson gave up his efforts to discuss his views through normal military channels and instead went public. How will it serve morale, fighting spirit? Can it serve but to discourage the men aboard those ships? Can it but give aid and comfort to the enemy for him to hear that we regard our own ships as admirals' toys, sitting ducks, deathtraps?

"Your honors, I will present no witnesses. I could exhaust us all with a stream of experts on strategy and tactics who would confirm what I have said, and then the defense would dredge up its own experts to refute me. I could call Captain Josiah Robinson, the commander of the *Eagle*, and he would be happy to tell you the high state of readiness his ship is in, and how his men are reacting to Commander Larson's statements. But you are all naval officers, and you know all these things.

"The one witness I would call, if I could, would be a naval commander—a *Guardian* naval commander. We must assume they have their spies here on Kennedy, watching us. The Guardians, on their hidden planet, Capital, perhaps have already viewed the recording we have just seen. If I could put a Guardian naval officer on the stand, under oath, I would ask him: Did Commander Larson's statements reveal weaknesses of which the Guardians were unaware? Did he make *their* forces more confident? Was what he said good for *their* morale?

"We have heard a great deal about duty today. We have been told that Commander Larson felt it his duty to speak, a higher duty than that he had to Navy regulations. Was it not a higher duty still to keep silent? He has hurt our perception of our strength, our morale—and aided that of the enemy? He has told us of a danger that it seems only he can see. Assuming the danger exists at all, has he not made that danger greater by pointing it out to the enemy? But speaking out on this 'danger,' has he not increased all our other dangers?

"This man has displayed courage, enormous courage, both in battle and in coming forward to say what he has said. But has he displayed good judgment? I think not. Your honors, I ask you to demonstrate your own judgment and find for the prosecution. In the old days, the wet navy days, they said that 'loose lips sink ships.' In our present day, loose lips might serve to *vaporize* ships. Do not encourage the practice of loose talk by letting this man go free. Yes, he is a hero. But heroism is no excuse for making a terrible mistake of judgment.

"Your honors, the prosecution rests."

Leventhal banged down his gavel. "Very well. This court-martial is adjourned. The court will withdraw to reach a verdict. This court-martial will reconvene at 0900 hours tomorrow morning."

Mac might have been confined to quarters in the Navy Castle, but at least he was confined to comfortable, if not downright imposing quarters on a high floor of the Tower. The rough-hewn walls of the semi-circular room were hung with paintings of great ships and admirals, the furniture was from the captain's cabin of an old U.S. wet Navy battle cruiser, the floor was covered in a rich, solemn burgundy carpet. Pete was pleased by the room. They only put high-class prisoners here.

The Navy Castle had not been built by some romantic architect to look like a fortress—it *was* a fortress, with stone walls three meters thick at the base, internally reinforced with steel and modern graphite composites. The walls would defend against mobs and most conventional attacks, and the bomb shelters drilled into bedrock a kilometer below could hold out long after the Castle proper had been vaporized. The Castle was designed to do more than just survive an attack, of course. It could fight back, with an armory full of rifles and side arms and supplies for a siege. There were other weapons tucked away inside the great building, which no one talked about much.

The Navy Castle had been built seventy-five years before, in quiet and peaceful days—at least they had been peaceful days on Kennedy. The ROK Navy was busy back then, as it was now, frequently being dispatched in answer to League requests: police actions, rescue missions, and even the transportation of riot police from one star system to another. The League had been formed largely in reaction to the economic and political disarray on far too many of the settled worlds, and it fell to the navies of the strongest powers to effect and enforce the League's decisions. The ROK Navy had been there in the evacuation of New Antarctica, literally on day one of the League's existence. The Navy had flown relief supplies, bombed one side or another in the midst of revolts, arrested arms runners and drug smugglers, done too many dangerous things to trust much to days of peace. Only now, in the fight against the Guardians, did the ROK Navy find itself in its first war, but it had experience enough of fighting.

So headquarters was built inconveniently far from town—near but not at the spaceport, in sight of but not on the coast, on the brow of a hill in the middle of a large and carefully tended clearing. It wasn't due to chance that the view from the Tower was superb, nor due to the prestige of the unit that the First Marine Battalion was stationed there.

There had been scoffers who laughed at the egos that needed such a huge building, and a few Army types pointed out that the Castle cost more to build than most of the Navy's ships. Then the Fast Plague fell and madness literally became a contagious disease. When the cure was found, and the riots were over, the Castle was still there, with only a nick or two and a few scorch marks to mar the outer stone facing. The Army's gleaming, modern, downtown HQ Center had to be torn down and rebuilt altogether.

The builders of the Castle were more farsighted than they were optimistic.

The view from Mac's cabin (which Pete insisted on calling a room) was spectacular. Brown and Gesseti joined Mac for breakfast there the next morning. Mac couldn't eat much. He was too drawn by the view, the things to see. The coastline, the skyline of Hyannisport, the broad plain of the spaceport, were laid out in a magnificent panorama. It was the spaceport that Mac stared at. As he watched, a ship, a small winged job, made a horizontal launch into the perfect blue morning sky and rushed for orbit, the dull yellow of its air-breathing engines suddenly flaring into sun-bright specks as it shifted to fusion power. Mac watched it climb to orbit, to space, to the dark between the suns, and thought of Joslyn, his wife, once again so far away.

"I should be out there, Pete," Mac said at last. "There's work to be done and I'm one of the best qualified to do it, and I'm cooped up here."

"You'll be out there soon, Mac. The judges will pass their verdict, this whole farce will be over, and you'll be back at it. Besides, you're only locked up here because you had a job of talking to do that you thought was pretty damn important. And you were right."

"Maybe," Captain Brown said, carefully refilling his coffee cup, "you even did some good, though I doubt it. And Pete, we gave it our best shot and did pretty well, but I've never had much hope of getting Mac off. The regulations are pretty clear, and I can't see Leventhal and company being thrown by a lot of verbal flourishes."

"Why do you doubt I did any good?" Mac said.

"Because you're a lousy politician and you didn't know the right people. Oh, I don't think you had much choice, and you did get your case heard, but all that accomplishes is getting the brass with their backs to the wall. They can't lose face by admitting you're right. They want to prove *they're* right—"

"And the only way to do that is to deploy the damned carriers. But I had to try, Captain Brown. For all the reasons you talked about in court."

"Yeah." Brown was angry, though he couldn't quite explain at what. But Terrance MacKenzie Larson was not the sort of man who should be hung out to dry. It was only the higher ranks, the admirals who loved their big ships too much, who felt the need to punish him. They left the dirty work to the Tsungs and the Leventhals, honorable officers honorably and reluctantly doing their duty. And Brown felt he never wanted to hear the word duty again.

There was a polite knock at the door and the very

respectful white-gloved marine informed them that the court-martial was ready to reconvene.

They descended in the sleek, silent-running elevator, and were led the familiar way to the courtroom by the marine guard.

There was shuffling of papers, and rising for the court, and finally it came, unwilling, from Leventhal's lips.

One word.

"Guilty."

CHAPTER FIVE

March, 2116

Guardian Contact Base on Surface of Outpost

The day dawned as most of them did in this clearing, with a mist-shrouded sun easing its way through the knotted, roiling clouds and the tangled limbs of the surrounding forest. Two camps, one human, one Outposter, stirred and began their morning routines as the sun burned off the mist and the clouds and the dew dripped off the plant life.

C'astille opened her eyes, uncurled her legs from beneath her long body, flexed her tail, and stepped out of her field shelter into the clearing. She sucked in the fresh morning air through her blowhole. The morning air smelled good, invigorating. She stretched her arms and flexed her long fingers. It would be another good day. She went to the camp kitchen in search of breakfast.

On the far side of the clearing, inside one of the humans' pressurized huts, Lucy Calder slapped at the alarm clock with somewhat less enthusiasm for the day. With the dim thought of a shower and coffee, she stumbled out of bed. She had been up late again the night before, working on her notes. And Outpost's day was only nineteen hours long. It took getting used to. And C'astille would beat her to the Crystal Palace, as usual. She had given up trying to be early for their meetings—C'astille would simply be earlier still the next day. Calder liked her counterpart, and even felt in some strange way that she had something in common with her, but a little less enthusiasm for early morning work wouldn't be amiss. Coffee. That was the main thing.

Neither side was consciously aware of it, of course, but each had done the same thing, or had at least arrived at the same result: Young, open-minded, highly intelligent, and quite expendable individuals represented both species.

The Guardians hadn't made any immediate, deliberate decisions to put Johnson Gustav or Lucy Calder on *Ariadne* at the moment of First Contact. However, human traditions of exploration and military service, formed by decisions made and lessons learned over thousands of years, favored the practice of using young, still-flexible personnel, people with few immediate dependents to lead expeditions to the unknown or the unpredictable. It seemed to be what worked best: More explorers and soldiers came back when the leaders were young and smart and had few attachments to the outside world. Given that tradition, persons like Gustav and Calder were the most likely to be thrown into situations where a First Contact might occur: for example, on board a station orbiting a largely unexplored world. If humans had found that older left-handers who lacked a sense of humor did better in hazardous situations, the Outposters would have faced some aged and stern-faced southpaws instead of Gustav and Calder.

But fresh, sharp, and flexible minds did work best, and not just for humans. C'astille's mind fit that description just as well. C'astille's people had no concept corresponding to that of a military, though hers was not a particularly peaceful race. She knew what exploring was, though, and had dreamed of being the finder of a new thing. As a youth, she had at times worried that the world was too well known, that there would be no discoveries or explorations or new things to learn. All that had changed now, of course, and certainly there were now to be strange new things to fill more than a lifetime.

She found the humans themselves the most interesting. Even now, long after she had first set eyes on them, the sight of humans, especially walking in their bizarre bipedal gait, fascinated her. The sight both mesmerized and repelled practically any Outposter not used to it. A human parallel to this reaction could be found in the unpleasant, creepy thrill some humans got out of touching a snake. A nastier, more accurate, and more compelling analogy might be the giddy, horrified, stomach-knotting reaction humans often have when they see a member of their own species, unfortunate enough to have both legs amputated, forced to walk on hands instead of feet.

To the Outposters, the humans looked mutilated, a front half of a creature chopped from the whole. Given the cultural and biological background of the Outposters, the very sight of a human brought a whole constellation of unpleasant things to mind.

It *took* a flexible, educated psyche like C'astille's to accept the fact that these were natural, whole, and healthy creatures—probably evolved in a process similar to that which produced C'astille herself—and not monsters.

Calder and the other humans had an advantage without realizing it: They were used to the idea of seeing a creature that walked on four legs, and even had the comfortable, familiar, and not unpleasant legend of the centaur to help them get used to the shape and movements of the Outposters. The Outposters had no such comforting images. To C'astille and her fellow Low Assistances, the humans did not bring to mind a more-or-less friendly sort of mythical beast. A very mild analogy to what humans reminded them of would be the front half of Frankenstein's monster lurching off the laboratory slab.

Humans took some getting used to, and the older Outposters happily left direct contact with the halfwalkers to the younger set.

Her meal quickly finished, C'astille cantered across the clearing from the Outposter camp to the Talking House. The halfwalkers had built their part of it first, not long after C'astille had first met the human Calder. The human techniques of building had puzzled the Outposters. The methods seemed highly inefficient, but the human structures went up quickly enough.

A Guardian Army engineer's platoon had poured a concrete slab foundation, assembled a rather large prefab hut and simply bolted it to the slab. The hut was meant to keep the rain off and nothing else, and the slab to keep the hut from sinking into the soggy ground. A quiet-running portable generator was installed and lights were hung. No effort was made to make the hut airtight, but inside it, a more sophisticated structure went up. The artificers assembled a room-sized box of very tough and transparent plastic. It took up about a third of the interior of the prefab hut and *was* airlocked. The artificers added a few conveniences outside on the slab: racks to hold equipment, a hose-down station to get the mud off a suit before entering the airlock. The whole interior of the box was always visible from the outside, except for a portable toilet which could be hidden behind a screen when in use. Calder quickly named the plastic box the Crystal Palace, and was delighted to have it. Learning and teaching a wholly novel language was rough enough without having to stand in the middle of a soggy field in a pressure suit to do it. Gestures, expressions, movement were essential to learning, and all were infinitely easier out of a suit.

Of course, there was no practical limit to how long a pressure suit could be worn if survival was the only criterion. But the suits were heavy, tiring, restricting, they limited vision, and the speakers and mikes were only so good.

In the Palace she could relax, pace, even take a nap or go to the head between language sessions, grab a snack from the compact refrigerator or make a cup of coffee. Far more important, she could see and be seen. Pantomime was often vital to making sure she understood what a word meant, and it was a hell of a lot easier to have the props of language-learning—a drawing board, objects you wanted the names of, notepads and recorders and so on—safely under weatherproof conditions, and it was a double pleasure not to have to handle a pencil through a pressure suit's gloves.

C'astille understood the advantages of getting in out of the rain as well as anyone, and once she had gotten an accidental whiff of what the humans breathed for air she understand why they needed to stay in a suit or a glass box. Unlike humans, the Outposters could smell and taste carbon dioxide and nitrogen. Human air had too little for the former and too much of the latter. She too was glad to get her drawing and writing and recording things out of the rain, and even took the human lead in making the Outposter half of the Talking House as comfortable as possible. She and the other Low Assistances brought in work tables, lights, rest couches, and their own food stores and portable power sources.

As the language lessons went on, it became clear to both sides it would be wise to concentrate on teaching the humans C'astille's language. Things simply weren't working going the other way.

The Outposters had so much trouble learning English that at first Lucy Calder thought they were "hard-wired," as she put it. It seemed possible that Outposters inherited their language genetically, and were no more capable of learning an alternative to the sense of smell. Calder would have been pleased if that idea had been correct; it would have meant one language would be usable across Outpost.

But the Outposters weren't the problem; English was. The Outposters just couldn't seem to get the hang of it. Calder concluded the problem lay in the structure of English, the parts that tone and sound played in meaning. She had a hunch that the 'Posters would do better learning Chinese, but there was little point in teaching them a language no one else in the star system besides Cynthia

Wu understood. Might as well teach them one of the Australians aborigine dialects. Come to think of it, Calder had a feeling C'astille would do pretty well at the abo languages. But not at English.

So Lucy did the learning, slowly, gradually. More of it today, and she had some questions to ask. Dressed in a lightweight pressure suit, she walked the paved path from the human camp to the Crystal Palace. C'astille was there, her tail flicking with eagerness to begin. Calder grinned and waved. Every morning it was the same; the moment she saw the young Outposter, she was caught up in the other's unflagging enthusiasm for their work. She hurried through the lock cycle, stripped her suit off, and sat down at the field desk inside the Palace. She cleared her throat and forced her voice into the odd resonances of C'astille's tongue. "Your presence is sensed, C'astille." It made as much sense as "hello," and meant as much.

"And yours is sensed as well. Talk starts?"

"Talk starts. But word-learning remains deferred," Calder said. It was the passivity of the language that was the most difficult and bewildering. It was hard for her, and hard for her human students of the language, to bear in mind that action must be placed away from the speaker, or better still, removed entirely and the verb used to describe a state of being rather than an action. "Absence of knowledge continues for my Guidances. And yet word-learning and word-puzzlement are at its center. A thing is pointed to—this structure, my clothes, our vehicles, our path to the Talking House—and the humans say they got there by being made, or built. Sometimes the Outposters have things pointed to and it is said they are grown. Your recorders, your structures, your couch are called 'grown.' Is it that verbs 'grow' and 'make' or 'build' are the same, or are so many of your things formed from live things?"

" 'Grow' is not 'build.' My couch is grown, my house is built from walls and other parts of a material grown in sheets. But walls not *precisely* grown. Never living, but made by living things not of my species. Species are caused by my people, and these species are makers of much of our things."

That was tangled, but Calder thought she had the gist. "And the new species that are caused. How many—" Lucy quickly checked her dictionary. No, she didn't have the word for "generation." "How many cycles from parent to offspring between the old species and a perfected new one?"

C'astille pulled her head back on its long neck, an involuntary gesture of surprise. "Why, none . . . or perhaps accurately one. The old form is taken, the changes are made on its—again, the word is not yet given to you. It is *lasut*. Do you have the concept of small structures that are controllers of what a live thing is?"

"Humans have known of this concept long years."

"Here they are called *lasut*." Calder noted its phonetics down, had C'astille repeat it so she could record it and practice it later, and the conversation went on. Both were used to such circumlocutions and pauses by now.

C'astille continued. "The genes are changed, and the next thing to come from them is what is wanted."

"That is not our way," Lucy said. "Human skill with changing these genes exists, but I have suspicions it is quite modest when compared to yours. Much time, many tried, many cycles of parent and offspring between first effort and success. Also, humans seek not to bring forth a wall-growing life form, but just a stronger animal, a plant that will give more food."

"So are all your things made, as has been seen?"

"Highly close to true. A human is the maker, or the maker of a machine that is the maker of nearly all our things."

"Even your *secu werystlon*?"

A tricky term. Literally, it translated as "outer memories," and seemed to cover both sound and sight recorders, computers, perhaps some other gadgets, perhaps even pencil and paper. It occurred to Lucy that the term was a bad fit. It was their name for a class of things that had some equivalence to computers, and recorders. "Yes, if I understand with precision," Lucy said carefully. "These are not grown, but are themselves machines."

"Many of ours live."

Lucy had the sudden and ghastly vision of a disembodied brain inside a glass jar, hooked up to wires. No, it wouldn't be like that. But the image wouldn't fade. *You learn something new every day*, she thought, and the two of them got on with the language lesson.

The days passed, and both sides learned.

Gustav pounded away stolidly at the keyboard.

Alien Contact Status and Action Report 137

General Summary: Once again, no major changes since last report. CI Lucy Calder continues to make gradual progress on Outposter-1 language. The Outposters have confirmed her earlier understanding that there are any number of different languages spoken by the Outposters, many of them mutually unintelligible. Previous theories to the contrary must be abandoned. Orbital examination and mapping of the surface continues to be hampered by cloud cover, but orbital work has located about 100 probable city sites on the planet, in widely scattered locations. Recent low-altitude atmospheric overflights, launched from Orbital Station Ariadne, of many of these sites have located definite small settlements. Many appear to be abandoned. The largest of these seems about as large as a human village of a few thousand. We at Contact Headquarters once again urgently request that these overflights be suspended, as they must be disconcerting to the locals. We do not wish to adversely affect relations with Outposter groups we have not yet met, and these overflights can tell us little more than they already have: that the Outposters have very many small settlements.

Specific Summaries:

Language: Calder has done excellent work, and has now established a reliable basic vocabulary of Outposter-1. At my instruction, she now divides her time between learn-

ing more O-1 and teaching what she has learned already to the trainees sent from Capital. These trainees are already capable of some conversation with the locals. She is also involved in the effort to get a computer to serve as a translating device. All of these efforts will eventually succeed: Calder will become more fluent in O-1 and she expects to be able to talk in related dialects; the trainees will learn the language as well; and the auto-translator device will be perfected. However, I must emphasize once again that all of these projects involve the most gradual and painstaking effort. By the very nature of the work—in large part patient trial-and-error—breakthrough simply are not possible. With all due respect, the work cannot be rushed, and I can assure everyone involved that we at Contact HQ are as eager for more results as anyone. But patience is required. We will be learning the subtle points of O-1 for the next generation at least. Calder deserves nothing but praise for her efforts.

Culture and Technology: I am forced to make the same report I have made so many times before. The level of culture and technology is undetermined but high, and probably higher than thought at the time of my last report a few days ago, particularly in the biological sciences. Apparently, the Outposters can "custom-tailor" the local equivalent of chromosomes on a rapid and routine basis. What would seem a staggeringly difficult job of genetic engineering to us, they can do with casual ease.

At this point, I feel compelled to repeat a caution I have made many times before: It would be a great mistake to assume the Outposters are primitive because we locate no huge cities from orbit, or because they appear semi-nomadic, or because we do not detect powerful radio or electric power generation. We have by no means begun to understand these beings, but I can at least offer a theory. Humans have always assumed that cities, preferably large cities, are the centers of culture, and humans have always assumed that cities are permanent. The Outposters make neither assumption. I believe this is a key dividing point

*in the development of our differing cultures. Insofar as the
connection between culture and technology, I submit a
statement that should have been obvious before we found
the Outposters: There is no such connection. To cite but
one example: The ancient Greeks certainly had a lower
technology than many subsequent civilizations, but certainly they had a higher culture than most. . . .*

There was a muffled *thud, thud* on the bulkhead, which
was what passed for a knock at the door of a pressurized
prefab hut. Gustav, glad of the break, hit the *lock cycle*
button and spent the next two minutes straightening up
the papers on his desk. One nice thing about airlocks—it
was just about impossible for anyone to barge into his
office.

A long series of thumps, clumps, and bumps further
heralded the arrival of a visitor. "Hey, Johnson," Lucy
said, her voice muffled by the breathing helmet, as she
came into the room.

"Hi, Luce. How's the day so far?"

"Good," she said, pulling off her helmet. "I get two
kinds of days—the kind where I wonder why it has taken
us so long to get so little, and the kind where I'm amazed
at how much progress we've made in so short a time.
Today," she said with a grin, "is a Type Two day. The
Outposter voice-recognition program seems to have most
of the bugs out of it, finally, and that's progress. Making
out the next report?"

"Yup. The top brass still want us to hand them a perfect
auto-translator instantly, and can't believe we can't just
pull it down from the shelf. I'm sticking my neck out to
explain why it can't be done in slightly firmer and less
oblique language this time."

"Damn bureaucrats. Yours are the same as ours."

Gustav grunted and said nothing. Lucy was still like
that, probably always would be. She could not or would
not identify herself as a Guardian. Even wrapped in all the
excitement and challenge of this wonderful chance find,

even granted all the privileges and freedom she needed to do the job the Guardians wanted of her, she refused to forget she was a prisoner.

It made things tough for Gustav because it threw both their motives into question. In his soul, he knew himself to be just as much a prisoner of the Central Guardians and their endless, desperate ambition. When, as he frequently did, he asked himself why Lucy went on, he was forced to ask at the same time why he went on.

Because it's an incredible opportunity, not to be refused. Because the dream of meeting the alien is what makes kids join the Navy in the first place. Because we're doing it for our species, not for whatever grubby party goons are living in Capital Palace at the moment. Because to say no would be suicide. Because someone else would do it for them anyway, if not as well. . . . And from there on down the reasons got less convincing, more uncomfortable. Though Gustav couldn't answer why he went on, he thought that Calder might be able to. Which meant there was a limit to how far he could trust her. Gustav didn't like that, because Calder had become what no intelligence officer could afford, even an ex-Intelligence officer: a friend in the enemy ranks.

Gustav broke the silence at last with some comment about his report. They chatted about the routine affairs of the camps, and the progress of various language trainees, and the need to shut down the overflights that damn fool Romero insisted on making. At last they found themselves, as always, coming back to the central and endlessly exciting topic: the Outposters.

"I like them, C'astille especially," Calder said. "Using that damn language is like trying to wrestle wet noodles, but she and I can communicate, and either I'm getting better or she's learning to explain better."

"What does the language itself tell you?" Gustav asked. "I mean about the 'Posters?"

Calder just shrugged. "I'm no xeno-psychiatrist. I'm not an ethnologist, or even a real linguist. The two glaring differences are the sound structure and the bias toward making passive statements. You've seen my translations. They are awkward because O-1 is clumsy for statements of action. English is clumsy for passive statements. Where we'd say 'she came through the door,' they might say—" Lucy shifted to the local tongue and said a few words. "Now that can be translated to English as, 'The door was at the location passed through by the person,' and that's a mess. But the *way* of stating that very passive concept is very direct and succinct in O-1. The verb form is all one word with the proper prefix and suffix and intonation to give just that meaning. To state it in the typically very active voice used in English or most human tongues is very close to impossible."

"And you don't think that says anything about our local friends?"

"It does, I'm sure of it, but I simply don't know *what* it says. It would be real easy to hand out some guff about they're being 'at one with their world' and not divided out from it. Some of the kids back home make that distinction between the aborigines and the Europeans. Mom's the abo and Dad's the Brit—they *both* laughed at that one. I have the distinct feeling the Outposters manipulate their environment for their own convenience just as much as we do. But their needs and methods are both different from ours."

"That's a long-winded way of saying, 'I don't know.' "

Lucy Calder grinned. "Or, to translate from O-1, 'The absence of knowledge is retained in my mind.' "

"Oh, shut up. Let's get some dinner."

CHAPTER SIX

April, 2116

The Planet Bandwidth

With a moody, methodical air to his actions, as if he had been planning it a long time, Commander Randall Metcalf, United States Navy, pulled the bartender's head off.

George Prigot shifted uncomfortably on the next stool and looked around nervously. "Randall, I don't think that's allowed."

Metcalf ignored his friend and carefully set the head down on the counter. It resembled an oversized doll's head, with slightly glazed eyes, waxenly pink skin, and slightly overperfect rosy cheeks. The handlebar moustache looked as if it had been stamped out by a machine—as indeed it had.

"I have been," Metcalf said, pulling out a small tool set, "stuck on this automated hell-hole for over six thousand hours. I have had my hair cut and my food cooked and my pants pressed and my pizza delivered by robots. I have been given exactly accurate directions to and fro by robot cops." Metcalf pulled the wig off the bartender's head, found an inspection plate, and began unscrewing screws. "I have been asked how long I will be gone by parking meters. I have been spoken to by doors, walls, taxis, airplanes, showers, clocks, and elevators, all warning me to use care, not to be late, not to forget, to be sure and look both ways before crossing." Metcalf pried the plate off and peered inside. "I have spent whole days engaged in conversation, without once talking to a human being. Every time I make a purchase my receipt tells me my remaining bank balance, to four utterly meaningless decimal places, not only in the U.S. dollars paid into it by the Navy, but in Bandwidth CashUnits and six other major currencies, based on the exchange rates as of a millisecond before. Every morning and night the damned mirror in the head in my hotel room reminds me to brush my teeth." Metcalf selected a set of wire cutters. "I," he said, snipping the leads to the speaker behind the bartender's smiling mouth, "have _had_ it with all the nag, nag, nag, nag, nag."

"I dunno," Prigot said, still a little nervous and trying to soothe his friend. "I kinda like it. Attentive service, everything works."

"You, old pal, are an engineer. The damn robots don't bother you. You _like_ machines—but would you want your sister to marry one? That's the only damn thing they haven't automated here—yet."

"I don't have a sister."

Metcalf looked up from his work to stare pityingly at Prigot. "Then, to paraphrase the immortal Marx, she's a very lucky woman. You don't get the point, do you? At least here, in the bar we come to every day, I want a machine that will shut up and just pour the booze and leave me alone."

"Ten C.U. says the maintenance machines have it repaired before you can order your next drink," Prigot said.

"You're on. Because I have also just cut the maintenance request caller inside this gizmo's head." Metcalf closed up the inspection panel, replaced the wig, stood to reach over the counter top, and shoved the head back down on the bartender's neck-pivot.

The bartender's body twitched once as the head's circuits linked back up with it. The head swivelled through 360 degrees, then the eyes seem to lock and track. The bartender turned, and its arm came up to shake a finger at Metcalf. A deep bass voice rumbled up from its chest. "Please use care in future, sir," it said. "If not for the back-up speaker in my body cavity, I could not now talk to you, and thus could not serve you properly."

Prigot roared with laughter as Metcalf glared at the robot. "Tomorrow," Metcalf said. "Tomorrow I come in here with a shaped thermite charge and melt you down. Now go get me a double Scotch."

"Draught for me," Prigot said cheerfully. "On your tab. Gotta start spending those ten C.U."

"Thank you. I will get your orders, sirs." The robot rolled down to the other end of the bar.

"Damn it, George." Metcalf stared into the mirror behind the box. "Damn it, George. *Nothing's* going right."

The robot delivered their drinks. Prigot reached out a graceful, long-fingered hand and took up his tankard. That was another thing he liked about Bandwidth: you got a really good-sized beer. Prigot carefully sucked some of the foam off the head, caught Metcalf's eye in the mirror behind the bar, and grinned as he raised his glass to him.

George Prigot was the shorter, chubbier, more relaxed of the two. His brown hair had been bleached almost to blond by Bandwidth's sun, and he had put on a kilo or two. He had grown a beard, too. It was an improvement, and gave his face a maturer look, hiding the almost childlike delight that lit up his face whenever something interesting happened. He wore a rumpled old coverall covered with pockets and zippers and velcro. He seemed relaxed, comfortable. "Come on, Randall. It's not that rough."

Metcalf hadn't fit into Bandwidth as well as Prigot, to say the least. He had the air of a man forced to hurry up and wait, who needed to check the time every three minutes. He was tall, skinny, pale-skinned, with black hair and bushy black eyebrows. His fingers drummed on the counter top, and he leaned his bar stool back on two legs, threatening to overbalance and crash to the floor. He wore his non-dress tropical khaki uniform, with a line of ribbons over his breast pocket that would have deeply impressed anyone who knew what they all meant. "I take it you haven't heard the latest, then," Metcalf said. "I got it through the Navy scuttlebutt. I doubt it'll hit the news services for a day or two. They convicted Mac."

"My God."

"Busted him back to lieutenant commander, confined him to base at Columbia at the Survey Service training center. He's going to be a prisoner and an instructor there at the same time. *He* suggested the sentence *himself*, of course, as the best way he could still serve the war effort while doing his time."

"But why did they do it?"

"We've been through this. Because Mac said they could blow the *Eagle* the way we took out *Leviathan*."

"I know what the charges were. I just can't believe they'd really do it."

"That's something you've got to learn, George. You want to think we're all angels in white at this end. Well, you keep telling me there are decent people among the Guardians, and I believe you, because you're one of them. Here's proof that we've got some flaming bastards on our side."

George Prigot grunted and sipped at his beer. Suddenly his good cheer was gone.

Prigot was a Guardian, born and bred on Capital. He had met Mac Larson on New Finland, become his friend, fought at Mac's side, against his own people, when the brutality of the Guards became too much for his conscience. Prigot *needed* to believe in the rightness of his choice, and that made it difficult for him to accept that

League people could pull a rotten stunt like throwing the book at Mac. Illusions die hard with George.

Metcalf sipped at his Scotch. He had been on New Finland too, had earned his Distinguished Flying Cross there. He knew Mac, could very easily understand George's loyalty to the man—because he felt it himself. He thought back to the time when Berman had died, and Mac found himself forced to take up the command he had never wanted. Mac had saved them. The League forces and the Finns had wanted to curl up and die then, but Mac—Mac had found the way to pull them all together, had found the reserves of courage and hope that hadn't even been there before Mac went looking for them.

Metcalf had good reason to share Prigot's loyalty to Mac. Without Mac, they'd both either be dead or Guardian prisoners right now. Metcalf felt a strong urge to *do* something about Mac, help him in some way. But there was nothing he could do. Except maybe fight the war. And there was no war to fight—and wouldn't be until the bright boys found Capital.

Supposedly, he and George had been shipped to Bandwidth for reasons that had something to do with the search for Capital. No one had quite known what to do with George after New Finland, and Metcalf half suspected *that* had much to do with why the two of them had found themselves on Bandwidth.

The whole thing was a military jury-rig. Certainly there was value in questioning prisoners, and there were any number of Intelligence officers from across the League right here on Bandwidth, very happily doing just that. Whatever prisoners of war from New Finland that could be pried loose from the Finns were here. But there hadn't been many prisoners to start with, and the Finns, as the party most aggrieved by the Guards, were reluctant to give many up. But here the available P.O.W.s were. And so George was here. Perhaps there was even value in having George around as a tame expert, catching the P.O.W.s in lies and suggesting questions that might be asked of them. It might even make sense to have Metcalf there, because he had experience in Guard battle tactics and might have something to contribute. Metcalf rather suspected he was really there because there wasn't much call for fighter pilots at the moment and because the higher-ups wanted some around who could keep Prigot company—and keep an eye on him. George, after all, was a turncoat, and he might turn again. . . .

But Prigot didn't seem to need much watching, though he was glad of Metcalf's company, glad to have a familiar face around. Still, there wasn't much for Metcalf and him to *do*.

Metcalf took a long pull at his drink. They had been cooling their heels, with little to contribute, for close to ten months now. The war had dragged to a halt for lack of an enemy to fight.

And all they had to work with were the prisoners, and the prisoners didn't talk much. When they did talk, it turned out they didn't know much. The Intelligence officers didn't seem to mind. As far as Metcalf could see, most of them saw interrogating the prisoners as a career choice with good job security, rather than as a temporary assignment. They went gaily on, asking the same things again and again, charting responses, correlating results, writing summaries of evidence that were longer than the evidence itself. Metcalf could almost sympathize with the Intelligence team. These were the only enemy troops they were going to milk the chance for all it was worth.

But all that to one side, there was no progress whatsoever on the central question: *Where is Capital?*

The Guardian leadership, very wisely as things turned out, had practically made astronomy a state secret. None of the prisoners had ever seen a star chart. None of them even knew there were grid reference systems to locate stars relative to each other. None of them knew that stars *were* differing sizes and colors. It made asking where their sun was, or what mass and spectral class it was, a stunningly futile undertaking.

As Metcalf was fond of pointing out, rarely had so few who knew so little been asked so much by so many for so long. When he said that to George, George replied, "So what?"

Metcalf didn't have an answer for that. He ordered another double Scotch.

CHAPTER SEVEN

Chralray Village: the Current Nihilist Camp

D'eltipa had a great desire to be found anywhere but where she was. But it was this village, that they had tarried in for far too long, and this hall, and this time, and she had no choice but to meet with her First Advice, Nihilist M'etallis. D'eltipa found irony in M'etallis's title. As Primary Guidance of the Nihilists, she had never accepted a syllable of M'etallis's advice. And now M'etallis would succeed her. M'etallis would be the one to deal with the halfwalkers.

The aliens, strange as they were, strange as they had to be, represented so much change and renewal to come—they were hope itself—and yet they could not have brought their remarkable flying-carrying machines down out of the sky at a worse time. Even without the halfwalkers, the situation would be explosive. And the halfwalkers, weird creatures that they were, represented infinite complication. No one had made sense of them yet. The aliens seemed to have no desire to *go* anywhere. And they did things in such strange ways. D'eltipa found herself forced to believe the reports of the learners, but she still found it fantastic that such a complex thing as a spacecraft was *built* and not grown. Perhaps, the learners suggested, it was actually impossible to grow one, or grow the parts of one to be assembled. Something about stresses and pressure and heat. The halfwalkers could build those things and yet seemed to have no skill of biology at all. Strange indeed.

She felt her mind straying, and almost allowed it down the side path. But the *humans*, as they called themselves, were not the central problem, though M'etallis no doubt had schemes already that involved them. M'etallis herself was the problem—a problem just waiting to happen. No, that was too gentle. M'etallis was a disaster *impatient* to happen. And D'eltipa could see no way that would keep M'etallis from the post of Primary Guidance. D'eltipa had even given up her hopes for a splitting of the path, of disciples of *her* Guidance being there to start anew down the correct course after she was a suicide or had been Divided from her people. And that time would be soon. She understood fully that she should have surrendered Guidance and taken her own life long ago, but she had remained, desperately hoping for some other inheritor than M'etallis. But D'eltipa's nearest followers were all dead—suicides, the kindly, dignified, death Nihilism had been founded to grant. And D'eltipa hung on, past all hope, until it was too late, until she herself felt the coming of Division. And, for the founder of the Nihilists, that was an irony far too cruel.

M'etallis! Nihilism would be so perverted under her that it should not be called by that name. Murderism, or Annihilationism, perhaps. But there would be no peaceful endings, no aid for the fearful under the next Primary Guidance. The upstart was not interested in easing the way out of life. She looked only for power. And soon she would have it.

That last point was one of the few on which M'etallis would agree with her Primary Guidance. The old fool was headed straight for Division—and undoubtably knew it. M'etallis felt a sudden acute shock of her chronic impatience. All the cantering about in circles, all the subtle—and unsubtle—suggestions to certain Nihilists that their proper time to die had come, all the agreements formed and broken, all the efforts meant to put her in her present place, all of it was at last to pay off. M'etallis was certain to take control and get this absurd little sect to be something worthwhile. And now D'eltipa courted the final humiliation, for no other possible purpose than to hold things back from their inevitable resolution.

M'etallis blew an angry snort through her blowhole at the thought. All the time that had been wasted! Why couldn't the old spread their wings and give over to the young without all this interference?

M'etallis paced back and forth down the long, low halls of Chralray's Second House. It was almost time to go and meet with D'eltipa at Guidance Hall. But wait. Delay a moment. Let D'eltipa fidget a while too. Time was on M'etallis's side, and it might as well be used.

She trotted out to the south windows that looked toward the meadow and the halfwalker's camp. Plain old bad luck that it had taken so long to clear the vermin out of the area when the humans first arrived. The humans had very prudently stayed in their carrier—*ship* was one word for it, and *lander* another—until their hosts could wipe out the more energetic—and hungry—animal life. Hunters and beaters still worked endlessly to keep the perimeter clear. M'etallis wondered if the halfwalkers appreciated the trouble it took to keep such a large clearing safe. Perhaps they did. The humans seemed to be making a very permanent job of that camp. They remained, and built as if they intended to stay forever. There was no sign of their looking toward the Road—but then the Roads they travelled across the sky must be long enough indeed.

M'etallis stamped her left forefoot. *She* could do with a bit of travel now. The Nihilists had stayed too long in this place. Time to strike camp, time to find an empty village or build a new one for the next season. She couldn't remember any Group spending this long in one village. Chralray might even spring up into a permanent city, fate forbid.

But the aliens were too great a chance to pass by. It had been M'etallis herself who had heard third-hand from a sojourner that some big metal shape had come back from the sky and come to rest near Chralray, stayed a bit, and then left with a great noise—that some odd creatures had been seen around it. That was why M'etallis had chosen Chralray Village for the season. M'etallis was not one to let new things slip by.

But now it was well past time for the meeting with D'eltipa. The skin around M'etallis's eyes crinkled in the Z'ensam equivalent of a gleeful smile, and she galloped off toward Guidance Hall.

The Z'ensam are the descendents of migratory herd animals and, like most migrators, are not a territorial species. The concepts of personal property, and money, and trade certainly exist, but do not hold anywhere near the emotional importance they do for humans. These are important only insofar as they helped to establish rank, a pecking order.

Their property is generally portable, for the very good reason that it has to be. The Road would call, the eyes would yearn for new vistas, and it would be time to move. It took the strongest discipline and the most compelling of reasons to keep the Z'ensam in one place for long. But the halfwalkers seemed prepared to stay where they were indefinitely, and *that* qualified as a compelling reason.

To the Z'ensam, it was natural to abandon a village and move the Group to a new site—either an existing village some other Group had abandoned, or a virgin site where a new village would be grown. Indeed, the villages were more for the sake of protecting property from the weather and keeping Groups organized than they were for the comfort of individuals. Humans are a tropical species, while the Z'ensam evolved in a fairly harsh temperate zone. The latter are therefore better adapted to extremes of cold and heat and rough weather, and tend to bother far less with heating and cooling.

M'etallis walked straight into Guidance Hall without a knock, a pause, or the slightest formality. A great deal of human etiquette and ceremony and law deals with the circumstances under which one can and cannot or must or must not admit or deny another to one's home territory. Such questions simply did not enter into any Z'ensam society.

A human second-in-command, especially a rebellious one, would have been stopped by an underling and announced, delayed, be made to wait, perhaps even led through guards and fortifications—symbolic or functional—before arriving in the presence of the Leader. If such things had been absent in a human meeting, there would have been a great show *made* of their absence, a demonstration that the visitor was welcome and trusted in the Leader's territory. But the Z'ensam lacked the trappings of the territorial imperative, along with the imperative itself. M'etallis simply trotted through the doorway of the Guidance's hall and wandered about until she found D'eltipa impatiently pacing down one of the corridors. The older Z'ensam pulled herself up short and glared at her subordinate. At which moment M'etallis had to physically restrain herself from rushing outside to gallop around the building and crow with delight. D'eltipa actually had a long red *welt* down the length of her back! She was already *in* the first stages of Division. She was practically ready to keel over then and there! M'etallis held her emotions in check and contented herself with a merry flick of her tail.

"Your presence is sensed, Primary Guidance," M'etallis said, in what she hoped was a calm and neutral voice.

"And yours, First Advice. Nothing can be hidden at this point, I know my condition as well as you. You need treat me with the dignity due wisdom only a little while longer. But I still have time for talk. Come, let us be found in the garden."

"As your Guidance is pleased," M'etallis said. The garden was surrounded by a low wall. They would be unseen there—and that was just as well; D'eltipa's appearance was not suited to being seen in public. M'etallis was surprised to find herself concerned that the Guidance not be humiliated. She twitched her tail, and realized she still had feelings for her old teacher. She felt a sudden twinge of guilt that she had driven D'eltipa to the extremity of accepting Division. But the change must come. New thoughts must lead Nihilism, and D'eltipa of all Nihilists must accept that each person choose her own mind's way out of the world. But it was sad that things had reached such a crossroads.

M'etallis could not admit it herself, but she was unnerved to find principle, and tenderness, and regret at unfortunate necessity, still in her soul. She had sought power so long, she had almost convinced herself that power was all she cared for. Perhaps one day it would be. She would be by no means the first being seduced away from a goal by the means of achieving it.

The older Nihilist led the way into the garden. It was a lovely spring day, a good day to enjoy with time so short. "So, M'etallis, soon you shall be called by a different name. Are you practiced, so you will answer when someone calls for D'etallis?"

M'etallis chose not to respond to such needling. "Not as such, but I have trust that my new name will be familiar to me."

"Yes, you are practiced, then. And you have been ready for a long time, as well. But you are not called here for teasing, but for schooling, and warning. This has been said before, but hear it again: Change is like any tool; not good, or bad, but only a thing which can be suited to many purposes. Use it, but wisely. I fear you will not."

"Guidance. Let us not have platitudes or wasted time and words. You left with me, years ago, when I ended my sojourn at your side, the knowledge that the curse of our people was in knowing their fate. All other living things, plant and animal, wild-evolved or guided and bred by us down a path of our choosing, did not know of their doom. Even the animals whose life cycle parallels our own do not experience the loss we do. Only our kind, the Z'ensam, have ever known the pride of having a full name—and so only our kind are haunted by the fear of losing it—"

"Gallop on, say it. I know my fate. Losing it to be Divided out from thought and knowledge. But you have taken that teaching to extremes, leaving it perverted. I had only the goal of aiding those who so wished a chance to pass from life painlessly, with mind intact, still bearing a full name. *But each must choose for herself.* You would have us *all* swept away. Can you not seen the paradox you find drawn around yourself? You have used the power of your own mind to reach the conclusion that sentience— the power of mind—is an abomination! You seek the extinction of your own people."

"I seek the perfection of nature," M'etallis said primly. "All life is beautiful. Death is ugly. Therefore the *knowledge* of death is ugly. And, that knowledge of our own doom is ours alone. The heritage of all other living things is to grow and live and prosper and multiply—until death, unknown, unseen, unlooked for, takes one life to replace it with another. A flower, a bug, a cartbeast, have no realization that they will die, and so for them the ugliness of death does not exist. The heritage of all the Z'ensam is a grim and terrible choice: an early death, or to let the cycle of life debase us—" M'etallis drew up short. "Guidance, pardon. The heat of my feeling, I did not recall your circumstance. . . ."

"I find relief that you can still feel embarrassment. There is kindness still in your soul. But it only strengthens my question: You seek the *power* to do so, but would you use it—would you truly wipe out your own kind?"

"What is the better alternative? We are trapped. We might go on and on, yes—but to what end? What goal? That the unborn generations can grow to find the ugliness of death or division to snatch at them? I would have the melancholy of the Z'ensam over and done, not drawn out over the endless generations. And, Guidance, I must add a further point. It is not my own kind I would wipe out. It is *mind* that perverts nature and life with the knowledge of death and the end of things. It is *mind* I would wipe out: mind wherever it is, wherever it comes from, doing so by any means possible. And you call me cruel, cynical, jaded already, so this next will seem in character. It will require power to wipe out the Z'ensam, but we cannot gain power by killing those we would have power over. A grand paradox. But now we are presented with a far easier, far more palatable way to kill our way into great power."

D'eltipa looked at her successor in stunned silence. There was a dull, rumbling roar from the meadow. Both of them turned to watch the human's lander rise into the perfect spring sky.

CHAPTER EIGHT

Guardian Contact Base, Outpost

Captain Lewis Romero was a dangerous man with an idea, the way an unskilled pilot was dangerous with a spacecraft. The pilot had no idea what his ship could do, and Romero hadn't thought his idea out past the end of his nose.

He was also ambitious. *Ariadne* station was a busy place these days—new battle fleets were forming and training, and they made much use of the station's communications and supply capabilities. *Ariadne* was also charged with supplying the contact base on Outpost and handling the scientists' ever-growing demand for communications and information. Romero's command was doing useful work, his people were accomplishing things—but it wasn't enough. Romero had finally come to the realization that he had been deliberately stuck in a backwater post, and that the Outposters were more than just of interest to the scientists: They were a golden opportunity for career advancement. He had been a good little sailor long enough. None of the excitement going past was doing him any good, and it was time to change all that.

That was why he had come down to Outpost. Ostensibly, it was a courtesy call, a chance for Romero to see after the supply situation, make sure that all was going well, a chance to listen for complaints or suggestions. All that would do as an excuse. Romero had to admit to himself that Gustav seemed to have things well in hand. The camp was in excellent condition, clean, well laid-out, and the enlisted men, officers, and civilians all seemed quite satisfied with the physical conditions they worked under. Romero strolled the camp, watching humans and Outposters working together. He had never seen a native in the flesh before; they seemed quite surprisingly large. Romero was upset to see everything working smoothly, good progress being made everywhere. Damn! He should *never* have let Gustav take command of the contact base—though with Gustav's Intelligence background and the shortage of personnel, there had been very few other choices, and there was no way Romero could have relinquished his command of *Ariadne* to do take the job himself. More galling still was the way Romero's job on *Ariadne* was suddenly so much more difficult with Gustav gone. Officially, Gustav was still the station's executive officer, on detached duty, so Romero couldn't put in for a replacement XO. The personnel shortage again. But there was so much *work* to do with Gustav gone! Damn his luck for being handed a prize like First Contact! *He'd* be promoted, he'd be in the history books, and Romero would be stuck on *Ariadne* for twenty years!

Romero needed to talk directly with the Outposters to get his plan started. He needed *all* the credit. If Gustav got his nose into it, no one would ever notice Romero at all. So Romero had fussed and fumed and waited until the computerized auto-translators were ready. He had been one of the main sources of pressure for getting them done—though he had been very backroom about it all, very careful to see to it that no one realized *he* was eager. He had never personally urged the techs to finish fast, but had gotten others to do that for him. If the Outposters were the biological geniuses everyone claimed, Romero knew he was a made man.

But how to get in touch with the Outposter leaders?

Romero had worried over that point for endless hours, and had never come up with anything better that stopping the first native he saw and handing out that centuries-old saw, "Take me to your leader."

Which is exactly what he did with the next 'Poster that went past, and the black box of the auto-translator blatted and hooted out his meaning in O-1. As luck would have it, the 'Poster was C'astille, the native most used to humans and their ways. If humans had had almost no luck figuring out the Outposter social structure, the Outposters had had just as little success understanding human rules for living. But both sides had tried, and Lucy Calder had explained military ranks and insignia as best she could, even using a wall chart to show which was higher and lower. The insignia this human had painted on her pressure suit denoted a higher rank than any a Z'ensam had ever seen. Perhaps *this* one should be addressed in the senior mode. C'astille decided to play it safe and use the *D'* prefix. And she was new here: The auto-translator had barely made sense of the human's words. It took a while for the halfwalkers to understand the limitations of the device they had built themselves. Only after she had considered all that did she think on the actual request the human had made. Certainly if this was a human Guidance, come at last, M'etallis—no, *D'*etallis now that Eltipa has divided and no longer had a full name—D'etallis would want to see her. C'astille decided she had best cooperate.

"Our Primary Guidance, D'etallis, would be honored," she said. She spoke in careful Australian-accented English, startling Romero. "I feel certain that she would wish to know you. May I have knowledge of your name?"

"Romero. Captain Lewis Romero," he said nervously.

"Honored D'Romero," C'astille said, "you shall soon be with D'etallis. The Talking House is unused at present. If you would accept waiting there, I would bring D'etallis, and thus both sides could talk in comfort."

"That would be good."

"Then D'etallis shall soon be there. The two of you shall

sense each other soon." With that, C'astille turned and walked away.

Romero's heart hammered in his chest. It shouldn't have been that easy, but he wasn't going to argue. The first hurdle was cleared. Maybe his idea would actually work.

The two sides misunderstood each other, and this worked to their mutual advantage. Romero was being furtive, hiding his intent from his subordinates, trying to get around the rules, doing something far beyond his authority. He was surprised that the Outposter had accepted him at face value, instantly. For her part, C'astille was delighted to be approached by a senior human eager to get right down to talking. The Z'ensam had been impatiently waiting for something of substance from their visitors. Chains of command, orders from above, the inertia imposed by a large organization, the delays of distance; these seemed inexplicable excuses, stalling. Finally, it seemed, the humans had sent someone who could do more than hold language lessons. C'astille felt D'Romero was the first human she had met who *wasn't* being furtive (besides Lucy M'Calder, whom she trusted even if she didn't understand her status). Finally, someone in charge was here. Maybe this D'Romero wouldn't wait for orders from above—a concept the Z'ensam were just barely beginning to understand—before he *did* anything. Leader to leader, directly, immediately, that was the way the Z'ensam did things.

D'etallis was as eager as C'astille. *Now* maybe they would get somewhere. She hurried to the Talking House, and found this D'Romero in the boxy transparent room that held the human air, folded up in their strange way into that support thing they called a chair. D'Romero saw her and stood up.

"D'Romero. I am D'etallis, Primary Guidance of this Group. Your presence is sensed."

"And yours as well." That much etiquette he had learned,

anyway. "I come to ask questions, and perhaps to offer trade."

"Good. There are items you make that we would have."

"Ah—yes. Let me see if I can explain. I have put several things on the table on your side of the pressure wall." Romero pointed to the table. There was a League pressure suit, a section of plastic bulkhead cut from the *Venera*, some samples of League electronic equipment, a few other things.

D'etallis turned and looked. "I sense them."

"Good. Now then. Here is my question. I am told that your people are very wise in the life-sciences. That you can cause living things to breed and grow as you desire." ·

"Certainly."

"Very good. Now then. Can your scientists create living things that can eat any or all of those materials, live on them, breed and grow very quickly?"

D'etallis went over to the table and barely glanced at the things on it. She picked up the suit and set it down almost at once. "Absolutely. They could be bred in a few weeks at the most. Eaters are used to dispose of unwanted things already. Simple modifications of these beasts would suit your need."

"Wonderful!"

"We would want things in return."

"Of course." Romero waited for it. If they wanted something he couldn't promise. . . .

"But let me understand clearly before you hear my bargain. I have toured one of your *landers*"—D'etallis used the English word—"and I have seen of what they are made. I am told that you have much larger vehicles, *starships*, that are so big they cannot leave space to land. All these pieces you show me seem to be from a lander or a starship. If properly bred Eaters were let loose on a starship made of such materials, they would wreck it in days, perhaps hours."

Romero hesitated. "Yes, that is true."

D'etallis flicked her tail. "You seek living weapons, then.

You seek such simple things because you humans know all but nothing about life-science, and your enemies, familiar with your other ways of fighting, would have no defense against such things."

Romero found himself in a cold sweat, but he could see nothing to be gained by lying. This D'etallis saw the whole thing. "You are correct."

D'etallis's face wrinkled in pleasure. These humans were ready to help her! And in so doing, they would teach her all their own weaknesses. "I face a similar problem, halfwalker. I want *your* weapons. I have seen the ones your people carry, and I am sure ours are crude and powerless in comparison."

Romero almost fainted with relief. He was going to pull it off! His future was assured. Now all they needed to work on was the details. He ran a supply depot. Weapons he could supply until he had enough bioweapons to show the brass—and once they saw bioweapons wrecking a ship, they would back him all the way. The two of them talked on.

Lucy Calder didn't discover that she had left the voice-actuated recorder on all night until she ran the tape next morning.

CHAPTER NINE

Guardian Contact Base, Outpost

Lucille Calder was sitting in Gustav's office when he arrived the next morning. Without any preamble, she rose and spoke. "Johnson, I'm about to take a terrible risk. And I might be putting you in terrible danger. It might even be treason. I don't know. But I don't see any choice. You're the only person I can trust," she said, holding up a recording tape. "You've got to listen to this. I left the voice-activated recorder on by accident overnight, and it picked something up."

Johnson Gustav didn't know how to react. He was having an increasingly hard time knowing how to deal with Lucy. Technically, he was the officer in charge of this CI, the warden of her prison, or to put it in less prettied-up terms, her slave master. But he was also her partner in an exciting piece of research, her chief scrounger in the constant fight for equipment, the assistant coordinator of all the projects she was involved in. And whatever had brought her here this morning didn't seem likely to simplify matters. He sighed and asked, "What's going on, Luce?"

"Something that could make the war worse. Spread it to the Outposters. Johnson, I know you and I never discuss the war, or politics, unless we really have to. But I know neither of us wants the killing to spread. And it might, and

I need to talk to you, and you have to listen to this goddamned recording!"

The Guardian Intelligence officer looked over the Conscripted Immigrant. It was hard, even impossible, to think in those terms about Lucy. He looked again, harder. There was barely controlled fear, even horror, in her face. Whatever this was, it was bad. And he was her friend. That much he knew, whatever the rules told him. "Okay, so I'll listen to it. You aren't the sort who'd put both of us at risk for no reason. I trust you."

"Thank you, Johnson. I hope you don't regret it." She pulled a portable recorder out of her equipment bag and slipped the tape into it.

Gustav went through the motions of filling the coffee pot and getting a pot started as Lucille fussed with the recorder, finding the right spot on the tape roll. Finally she found what she was after and let the tape roll. Gustav froze when he heard Romero's voice. He turned away from the coffee machine, sat down behind his desk and listened carefully, the color draining from his face. When it was over, he shook his head and spoke in a whisper. "No wonder he wanted to make this damn fool inspection trip. Jesus H. Christ. Romero, you stupid, stupid idiot."

"Johnson," Lucy said, her voice quivering on the edge of hysteria, "*those bioweapons are to be pointed at my people*. If Romero's idea works, I'll have helped kill them! I can't go on with my work here and tell myself that learning to talk to the Outposters is for all humanity if the result is a thug like Romero and an alien meglomaniac sitting around planning massacres!"

She stopped, breathed in and out deeply for a moment, making a visible attempt to regain control of herself. She straightened her back and looked at Gustav, straight in the eye. "Lieutenant Gustav, on your honor—*tell me the truth*: Was Romero speaking for himself, or was the deal he offered Guardian policy? If the bloody Central Guardians are behind that horrible plan, *you have to tell me*."

Gustav felt sick inside. The last of his faith was gone.

The whole thing was rotten. He could give her a precisely truthful answer, but he knew the scuttlebutt, he knew what had been going on, he knew what manner of men had survived the purges and the shake-ups. And he knew how they would respond to Romero. He shut his eyes, cradled his face in his hands. "It is not Guardian policy," he said, his voice muffled by his hands. "Not yet. But it will be. You're right, you and I never talk politics, but I guess it's time to start. The bloody stupid bastards were wiped out on New Finland. The invasion failed. *No one* made it back. And every source we've got says the League will be out looking for us in force. They know we exist now, and they're scared of us. That changes *everything*. They know we're out here, they know we've killed a lot of people, and every resource they've got will be put into finding us. It means they *will* find us. Our leaders have finally admitted that to themselves, and they're in a panic."

He paused for a long moment, and then went on in a bitter, angry voice. "And our courageous, idiotic Leader of the Combined Will, General Jules Jaquet, who got us into this mess, also got himself into some very big trouble. There was a quiet little coup attempt and he just barely hung onto power. Now he's got to show he's tough and capable and ready to fight the defensive war he's forced on us, or else he's out on his ass. And the people he has to impress, the admirals and the generals and the pols, are brutal, crude. Barbarians. Jaquet and his crowd shot all the decent men still in the government, or threw them in jail. Most of the better ones resigned long ago."

"But what happens now?" Lucy asked.

"Romero's probably already en route to Capital. He'll talk up the idea of bioweapons at anyone who'll listen, and the brass are desperate enough that they *will* listen. Jaquet will *love* the idea. There is no way we can stop them. They have the auto-translators, and people who know O-1. The situation is completely out of our control. Oh, I could hand you some piece of nonsense that maybe the government wouldn't stoop that low, but the Centrals are scared silly. They'll try anything." Gustav suddenly slammed his fist down onto the desk. "The stupid, stupid, *fools!* We have no idea about these Outposters, what they are, what they think, what they want—and the higher-ups want to give them lessons in how to kill humans and wreck ships!"

Lucy stared at him. She knew, and Gustav knew, that he had just crossed a point of no return. He should have had her arrested for spying, had her confined already, the recording destroyed. "Thank you for telling the truth, Johnson. And thank you for having the decency to be horrified."

"I wish I wasn't so easy to horrify," Gustav growled. "I'd sleep better. But wait a second—is there any hope on the other end? Is there any chance that the *Outposters* can't do it? That they can't deliver?"

Lucy thought hard for a moment and shrugged. She felt very tired. "I don't know, and I don't think any of your technicians or scientists could answer that—"

"And even if they could, I couldn't risk asking them. Loyal Guardians all. No Settlers here, thank you. Besides me, I suppose."

"What's a Settler?"

"People back home on Capital who want to plant some crops there instead of trying to conquer the universe. Not important now. But the point is we can't ask the techs."

"I trust C'astille," Lucy said suddenly, firmly.

"How? Why? Isn't she one of these Nihilists or whatever that religion of D'etallis's is?"

"It's not a religion, or a philosophy. And C'astille isn't one of them. She's a sojourner."

"Say again?"

"A sojourner," Lucy said. "I don't quite understand it all myself, so I can't explain it very well. Nihilism is a Group, and a Group is sort of a small nation, or subnation, except territory isn't involved, and I have no clear ideas about what the supernation is that oversees it all. Anyway, let's say you didn't like your Group, that you didn't agree with the ideas the Group shared. You'd leave and get on the road and find another Group. Easy to do. They have excellent roads, and communications are good. You know they have radio, and the equivalents of books and maps. If you find a Group you agree with, you can drift into it as it travels the road. If you disagree, you vote with your feet again and find some other Group, until you're travelling with a crowd that thinks the way you do. And they certainly travel. All the phrases and sayings about roads and journeys show how important movement is to them. It's very unusual for Outposters to stay in one place as long as they have here, incidentally; we're *important* to them. And since the Nihilists have *us*, that makes the Nihilists important, and they've attracted a lot of new members who are curious about us. And lost a few who just got restless and hit the road again."

"But you were explaining why you could trust C'astille," Gustav said.

"Right, I'm getting there, but it takes so much background . . ." It seemed strange to be giving a lecture on Outposter society at a time like this, but Johnson had to *understand*. "More or less in what corresponds to late adolescence, a young Outposter is expected to wander off from his Group and spend time travelling with other Groups. Sort of exchange students, I suppose. A wanderjahr. They aren't expected to join the other Groups, though they can if they wish. Usually, you finish your sojourn and go find your birth-Group. And C'astille speaks of her Group, which is north of here at the moment, as if she still wants to get back there someday. She definitely has no interest in being a Nihilist. And before you ask, as far as I can make it out, a Nihilist is someone who believes in committing suicide before going mad, or suffering senility, or something. Apparently there's a high incidence of mental disease among the elderly. They don't like to talk about it much, and when they do it's pretty oblique stuff, even for Outposters. C'astille very strongly does not believe in Nihilism. She was more or less just passing through when we landed, and she stayed around out of curiosity. I might add that she seemed worried when the old leader died and this D'etallis took over."

"Do you think we could talk to C'astille? Play her the tape, ask her if such bioweapons were possible?"

"Yes—and more than that. I think we owe it to her. Don't forget, in exchange, D'etallis wants human weapons to attack Outposters. The other Groups have to be warned."

"Then let's find her," Gustav said, rising.

"Okay," Lucy said, and suddenly the brittle calm that had sustained her collapsed. She felt afraid, more afraid than she had been since the *Venera* was hijacked. "Johnson? If it's true—what can we do about it?"

Johnson Gustav looked at the coffee maker. He had forgotten to switch it on. "I don't know, Lucy. We need time to think. But we're in this, even if we don't like it. Let's get suited up and find our friend."

They found C'astille without too much difficulty. She was fascinated by all things human, especially construction, and was developing into a highly qualified sidewalk superintendent. It had been getting more and more difficult to find a place to land supply craft as the Contact Base grew, and so a team of Guardian Army engineers was pouring a reinforced concrete landing pad in a nearby clearing. Suspecting that the native would take an interest in the proceedings, Gustav and Lucy drove a jeep over to look for her, and sure enough, C'astille was there to watch the engineers at work.

C'astille was glad to see Lucy, and surprised to see Gustav. For his part, Gustav was just as glad to find C'astille well away from the main camp and prying eyes.

"C'astille! We need talk with you," Lucy called in O-1 as she jumped from the jeep. She stumbled just a bit as she hit the ground—she had never gotten exactly *graceful* in a pressure suit, even in one of the lightweight models they had finally gotten. A few of the Guardians engineers went without suits at all, and just used respirators or air helmets. But Outpost smelled a lot worse than it looked. That incredibly rich moldy odor crept past any respirator seal, and permeated any clothing worn outdoors. It was easier to go with a suit and leave the smell in the airlock. And it made you a lot more popular in crowded areas. Even with airlocks and filters, enough Outposter air leaked into the mess hall to make it smell like a pile of steaming compost. But noses got used to it.

C'astille waved—a habit she had picked up from the humans—and trotted over to Lucy.

"Hello, Lucille and Johnson. I am glad to see you," C'astille said carefully. She was justifiably proud of the English she had learned. She did better than any other Outposter. Lucy was by this time convinced there was no single cause for the problems the 'Posters had with English. It was a combination of the sounds they could produce, and language construction, and viewpoint, and who knows what else. Lucy often wondered how bad her own O-1 accent was, though now wasn't the time to worry about it. But C'astille's Aussie-flavored English was an odd touch of home.

"C'astille," she said in the native language. "You are sensed. M'Gustav and I are here for talk. He does not have many words of your tongue, but of course can hear and talk through the translator machine he carries." She paused. How to explain? "We have accidentally learned a thing, and it is most urgent that we know if it is true or not. Come take a little walk with us."

C'astille looked at the two of them. Something was strange. Then it came to her. They had something to say they wanted no one else to hear, not even other humans. The idea was exciting. "Fine," she said, eagerly sweeping the ground with her tail. "The forest is safe of Hungry Ones for a good distance. Let us be in the trees."

Lucy began to speak as the three figures moved into the brush. "We want you to listen to a recording of talk between your Guidance and ours. The recording happened accidentally, no one *sought* to ah, hear this, but it happened, and when it was heard. . . ." Lucy found her voice trailing off as she ran out of excuses.

"It happened. It doesn't matter how it came to be," C'astille said.

Lucy shrugged. If C'astille didn't mind, she wasn't going to argue. She wasn't even too surprised that C'astille wasn't upset at a case of spying on her leader. It fit with the Outposter viewpoint, somehow. "So, listen." She unslung her equipment bag, dug out the recorder, and punched the play button.

C'astille bent her head forward to hear better and stood, stock still, while the voices of human, Z'ensam, and the translator machine talked.

Finally the tape ran out. She gave a low snorting noise, shifted on her feet, and said, "I have heard. What more would you know?" Her voice was suddenly flat and nasal, her whole body seemed strangely stiff and unmoving.

"Can your people make such creatures, that will eat such things?"

She wobbled her head back and forth on its long neck, a nervous fidgeting movement. "Yes, we can. As D'etallis said, it would be easy to change them from creatures we already have. This does not mean we *should*. Your people have no experience of our fighting. There would be great destruction."

Gustav thought of nuclear bombs, lasers, automatic weapons, and spoke through the translator for the first time. "The same could be said of your people facing our weapons."

"D'etallis seeks power and control and the expansion of her Group," C'astille said. "She is a dangerous person, and I do not doubt that she would be willing to use any weapon she could get at, against anyone she could get. If she gets a weapon from D'Romero, she will not hesitate to turn it on Romero. What drives your Guidance to do this foolish thing?"

"In all accuracy, we must call him M'Romero, for he is no true Guidance, no Leader," Lucy said. "He will go to those in power, and seek power from them in exchange for the living weapons."

"This should not be what occurs." C'astille said.

Lucy couldn't tell if C'astille was simply speaking in the normal passive voice of O-1, or if she was deliberately speaking ambiguously, trying to learn what the humans felt before she gave too much away. "M'Gustav and I agree. But we do not know how to stop it. M'Romero is gone, and has already spread his message—and D'etallis will have done the same."

"Yes. She would not wait," the Outposter agreed. "Then we must warn others. I must be with my Group and give warning. But I have no understanding of you two. Is not M'Romero of your Group?"

Lucy paused again. How to explain? There wasn't time for the complicated truth of the League and the Guards and Gustav's Settlers, whoever they were. But she couldn't lie. "We do not share the words for me to make all clear, and accurate. But this is close to truth: I am not of M'Romero's group, the Guardians. I am a sojourner, like you. I travelled here against my will, and was delighted to find your people at the end of the trip. I have helped these Guardians to speak with you, because I was curious and sought knowledge, but I can do so no longer. These weapons will be used against my Group, and so I have hurt my own people. I must stop."

"I am of the Guardians," Gustav said, his translator's words carrying none of the complicated emotion Lucy could hear in his own voice, "but I must take a new road, try and stop what the Guardians would do. Lucy's Group is at war with mine. If my Group attacks her with terrible new weapons, that will only make her side strike back at my side the harder. No good can come of making that war bigger. And there must not be war with your species helping to kill mine, or my species helping to kill yours. Begin that now, and humans might be trapped into hating your kind, being afraid of you. And they might decide to kill all of you," he said, and then hesitated. "Which they could do."

"I believe you, human. But I have often sensed that you think us not as clever as you, because you can do things we cannot, or because you choose to do things we choose not to do. I understand your people are spread across the sky, and our astronomy is good: I know how vast the sky is. *But our machines are living things that grow, and breed, and reproduce.* If we make two, we have made millions. D'etallis has a strange vision of Nihilism. The idea has been passive, she would make it active. Again, you and I do not share the words to say *why,* but she seeks to kill all the Z'ensam, all the Outposters. When she had only the weapons and the knowledge of all Z'ensam, she was no great danger. The other Groups could counter her moves. With human machines behind her, she will walk far down that killing road. But do not imagine you are safe in all your worlds. You *must* understand, and believe, hard though it might be. If she became the leader of all the Z'ensam, and decided her ideas called for the death of humans, she could kill all of *you.*"

The two humans were silent.

"I believe you, C'astille," Lucy said at last.

"That is good. But what is to be done?" C'astille asked.

"I have to stop my work here, immediately," Lucy said. "The best hope we have is delay, and the only way to delay is by not helping. There are very few records that haven't been copied or passed along yet. Not more than a day or two's worth. Those can be destroyed."

"Can the two of you fake things?" Gustav asked. "Create confusion with bad translations or something?"

"No," C'astille said. "There are too many others who would find the mistakes too soon. M'Calder is right. All we can do is stop. And then I must leave for my Group, warn them."

"That'll have *you* safe. But what about M'Calder?" Gustav said. "I can cover for you for a few days, Lucy. Maybe you could fake being sick, or something. But then what?"

Lucy shifted her feet, tried to scratch her nose, and bounced her fingers off the pressure suit's helmet. She wished they could sit down comfortably and think and talk. But the only place where all three of them could be comfortable was the Crystal Palace, and that wasn't safe. She shifted to English, and let Gustav's translator keep C'astille up to date. "Can I pretend to be sick enough to be pulled back to *Ariadne*?"

Gustav thought about it and shrugged. "I suppose. We don't have a real doctor down here. But what's the point?"

"Well, you said that the League was bound to find us, sooner or later. When? How long do we have?"

Gustav made a vague gesture with his hands. "Tomorrow. Ten years from now. They've got a lot of ground to cover. But now we've given them a reason to make the effort."

"Okay, I'm thinking out loud. Suppose we gave C'astille some sort of homing beacon. Something that would give out a signal we could track on a frequency the Guards aren't likely to monitor. Then she could go off with her Group and we fould find her later on."

"Yeah, so?"

"So when the League arrives, they're going to want someone who can talk to the Outposters, and they'll want some Outposters to talk to. I could be their link, their ticket in. Say I get caught without a helmet and *get* carbon-dioxide poisoning. I get sent to *Ariadne*, deathly ill. The doctor there looks me over, and pokes me and prods me and makes me feel better. When I recover, I steal a lander and make a break for it. I land near C'astille's beacon and wait for the League. When they come, I contact them."

"How?"

"If the lander's still functional, I fly. If not, the lander's radio, or the 'Posters have radio."

"But what about life support? For years and years, probably? You can't eat Outposter food. You'd die of carbon-dioxide poisoning if you tried to breath their air.

You'd have to live in the ship, or a pressure suit. And those would give out."

"Pauze," C'astille said, having a little trouble with the English word before she shifted to O-1. "If I have understanding, there is no problem. Our people could provide air and food that would suit you. Be sure of it."

"There you are, Johnson. Do you think I could get away? Don't forget, *Ariadne*'s radar operators are all CIs."

"Mmmph. I had almost forgotten that. With that working for you, and if we timed it just right, you'd have a chance, though God knows you could be shot down for real."

"I almost don't mind that. I just want to be safely dead in the eyes of the Guardians. I don't want them to come looking for me to get more out of me."

"And suppose you really end up dead? Will you feel better then? Getting yourself killed won't undo what's happened."

"I know that! But I—"

"Lucy, listen to me! *You did not deliberately hurt anyone*. You were trapped here, in our star system, with no way out, ever, and you lucked into an exciting chance that should have had *nothing* to do with war. You were learning a language, and it's not your fault what is said in that language. You weren't telling me where League bases were, or building bombs—"

"Johnson! Stop it! I know I didn't do it intentionally, but facts are facts, I must live all my life knowing that my people are going to die because of what I did in all my innocence. I betrayed my trust—"

"Then you are not alone," C'astille said in O-1. "I choose you grotesque aliens over my own kind, and side with you against the leader of the Group that protects me. And M'Gustav deliberately chooses to betray *his* Group. You are the lucky of we three: You betrayed by accident. M'Gustav and I know what we are doing before we do it. But we are all traitors."

And all the pretty speeches and ethical standards and

codes of honor and ideas about right and wrong won't change that, Gustav thought. "Lucy. I'm sorry. I think your plan might work. You know what you're asking of yourself. You could easily get killed or be marooned somewhere on Outpost and watch your air run out. But I think we have to try it."

"But where does it leave you?" Lucy asked.

"I don't know. They might catch me and shoot me. If not, I'll still be here, or on *Ariadne*."

"Run things, then. Stay alive. I'm burning all my bridges. One of us should keep some options open."

"You're pretty easy on me."

"Gustav, you are my enemy. We are at war, you and I. But I want you alive, and well. I'd feel a hundred time worse a traitor if I got you killed."

C'astille looked on in confusion as M'Calder took M'Gustav's hand in hers and squeezed it, for the briefest of moments, before she let it go. The two humans looked at each other in a most peculiar way for a moment, then drew apart, seemingly very upset about something.

"It can't be, Lucy. But God, I—no, I can't even say it."

"Neither can I, Johnson. Neither can I. We'd better get back before they miss us." The humans said their goodbyes to C'astille, arranged to talk with her the next day, and went back to the jeep.

C'astille, watching them go, could make nothing of it. But there was something about that moment when the two humans touched that seemed perverse, as if the two of them wanted to—but C'astille couldn't think *that,* even to herself. Alien or not, they couldn't be monsters. And there was something else that disturbed her greatly. The translator hadn't be able to make complete sense of the English-spoken conversation, and she had to take that into account. Yet she had gotten the strong impression that the humans were discussing medicine—and not as a bizarre, horrifying, and dangerous thing, but as something quite normal and routine.

She started back toward the clearing where the engineers were still hard at work. Every time she thought she was used to the humans, had finally made sense of them, this sort of thing happened. Only in the last few weeks had she become certain that they were all one species, instead of a vast number of related species that worked together. But they varied so much, in height and size and color and shape, and in a hundred details. No animals species on her planet had such a wide range of variation. She had thought for a time that they were all mutations from some true breed, and she had worked out a complicated social theory to account for it, of a race that got some use out of its mutants and sports by sending them on risky jobs of exploring and so forth. But that hadn't made a great deal of sense, and all the humans seemed far healthier than mutations usually were. There was a lot to learn about them, and learn from them.

If D'etallis didn't wipe them out first.

CHAPTER TEN

The Planet Bandwidth

It was only when he was behind the door of his office that Randall Metcalf felt really safe. The Navy had assigned him an overly automated hotel as a billet, and there was little he could do about the hyperactive robot service there, but in his office, inside *those* four walls, *he* could call the shots and choose the equipment. There was no machine more complicated than a pencil there, no technology higher than an electric light. He could hide alone behind his reports, slogging through another day of flying a desk, sifting through transcripts of interrogation, searching for some morsel, some clue, that would be of use in the fight to come. If they ever found anyone to fight.

But today, as usual, there was nothing in the reports. The prisoners had been squeezed dry, long ago. But orders were orders, and reading the interrogations was the job at hand. It sure as hell killed the day.

Metcalf was very glad to hear George knock on his door at quitting time. He eagerly closed up his work and they left the office together. George was as bogged down in busy-work as Metcalf, generally sitting in on interrogations that went over and over the same ground again and again. The Intelligence types had theories about long questioning sessions being the most effective.

It turned out to be a pleasant evening, with a freshening wind blowing in off the Straight Straits, and Metcalf had had enough of the corner bar for a while, so they decided to grab some carryout from the robot in the lobby and eat in the park.

Ivory Tower, the largest city on Bandwidth, was a forest of tall buildings set in generous parkland; towers and pylons and skyscrapers in every imaginable architectural style all caught the eye. It seemed a far more mature city than it should have been, but robots could build fast. Twentieth-century-style glass boxes shared the skyline with gaudily baroque piles based on medieval cathedrals, scaled-up pagodas, and copies of the Eiffel Tower and the Washington Monument and the cliff-dwelling blocks that were the latest style on Earth. It kept the eye busy. Smaller buildings, more modest in scale but equally varied in style, were set along the wide boulevards. Trees, grasses, and flowers imported from Earth were planted in the parklands, and real, honest-to-God ducks quacked and fussed and paddled around the ornamental ponds and lakes. Metcalf liked to sit on a low hill in Unity Park, near the League HQ tower, and look out over it all. Even he had to admit that Bandwidth had spent its riches well.

It was a perfect evening, the sun still reddening the sky, a hint of the enticing spicy odor of the Sea of Ness in the air, the stars just coming out in the purpling east. Lounging back on the grass, staring out over the park and the skyline, munching on a kosher hot dog that would have done New York proud, and with his beer still cold, Metcalf concluded that Life was Good. He looked up at the sky, and a familiar thrill ran through him. "Just look at those stars, George," he said in a near whisper, all the usual bantering tone gone from his voice. "They're so damned far away—and they're *people* out there! We've crossed that distance. Makes me feel sort of proud and small all at once."

"I know what you mean."

"Maybe ten years after they got the C^2 drive running, they flew a ship to Rigel. The light that shone on that exploring ship won't reach Earth for more than another century! Jesus, it makes me proud. We're not just some bunch of geeks standing around on street corners! We can reach the stars!"

Neither of them spoke for a long time. The sky grew darker, and the stars came out in all their glory. Meteors zipped across the firmament as lights came on across Ivory Tower, subdued enough not to disturb the splendid skies, but artfully placed and aimed to set the great buildings off from the surrounding darkness.

"The stars are different here," George said.

"*That* much, we know," Metcalf replied with gentle sarcasm. None of the Guardians had recognized the night sky as seen from any world. "I remember back at Annapolis, back on Earth. I had put in for Space Fighters the first moment I could, and the night the word came through! We all went down to the shore and pointed out the stars to each other. We kept telling each other—'see that one to the left of the Big Dipper? I'll be there!' "

"The Big Dipper?"

"One of the constellations as seen from Earth."

"Okay, I'll bite. I forget what a constellation is."

"Whoa. You're kidding. You know, connect-the-dots between the stars and imagine a picture there."

"Oh, okay. That's right. Mac explained that, and the Intelligence guys asked me about 'em once. Didn't seem surprised when I couldn't quite place the term."

"Wait a minute. You guys don't even have *constellations*?" Metcalf asked. *Every* culture made up constellations. Anyone with a normal imagination would find patterns in the sky and name them.

"Yeah we did. We just don't call 'em that. Called 'em sky pictures. We didn't have any *official* ones, of course, but all the kids made up their own."

Metcalf grunted. That made sense, in a twisted Guardian sort of way. If you didn't want people to learn astrogation, you didn't teach them astronomy. If you didn't want them to learn astronomy, you didn't encourage people to make up pretty pictures in the sky. But they'd do it anyway. Who could enforce a rule against looking at the sky?

"Doesn't really matter, anyway," Metcalf said. "Stars is stars, and stars is pretty."

They were both quiet for a while.

"I wonder what the new stars will look like," George said at last.

Metcalf suddenly sat bolt upright. He had the feeling that George had just said something very important. "What do you mean, George?"

"You know, the new stars that appear in the southeast."

"It's summer here, now. Do you mean the winter stars? These stars will come back next summer, and so on."

"No, but come to think of it, that might be what the interrogators thought I meant, too."

"Well, what do you mean?"

"I mean the sky pictures—the constellations—that no one has seen yet. Every year there isn't just the move back and forth between the winter and summer stars. Every year, every summer, New Stars that no has seen appear east, and Old Stars vanish in the west. They used to tell us kids that the Old Stars were old dreams, and the New Stars were new dreams. The old dreams pass through the northern lights and are reborn as new dreams, new stars to wish on."

"Hold it. *Northern* lights? You said you lived in the southern hemisphere and the north was unsettled. And you said you had northern lights. That'd mean lights coming from the *equatorial* sky, and that doesn't make sense. Northern and southern lights are linked to the magnetic poles. Charged particles are pulled in from outer space by the planet's magnetism and sucked in toward the poles. The charged particles zip into the atmosphere, and hit an air molecule, and that sets off sparks of light—the aurora.

If there were enough charged particles hitting the equator so they could be seen in the south, then the whole planet would glow in the dark—and so would the people. The radiation would kill everything."

"I could say you're glazing my eyes over, but I'll leave it at a simple 'huh?' "

"Sorry. Trust me, equatorial aurora don't make sense."

"Whatever you say, but every night back home, there was always a strong glow of orange light, all along the northern horizon."

"Always the same brightness?"

"Pretty much. It follows the same pattern every night: The northern sky starts out pretty bright, gets darker until the middle of the night, and then gets lighter again, until it's lost in the glare of the rising sun. The lights get hidden by weather, of course, but they're more or less always the same."

"Hmmm. That's not aurora, anyway. Aurora aren't constant, they come and go, flicker for a few hours or days and then fade."

"Fine. Now I'll know aurora when I see it. Why are you all excited about this stuff?"

"Because it all sounds very unusual. It means there's something odd about the skies of Capital. And that means there might be something odd, maybe even unique, about Capital, or space around it—"

"And that might help us find Capital."

"Right. So let me ask a dumb question," Metcalf said. "How do you know for certain that north was north and south was south. Couldn't the Grand Wazoo or the Imperator of the Grand Bugaboo—"

"You are referring of course to the Most Honorable Leader of the Combined Will, long may he lead us, etcetera, etcetera. Did you get the last pickle?"

"Yes, sorry. Whatever you call him. Couldn't he or some guy a hundred years ago have decided to fool all of you and tell you south was north, just to confuse the issue if you tried to help us barbarian hordes find your home?"

"Well, Mr. Barbarian Horde, they could have, but they didn't. The birds flew north when it got cold. Toward the equator. My mouth was all ready for that pickle."

"Ah. They couldn't have fooled the birds, I guess. So let's see: We've got a glow in the sky toward the equatorial horizon and Old Stars that vanish over the southern, polar, horizon, never to be seen, and New Stars that pop up in the northern sky. I'd say that's weird enough to rate comment. Gives me an idea, but I'm no expert. Let's go scare up an astronomer and see what he has to say."

Metcalf left the job of finding an astronomer to George, and George had led him back to his office. Compared to the barren cell Metcalf hid himself in, George's workshop was a madhouse. George fell in love with every gadget and put them all to work in his office. The chairs were self-adjusting, the lights came on automatically, a grabber was ready to find any book on the shelf and hand it to George. There were keyboards and terminals hooked into a half dozen computer grids, and old coffee cups and printouts were everywhere. Metcalf found himself wishing George had one more gizmo—a cleaning robot. But before Metcalf could shove the magazines off the chair and sit, George had dipped into the professional directories and retrieved a list of the astronomers currently on-planet and in Ivory Tower. A hard copy of the list in hand, they were ready.

Metcalf toyed with calling one of them up, but then decided to just show up. It was always harder to say "no" to someone in person, and the odds of getting a "no" seemed pretty high with such sketchy information. Who'd want to waste their time on it? Besides, if they blew it, they could just try the next name on the list.

Metcalf didn't realize it, but he was lucky to have such an embarrassment of riches. On any other planet, finding even one astronomer to consult would have been a challenge. Very few of them were *on* planets anymore. The opening of interstellar space had hurt astronomy in some unexpected ways: the discipline had become fragmented and specialized. The traditions of the old science were that of the utterly passive observer, cut off from the object of study by light years, forced to glean every scrap of information from whatever miserly number of photons the instruments could capture. Not anymore. People interested in planet formation or atmospheres didn't become astronomers at all—they went out and found a planetary system forming or an atmosphere that they could study. Stellarists interested in a particular star would load their instruments onto a ship and launch for the object of their interest. Scientists were widely scattered and communications weren't good enough. Results were frequently published long years after the work was done. Many results were lost altogether, along with the experimenter. Astronomers weren't good ship handlers, and they had an unfortunate tendency to get "just a bit closer" to some rather dangerous objects—like stars.

The scientific establishment of Bandwidth couldn't do anything about vaporized stellarists, but it could correlate results, and the computers were there for number crunching problems where the number of variables was itself a large but variable number. The field astronomers looked down on their ground-based colleagues, the theoretical astronomers, and harbored a suspicion that they were little more than computer programmers and librarians—but then, scientists had never really understood how much they relied on those two professions. Dr. Raoul Morelles liked to think of himself as a spider at the center of its web, all the threads leading back to center. Bandwidth and Earth, there were the two places the data came, and maybe Earth has computers as good—but try getting at them! Bandwidth was the place to work. Interesting problems cropped up all the time. Morelles didn't look like a spider—closer to a praying mantis. Very tall and thin, with a shock of white hair that stood straight up from being endlessly shoved out of his eyes, large, serious eyes, and long arms and legs, with delicate, almost frail-looking hands. He seemed always to be deliberately holding himself very still, as if he was concentrating on something that might vanish if he looked away. His clothes were worn and spare, the old workshirt and the khaki trousers that he found most comfortable, a pair of slightly shabby slippers.

When he answered the doorbell to find two slightly embarrassed young men, he had a hunch that he was about to find himself in the middle of a very interesting problem indeed. They didn't seem the usual sort of visitor. They weren't grad students trying to butter him up in his capacity as a professor, anyway. No naval officers at the school.

Mostly out of curosity, he let them in. They got the introductions out of the way, Morelles ordered the kitchen to make coffee and deliver it to his study, and they sat down to talk.

"It's this way, Dr. Morelles," Metcalf began. "As you might know, there's a lot of effort being put into finding the planet Capital, where the Guardians come from."

"I don't follow the war news much, but I have heard something about it, yes. Do go on."

"Well, George here is from Capital, but he's working with us. He and I were talking tonight, and it struck me that we've been going about it all wrong. The Intelligence teams wave star charts and ask about spectral types and so on, but it doesn't do any good. The prisoners they're interrogating don't *know* any of that stuff. I was talking with George, and he got to describing the night sky, the way the people see it and understand it, and their assumptions about the sky and how it worked. What I want is to work backwards. I want to figure out what must be in the sky for it to look and move the way it does. Like the ancients figuring out the Earth is in orbit by seeing the Sun rise. I want to find the pattern to fit the facts, instead of just casting blindly about waving star maps at the prisoners."

"It would have to be a very unusual sky for that to work," Morelles said doubtfully.

"I think it is, Doctor. Tell him about it, George."

George, with plenty of interruptions from Metcalf, and many questions from Morelles, described the strange behavior of his planet's night sky.

"Hmmmm. All right," Dr. Morelles said. "If that isn't strange enough to give us some clues, than it certainly ought to be. I must say, though, that the strangest thing is that none of this came out from all that interrogation you mentioned."

"Well, maybe the powers that be were smarter than anyone thought in putting me on this damned planet," Metcalf said. "I'm the only pilot, the only person who makes his living—and *stays* alive—by looking at the sky and wondering what's out there. The Intelligence teams are trying to backtrack by figuring out the travel times and the number of C^2 jumps the prisoners experienced between Capital and New Finland. *That* won't do them much good. I think that if we can figure out what all this stuff about equatorial lights and vanishing stars *means*, what sort of objects moving how in the sky are required to make things look that way, we can dig through the computer commander and maybe find a system that matches it."

"Yes. I see. You have something there. Please help yourself to more coffee. Let me work on this."

George expected Morelles to go to a computer terminal and start tapping in queries, or at least pull some huge book down from a shelf and mutter to himself as he flipped through it. But Morelles simply leaned back, propped his elbows on the chair arms, cupped his chin in his hands, and stared at the ceiling. The astronomer didn't move but to breathe or blink for a disturbingly long time, until George had thought Morelles might have had some sort of silent stroke and died.

"Were any formal star charts made by the people on Capital?" Morelles asked, interrupting the long silence so abruptly that both George and Metcalf jumped. "Did anyone keep permanent records?"

"Ah, no. It wouldn't have been allowed. We aren't supposed to make up stories about the sky, in the first place. The Central Guardians ruled that folk tales and superstitions were misleading and time-wasters and declared them illegal."

"That sounds like the most unenforcable law I've ever heard," Morelles growled. "Either your leaders were very sensitive about such things, or they know nothing about psychology."

"I suppose, sir," George said uncomfortably. It was okay when Randall kidded him about home, but he still squirmed when a stranger sneered at the Guardians like that. The evidence of his own eye had forced him to decide the Guardians *did* bad and dumb things, but he couldn't admit they *were* bad, or dumb.

"Do you have any rough idea of the average life span of people on your planet?" Morelles asked.

This guy Morelles must have learned to ask oddball questions in that same place Metcalf had, George thought. "Not really. Not more than seventy or seventy-five in Earth years, I guess. It's news when someone reaches the equivalent of eighty-five or ninety."

"I see. Than we can take perhaps seventy years as the basic upper limit for the survival of knowledge about one certain patch of sky. Do you see why that's important?"

"No sir," George said.

"I think I've got it, Doctor. Stars don't just appear and disappear. They're permanent. There must be some cyclical pattern of motion of Capital's sky that makes new stars appear and the old ones vanish. This year's new stars *had* to have come by before. If no one remembers seeing the new stars, a human lifetime gives you a lower limit for how long it takes the stars to move once completely around the sky."

"Exactly. I assume that if a person saw a constellation vanish in the west one year and saw an *identical pattern* appear in the new stars of the east, many years later, he could realize that they were one and the same. That seventy years gives me a lower limit for a cycle, three hundred sixty degrees of motion."

"Aha," George said. These guys had lost him again. George was smart enough, plenty smart enough, to understand the motions of the sky, and once he thought about it, it was obvious that stars didn't just vanish. It was just that he never *had* thought about it. Just as the Central Guardians intended, he had never really believed that the points of light in the sky were mighty suns.

"So what is that cycle?" Metcalf asked.

"I should think that would be fairly obvious."

"So call me stupid, Doctor," Metcalf said evenly. "What is it?"

"I would say that Capital's sun is one of a binary pair."

"But sir!" George objected, "even I know what a binary sun is—two stars in orbit around each other. No one back home has ever seen another sun—or even particularly bright star."

"Oh yes you have. What about that glow coming from the north, from over the equator?"

"That's from another *sun?*"

"I expect so. Does all this make sense to you, Commander Metcalf?"

"Yessir." Metcalf paused and thought it through. "Except what you're saying is that Capital's north pole is always pretty much pointed at the other star. That's the only way the other star would never be visible from the southern hemisphere of Capital."

"You're quite right, and that *does* suggest a rather odd structure to Capital's star system," Morelles agreed. "But I don't see anything else that fits the facts."

"Sir, if you don't mind my asking," George said, "what sort of odd structure are you talking about?"

"Let me see if I can sum it up. Capital's sun—what do you call it?"

"Nova Sol."

"There must be a dozen stars with that local name in the League. People aren't very original. Very well, Nova Sol is in a binary relationship with another star: The two of them orbit around each other, or more accurately, around an empty spot of space midway between them, where the gravitational attraction of the two stars is exactly balanced. That central balance point is called the barycenter. The two stars revolve around each other in no less than seventy years. Do you understand that so far?"

"Yes. But I can't see how the other star would be hidden all the time."

"Wait a minute, Doctor," Metcalf said. "I think I've got it. Capital's orbit—not the planet, but the *orbit itself*—is precessed, so the orbit is always face-on toward the other sun."

"Precisely!" Morelles grinned with delight. He wished this young naval person was in one of his classes. He was a good thinker.

"Sir," George cut in, "I hate to say it again, but 'huh?' "

Morelles sighed. *That* was more what he was used to. No wonder he preferred research. "Let me see if I can explain." He got up suddenly, went into the next room, and returned with a big sheet of stiff posterboard paper, a pair of scissors, and a marking pen. "I keep this stuff around for notices and posters in the class," he explained. Morelles shoved everything else off his big round coffee table, and George and Metcalf rescued the coffee cups just in the nick of time. Morelles lay the sheet of posterboard down on the table. "All right, now I'll draw this out on cardboard, since I left my blackboard at the classroom."

Morelles, already sketching rapidly on the posterboard, didn't notice that neither of his listeners laughed. "Now then. The usual thing for a solar system is for everything to move in the same plane. I've sketched some of the major element of Earth's solar system here. If you want to represent the orbits of all the planets, except for Pluto, you can just draw them on a flat piece of card as I have done. Within a degree or two, all the orbits are in the same plane. Pluto is the exception that helps explain the rule. Pluto's orbit is, oh dear, what is it? Oh yes, about seventeen degrees away from the plane of the others. If I wanted to show *its* orbit accurately I'd have to take a loop of wire or something and poke it through the cardstock so half the wire loop was above and half was below my flat plane, and then I'd have to set that orbit—that loop of wire—so it was at a seventeen-degree angle to the paper representing the plane of the solar system. Does that give you an idea about the planes of orbits?"

"Yes, I think so," George said. He was beginning to understand, and beginning to be annoyed at the teachers who hadn't shown him this. George, a lover of gadgets and machines and machinery, was getting his first introduction to the greatest clockwork toy there was—the complex and orderly dance of the skies.

"Good," Morelles said. Unconsciously, he had taken on his classroom persona, and all his words and movements became more and more exaggerated. Twenty years of dealing with students had taught him the value of a loud voice, careful enunciation, and expressive hand gestures. "Now, since we've got a large enough piece of card, I can draw a whole other solar system on it, with a sun and planets and satellites and so on. Notice it's all still on one flat piece of paper, everything still moving in one plane. Now I've drawn in the orbits of the planets around the second sun. Let me drawn in one more orbit."

He started his pencil on one of the two suns and drew a wide circle that went through it and the other sun, so that the two of them were one hundred eighty degrees apart. Directly in the center of this big circle, he drew a dot. "That dot is the barycenter, the center of gravity, the balance point for thewhole system. Now, imagine the two suns orbiting each other around that barycenter, and the planets orbiting their respective suns, everything in the same plane. This sort of arrangement is what most binary star systems look like. That's clear enough to see. Here's where we get to the unusual features of your Nova Sol system."

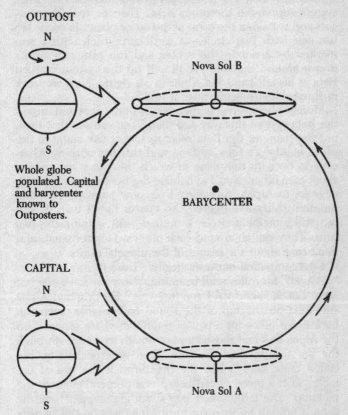

OUTPOST

N

S

Whole globe populated. Capital and barycenter known to Outposters.

Nova Sol B

BARYCENTER

CAPITAL

N

S

Nova Sol A

Only southern hemisphere populated: outpost never visible.

Nova Sol B is only visible from the uninhabited northern hemisphere of Capital. Nova Sol B is never visible from the inhabited southern hemisphere of Capital.

Morelles took his pencil again and marked one solar system *Alpha* and the other *Beta*. Then he took the scissors and cut along the orbit of the outer planet in each. He was left with two circles of cardboard, each with a sun marked by a dot in the center and the planetary orbits drawn around the sun. He picked up the system marked Beta in his left hand and Alpha in his right. "Now we work in three dimensions instead of two."

Morelles held Alpha perpendicular to the floor and turned the Beta system this way and that. "You can see that I can put the plane of the Beta *solar system* at any angle to the plane of Alpha's solar system, and this has nothing whatever to do with the plane in which the two *stars* revolve about each other. Now I'm holding the Beta system at ninety degrees to Alpha, now forty-five, now parallel, now one hundred thirty-five degrees. No matter how I turn it, you can still imagine a circle, a mutual orbit, joining the two suns. They can go around each other no matter what, and don't care about the planes of the planets' orbits."

George nodded enthusiastically. "I see it."

"Good!" Morelles said, beaming. "Now, we have one last step. Let me see. Ah! I see the way." He dropped Alpha and Beta on the top of the round coffee table, then ran back to his office for a pair of thumbtacks. He scooped up the Alpha disk and shoved a pin through its center, through the dot that marked the sun. Then he crouched by the coffee table, and poked the pin through the rim of the table, so the piece of cardboard was perpendicular to the tabletop. The table was a lazy-susan arrangement, and he spun it around on its pivot until Alpha was on the far side of the table from him. He poked another pin through the Beta system's sun, and shoved that pin into the rim of the table as well. He gave the tabletop another push, and it spun round and round.

Two disks of cardboard, directly across the diameter of the table from each other, held perpendicular to the tabletop and parallel to each other, whirled around and around.

As each went past him, Morelles reached out his hand and set the disks spinning around their pushpins.

"There you have it, gentlemen, a first crude armillary, a mechanical representation of Capital's star system. The two stars, which are represented by the push pins, revolve around each other in their mutual orbit, the circumference of which is the rim of my coffee table. The planets orbit around the stars, the pushpins, in the planes of motion represented by the two cardboard disks. The orbital plane of the solar systems are, as Commander Metcalf noted, precessed. They are firmly attached to the rim of my coffee table, and move as it moves. As the two stars revolve through three hundred sixty degrees, a full circle, in their mutual orbit, the orbital planes of the two star systems rotate three hundred sixty degrees."

"Hold it," George said, staring at the model. "If I've got this straight, that means the *northern* hemisphere of Capital is always pointed at this other star? The other star is always visible from there? And the southern, populated hemisphere is *always* pointed away from it—which is why we never see it?"

"Right. And the northern lights are like a dawn that never happens—the other sun is just below the horizon, lighting up the sky but never rising," Metcalf put in. He gave the table a spin, and stood up. "Doctor Morelles, I thank you. You might have just solved a big problem."

Metcalf and the astronomer shook hands. "What will you do now?" Morelles asked.

"Start a search through all the catalogs, I guess," Metcalf said. "We'll look for pairs of distant binary stars where one of the stars is the right mass and temperature to support life."

Morelles smiled. "That is *my* proper work. With all due respect, I am sure I could do a far more sophisticated search than a non-astronomer. Please allow me to do the job. I'd be delighted to do so—and before you say it, I know they'll slap a Top Secret on this at least, and that's fine. I have clearance. I'll get started on it right now."

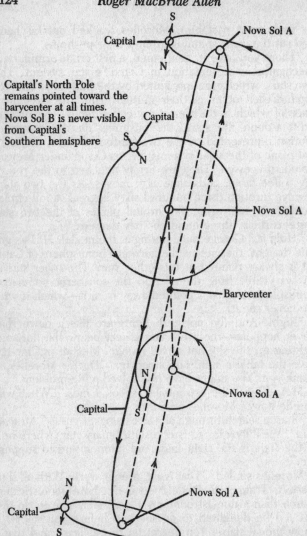

Capital's North Pole remains pointed toward the barycenter at all times. Nova Sol B is never visible from Capital's Southern hemisphere

Movement of Capital around the barycenter of the Nova Sol System. Nova Sol B and Outpost are omitted for clarity.

"Doctor, it's urgent but it isn't *that* urgent," Metcalf said. "It can wait until morning."

Morelles smiled. "You're forgetting, Commander. Astronomers always work nights."

CHAPTER ELEVEN

Aboard *Ariadne*

"Gee, Doc, all over a sudden I'm feeling much better."
Lucy threw the sheets off the stretcher, got to her feet,
and produced a gun out of nowhere in one fluid motion.

Dr. Angus Willoughby found himself with the slim barrel of a laser pistol stuck up his nose. Instinctively, he
tried to step back, but Lucy tugged on the pistol and he
came back to where he was.

Ariadne's sick bay wasn't much, and neither was her
doctor. Willoughby meant well enough, and cared for his
charges as well as could be expected, but he was a short,
middle-aged, pale, chubby sort of fellow, more given to
blubbering than blustering when faced with a crisis.

Lucy knew all that and was glad of it. Pulling her off
Outpost hadn't been rough; illness was easy to fake, especially with Gustav to back her up. Getting rushed to the
infirmary was straightforward, and Willoughby was easy
enough to scare. But if he had been made of sterner stuff,
there could have been problems.

And Lucy had problems enough as it was. But one thing
at a time. "Okay, Doctor." She pulled a pressure syringe
out of her hip pocket. "You get a double dose of some
feelgoods, and I'll be on my way. Roll up your sleeve."

"But I ah—ah—"

"Do it, or I clean out your nasal passages." Did that sound dumb to him, too, or was he too scared?

Willoughby pulled his shirt sleeve up without further debate. Lucy slammed the hypo down and the powerful narcotic forced itself through his skin and into his bloodstream.

He dropped a little faster than Lucy had figured. Maybe he just fainted.

That was square one. She stood in the tiny room, waiting for long moments. No sound. She opened the door a bit and peeked out into the corridor. The stretcher-bearers were gone, back at their regular duties. There had been enough cases come up from Outpost, cuts and burns and carbon-dioxide shock, that it was all pretty routine to them. Pull the casualty off the lander, get the stretcher to the doc, and then back to work.

She locked the door, shoved the laser pistol into her belt, and checked on dear old Doctor Willoughby. He was folded up in the corner, gently snoring, out of the game for quite a while.

Now started the scary part. The sick bay had a standard terminal station, hooked into *Ariadne*'s computer systems. The CIs had been working over that computer system for quite a while now. Lucy powered it up, requested the calculator, tried to figure the square root of negative 43, then asked for the base-8 equivalent of her parent's phone number back on Earth. Then she typed in:

Operate Gremloid

There was a brief delay, and then the computer responded.

EXPOSE YOURSELF

Sydney Sally

ALIAS?

Ned Fine

PROVE IT—WHERE WAS YOUR FATHER BORN?

Liverpool, Pommieland

WE'VE GOT YOU LINED, SAL. WHAZZUP?

The whole Gremloid system was like that, with the

computer handing out and expecting slang and inside jokes. Gremloid was buried deep inside the computer system, and only after one of several cuing routines would the computer system even admit it existed.

But even if Gremloid was buried deep, he could reach into lots of places.

Lucy typed in:

Looper Snooper Straitslace Sue

SHE BE LINED.

Good. Straitslace Sue—more commonly known as Cynthia Wu—was at a terminal somewhere, working. Now to get Gremloid to send her a message. So far no one aboard *Ariadne* knew who had been aboard that medical shuttle. Lucy had to let Cynthia know what was up.

Gremloid, C.Q. Straitslace Sue

IT'S IN THE HOPPER—COOL YOUR JETS

There was a brief pause, and then a new line popped on the screen.

S. SUE RESPONDS: WHO AND WHAT IS IT?

Gremloid had cut into the regular operations of Cynthia's terminal, told her someone on the Gremnet wanted to talk to her, and sent her reply back.

Lucy had no time to jigger around with the usual jargoned-up lingo of the Gremnet. She had to get some very precise information across.

Cyn—this is Lucy. No time to explain why, but I came here to steal a ship and land it on Outpost. Once there, I will use a beacon set at a frequency equal to your birthdate, Earth calendar, divided by three. No time for questions. I'm in sick bay. Where is closest prepped lander and can you create diversion to draw sentries from same? There was a longish pause. It might have been Cynthia thinking, or a Guard asking her what was going on, or Cyn carefully checking the computer files to see what landers were where. Lucy didn't know or care. She just prayed for Cyn to hurry.

Cynthia Wu felt the bottom drop out of her stomach. The Gremnet always had that effect on her, as if she was talking to a ghost, a disembodied voice, but this was worse than usual. Lucy was supposed to be a thousand kilometers away, straight down, on the planet's surface. Cynthia was at her regular post in the radar room, monitoring the comings and goings of ships. It was a lonely post, especially during the night watch. No one else was on duty, just Cynthia and her keeper, a Private Wendell.

She glanced up at him, then looked back at her console screens. What the hell was Lucy doing here? But it wasn't time for questions. She used Gremloid to call up the sabotage and surveillance files. The s&s files were the most carefully hidden part of the CI's underground computer net. The names, the call-up procedures, the security techniques, were constantly being changed. That was part of how they maintained its security. Lucy had been away far too long to know how to use the current incarnation. Come on, come on—ah, there we go, a lander nice and close in Bay Three. Cynthia keyed in her reply, willing that her sentry stick to his comic book for another five minutes.

THERE IS A HERO-CLASS LANDER AT LOCK 6, BAY THREE FUELED AND AT GO. I WILL INSTRUCT COMPUTER TO WARN OF FUEL LEAK AND EXPLOSION DANGER IN THAT COMPARTMENT IN TEN MINUTES. GO NOW. GOOK LUCK.

Lucy breathed a sigh of relief. *That* was why she had tried Cynthia first. No gush of questions to slow things down, she was just ready with what was needed when it was needed. Levelheaded common sense taken to an extreme state.

God bless you, Cynthia. I'll explain some day, if I can, Lucy typed.

I KNOW YOU WILL. GO NOW. HURRY.

Lucy cut the power on the terminal and slipped out into the corridor. It was the night shift on *Ariadne*—all the corridor lights dimmed, the constant background noises of the station's machinery subdued. All was gloomy and still. Quietly, quickly, going by side corridors and ducking out of sight whenever she heard a noise, she made her way toward the docking bays in the zero-gee section.

A Hero-Class in Bay Three. And the sentries ought to be scared out of there in about seven more minutes. That only left a few problems—like operating the Guard controls—she had seen them, but never run them—and making a landing someplace where C'astille's people could find her. And convincing the Guards that she was dead and not worth going after. There was a way, but it was tricky. Dangerous. But grabbing a Hero would help. The Guard pilots had nicknamed them Neros, because the ships had a tendency to burn. No doubt that was part of why Cynthia had chosen a Hero for Lucy.

Through this corridor to the elevator banks—good! There was a car waiting. She rushed from a shadowy corner into the car and punched the button for the zero-gee section. The door shut and up she went.

The elevator travelled up to the zero-gee section and the doors opened. The lights were dimmed here, too, and Lucy felt a cool, metallic tang in the air, as if she could sense the vacuum held back by the airlocks. A silly idea. Her head seemed to be full of them tonight. She had just about three minutes to get herself inside Bay Three before Cyn's bogus explosion warning would scare everyone out. No time to hide and skulk in corners at the sound of a voice now. She had on the right sort of uniform. She'd just have to trust to the gloomy lighting and hope that she didn't run into a Guard who would recognize her face.

Lucy rushed along the corridors, swarming along the handholds at top speed. She hadn't been in zero-gee for months, but it all came back to her now. Like riding a bicycle, or so went the expression. Lucy hadn't ever learned to ride a bike.

Bay One. Bay Two. Bay Three. Here. In here.

Lucy stopped herself and hung in mid-air at the personnel hatch to the bay. Bay Three. This was where the

CIs—no, they had still thought of themselves as Survey Service back then—this was where the Survey Service group had been put aboard *Ariadne* when they were taken off *Venera*.

Well, if this was where she got on, it was also where she got off. And no way to sneak in. There was a small viewport set in the hatch, and Lucy cautiously peeked into it.

The interior of the bay was in darkness. One small light shone in the corner—the two sentries playing gin rummy being very careful of the cards in zero-gee. Good. Their eyes would be adjusted for light, not dark. Lucy took as good a look as she could at the dim interior. When the *Venera* survivors had been piled in here, the vast storage and transfer space had been completely empty, stripped bare. Now there was cargo stored everywhere, in crates and cases and pressure vessels lashed down and stacked and secured on every inch of deck space. It was a maze of hiding places.

The hatch was closed but not dogged shut. Slowly, with exquisite care, she opened the hatch. It creaked just a little as it swung outward, a bare little chirp of a noise. She swung the hatch open just far enough to let her slip through it. Hugging close to the deck, she pulled it shut behind her. Floating noiselessly through zero-gee, she pulled herself along the deck and hid behind a convenient stack of cases.

Now it was time for Cynthia to come through.

At that moment, Cynthia was in a cold sweat—doing her best to have a pleasant chat with Private Wendell, who had suddenly tired of his comic. He was a nice enough kid who probably had a crush on her. She blanked her terminal's screen the moment he had come over to talk about the movie that had been shown the night before, a rather pedestrian Guardian comedy that had proven humor was incompatible with censorship. Wendell had loved it, which probably proved that taste was likewise incompatible.

She tried to shut him up politely, get him back to his reading "—Listen," she interrupted gently, "I've *got* to watch my screens, or else get shot when some pair of ships crack up out there."

"Huh? I thought things were pretty quiet tonight."

"They are, but I want to keep it that way. And with one thing and another I've barely had a chance to monitor. I've really got to pay strict attention for a while, until I know what's going on out there. I need to get caught up."

"Okay. Could I maybe get you a cuppa coffee? It'd gimme something t'do."

Please, please do, you silly kid. Anything to leave me alone, Cynthia thought. But she couldn't seem eager. "Isn't that against regs? You're supposed to be keeping an eye on me."

"Hell, you've been here close to a year and you've never tried anything. I'll just go to the galley and back. Stretch my legs. Be back in five minutes."

"Wellll—how about tea instead?"

Wendell displayed a grin full of buck teeth. "Sure. I'll go get it."

Cynthia called up Gremloid before he was out the door. What the hell was Lucy doing back on station? Where had she come from? And what the devil did she need to steal a ship for? No time for that. Cynthia hurriedly instructed Gremloid to slip the bogus emergency to the main computer through the ship's environmental monitor circuits.

Lucy was probably in or near Bay Three by now—the sick bay was close to the elevator banks, and Luce was fast in zero-gee. But Cynthia didn't dare stage a phony alert in the time Wendell was gone. Too suspicious. She told Gremloid to run the fake in ten minutes. That would give Wendell plenty of time to spill the tea, mop it up, make it again, and bring it to her.

Lucy knew how slowly time moved for her when she was waiting, but this was ridiculous. Though it was too damn dark to check her wrist-aid for the time, she was sure more than ten minutes had passed. There was nothing she could do but wait in the dark, and mentally rehearse the moves that would get her to Lock Six. As best she could remember, Six should be on the opposite side of the deck.

"Here's the tea," Wendell announced in a loud, clear voice as he came in. Cynthia nearly jumped half out of her skin.

"Oh—you startled me," Cynthia said, trying to regain her composure. She took her tea and smiled at him. "Thanks."

"No problem. So how's it look out there?"

"Very quiet. No one changing orbit, so far as I can see."

"Good. So I guess we can talk a bit, then, now that you're caught up."

That was exactly the last thing Cynthia was in the mood for, but it would cover for her when all hell broke loose in a minute or two. "I guess so," she said, smiling. She was just beginning to strain her imagination, trying to think of a topic she could possibly discuss with him, then a shrill *beep, beep* came on at the radar room's security console.

"Oh, hell," Wendell said as he crossed to see what the alarm was.

"What is it?" Cynthia asked. Either they had caught Lucy or Gremloid had just tossed his diversion into the main system.

"Hold on a sec—I'm not that good with this thing. Ah—oh, no big deal, not our section. Fuel leak in the zero-gee section. Happens all the time. They'll get it fixed."

"Oh."

"So, anyway," Wendell said cheerfully. "y'know what I really liked about last night's show?"

"Tell me."

The alert might not have bothered Wendell, but the two sentries in Bay Three got pretty excited. It was more than a *beep, beep* to them. A huge voice shouted down at them, "Evacuate and seal off this compartment. Explosive fuel leak detected. All personnel evacuate this compartment." A siren started, and the booming warning voice repeated again and again. The two of them were out the personnel hatch in nothing flat.

Lucy watched the two of them get out and dog the hatch behind them. Then she pulled herself up from behind her packing cases and kicked off toward Lock Six. Everything going well so far—

There was a clank and a thud as the personnel hatch was pulled back open. Lucy grabbed at a handhold and pulled herself down, taking cover behind a pressure vessel. The main lighting came on, dazzling her eyes.

"We saw you, whoever you are. You should have remembered that hatch has a viewport. Come on out."

"Sergeant Mosgrove, that could be a real leak warning. It's still repeating. Let's get out of here."

"Shut up, Sammy. Whoever is in here jiggered that alarm to get us to leave our posts. You want to steal a ship? Go ahead and try, you lousy CI bastard. I knew you creeps couldn't be trusted."

"How do you know it's a CI?"

"Who else would be after a ship?" Mosgrove growled. "Come on out, 'cause we're coming in."

Lucy's heart was pounding fit to break through her ribs, and she found her gun in her hand. She pulled herself along the ropes and cables that held down the cargo, peering around the packing cases, trying to get a sight line. The booming voice repeated its warning. Soon other sentries would come, to check on their comrades. She didn't have time to fight these guys. If she could get to Lock Six . . . It should be a small lock, its hatch set flush with the deck. There. Ten meters away, across open deck—

She spotted one of the Guards and fired before she could think. A young kid, maybe nineteen, and he screamed as her laser chopped his hand off.

Mosgrove, a sour-faced man of indeterminate age, came

up behind the younger man, and Lucy felt a terrible pain in her left hand and caught a whiff of cooking meat. Mosgrove had fired and hit her. She fired her own weapon right in his face, and her enemy became a corpse before he could lift a hand to shield himself.

Lucy forced herself to take their guns. She might need weapons where she was going.

Ninety seconds later she was cycled through Lock Six and strapped into the pilot's chair in a Hero-Class lander.

She thought of two men, one dead and one maimed, and she didn't feel very hero-class herself. Then she started flicking switches and trying to remember what she could about how the Guards flew these things.

The radar room was wired into Launch and Recovery Control, of course. Cynthia's own radars were watching a lot further out than the skin of *Ariadne*. L&R would call her, ask to confirm an unauthorized launch the moment it happened. Cynthia chatted aimlessly with the endlessly dull Wendell, waiting for the call. The comm light lit up. "Excuse me a second, Wendell." She hit the answer key. "Radar room here." She had to keep her voice calm.

"Cyn, this is Schiller over in L&R. We've got a sensor light here showing an open docking collar where a lander's supposed to be. Is that a bum sensor or did a ship really drift loose over there?"

"Hmm. Stand by. I'll have to reconfigure for a close scan. But we got a reading of a fuel leak over there."

"Yeah, we got that too. Sounds like a right nasty malfunction."

"Could be the lander's pilot cast loose to get clear of a possible explosion."

"Yeah, we thought of that. Got it yet?"

"Hang in there Sam. The controls seem a little sluggish for some reason."

Sam Schiller wasn't especially concerned up until that moment. Little malfs like this were what he was here for.

But then something strange happened. As he listened over his headset, Cynthia started whistling, badly.

Cyn *never* whistled. It wasn't in her character. Neither was the tune, a breezy little bit of froth. Cyn was big on the classics, and on the Atonalists. But that tune sounded familiar. A very old pop song that had been dredged up out of someone's memory for some reason. What was it? Schiller remembered some of the CIs singing it to tease—

Whoa. That was it. *Lucy in the Sky With Diamonds.* They had used to kid Calder with it, back on the *Venera*.

And Wu was no kidder. Schiller had been, once, but living in the enemy's lap had drained that from him and left a residue of paranoid imagination. "Ah, Cynthia. I've got a lot of what sounds like room noise on the line. Please switch to your headset, and I'll do the same."

"Stand by." There was a click. "On headsets now."

Schiller plugged the tiny speaker into his ear. "Okay, if I keep my voice down we're private at this end. You trying to tell me something?"

"Affirmative."

Great. Some Guard was breathing down her neck. At least the L&R sentry was across the room. "Understood. Something's up, but you can't tell me because of our babysitter. He can hear what you say, but not what I say."

"Affirmative," Cynthia's voice said, a strange, false light-heartedness in her tone.

"So who the hell is on that lander?"

"You'll have to trust the readings I just gave a bit longer, Sam. Let's just take our time and do it right, so we don't lose one."

"Okay, Calder's on that thing, somehow, and you want me to stall. What the hell is going on?"

"No info yet, Sam. Stand by." There was a long pause. "I have some sort of very close-in radar contact. We might need to put in a call to Search and Rescue."

Sam Schiller wasn't very good at this sort of thing. He was glad Cynthia could think fast. Search and Rescue was one banged-up old cargo ship and whichever two Guard pilots who wanted a chance to catch up on their sleep. The longer it took to rouse them, the longer it would be until someone figured out there was an escape in progress and called Fighter Command. And the way Cynthia was running things, there wouldn't be anything on the record to show the CIs had aided the escape or impeded the Guards.

Unless they were tapping the intercom, in which case Schiller knew he was going to be shot. Schiller reached for the S&R phone and swore to himself. He didn't *want* to be good at this sort of thing.

At least laser wounds didn't bleed much, though this one hurt like hell. It really didn't look too bad, a slash of angry red along her wrist and her pinky. There were already signs of some nasty blistering, though.

There wasn't time for painkillers or first aid. She had to get this tub out of here, below the radar horizon. And this was the second time she had ridden a Guard ship without knowing the vehicle's name. If Hero-Class boats even rated names. Might just be a number.

She had kicked free of *Ariadne* with maximum thrust of her maneuvering jets. Now she spun ship and set up for retro-fire. Get down, get away, then worry about fancy stuff.

She punched some buttons and brought up the inertial tracker in a set of ground coordinates. It had taken hours with C'astille to figure out the coordinates of Lucy's landing site. The Outposter had some trouble with human mapping conventions, but nothing compared to the trouble Lucy had with the native's charts. C'astille wanted her several hundred kilometers north of the Guardian contact site.

Lucy knew that if she missed that landing site by too much, she was a dead woman.

With any luck, the landing site would be on the far side of planet from her current position, with the bulk of a whole world to hide her movements. There hadn't been any way to time it out. She swore a blue streak when the navigation computer showed her that the landing site was, at the moment, almost directly beneath her lander. The Guards would have perfect line-of-sight on her all the way in if she made a direct approach. So much for luck.

Okay, it was bloody well time to work with what she had. A minimum power reentry would land her about one hundred eighty degrees away from where she was now. She checked the map display in the inertial guidance computer. There was open ocean on the opposite side of the globe. That was a start. Two minutes later the nameless lander fired its engines in retro-fire.

Twenty minutes. Cynthia Wu felt the sweat coming out of every pore in her body. Twenty lousy minutes was all she and Sam had been able to buy for Lucy. Now all hell was indeed breaking loose. One dead, one badly injured in Bay Three. Fighter Command, up on *Nike* Station, had jumped with both feet four minutes ago and would have their fighters scrambled in another two. They had patched into the radar feed from *Ariadne*, and Cynthia had no way of cutting the feed. They were running her radars by remote now, combining her radar returns with their own. All Cynthia could do was watch the radar screens and pray that Lucy could get herself lost. And fast. If she could hit atmosphere, get behind the planet, out of line-of-sight, she might pull it off.

First the *Ariadne*'s beacon slid behind the planet and winked out, then *Nike*'s. Loss of signal. Over the radar horizon. Thank God. If she couldn't see them anymore, then they couldn't see her. Lucy rode her lander down, and finally the damn thing hit air. A plume of superheated air grew around her, became ionized, glowed fiercely in the darkness as she slid into the night side of the world below. She had to assume some ship or station overhead would spot so bright a thing as a night reentry. But without good radar and careful tracking, things that only *Ariadne* and *Nike* were equipped for, the Guards wouldn't have enough to find her, especially if she were maneuvering in the atmosphere—something she very much intended to do.

She wanted to try an old idea, dreamed up in the very beginning of space flight, or perhaps even earlier. Rock skipping. Instead of plowing straight down into the atmosphere, she would use the lander's energy of velocity to bounce in and out of the upper atmosphere several times. It would play hob with her heat shield, but she only wanted to use the thing this once. She pitched the lander around until her conical shape produced more lift than drag and started gaining altitude once more, until she was flung clear of the sensible atmosphere. Back in vacuum, her lander again became a purely ballistic vehicle, her velocity still very high, in the thousands of kilometers an hour, but just barely sub-orbital. The little craft soon began to fall again, this time half way around the world from her first entry. Lucy swung the nose around again, the conical lander in effect becoming a large, crude airfoil. Again she was flung clear of the air, but this time not so high, not so far.

She checked the situation in the guidance display. Outpost was spinning on its axis, and the Guardian orbital stations were moving in their orbits. Her planned landing site was now well out of their line-of-sight. And her odd-ball entry was probably enough to lose any fighters they might have scrambled.

The landing site was barely in range for a gliding reentry. Her lander started to fall in toward the planet again, for the last time. She was going to make it. Then all she had to do was sit tight and wait for C'astille's people to find her. She hoped they took their time. Lucy felt about due for a breather.

Fighter command never tracked her second and third entries, just the first. The computers tracked that one as terminating in open ocean, and a human couldn't survive long on Outpost anyway. The Guards listed Calder as died trying to escape.

Cynthia and Sam were afraid they were right.

CHAPTER TWELVE

Aboard HMS *Impervious*, in Orbit of Britannica

Commander Joslyn Marie Cooper Larson, Royal Britannic Navy, couldn't help liking the poor old dear. Oh, there was no doubt that he had a strong fondness for the bottle, and there was probably truth to the rumor that he had been posted to Britannica thirty years ago to keep his slightly drunken self as far as possible from London society and politics. But none of that mattered. Great Uncle George—or Captain Sir George Wilfred Thomas, when they were in uniform—was a most courteous, thoughtful, and hospitable man.

If the mark of a true, blue, gentleman was the ability to behave well under trying circumstances, then Sir George had proved himself to be among the truest and bluest. He was master of the HMS *Impervious*, one of the carrier ships Joslyn's husband Mac had campaigned against. Sir George had been the reserve captain, charged with maintaining her in storage, for the last ten Earth years. And yet Sir George hadn't held Mac's words against Joslyn, though she couldn't have blamed him if he had. Instead, he had most gallantly asked her to serve as official hostess at tonight's reception. A visiting delegation of flag-rank officers from half the members of the League was there in celebration of the *Imp*'s recommissioning. If anything, Sir George seemed delighted at the chance to twit the stuffier officers with his choice of a hostess.

Sir George himself was splendidly turned out in an elegantly tailored formal dress uniform, a chestful of ribbons for who-knows-what glittering against the sleek black of his jacket, all his braid and insignia brushed and polished and perfect. He smiled and joked with everyone as the reception line moved past, the picture of a hale and hearty old man, his tall, thin figure the natural focus of attention. There was not the slightest hint of a hair left on his smooth-polished scalp, and his snow-white eyebrows bounded up and down as he talked. The only wrinkles on his face were crow's-feet and laugh lines. Fondness for the bottle or no, his complexion was fresh-scrubbed, pink and healthy, with no trace of the mottled skin or liver patches one might expect, and the grip of his handshake was still firm and strong.

It was a festive night. Hangar One, decorated with bunting and flags, with thick carpeting rolled out, a walnut dance floor laid over the steel decks, and a Navy band playing an elegant old refrain, looked as if it had been designed to double as a ballroom—as indeed it had.

Joslyn looked lovely that night, and knew it, and enjoyed the fact. The Royal Britannic Navy didn't have a uniform for officers, female, formal evening, but instead expected its female officers to "select a gown of color, cut, and style suitable to the occasion." It was one of the few regulations Joslyn actually enjoyed obeying. She had literally let her hair down, out of the usual tight braid, and it fell in long, full, golden-brown waves to lie on her bare shoulders. She wore a flowing, strapless evening gown of midnight black, woven of a sheer, glistening fabric that caught the light as she moved. She was tall and slender, and the gown suited her exactly, adding a special grace to her every move. She wore a single strand of pearls around her throat, and matching pearl stud earrings. Her blue eyes and peaches-and-cream complexion completed the picture of a charming and lovely young upper-class woman. She was that, but she was also a skilled pilot, and perhaps the most experienced combat veteran aboard the *Impervious*. She had killed her share of Guardians, a hard fact to keep in mind as she greeted the guests with a charmingly shy and youthful smile.

Joslyn was glad, now, that Uncle George had asked her to play the part of hostess. She didn't know or care if it was some complicated political ploy of his, or if he simply thought it would be fun. Joslyn herself could have held a few grudges against a few people, but she had concluded it wasn't worth the effort. The Office of Personnel for one, but then they had only cut the orders the Britannic High Command had told them to cut, if the scuttlebutt was to be believed. She greeted Admiral Samuel Whitmore of the High Command with a smile, and thought daggers at the bugger, just in case he had been the one with the gallows sense of humor, posting her to a ship her husband said was a deathtrap.

She didn't so much mind being posted away from Mac. Oh, she missed him terribly, of course. And she was furious at Whitmore and anyone else in the Royal Britannic Navy who might have been behind the order that had yanked her home and away from the Survey Service. But she was Navy, from a Navy family, and one had to expect to be separated from a husband in wartime. That came with the territory of military life. If Mac had been a civilian, they'd probably be just as far from each other right now, for all practical purposes.

And she had the comforting knowledge that Mac was *safe*. For far too long in those dreadful months in the New Finnish system, she had been alone in the *J.M.*, waiting, never knowing from moment to moment if he was dead or alive, knowing only that he was in constant danger.

At least now she knew he lived. And they could write each other, send recordings. That should have been enough. But she loved him very much.

Yet it *was* good to be home, or at least in orbit around home. And she could catch a shuttle down to Kings Town Field and be home with Mummy and Dad in twelve hours whenever she could wangle a pass. She felt more *British* than she had in a long time. She had travelled widely, seen many ways of doing many things, but it was good to be *home,* and be surrounded by the ways she had learned as a child. It was good to be where everyone knew the importance of warming the teapot properly, and trivets and elaborate gardens and digestive biscuits and driving on the left side of the road were quite normal, the done things, rather than quaint, charming old customs, survivals of an earlier age.

And there was work, a therapy that had always helped Joslyn. There was a lot to do aboard *Impervious*. The ship was a huge cylinder, a thousand feet long and three hundred fifty feet in diameter. Fifteen huge fusion engines were clustered on the aft end, and the circumference of the hull was a forest of detection gear, antennae, gunnery, hatches, and inspection ports. The bow of the ship was a flat disk. In its center was a large circular hole, a launch and recovery port. Even if the ship was under spin *and* under thrust, it was just about possible to bring in a fighter or other smaller vehicles there, and a system of elevators could then move the ships to the *Imp*'s circumference. Every ninety degrees along the circumference of the bow end were launch tubes for the fighters, the Wombats and SuperWombats. The bow holes of the launch tubes led into tunnels that ran half the length of the ship. The launch tunnels were normally in vacuum, but the One and Three tubes were being worked on at the moment, and were sealed and under pressure. Inside the launch tunnels were great electric catapults—linear accelerators—that could take a fighter and fling it clear of the *Imp* without either ship firing its engines and damaging something. The launch tunnels could also be used to move ships much more slowly between the bow centerpoint launch and recovery port and the hangar decks.

There were four hangar decks, one for each launch tunnel. These took up the entire circumference of the *Imp* amidships. Since the One launch tunnel was out of action, Hangar One had been done over for the reception. The ship was under spin at the moment, of course, and the hangars was under about three-quarters of an Earth gravity. The hangar was high-ceilinged and went through ninety degrees of the ship's circumference. It was disconcerting to see handsomely dressed ladies and gentlemen calmly strolling or sitting on a deck that was curved about halfway toward the vertical.

The other side of the steel deck beneath the dance floor was the outer hull of the ship. There were great hangar doors, large enough to move a SuperWombat through, and Joslyn couldn't help imagining some practical joker opening the doors beneath the wooden dance floor, and all those old stuffed shirts dropping straight through into space. . . . But even the most ghastly bore didn't deserve that fate. However, if the hangar decks were in vacuum, and the ship were under spin, the fighters could be simply dropped through the hangar doors. When so dropped, they would move away from the ship at the speed the ship had been spinning. If the ship weren't spinning, the fighters would use their own maneuvering jets to get on or off the ship.

The *Imp* had been mothballed thirty years ago—left in a distant parking orbit of Britannica and more or less forgotten about, until the message torp had come in from the Finns with word of the Guardians. *That* had set off a panicky rearmarment program, not just on Britannica, but throughout the British Commonwealth—and the League. The *Imp* was Britannica's ship, though, and it was a Britannic decision to dust her off and get her battle-ready.

It wasn't easy. Thirty years was a very long time in the art of shipbuilding. The words "obsolescent" and "obsolete" didn't quite cover the situation. The *Imp* could more accurately be described as a fossil. She practically had to be stripped down to the hull. The computers had to go.

The communications equipment was hopeless. The laser cannon and torpedo tubes had to be pulled out and replaced with modern equipment. And of course the power plant had to be radically upgraded. A modern fusion generator was half the size, was far more rugged, and could give twice the power as the old monster aboard the *Imp*. And the engines . . . good lord. From what Joslyn heard, dealing with the engine problem was more an historic epic than an engineering challenge. Modern engines of the size originally fitted on the *Imp* gave twice the power, but unfortunately they couldn't be used—the *Impervious's* hull and superstructure couldn't withstand the increased thrust stresses. But the old engines couldn't be trusted. They had too many hours on them, and were a plumber's nightmare besides. The only people who knew how to maintain them had retired ten years ago. And no current engine model had anything like the proper thrust ratings to be a direct replacement.

But somehow it was all getting done. Joslyn was on the periphery of it all. Her direct concern was with the fighters that would be carried by the *Impervious*, and that was trouble enough. She was doing her part, making a real contribution. She had more actual experience directing fighters in real combat operations than anyone in the Britannic Navy. From time to time it struck her that the Office of Personnel had simply done its job and put her exactly where she could do the most good. She was certainly whipping the *Imp*'s fighter wings into shape.

The last of the guests filed through, and it was time for the dinner to begin. The ship's cooks had done themselves proud, as if eager to put the lie to the old saw that the British couldn't cook. The appetizer, the soup, a lime sherbert to cleanse the palate, the meat course, the dessert, coffee—all of it was delicious.

Joslyn sat at the head table with Sir George at her left. At her right was a rather handsome young officer, a Captain Thorpe-Peron of the RBN. He seemed rather young for a captain, a short, almost pudgy sort of chap, with white-blond hair and brown eyes. He was slightly round-faced, and seemed soft all over, somehow.

Thorpe-Peron was fascinated by anything to do with the *Impervious*. What did the pilots think of their fighters? How was the refitting going along? Were the flight-deck crews ready? How much training in pressure-suit work did they have?

Joslyn never enjoyed talking shop during a social occasion, but she did her duty as a hostess and chatted cheerfully enough. She didn't notice at first that Admiral Whitmore had left his seat to whisper in Sir George's ear. Whatever it was Whitmore had to say seemed to upset Sir George terribly. After Whitmore left and returned to his seat, Joslyn was shocked to see Sir George call for a steward and have a decanter of port brought out, long before the guests were finished with their coffee. It wouldn't do, she decided. Better to get him away from table and fuss at him than let him get an early start on a drunk, tonight of all nights.

"Captain Thomas?" she said to him, standing up. "I believe a tiny problem has come in the choice of dancing music. I wonder if you might come with me to have a word with the musicians." It wasn't much good as a lie, but it was all she could think of quickly and it was far better than having him pass out in a dead drunk two hours from now.

"Beg pardon?" Sir George answered, his glass halfway to his lips. "Ehh? Oh, of course, of course." He rose, glass in hand, and followed her away from the table.

Where could they talk privately? Not the galleys or the passageways. Too many people coming and going. Hangar Two, then. The hangar decks were separated by a single bulkhead. Joslyn led the way through one of the personnel airlocks. There wasn't any pressure difference between the two sides, so she didn't have to cycle the lock, but she was careful to dog both doors shut after they were through. Careless pilots didn't live long.

Hangar Two was the twin of the deck now being used as

a ballroom, but where on one side of the bulkhead were gaiety and music, on the other side were gloomy, echoing spaces and the machines of war. It was crowded in there—the fighters usually carried in One were in Two.

Sir George looked around the space with a distracted look as he sipped at his port.

"Uncle George, will you for God's sake put that stuff away!" Joslyn shouted at him, as she grabbed the glass and threw it across the deck. It smashed out of sight in the shadows. "You are the *host* at this party, and I will not let you get to be a fallen-down sodden drunk by the time the dancing starts! What host has ever had booze brought to his own table while the guests were taking coffee! How insufferably rude can you be! And manners like that from the captain of the ship, no less—"

"I'm afraid I'm not the captain any more, my dear," Sir George said, very gently. "Though you are quite right to stop me drinking so soon. It wouldn't do at all."

Something froze inside Joslyn's gut. "Not the captain?"

"Oh, I suppose I still am, officially. But good old Joe Whitmore just let me know that it might be nice for me to make a toast to my successor—lovely way to let a fellow know, isn't it?"

"Oh my God," Joslyn said, all the anger washing out of her. "Oh, Uncle George, I'm so sorry. It's that doughy little man Thorpe-Peron, isn't it? I should have *known* why he was pumping me for all that information." She threw her arms around her great-uncle and hugged him. "Damn the bastards! It's just not *fair!*"

"There, there, my dear. Commanders shouldn't hug captains, even under *these* circumstances." Joslyn smiled, and Sir George gave her a pat on the back. "Do settle down. I must admit that I am nowhere near as surprised as you. I've been waiting most of a year for them to put me out to pasture. You give a grand old girl like the *Imp* to an up-and-comer like Thorpe-Peron, not a broken-down old sod like me. Now, now! Don't say anything. And let me just tell you that your doughy-faced young captain is a fine officer—a fine, fine—"

Sir George's voice broke, and he stepped away from Joslyn into the lurking shadows of the hangar deck. "Damn the luck?" he shouted into the echoing silence. "I've been little more than a caretaker all my life, a placeholder, keeping a chair warm until the other fellow wanted it. They got me out of England because of my drinking—and they thought that putting a man on the backside of no-where was a way to take his mind off drink. I decided to make do, settled down permanently, put in for emigration—and got it. I watched Britannica grow into a worthwhile place. And I joined up, got my commission—and this old hulk was my first command. I have taken care of this ship for ten long, lonely years since the old reserve captain cashed in his chips in his sleep. I did my job right. I checked over every inch of the old girl myself, learned what was too old, what was still good, what would be needed—and kept the whole thing up-to-date, once it was done. When they asked me what it would take to get her ready for battle, a year ago, I had the answers ready . . . right there under my arm, in detail. My staff—all eight of them—had wondered why I fussed so hard over a ship that no one would ever use—but by *damn* she's ready for a fight a year sooner than expected, because I did my homework!

"And they're taking her away from me and giving her to some pasty-faced, public-school boy so he can punch his ticket with a major command on his well-charted way up to full admiral." Sir George's voice was bitter and angry. "And I'll be posted somewhere else where they think I can't do any harm. And everyone will watch, and wait for me to crawl deeper down inside the bottle—"

"Captain to the Bridge," a disembodied voice boomed out. "Red Alert. All hands to battle stations. We are under attack. This is not a drill. Captain to the Bri—"

The first impact was felt, more than heard—a booming, shaking roar that knocked them off their feet. The lights died and, through the bulkhead that led to Hangar One, they heard the horrible sound of air whistling away into space, of screams and cries and alarm bells dying off when the air that carried them had vanished into space.

"Oh my God; they've hulled Hangar One," Sir George said, his voice deep with shock, echoing in the absolute darkness. "They're all dead in there. My God."

Joslyn climbed to her feet—and then got back down on her hands and knees. No sense getting knocked down again, banging around in the dark, waiting for another hit. The gloomy red of the emergency lighting system flickered on, and she saw Sir George striding purposefully across the deck, toward the airlock at the aft end of the nearest way to the Bridge. Now that she could see, she got carefully to her feet and kicked off her high heels. She wasn't about to try *that* balancing act in a ship under fire.

WHANG! A huge noise like the greatest-of-all bells being rung blared out, and the deck shivered. Joslyn fell again and got back up. Something, a missile that misfired, a piece of debris, had bounced off the hull beneath their feet. There came another rending crash, followed by the deep, roaring shout of air rushing out into space. The sound seemed to come from deep inside the ship.

Alarms came on again, pilots and personnel came rushing into the hangar from the airlock. Voices began to shout and a mad tangle of frantic activity tried to sort itself out, as hangar crew and pilots readied for combat in the overcrowded space. Sir George was glad to see them get there fast. He was the one who had seen to it that pilots and hangar crews were billeted near their battle stations. It saved time—and they needed all they had.

Joslyn's fighter, a command SuperWombat, was across the bay. Barefoot, in a ruined evening gown, her hair streaming behind her, she made her way through the confusion to her post.

Sir George barely noticed her as he made his way through the growing press of bodies to an intercom post. He used the captain's override and punched up the Bridge.

Nothing. The Bridge didn't respond. Damnation! He tried the Combat Information Center. Nothing. Was the intercom out? He tried another code, the Damage Control officer. The D.C. officer could be anywhere in the ship, but the intercom computer was supposed to track him or her at all times. The intercom squawked and answered. "Commander Higgins, at post in aft damage control center," a perfectly calm voice with an odd, rolling accent answered. "What is your report?"

Thank God. Higgins was the man for a moment like this. "This is Captain Thomas. I am on Hangar Two. Hangar One has been hulled. I cannot raise the Bridge. I cannot raise the Combat Information Center. Can I get through the corridors to the Bridge?"

"Captain. I am glad you are alive. I assumed you were in Hangar One. Sir, I lost all status reports on the Combat Information Center and the Bridge immediately after the first impact. I must assume they are out of commission. We were hulled twice and took some glancing hits. There seem to have been no explosions, however. I can't be certain yet, but I believe there is no corridor still under pressure that could lead you to the Bridge. I am sending runners in pressure suits to inspect."

"Very well. What sort of outside communications do we have?"

"None at the moment, Captain. Outside comm is normally channelled through the Bridge. We should get backups soon, routed through the auxiliary command station, which is functional but not yet manned."

"Very well. Commander Higgins, for the moment I have no tactical information, I'm trapped on a hangar deck, and I have a battle to fight. Assume that the aux control crew cannot reach their posts, or are dead, and get some of your personnel there on the double. I will contact you soon, Commander."

"Yes, sir."

Normal lighting came back up. Crews were sorting themselves out, looking sharp, all things considered. Where should he be? Number Two Hangar Control. That was the spot, just across the deck. Sir George quick-marched to it, keeping well out of the way of the crews prepping the Wombats.

The four Hangar Control stations were always manned, behind sealed airlocks. Thereby, in theory, their crews could get some birds launched at any time. Captain Thomas hoped the theory held up. He undogged the outer door to the Control station's lock, cycled through, and hurried up the gangway. Hangar Control was high up on the aft bulkhead of the hangar, with big quartz ports that overlooked the entire compartment and let the Hangar Boss see everything that happened.

"Captain on the deck!" a rating called out.

"As you were. Hangar Boss, report," Sir George said.

"Sir. Our Forward Launch Tunnel is out. We are at Go for radial launch. We're ready to lift and drop Wombats through the hull doors as soon as we have the hangar in vacuum. Ready to button up in three minutes."

"Very good. The other hangar decks and Central Launch and Recovery?"

"Sir. CL&R does not respond. Four is at Go for radial or forward launch. Three was on standby, with no fighters in bay, with skeleton crews in Hangar Control. Fighters normally in Three shifted to Four. Likewise in One—and the crew in One says they are the only people still alive in the hangar. They were buttoned up, behind their airlock, when the deck was hulled."

"Very well. God help us all." It was beginning to sink in that the entire Britannic fleet had been decapitated. All the fleet's captains had been at the ball, all the flag officers, all the visiting bigwigs. Dancing four minutes ago, all dead now. The fleet was under attack and under command of junior officers. Sir George realized he might well be the senior officer left in the fleet. There was little time to think. "Can you patch comm with all the fighters through here?"

"Yes sir."

"Lieutenant, instruct Hangar Four to prepare for radial launch. The *Imp* has taken too much damage to trust the launch tunnels, whatever the readouts say. The Bridge is out for the moment, and might have been destroyed. I will command this ship from here. Hand over whatever operations you can to Hangar Three and clear some of your consoles for combat control. Advise Damage Control of the shift. In fact, give Damage Control a direct audio feed from here. Tell them I am here and that I expect a report as soon as aux control is manned and ready."

"Sir."

Sir George stepped back and let the lieutenant and her enlisted personnel do their jobs. There was no point in rattling off a string of commands to do this and that about the ship. The crew needed time to sort itself out and get to stations. He stared out at the hangar. Joslyn—Commander Larson—had earned her pay. That crew was sharper than it had any right to be.

Six minutes had passed since the first explosion.

Joslyn swore bitterly to herself and decided an evening gown made a rotten uniform after all. The damn thing was so tight across the hips she couldn't climb the boarding ladder. Finally, she said the hell with it, bent over, and ripped open the seam from hem to the waist. Let the hangar crew see a little leg, she had work to do. She scrambled through the hatch into the cockpit and started button-up, wishing there was time to get into a pressure suit. Just hope to hell the cabin pressure held.

Oxygen, fuel, fusion source, laser pack, missiles, gatlings, maneuvering jets, main engines, comm unit, battle computer, flight command computer, tactical computer and downlink, all backups. She checked everything, and checked it all again, and again, until a loud *clump, clump* told her the overhead grapples had latched onto her SuperWombat. She looked up through the overhead quartz viewport. The pair of huge ceiling-mounted grapples had locked properly into the hardpoints. She gave the hangar crew a thumbs-up and felt her SuperWombat lurch slightly to one side as the grapples lifted her off the deck. She retracted the landing skids as the grapple unit moved on its overhead track, carrying her toward the hangar doors.

She pulled off her earrings, grabbed at a headset, put it on, adjusted the mike and earphone, and keyed in the radio. "This is A for Albert Leader, buttoned up, grappled and hanging, Go for launch. Albert craft, give me status by the numbers."

"Albert One, ninety seconds to button-up. Grappled and hanging."

"Albert Two at Go."

"This is Launch Boss. Albert Three not accounted for."

Damn, Joslyn thought. Mawkly had been two tables down from her at dinner. "He's dead, Launch Boss. Pull his ship for reserve."

"Will do, Albert Leader."

"Albert Four at Go."

"Albert Five. I have a yellow laser pack, but otherwise grappled, hanging, at Go."

"This is Albert Leader. Five, we're going to want you out there."

"Right-o, Joslyn. But don't count on my lasers. Maybe the back-ups will kick in, but not so far."

"Albert Six at go."

"Albert Leader to Hangar Two, Launch Boss. Albert Three has no pilot, all other Flight Albert craft at Go for radial launch."

"This is Launch Boss to Flight Albert. All green at this end. You are Go for rapid radial launch. All birds grappled, hanging, and ready for drop. Stand by for radial launch under spin. This is Launch Boss to all hangar personnel. We will dump air pressure at combat speed in one minute. All personnel behind a pressure door or in pressure suits. Hang on against the suction during pressure-drop. Vacuum in forty-five seconds."

A new voice in Joslyn's earphone: "This is Captain Thomas to Albert Leader and Flight Albert. Commander Larson, you will be patched through at all times to me personally. We have no information about this attack. All radio is out. We're deaf, dumb and blind. As yet, no ship-to-ship communication. Yours is the first Flight to launch. I want you to set your birds in a defensive shell around Albert Leader's ship. Commander Larson, they are to keep trouble away from you so you can find out what the devil is going on. Do your damnedest to raise any other ships you can. We have no tracking or plotting on the enemy ships. We have no intercept vectors. Nothing. You must depend on your own detection equipment, and on what ships in better shape than the *Imp* can tell you. You will have to be my eyes and ears, and that's as important as shooting down bandits. I expect you to engage the enemy in self defense, but we need data to fight."

"Aye, aye, sir."

"Launch Boss," Sir George said, "you may launch Flight Albert at will."

"This is Hangar Two Launch Boss. Section leaders report all personnel protected from vacuum. Stand by for combat emergency pressure drop. Ten seconds to air dump. Five seconds. Air dump. All air spill valves open."

There was a tremendous roaring *whoosh*, and Joslyn's SuperWombat rocked slightly on its grapples as the hangar released its air into space through half a hundred relief valves. There was a brief whirlwind of dust and bits of paper, and Joslyn saw a suited figure hanging onto a stanchion as the suction tried to pull him off his feet. The Wombats were, like the *Impervious*, basically cylindrical. The pilot sat at the bow, surrounded by tough quartz viewports that allowed vision up and down, port and starboard, and to the fore. Cameras and monitor screens gave a view aft and could zoom in on interesting details in any direction. Three fusion engines at the aft end provided main power, and smaller chemical jets around the circumference were used for maneuvering and course corrections. Joslyn's SuperWombat was a stretch of the standard design—longer on its axis, with better delection and communication equipment, large fuel tanks, and a fourth fusion engine to compensate for the greater mass.

"Hangar Boss here. Hanger at vacuum. Open Hangar Door 21. Flight Albert to start radial launch in ten seconds."

Joslyn did a last meaningless check of the major systems. It was too late to abort the launch now, anyway. Nine minutes had passed since the first impact.

The grappler rolled forward again, until Joslyn's fighter hung over the two great hangar doors, each twenty meters long and ten wide. Hinged to open along their centerline, they swung open to the darkness of space. The last puff of air scooted out the doors, rippling the magnificent view for a moment.

The stars swept past the doors as the *Impervious* spun on her axis. The lovely, far-off blue-and-white ball of Britannica swung into view for a moment, then vanished as the great ship wheeled on.

Suddenly Joslyn felt as if she was falling down the biggest elevator in history. The grapple had released her bird and she fell out through the hangar door, suddenly weightless, bursting out of the dim recesses of the ship to the brilliant sunlight that blazed across the darkness.

She fell away from the ship and looked up through her overhead viewport to watch the rest of Flight Albert unload from the *Imp*. The carrier was spinning once every forty-five seconds; all that was required to keep Flight Albert together was to drop one Wombat every forty-five seconds. It was a good drop; Flight Albert lined up nicely.

"Flight Albert form on me. Hedgehog formation, and give me a two-mile distancing," she ordered. They moved into position crisply, no wasted moves or fuel. Good kids. "Albert Leader to *Impervious*. All birds green, in formation."

Time to take a look around. Joslyn kicked in the tactical radar. She didn't bother checking the viewports—the naked eye was of very little use. Radar and radio were what she needed.

Wherever the enemy were, they knew well enough where the *Imp* was to score at least two direct hits on her.

No sense in worrying about their detecting anything. She cranked up the radar and set it to maximum power and rapid pulse. The holo tank immediately started forming an image. There were the Flight Albert birds, there was the *Imp*, right overhead. Lots of other big blips, coded red for unknowns, bogies, and a stream of much smaller, faster-moving blips. The comm computer got to work, sending Identify Friend or Foe signals. The IFFs came in, blips turned to green for friendlies, and ship names started to appear in the tank by the blips. The little ones stayed red. There were a hell of a lot of bandits out there.

"This is *Impervious* Launch Boss. Flight *B* for Bertram unloading from Hangar Four, *C* for Cuthbert ready for drop from Two."

The small blips was staying stubbornly red. No response to IFF. They didn't seem to be maneuvering, though some of them were mighty close, and on courses that threatened collision. "Bandits on screen," Joslyn called. "Altitude one hundred twenty-one degrees, azimuth two hundred ninety-one. Four bandits at that bearing."

"This is *Impervious*," Sir George's voice announced. "Flight Bertram, track and intercept."

"Flight Bertram on intercept, sir."

Joslyn forgot about the bandits. Bertram would handle them, or else her own kids would keep them out of her hair. She had to get Thomas some data. She checked her radar tank again.

There was the *Lord Mountbatten*, a heavy cruiser. Maybe they had held together. "*Impervious* Flight Albert Leader to *Lord Mountbatten*. Come in, please."

"This is *Mountbatten*. Come in *Impervious* Albert."

"*Impervious* has lost main ship-to-ship communications and Combat Control. I am relaying for Captain Thomas. Report on tactical situation."

"Stand by. Thank God you're there, Albert. Thought we had lost the *Imp* altogether." There was a pause and the same voice came on again. "Eleven minutes ago there was suddenly a swarm of radar contacts. They're still coming in, though the worst damage was done in the first moments. We're shooting up most of them now. The computers report over two thousand contacts, possibly many more smaller contacts. The bandits do not maneuver, and they were very small and fast. They are going right through the fleet and have hit a lot of ships and stations. Some impacts on the planet. Everyone's damage control is very busy. We are tracking the bandits that missed and they have not maneuvered. We haven't picked up radio or other transmissions from the bandits."

"Are you receiving, Captain Thomas?" Joslyn asked.

"Yes, thank you, Albert Leader. Please patch my audio through to *Mountbatten*."

Joslyn flipped some switches and listened in as she checked the radar again. Rocks. The little blips, the bandits, were rocks someone was throwing. They were all over the place, still streaming through the fleet. As she watched, the image in the tank shrunk and new images showed up around the new, larger, perimeter. Her radar signals were still moving out, covering a larger and larger area, and the bounce-backs were taking longer and longer to arrive back at her ship. There was Wight, Britannica's larger moon, marked in red until the radar figured out what it was and marked it in the gray of a natural body. That was about the effective range of her fighter's radar. *Mountbatten* would have to do the *Imp*'s long-range work until the carrier could patch herself up.

But near-space was full of bandits. Joslyn didn't even bother to hope that the *Imp* was the victim of some random meteor shower. This was a softening-up attack. The Guards were out there, somewhere.

Sir George would have been inclined to agree. But the word from *Mountbatten* was that no enemy had been detected. Yet.

"Sir, all fighter Flights deployed and on station," the Launch Boss reported.

"Very good, Lieutenant," Sir George said. He turned

and spoke to the intercom. "Commander Higgins, are you there? If so, report."

"Yes, sir. I have a crew at auxiliary control. They have ship's conn, and are rerouting to get tactical and comm data there. The Combat Information Center is still out, but aux control says they will be ready to handle combat functions in five minutes. Sick bay reports many casualties and fatalities. Engineering and main ship's armament are green. I have runners laying comm cable to sections that are still out. One runner got to the Bridge and reports it destroyed."

Damnation! "Thank you, Commander. Tell me, is there a way clear to aux control from where I am?"

"No, sir. Corridors are blocked by debris and in vacuum. I will keep you advised if we get a way clear."

"I'll put on a pressure suit now, Commander. The moment a corridor is clear, I want to know it."

"Yes, sir."

Sir George punched up aux control. "This is the Captain. It appears that I can't get there from here. I am in Hanger Two Launch Control, and will command from here at present. Sooner or later, we will need to recover those fighters, and we can't count on getting the Bow Recovery Area up to snuff for a while—and I expect Damage Control would have an easier time of it in weightlessness. I want spin off this ship at combat speed. And order ship secured for maneuvering."

"Aye, aye, sir."

The overhead speaker blared a moment later. "ATTENTION ALL HANDS. STAND BY FOR COMBAT SPEED DE-ROTATION IN THIRTY SECONDS. SHIP WILL TAKE APPROXIMATELY ONE MINUTE TO LOSE SPIN. SECURE ALL LOOSE ARTICLES AND BRACE FOR DE-ROTATION."

Everyone in Launch Control grabbed a stanchion or strapped themselves in behind their console.

"DE-ROTATION COMMENCING IN TEN SECONDS."

"Hang on, lads and lassies!" the Launch Boss called. "Here's where Cook gets all his crockery smashed."

"DE-ROTATION COMMENCING."

A deep roaring noise came up through the deck and everything lurched to one side as the de-spin thrusters fired all around the circumference of the big ship. Structural beams groaned and creaked as the stresses shifted, and someone's clipboard slid across the deck to slam into Sir George's shin. He swore and kicked the thing away. It sailed halfway across the compartment. As spin was taken off, gee-forces fell and everything got lighter. Sir George felt himself getting a bit queasy and wished for a little drop of something to settle his stomach. Zero-gee didn't bother him any more than full gravity did, but he had never enjoyed what a spin-up or spin-down did to his inner ear.

"DE-ROTATION COMPLETE. SECURE SHIP FOR MANEUVERING."

It was fifteen minutes since the first impact.

"That's done, anyway," Sir George said to no one in particular. "One day some dull little sod in a dreary little lab somewhere is going to discover artificial gravity and save us all this mucking about with spinning ships. Get me through to *Mountbatten*. And dig out a pressure suit for me."

"*Mountbatten* here," a new voice answered, younger, more nervous than the comm officer who had answered before.

"Lieutenant Pembroke, is that you?" Sir George asked. A rating drifted over, dragging a suit. Sir George gestured for the man to help him on with it as he talked to *Mountbatten*.

"Yes, sir. I have the comm. Captain Sanji and Commander Griffith are aboard the *Imp*."

"That's right. Stupid of me to forget," Sir George said cheerfully. "Well, if they've left you in charge for the moment you might as well enjoy it. We still have no radar of our own, so we're going to be hanging on your every word. But have a listen first," he said in his best fatherly voice. "I'm afraid we've taken some damage and none of the flag officers can get through to take charge of the fleet. I'm the highest-ranking senior line officer anyone's been able to scare up so far, so I'm afraid I'm forced to play admiral for a bit. Do you understand?"

There was a pause before Pembroke answered. "Yes, sir. You are assuming command of the fleet. Very good, sir."

No doubt the boy could guess they were all dead, but breaking it gently would keep him from panicking. Couldn't be helped. Sir George stuffed his arms and legs into the suit and pulled the seal shut. "Right, then. Let's get to it. I'll give you my hunch, Pembroke. The 'bandits' that have hit us were rocks, thrown by a catapult, a linear accelerator quite some distance away. Perhaps from outside Alexandra's orbit. Rocks small enough and moving fast enough that our radar wouldn't pick them up until they were right on top of us. And they were thrown blind long before anyone decided to put the *Imp* where she is. We've gotten our nose bloodied by a lucky hit."

"But sir, if that's so, they must have been launched weeks ago."

"True. But if they were launched from much closer, we'd have spotted the linear accelerator. Linacs are bloody big things, huge radar images, with power sources and whatnot to detect. Now, they've done us some hurt, and we're using up ammo and power fending off rocks. Which means less to fire at the Guards' ships when they come. Relay an order to fire only on bandits that are on intercept courses. They can't maneuver and we can't waste our effort on the misses. Lucky for us, from that range they had to be firing blind, though they got off some lucky hits on *Imp*. What sort of damage have the other ships taken?"

"Well, sir, we're not configured for flag operations at the moment, but most of the larger ships seem to have taken at least one hit apiece. Some of the smaller ships got hit too, and they can't soak up as much damage, of course. *Hotspur* was wrecked. *Othello* is going alongside to look for survivors, but there's not much hope. Other than that, the *Impervious* seems to have had the worst luck."

"So she has. But trust in Higgins to patch her up. Which leave us with the question of what happens next. We can detect good-sized spacecraft that doesn't want to be found at least thirty million miles out, which means that our friends are at least that far away. We have some time. At least quite a few hours—possibly a day or so. They had a difficult timing problem, I must say. They had to synchronize the arrival time of the thrown rocks—which, as you say, must have been thrown weeks ago—with popping a whole fleet out of the C^2 at the right moment, in the right spot. They had to arrive as close in to the sun as they dared, which would be about one hundred fifty million miles out. Which means the enemy is *here* already, somewhere between one hundred fifty million and thirty million miles out, but we have not yet detected the light rays and radar reflections because we don't know where to look. But follow my chain of logic and make sure I'm not daft. They threw the rocks to soften us up, make us duck our head, force us to waste ammunition and fuel. The best time to do that is when it won't give away the 'surprise' part of their surprise attack. You know how the Guards love surprises. That means the rocks were launched weeks ago and have travelled billions of miles from their accelerator, timed to arrive just as the Guardian fleet can be detected from Britannica. Perhaps they've overestimated our detection skills. But we'll spot 'em at about thirty million miles or so—and thanks to what old friend gravity does to C^2 travel, they couldn't drop into normal space closer than that hundred fifty million miles from Epsilon Eridani. And it takes a lot of *time* to travel a hundred fifty million miles in normal space. They've been here a while, rushing for us."

"But why haven't we detected them?"

"Because they're just specks of metal, very far off. Any radar powerful enough to watch in all directions in space to C^2 arrival range would jam every other use of radio in the system. The Guards presumably have kept radio silence and haven't maneuvered. Once they light their fusion engines, we'll see 'em! I'll grant you that the rock throwing was risky. We might have spotted it, somehow— a ship happening across a stream of boulders hurtling straight for Britannica. But we didn't. The rocks added to our warning time—but the rocks have done damage to my ship, and others. A clever plan, and one that might be worth the extra effort, or might not. Does all this make sense, or have I gotten as blotto as the fleet scuttlebutt says?"

"Makes enough sense to scare the hell out of me, sir."

"Good." *And I knew that,* Sir George thought, *but if the next rock gets me, I want someone else in the fleet to understand the situation.* "Then here is what you are going to do. Leave ten fast frigates behind, and then I want you to lead the entire fleet out of Britannica's orbital plane. Launch *now* at flank speed north, off the orbital plane and to sunward. Disperse in a spherical formation, pretty widely, at least five hundred miles between ships. The Guardians will be looking to find our fleet at rest in orbit around Britannica, but let's not oblige them. Use lasers for communications if at all possible, maintain radio silence the best you can—and use frequencies that the sun's natural radio noise will drown out at long range. Hide. Now, we'll have the fast frigates' sensors, and I expect we'll have the *Imp*'s detectors up to par by then as well. When we detect the incoming fleet, I will transmit their heading to you. You will maneuver to put the fleet right in the sun's disk as seen from that heading. That won't hide you completely, but it will give the buggers some problems.

"*Impervious,* her fighters, and the frigates will meet the enemy fleet."

"But, sir—"

"But me no buts, Lieutenant. The Guardians are here to smash the finest fleet in the British Empire. Pearl Harbor started twenty minutes ago. This is a raid, not an attempt to land and conquer the planet. They wouldn't try *that* with Britannica. New Finland was a lot more weakly defended, and *she* was too much for them to swallow. No, they want to knock out our ships before we can go hunting for them. My job is to defend this fleet. So I mean you to go *out* of harm's way. If they move against the planet—and they won't—we can jump on them. But right now let's keep them away from their targets. Execute your orders."

"Aye, aye, sir. *Mountbatten* out."

Sir George stared at the microphone for a moment. It was the strange sort of moment commanders faced—the orders had gone out, were being acted on, all that could be done was being done—and the person at the center, calling all the shots, could do no more but wait. A younger officer might have worried, bothered his men, nagged at them, told them to do what they were doing already, but if Sir George had been taught one thing by his long and not-very-illustrious career, it was patience.

Sir George's ship was half-wrecked, all his superior officers were dead, a fleet of unknown power was undoubtedly bearing down upon him, and disaster was the most likely outcome. Yet he felt more alive and confident than he had in twenty years. Still holding the mike, he pulled a headset out of its niche and put it on. He shooed the communications rating out of his seat and sat down in front of the console, thought for a long moment and then spoke into the mike again, very quietly. "Commander Larson. Are you still on the line?"

"Yes, sir."

"Then cut your relay for the moment. I'd like a private word."

"We're private at this end, sir."

"And at this end." Oh, there might be a half dozen radio-detection technicians listening in, or the battle recorders might be putting it all on tape for posterity, but that didn't matter. No one around could hear, the techs and historians would be discreet, and the moment *felt* private. "Joslyn, my dear, we should both be dead with the rest of them," Sir George said, in barely more than a whisper.

"I know, Uncle George. But we're not. Call it the fortunes of war or dumb luck."

"All I know is my being alive is a direct result of your taking me to one side and bawling me out for being a drunken fool."

"Uncle George—"

"It's true, and you know it. Half an hour ago I was being kicked upstairs as an old incompetent, and now I've got greatness thrust most unwillingly upon me. And I wonder how I've done with it. You heard my reasoning and how I've chosen to deploy my forces. Have I done it properly, or gone quite mad? I would value your opinion."

"Sir. I believe you were absolutely correct in your analysis. I believe you are thinking clearly and well. I think you have responded to the situation in the best possible way."

"You've changed your tune in thirty minutes."

"And so have you, Uncle George. I didn't think you had it in you."

"To tell you a dreadful secret, my dear, I'm fairly certain I *didn't* have it in me, up until that rock hit us. Maybe I still don't have it, and I'm fooling us all with a grand old show. Time will tell. Now I've got to go breathe down Damage Control's neck and get this ship ticking along. Patch through all your radar information to us, and whatever you can get from the frigates' detectors."

"Good luck, Uncle!"

"And good luck to you, Commander! Captain out."

Joslyn smiled to herself and got down to it. He *was* an old dear. But that to one side, the main thing to do at the moment was watch her radar. There were eight flights of Wombats deployed about *Impervious*—Albert to the bow, Bertram to the aft, Cuthbert and Dagmar to port and starboard, Elton above, Farnsworth below, Gordon and Harold hovering well to the rear as reserves. Good formations, good deployment. But from what Sir George had said, it seemed likely that there would be nothing but rocks to shoot at for quite some time. Joslyn worked it out in her head. Even given a fairly close-in detection of the enemy fleet, and even assuming that the enemy, once detected, would move and maneuver faster than any ships ever had, the Britannic fleet would still have several hours warning. And they had just proven they could launch on fifteen minute's warning.

Joslyn decided to make sure at least some of her crews were fresh when the Guards showed up. "This is Albert Leader to Hangar Two Boss. Lou, I think we might as well get half my flights back aboard and into the sack. We'll start an eight-hour-on, eight-hour-off rotation right now."

"Right-o, Albert Leader. Stand by just a moment. According to what I've got, the *E, F, G,* and *H* Flights were just coming off duty when the fun began. Let's cycle them back in and get them tucked in while the rest of you lot patrol the dark reaches of space."

"You've been reading too many cheap novels, Lou, but that sounds good. We'll do radial recovery."

"There's a candle in the window for you."

The recovery went quickly and smoothly, all the off-duty fighters landed in under twenty minutes. Joslyn felt quite pleased with her kids. Good pilots all.

Flights Albert through Dagmar went rock shooting, with Joslyn picking the targets. Her radar was substantially more accurate than a standard Wombat's. Her problem was mainly one of spotting targets that would actually hit something: If they shot at all the rocks, they would have run out of power and ammo in two hours. But ninety-five percent of the rocks didn't even come close to a ship.

But that didn't stop Joslyn from respecting the rock-throwing tactic: It forced the Britannic forces to stay at alert a long time, always a wearing experience. It soaked up ammo, and did some real damage to ships.

That made it all wiser to move the fleet. Joslyn watched in her radar as *Mountbatten, Churchill, Princess of Wales, Determined, Warsprite,* and the lesser ships pulled away from orbit of Britannica, toward the sun and out of the orbital plane. *Hotspur's* wreck stayed behind, abandoned. Joslyn hoped that at least the dead had died quickly.

Ten of the fast frigates—ships of the same class as the *Joslyn Marie*—remained behind. The *Imp* had ten frigates. It seemed very little to meet the enemy with. Then Joslyn dimpled. Mac would have cheerfully pointed out that the *J.M.* had attacked *Leviathan* all by herself. The odds were a lot more even here.

The runner had made it—barely—through the wrecked corridors from aux control to Hanger Two. Sir George followed the runner's torturous route back, through improvised airlocks and wrecked corridors and burned-out compartments. There were grim sights to be seen on the way. Sir George was shocked to see dead bodies floating in the corridors, their young, ruined, lifeless faces staring back at him from the vacuum. "Fatalities" was such a tidy, hygenic term to apply to those horrors, those hideous slabs of meat that had been alive and laughing and full of promises such a brief time before. Sir George had never seen the bodies of the battle-dead before. For the first time, he began to get genuinely angry at the Guardians, and took his first lessons in hating them. Why had they done this?

War in space, battles between great fleets, had never been more than a theoretical possibility before the Guardians. Space war had been a game, a chess problem to Sir George. Neatly labeled spots of light that moved about in a display. Dead bodies floating in the corridors of the *Impervious*. That was real war, real death. Entirely too real. Grim-faced, the old officer struggled to keep up with his youthful guide.

Auxiliary control itself was in perfect shape, so clean and quiet and orderly that it seemed surreal. Technicians worked here and there in front of open access panels, talking in low tones, slapping in jumper cables, getting readings, pulling in control. The reserve bridge crew had finally gotten through the corridors and were at their stations, powering up the backup systems, setting things to rights, bringing the ship back to life—superbly British and phlegmatic in the face of disaster.

The main holo tank sprang into life suddenly, showed a scrambled mish-mash for a moment, then cleared to show a tidy, precise display of the tactical situation—neatly labeled spots of light that moved about in a display. Sir George sat down in the captain's chair, remembered himself, and shifted to the flag officer's chair. The captain's chair would have to remain vacant. Another little reminder of all the officers they had lost in the first thirty seconds. Sir George felt strangely wary, unsettled. All this studied, quiet, purposeful action, this cathedral of calm, was a fraud, a tidy lid atop the carnage of war. Dead bodies floating in corridors. He shook his head and began to take in the situation.

The *Imp*'s radar and passive detection gear was back on line. At least two of the four laser cannon were operable. They had half the torpedo tubes, and fish enough to shoot through them—though the age-old slang term seemed a strange one to use for torpedoes that never got wet. The *Imp* was showing signs of life, could still fight.

The main engines were dicey. All of them were fitted and supposedly ready for action, but only the even-numbered half had been inspected, tweaked up, and approved by the Chief Engineer.

"Helmsman. Bring all main propulsion engines up to standby. Prepare to maneuver using odd-number engines. If any of them blow, abort and shift to even numbers. Let's find out the worst now instead of later."

"Aye, sir."

"Lay a course directly away from the sun, flat as can be on the orbital plane. One-gee acceleration. Communications—relay same course and acceleration of escorting craft and order them to safe distances and positions for powered flight. Relay to commander of frigate group. Detach one frigate to remain behind in present orbit and link to *Impervious* through secure laser comm channel."

"Aye, sir."

"Detection. Patch in communications to the stay-behind frigate and all the orbiting stations. Order them to use active radar, powerful and frequent pulses. Maximum range and coverage. Assign pulse frequencies to all of them. Use our own active radar until we start to maneuver—then shut down and listen and watch only. Passive. Pick up any radar reflections off the pulses the stay-behinds send off. Use the optical systems to watch for the lights of fusion engines.

"Helmsman, come to heading and prepare to perform maneuver in four minutes."

"Coming about. Four minutes to main engines."

"Albert Five to Albert Leader."

Joslyn pushed a button and answered. "Albert Leader. Go ahead, Madeline."

"Skipper, maybe I'm dense, but I can't figure it all out. Why did the Guards throw all those rocks at us and give us warning that they were on the way?"

"The starting point is that it takes time to move around in a star system—and you can't pop out of C^2 too close to a star or else the gravity field fouls things up and you come into normal space a zillion miles off course or inside the star or moving at a hundred times the velocity you wanted. So the Guards had to arrive in Britannica's star system at least one hundred fifty million miles out from Epsilon Eridani herself. They are out there, heading for us, right now."

"And the rocks are just a diversion, to force us to keep our heads down?"

"Right. Except they must have timed the rocks to come about the same time we could detect them. But even after we detect them, we might have days before the two fleets are close enough to shoot at each other."

Madeline Madsen sighed, and spoke again. "It seems to me," she said, "that war must have been a lot simpler when you didn't have to travel so far to *get* to it."

"Wrong again, Maddy," another voice chimed in. "All this is just a classic version of the timing problems a mobile force has always faced."

"Ooh, Artie, don't *we* sound grand. Someone's been reading the cram notes on space strategy again, someone has."

"Oh, ease off, Maddy. At least some of us do read."

Joslyn let the good-natured bickering go on. It would let some of the tension bleed off, keep them from getting bored—or scared.

There was another rock, headed straight for the *Imp*. Joslyn fired her main laser, vaporized it, and wished the battle would hurry up and get started.

CHAPTER THIRTEEN

Aboard *Impervious*

The *Impervious* shut off her odd-number engines. The damn things had held out. Sir George called for tea and stared at the screen. The *Imp* had taken up a stable orbit about seven hundred thousand miles starward from Britannica—the frigates, their auxiliary craft and the Wombats hovering about her in space.

The rest of the fleet was lost in the flare of the sun, barely detectable even at this range, no more than a few million miles.

There was a job to do, still, for which Sir George had not provided. "Get me a secure channel to *Mountbatten*," he ordered. It took a little time. Finally the comm laser was locked on *Mountbatten*, and the answering beam had found the *Imp*.

"Pembroke here. Standing by for your response." They were far enough away that normal conversation was impossible. The laser light bearing Pembroke's words took about ten seconds to travel to the *Imp*, and it would take just as long to send a return answer.

"Thomas here. You're hard to find, which means you've deployed well. Retain this link to receive your detection information. I want a small, fast corvette detached from your fleet. She is to backtrack the course of the thrown rocks, move along that course to their launch point, and attempt to locate and destroy that accelerator. That accelerator could be a stay-behind weapon that will be harassing us until we put it out of business. It is vital that the corvette locate it, but I don't want them taking fool chances trying to destroy it. Obviously, it might have moved since it fired on us, but it still might be possible to spot it. Once we find it, we can smash it whenever we wish.

"A final point. If the *Impervious* is lost, or I am killed, the flag duty, the command of the fleet, reverts to you. I would strongly advise you start considering tactics to meet that contingency. Thomas out."

Four hours had passed since the first attack. The enemy fleet should have been spotted long ago. Either the Guardians hadn't timed it well, or they had overestimated the *Britannic's* skill in ship detection. At least the fleet was clear of the bloody rocks. The units still in orbit around Britannic reported the rocks were still coming, but the stay-behind frigates and the stations were getting to be increasingly good shots. None of the rocks had scored a hit in more than an hour.

"Captain, sir, we have an unidentified radar return," the ensign serving as detection officer announced calmly. Instantly aux control's constant low murmur of voices was silenced.

"Communications. Patch everything said and done in this compartment to *Mountbatten* over a secure laser channel—and send everything from the detection console as well. Detection, full report."

"Sir. Very faint return on last pulse—there it is again, a bit stronger. Epsilon Eridani Centered Coordinates: negative zero point nine EECC latitude, one hundred seventy-three point four EECC longitude. Request passive systems aboard *Mountbatten* and other ships center their search on that point and report to *Impervious* to provide parallax. Now have third and fourth pulse returns. Target is moving rapidly—toward Britannica. Velocity very high to show in so few pulses, but not yet determinable."

"Optical? Spectral?" Thomas asked.

"Sir, no optical detection, therefore no spectral readings."

"Then they haven't lit their engines yet. The fusion plumes would show, that's for sure. Communications. Order *Mountbatten* to commense maneuver at low power. Get the fleet in the sun's disk as seen from radar return. Helmsman. Bring us about to present our bow to the target. We're a lot smaller side-to-side than we are end-to-end. Keep our smallest cross section pointed through them. Communications. Use secure laser comm to repeat orders for radio silence to escort vehicles. Keep it quiet. Laser communications only. And keep laser to a minimum, too. In theory, laser comm can't be detected, but let's not test theory too far. Detection. Ensign McCrae, isn't it? What more have you got?"

"Sir. Awaiting data from *Mountbatten*. No significant changes in target. Range decreasing, and we'll have enough data for a doppler check soon. Not yet."

"Sir," The comm officer called. "Secure laser signal from *Mountbatten*. They are executing maneuver, and report it a minor correction. They were almost in correct position already."

Sir George allowed himself a brief smile at that. He had done some good guessing to place the main fleet there. He punched up the flag commander's strategic display in the holo tank. Very roughly, they were all strung out in a line: *Mountbatten* and the rest of the fleet about a million miles towards the sun from Britannica's orbit, then Britannica herself, then starward a bit from the planet, the *Imp* and her escorts, and then, far off starward at some unknown distance, a radar return, presumably the Guardian fleet. That's where he would have come in, straight from starward, the shortest distance from an arrival point to the planet. And that's where they had come in. Good.

"Sir," McCrae called. "Request that the high-power radar units around Britannica sending radar pulses shift from spherical search mode to a narrow beam centered on unidentified return."

"Denied. That would give us some detail we don't need yet, and tell them we've spotted 'em. Spherical search to continue. Work with what you've got a while longer, lad."

"Aye, sir. Sir, we have received parallax data from *Mountbatten*. Approximate range, awaiting refinement, thirty million miles. Velocity determination difficult because the target is moving straight for us."

"Well, thirty million miles is what they said it could do. It would appear that our radar is exactly up to spec." Sir George punched up the officer's mess on the intercom. "This is the captain. Send a steward with tea, coffee, and some sandwiches. We've got a bit of a wait yet, and there's no sense going hungry."

Reports started coming from all over the ship. There were, as expected, no survivors in Hangar One. There were one hundred fifty-seven dead there, and sick bay reported at least one hundred additional fatalities, possibly two hundred serious non-fatal casualties. Some forward compartments were still cut off from the ship's corridors by vacuum and there were certainly more dead and injured that had not been accounted for yet. Out of a normal ship's complement of one thousand one hundred, perhaps seven hundred fifty were fit, ready, and able to get to battle stations.

The damage control crews worked on. Work-arounds, backups, improvisations were plugged in, patched in, forced into place. Wreckage was cleared and either jettisoned or lashed down in Hangar Three for later salvage or use. Corridors were patched and repressurized. Main ship's weaponry was ready, too. The *Imp* could fly and fight. Sir George was satisfied with that. To his mind the rest of the Britannic fleet was now in graver danger than the *Imp*—and the greatest danger the fleet faced was the loss of its experienced commanding officers. That was a danger that a damage control team couldn't handle. It would take years, perhaps a generation, to wholly repair that catastrophe. Thank God the prime minister and the cabinet had turned down the invitation to the ball.

The poor old p.m., the whole government, in fact the whole planet, was sweating this one out. The fleet was ordered to radio silence when attacked. The Guards seemed to have a hell of an Intelligence service, and it had to be assumed that anything transmitted to the planet's surface would get back to the enemy, either through electronic taps or through plain old-fashioned agents-in-place. A civilian government, still largely geared to peacetime, and in a gossipy capital, was easy pickings for spies. The fleet didn't dare send news of how the battle was going.

They were probably more scared back home than the fleet was up here. At least the fleet had some idea what in blazes was going on.

Thirty million miles. It was a meaningless figure. Huge beyond imagining in everyday terms, but in the scale of interstellar travel, it was nothing, a distance traveled in less time than it took to say the words. Thirty million miles.

Even the measure was obscure. Only Earth's British Commonwealth and the world Britannica used "miles" anymore. Even the Americans had given up long ago and shifted to metric measure. These days, few non-British even knew that a mile was, by some vague amount, longer than a kilometer.

The Britannic fleet was learning just how real thirty million miles was.

Detection nailed down the Guard fleet's velocity: two hundred eighty-two miles a second, or just over a million miles an hour. A pretty hellish clip, but still it would take thirty hours for them to reach Britannica, even if they didn't deaccelerate at all.

The watch had changed while Flight Albert had been on patrol. Albert Leader's approach and recovery was a lot less exciting than her departure, which suited Joslyn just fine. She willed the hangar crew to hurry up, get all the ships in, seal the hangar doors and pressurize *fast*. She wanted food, and rest, and sleep, and she wanted to get started on them quickly, before another alert came and put her back in her SuperWombat.

For a wonder, there weren't any foul-ups, and the hangar was buttoned up and under pressure in record time. Joslyn had the hatch undogged and was already out of the ship and on her way along the handholds when she noticed the stunned silence around her. Only then she remembered what she looked like. Her long honey-colored hair streaming every which way in zero gravity; barefoot; dressed in the ruins of the evening gown she had ripped apart so she could get into her fighter; her careful makeup job undoubtedly sweat-streaked, blurred, and muddled into a fright show; more out of than in her dress. She blushed mightily, then laughed at herself and went on her way. "Let me tell you fellows, it was rough out there," she told the hangar crew. She hurried on to the pilot's mess. Time for food and then some sleep!

She had at least gotten a sandwich and a cup or six of tea when the radar contact was made. The word was passed along ship's intercom immediately. Joslyn swore to herself, headed back to her cabin and got into flight overalls. She knew what came next, and it did.

"Commander Larson," the intercom called cheerfully. "Captain's compliments, and would you please come to auxiliary control?"

"Duty," she said to the empty air as she braided her hair back into a bun, "thy name is lack of sleep." She decided she had time to wash off the remains of her makeup first, but not time for a full shower, and headed down the corridor to the head.

"Ah, Commander. Welcome to our Bridge-away-from-Bridge," Sir George said. "We're a bit cramped, but managing. I want you to take a look at the tactical situation and tell me what you think your friends plan to do."

"Captain. Well, let's see." She took a long hard look at the hologram tank and frowned. "I assume that we found them on active radar pulsed from Britannica's orbit. That wouldn't give our position away. The Guards haven't kicked out any radar pulses looking for us, have they?"

"That's right."

"Then they won't have spotted *us* yet. Not at that range. But they have picked up the pulses sent out from Britannica's orbital stations. Presumably Britannica's radar has been hitting them for a while, but the signals have only just gotten strong enough for us to detect them on return. They know we will spot them soon, but they can't be *sure* we've nailed them yet. Lordy, this sort of they-know-that-we-know-that-they-know makes my head spin. But they'll assume that we'll have maneuvered since the rock throwing, they know we'll be hiding, and that they'll have to find us. Detection officer. If you had the best possible equipment—optical, infrared, and so on—and didn't use active radar, how far off would you detect the *Imp* if she was rigged for quiet running?"

Joslyn took her first real look at the ensign sitting in as detection officer as he swung around in his chair and grinned at her. Presumably, the real detect officer was dead, wounded, or trapped in a compartment. The kid on duty was a fresh-scrubbed, cheery-looking lad with apple-red cheeks, black hair and brown eyes and snaggly teeth, far too young to really understand the stakes of the game he was in. "Well, ma'am, I assume you mean in the present geometry of the situation. The *Impervious* has her bow pointed through their location, and so shows them a small cross section, and that helps a great deal. And we're pretty much in the sun's glare—lots of background noise. And the blips I'm getting seem to be a large number of smaller ships—they probably don't have very large or powerful detection gear aboard. I would say perhaps ten million miles. But why *wouldn't* they use active radar—they would have detected the radar pulse that picked them up for us—they'd know we know where they are and—"

"Spare me the details. That's what I just said: They've been hit by radar pulses for quite a while. It's just that we haven't be able to pick up the returns from that radar because the returns have been too weak until now. They can't be *sure* we've spotted them yet. Maybe we can fool them. You've got enough data to plot their projected course and watch it optically, don't you?"

"Yes, ma'am. I wouldn't actually see their ships until they started maneuvering, but *not seeing* fusion lights would tell us they hadn't changed course. Just as good as seeing them."

Joslyn thought for a moment. "There are still rocks coming in toward Britannica, aren't there? Suppose we order all our radar to a narrow sweep of the piece of sky that the rocks are coming from. We have a ship in that area, the corvette that's supposed to track down the linear accelerator. It seems very unlikely to me that the Guards were able to track the frigate's launch. Here we go again with the we-know-they-don't-knows, but they wouldn't realize we are aware of the frigate's identity. The Guards will see us bouncing a radar reflection off that ship, and then focus our search in that area. We can act as if we had spotted that frigate, didn't know what it was, and were tracking it intensively. They'll think we're expecting them to come down under cover of the rocks."

"Which will make them think *we* haven't spotted *them*, and so we'll get *them* to not use *their* radar, so *they* won't find *us*," the ensign said with a laugh. It appealed to his sense of humor. "And once they start braking—and they *have* to—I'll be able to spot the plumes instantly. It'd work."

Sir George smiled. "Send the order to the radars around Britannica. And don't explain it, either. Just the bare instruction to redirect the radar. If someone is listening in, that might add to their confusion."

"I'm bloody confused enough for everyone," the comm

officer muttered under his breath as he set up the transmission.

The hours crawled by, the situation largely unchanged. The Guard fleet moved closer and closer—or at least the computer's projection of its course said the enemy was still headed for them. Ensign McCrae got increasingly nervous. He *knew* the Guards had to be where the computer said they were, that his equipment would spot the lights of their fusion plumes the moment they maneuvered, but he didn't really believe it. McCrae decided he was going to go back to studying Zen when this was over. The philosophy seemed custom-made for detection specialists.

Joslyn remained on the bridge, laying plans with Sir George, watching the tactical display. According to the computer, the Guards were still hurtling closer. Twenty million miles. Eighteen. Fifteen. Ten. The numbers changed meaninglessly. McCrae felt bored and tired and nervous and fidgety and eager and scared all at once. He wished the devil the sodding Guards'd get on with it. They had to start braking soon or they'd never stop in time. Maybe they had malfunctioned, miscalculated—

It took a full ten seconds for him to realize what the screens were showing him. "Sir! Fusion lights! They have commenced braking."

"There we go! You won't need active radar now, Ensign. Details as you have them."

"Yes sir. I count at least fifty fusion lights. Fifty ships. A variation of sizes. We'll need readings for a few minutes before I can give you masses and accelerations. Range at engine-light: approximately six point seven million miles."

Joslyn pulled herself over to the detection station and looked over McCrae's shoulder. There they were, right in the middle of the crosshairs. The computer had kept a damn good track all this time. And the Guards had never used their radar. The gag with the frigate had worked. "Captain," she said. "At the power levels they're using, their own engine exhaust plumes will jam all their detection equipment. There's a good chance we can stay hidden for quite a while yet."

"I was hoping for as much. Ensign McCrae. Tell me, your own opinion, formed out of your own vast experience: Can they see through the plasma their exhaust plumes are putting out?"

"Sir. As long as they are decelerating, they will not be able to detect us at any distance at all," McCrae said. "Their fusion plumes will jam all their radar and visual, right through to infrared."

"What fun. Then it might be time to arrange a reception committee to greet our visitors. Communications. Get me a link to *Mountbatten*. If this doesn't work, they'll be on their own. Flight Boss, recall all fighters. Get them aboard and refueled and ready for sortie. Secure the ship for maneuvering and get me a secure laser link to commanders of the escorting fast frigates. Commander Larson. What are our visitors going to do next? Is there any lesson for us from the attack on New Finland?" Sir George asked.

"No, sir. This is nothing like what they did there."

"Your own thoughts, then."

"Well, sir," Joslyn said carefully, "if I were the Guardian admiral, I'd head straight for Britannica and use her gravity well to maneuver, and do my detecting while in orbit of the planet. I'd knock out our radar stations there. Maybe I'd even do a very brief, token attack on the planet—that would force our side to respond, if it had gone off to hide. That's the one flaw in the tactic of not being there when they come after you—the planet must be defended. But *Mountbatten* and the rest of the fleet are well positioned. They could be there to interdict quickly. The Guards know the fleet will have moved, and they probably have a number of contingency plans based on where the fleet has moved to, though I can't say what those plans would be. There is one thing. How the hell are they going to get out of here? They'll have to brake in order to fight us—and then they'll have to accelerate like mad to get out of the system with us on their tails. That's a lot of fuel."

"Mmmmph. True. Very well." Sir George wanted more answers than that. "McCrae. What more have you got?"

"Quite a bit, sir. I'll be able to refine things more and more as we go on from here. We've got the target range and the temperature of the fusion lights now—those figures let us calculate the amount of power the engines are putting out. We've just gotten an optical track. That gives us a change-of-rate, and the doppler confirms the figures. They're slowing at about one-gee. Figuring one-gee into the engine temperature tells us how much power the engines are putting out, and *that* tells us what we really need to know, the mass of the ships."

"You're quite right, that is the only thing of all that I want to know. Well?"

"Ah, yessir. I beg your pardon. I now count fifty-five separate targets. Fifty seem to be the same mass—about twice the size of our fast frigates. Very crudely, that gives those ships a crew of about twenty to thirty, and potentially some pretty heavy armanent."

"The other five ships?"

"Are a puzzler. The engine temperatures are all different, much hotter, which means the engines are running much closer to their maximum power ratings. As if much smaller engines were being used to power the larger ships—and what I can pull off the spectroscopic scanners show a lot of impurities, as if the engines are old and worn and bits of the throat nozzles are vaporizing into the fusion flame. And those five ships must have ten times the mass the others do."

Joslyn looked sharply at McCrae. "Let me have a look at those figures, Ensign."

Sir George let his younger officers fuss with the technical issues. He had some thinking of his own to do. He intended to launch the *Imp* straight at the oncoming fleet, hidden from their view by the glare and the jamming effects of their own braking thrust. It was something of a risky proposition. He could not think of any detection system that could see through the fusion glare—the League

had been trying to develop just such equipment for years.
And a similar maneuver had worked against the Guards in
New Finland. But they *might* have come up with something. And they *might* shut off their engines for a bit, just
to do a bit of searching, right at a very awkward moment.
And there was the risk of plowing the *Imp* right into the
flame of an oncoming ship's thrust. But that wasn't a great
danger with a steady hand at the helm. He shrugged.
They didn't pay warship commanders to be overcautious.

The real danger was that the Guards knew perfectly
well they were coming in blind, and would be prepared
for such an attack. He had to assume they were so prepared. Very well, they would expect it. That was simply
one more thing to take into account. They would not know
where, or when, he would strike, or with how many ships.
How many he had already decided, hours ago—the *Imp*,
her fighters, and the frigates would go it alone.

When was the issue, then. There were arguments for
making a strike further out, and counter-arguments for
waiting until the enemy was almost in orbit of Britannica.
Sir George was inclined to strike as soon as possible, if for
no other reason than to give his sailors a psychological
boost, a chance to hit back. They had been waiting, sweating it out, feeling helpless and scared long enough. The
sooner they were busy, the better. He turned his attention to the flagplot tank and started playing with the
variables—looking for the advantages of one course over
another, intercept points, closing rates, fuel usage, thrust
levels. . . .

"Sir George, excuse me."

"Commander Larson," the old captain said with a start.
"You have something for me?"

"Maybe, sir. I've got an idea that the five largest targets
are fuel ships, expendable and possibly unmanned. We've
just gotten an optical reading, light reflected off the fusion
flames, and the five larger targets are *huge*, even for their
mass—which suggests that they are carrying a lot of something that isn't very dense."

"Such as liquid hydrogen to top off the tanks of the rest of the fleet so everyone can make their getaways!" Sir George said. "Splendid. It makes a great deal of sense. The ships come in, run their raid, refuel, and run like hell. We have nine frigates with us. We'll assign two to the attack on each tanker, and I want you to get Flight Albert out there alongside the last frigate to hit one tanker."

"Sir, there's one other thing: The tankers' engines appear to be running nearly at maximum temperature, and their spectra suggest they are old and worn. It's what I'd do. No sense using new engines on expendable ships."

"What are you suggesting?"

"That we fire the *Imp*'s laser cannon at the tankers from long range. With a bit of luck we'll overheat the engines and blow them—"

"Leaving the tankers with no way to slow down, so they zip across the star system never to be seen again, leaving the rest of the attack fleet with no fuel to get home. Joslyn, you are a true member of the clan. Only someone with a drop of Thomas blood in her would have dreamed up something that nasty. We'll do it your way, and then play shoot-'em-up with the Guards."

The *Impervious* maneuvered for the second time, fifteen hours after the rock attack. Sir George selected a fairly sedate five-meter-per-second acceleration, a two-hour burn, and ordered a course that kept the *Imp* out of the Guardian fleet's projected flight path for as long as possible. Sir George checked his tactical display. The *Imp* would intercept the Guard fleet six hundred thousands miles out from Britannica. Assuming the buggers didn't spot them and run.

"Detection, I want to hear the moment you think they might have spotted us. Any course change, any maneuver." The *Imp* had one great advantage. She had hours to track her foes, lick her wounds, carefully plan her counterattack. The Guards would be expecting some sort of move, but they would have only seconds to analyze the *Imp*'s attack and respond.

"Aye, sir."

Engine shutdown. Back to zero-gee. *Impervious* and the frigates flew on.

Sir George worked at his planning. The two fleets would pass through each other at a relative speed of about one hundred and five miles a second. The tanker-ships seemed to be well to the rear of the Guardian fleet, which meant there would be marginally more time to hit them before the Guards had passed through the *Imp*'s trajectory. Sir George ordered the ship brought about to aim her stern through the direction of flight—as soon as the *Imp* was through the Guard fleet, she would have to start matching velocity with the enemy.

The laser cannon crews were given their targets and ordered to stand by. The lasers would be effective at a range of no more than ten thousand miles—and that gave them just over a minute and a half to hit those tankers. Sir George ordered all debris and wreckage thrown overboard and dispersed as widely as possible. With a little luck, one of the Guard ships would run into something, anything. Hitting a styrofoam cup at one hundred and five miles a second could wreck a ship.

He looked around for Joslyn—she was a comfort, one of the few people he, the captain, could talk to. Oh, yes, she had to get to the flight deck and get her crews ready. It occurred to him that there was battle on the way, and his niece was on the front lines of it. He might never see her again—and he couldn't remember her leaving just now. Well, good luck to her. The way to make her safest was to do his own job properly. But he had already done all he could. It was time to wait again. And time for another bloody cup of tea.

All eight flights of fighters sortied again, an hour before intercept. They held station on the *Imp*, ready and waiting for action. The fast frigates each deployed their three auxiliary craft. Everyone got ready.

Time moved slowly, wearing on nerves, until the moment when it began to move all too rapidly. "At effective laser range in three minutes," the weapons officer announced.

Sir George thrummed his fingers nervously on the arm of the command chair.

"Two minutes. *Impervious* and escort craft all well clear of enemy ship's fusion plumes."

Good. Now if those bastards could keep from changing course for a few minutes, the *Impervious* might not get melted down to slag.

"Sir!" McCrae called. "I have just picked up a very jammed-up radar pulse coming from the Guard fleet. They'll have spotted us now."

"How could they spot us? Is it something we don't have?" Sir George asked anxiously. If the Guards could see through a fusion plume, the League might be in very serious trouble.

"No, sir. Brute force detection, that's all. They're pumping a hell of a big pulse through the radar and seeing if anything makes it back through the plume. Useless at more than this range, and at our closing velocity they don't have time to respond and maneuver anyway. It's an impact warning system, that's all."

"Good. Then you might as well crank up our active radar, Ensign, since they know we're here. Pass the refined targeting data along, obviously."

"Sir!" McCrae grinned. It had been frustrating as hell to sit on top of those monster radars for all these long hours without the chance to use them.

"One minute."

"And here we go," Sir George announced. "Put tactical on the main screen." The ship's computers drew a diagram that showed the *Imp* and her allies and antagonists. Neatly labeled dots on a screen.

"All four laser cannon trained on target one. Concentrated fire commencing—mark!"

"Detection—any effect on the tanker?"

"Temperature of target climbing rapidly. There's a brightness flare! *Something* has blown on it! Tanks, or the engines, I can't see."

"Laser crew! Shift to target two! Fire torpedo volley at target one, track it two ways, for constant thrust and for no thrust!" Sir George called, his heart pounding with excitement. Battle well and truly joined, for the first time in his long life.

McCrae was going happily mad, watching nine kinds of monitors at once. "Range to second target much shorter; *boom*! She blew already. Definitely an engine meltdown that time."

Sir George turned to the weapons officer. "Split your fire! Two cannon on target three, two on four! Torpedo volley on target two, as planned!"

"Sir!" McCrae was near a fit. "Incoming laser fire. They've ranged us."

"Intensity?"

"We can take it, and they're not holding target well. But you can bet there's more on the way. Boom *twice*! Third and fourth tankers blown!"

"Target five!"

The weapons officer shook his head. "Sorry, sir, we're already outside effective range for five."

Sir George looked again at the tactical display on the big screen. The *Impervious* had already flown clear through the opposing fleet. "Bloody hell. *That* didn't take long. I want torps chasing targets three four and five. Flight Boss. Are escorting craft at safe distance for maneuver?"

"Aye, sir."

Helmsman, you may commence planned maneuver on schedule."

"Sir. Attitude at thrust heading. Thirty seconds to throttle-up to three gravities thrust."

"Communications, warn all hands."

"ALL HANDS. STAND BY FOR THREE GRAVITIES THRUST OF PROLONGED DURATION."

"Detection. Damage to enemy fleet."

"Sir. Too soon to read it. Four of the five tankers are out, either wrecked or engines overheated and blown. All four are unable to maneuver. Our torpedoes still chasing them. It will take at least three hundred seconds to call hits and misses."

"And the attack fleet itself?"

"No hits as yet, sir. The frigates and the Wombats are chasing them."

"TEN SECONDS TO THREE GRAVITIES."

No chance to bother with using half the engines for safety's sake now. It was a stern chase, and the engines would hold or they wouldn't. Depending on how the Guards reacted, they could be under three-gees for ten minutes or three hours. The great fusion engines roared to life and slapped everyone down into their chairs. The *Imp* shed her velocity starward and headed back in toward Britannica. She would catch the Guards sooner or later, but she was out of the game for the time being. It was up to the frigates and the fighters.

Twenty-three hours had passed since the first rock had hit the *Impervious*.

CHAPTER FOURTEEN

Deep Space, Britannic Star System

Five gravities was no fun. Now Joslyn found herself wishing she *didn't* have a pressure suit. The damn thing was designed for use in high-gee situations, but it wasn't exactly comfortable. Joslyn hated high gravities, had wanted the retro-burn to be over the moment it had started. But the Guardian fleet was already far ahead, and it would take some chasing to catch them.

The Guardian ships were moving toward Britannica at about eighty miles a second now, still braking, slowing all the time. The *Imp*'s fighters had started their retro-burns while moving *away* from the planet at twenty-two miles a second. The fighters had to lose that speed, reverse course, and then gain speed moving the other way, chasing hell-for-leather after the invaders. It was going to be a long ride.

Joslyn watched the Guardian fleet in her radar. Now the gloves were off, as far as detection equipment went. Both sides knew exactly where the other was, and every frequency was full of radar. The Guards were holding formation for the moment—no, wait a moment.

"Albert Leader to all units. They're splitting their forces. Half the ships are decelerating at higher thrust, call it four-gees. They'll match with our velocity plenty damn quick at that rate. The second half of the fleet maintaining previous thrust—including the fuel ship."

"Albert Four here. Right-o, Joslyn. What's the plan?"

Joslyn checked the numbers. The fighters and the frigates were still in formation together, now headed sunward at about twelve miles a second, perhaps half a million miles from Britannica. The *Imp* was well behind them, just about dead in space and starting to gather speed back in toward the planet.

"They're the ones who are short of fuel, lads and lassies. We let them do the work. All ships, shut down all engines in thirty seconds from my mark—MARK. We let them come to us, take one firing pass through them, then relight our engines. We barrel on in toward the planet to take on the second team. We should be able to reform on the *Impervious* and move in as a fleet if we time it right."

Joslyn cut her engines with the rest of them, glad of an excuse to get back into zero-gee. Let the Guard fleets get tired and worn by gunning around at high gees.

But the second team, the half of the fleet following the fuel ship . . . if *she* had been coaching the opposition, she would have ordered the second team to cut their engines altogether. Without the braking thrust, the ships would have fallen in toward Britannica—and away from the *Imp*—faster. And the *Imp* was worth getting away from. So why had they kept to their plodding one-gee thrust?

Aha! Because if they delayed braking, they would have to brake at a higher thrust later on, to make up for the deficiency. And that fuel ship was barely keeping up the pace as it was. And they *needed* that fuel ship. It was their last ticket out of the system.

In other words, the fuel ship couldn't manage any better than one-gee. It was a fact worth remembering.

Second Lieutenant Madeline Madsen, Royal Britannic Navy, wasn't interested much in strategy or deception schemes or fleet movements. She knew only that there were twenty-five large enemy ships heading straight for her, intent on killing her.

She was interested only in her armament, her fuel, having her pressure suit sealed and ready. She wanted to stay alive, and that meant shooting her way through the Guardian fleet and coming out the other side. Simple.

In some part of herself, she wanted to get mad at the powers that be, because she was merely a pawn, a player's piece in all this—except Captain Thomas and Commander Larson were out here risking their lives too, and the p.m. and the governor general would die just as dead if the Guards bombed the capital. Every ship's commander in the fleet had been in that bloody hangar. They paid the piper, too.

Pawns weren't the only ones dying.

Madeline carefully watched all her screens, rehearsed her firing run, targeting, maneuvers, laid it all into the computer. If she went out, she'd leave the opposing side something to remember her by.

She knew her job—and knew that all the schemes, the strategy, the studies, the simulations, the training, the ships, the expense, the time, the whole damn Navy, had only the point of putting young women and men where they could fight. All of it, the great confusing, clanking, ponderous bureaucratic machinery, was there only so she could be here, to put a few ergs of energy or a few ounces of metal into the enemy ships.

At the moment, she would have been just as happy if the bureaucratic machinery hadn't worked. She was *scared*, actually aware that she might die, for the first time in her short life.

Time stopped meaning much. She was ready. All she could do was wait. The Guards were coming straight for the Wombats. Maddy swore to herself. They were still braking. The Wombats would be moving at less than five miles a second, relative to the Guards, when they passed through each other's formation.

And it started. Her first assigned target in range. Two

torps away and watch for incoming. There. Radar and optical were both tracking it. A torp coming right for her. Use the recoilless gatling guns, throw some metal at it. The gats fired two-ounce steel cylinders, and spread their ammo far and wide. You fired five thousand rounds and hoped one hit. One did. A flash of light, and radar said the torp had stopped accelerating.

But her IFF said someone had her lined. Time to randomize the situation. She kicked in her main engines at six-gees for ten seconds, then spun through ninety degrees and fired her auxiliary thrusters to confuse the track a bit more. Another target. Close enough for lasers, by God. She opened up, gave the target fifteen seconds at full power, then shut down and gave them a dose of Doctor Gatling for good measure.

They had had time and a half to get her lined. Without regard for heading or targets, she fired her mains again, full open, ten-gees for three seconds, then spun end-for-end and braked at ten for another three. That should get her off their screens for a bit.

Time to look around. Tally-ho! Short range—the target was braking, heading straight for her, its fusion plume actually visible to the naked eye.

She had two torps with ablative coatings that could survive, very briefly, in a fusion plume. Time to see if they worked. She loosed one of them at the plume, then maneuvered again, quartering around to get a clear shot at the enemy ship with a conventional torp—

—No need, up she goes! She wasn't sure her torp had had time to get there and hit. But good lord, that ship had been close! Not more than a hundred miles off, at most—

A jarring impact. Red light! Fuel tank two, damn. She was venting hydrogen, bleeding like a stuck pig. The auto damage control took over, pumped to the other tanks, shut it down. Still alive.

Maddy didn't stop to worry about how close the call was. Time to move. For all she knew, she had just flown right into her own gatling gun fire, or hit a random fragment from a blown ship—but she had to assume that a bandit had her lined and was ready to nail her.

Ten-gees again, at a crazy skew to her current course, twenty full seconds, and she wanted to black out and throw up at the same time.

Another target—no, the radar's IFF said it was an aux ship off one of the frigates. She pulled her hands back from the weapons panel and left the aux to her own devices. No radio calls on targets in a fight like this— though there had never *been* a fight like this before—but ships were too far apart, the complexities of ship-to-ship combat too much to worry about to allow time for calling in a bandit at twelve o'clock high.

And Maddy wondered where the hell she was, and where she was going—oh balls and bastards, she was headed straight out of the system, practically in formation with the Guards. Time to move. Two more bandits, two more torps apiece, and another rip from the gats. She took ten seconds out to take a proper bearing and slammed her engines into gear again, bringing her back to original course and heading in one violent, twisting corkscrew maneuver.

On the radar, dead ahead. A Guardian ship. A straggler. Derelict. Dead in space. Easy target. Was the ship already wrecked, all hands lost? Were they willing to surrender, prisoners to interrogate? Were they making repairs right now—would this be the ship that made the direct hit that blew the *Imp* when she passed this way? A sitting duck.

Maddy gave it thirty seconds with the lasers that ripped the hull open from stem to stern.

And then she looked up and space was clear. So that was battle. She didn't know it would be that easy. And suddenly she was thinking again, a human being and not a trained shipkiller. She looked to the radar where the derelict still showed, well behind her now. That was the only ship she was absolutely certain *she* had blown. Would they have surrendered? Battle. She didn't know it would be that hard, either.

Sir George frowned at his screens. Two frigates, three frigate's auxiliary ships, six fighters. Lost; dead. And twelve Guard ships blown.

That left thirteen ships waiting in the *Imp*'s path. And these Guardian ships were clearly designed for battle against big ships. They might have had trouble with the fighters, but they could out-maneuver the *Imp* easily.

A pincer. If the escort fleet was up to it. "Communications. Can we get a secure link to Commander Larson?"

"I'll try sir. The Guardianships are right between the *Imp* and Albert Leader. They might pick it up."

"That's what scramblers are for, Lieutenant."

"Yes, sir."

"See what you can do. Ah, another thing. Do we still have the link to *Mountbatten*?"

"Yes, sir."

"Patch it through to my headphones, if you please. This is Captain Thomas calling Lieutenant Commander Pembroke. Awaiting your reply." The laser beam would have to carry the message across a million miles of space, and then it would take a minute to get Pembroke on line. More waiting, and very little else to occupy Sir George's attention in the meantime.

He suddenly felt very old and tired. He hadn't slept since the night before the reception—over thirty-six hours now. It seemed more like a century before. This was a young man's game. And would have been, if the Guards had held off for a day. Young Captain Thorpe-Peron would have had the comm, with a full flag staff to run the battle with him, instead of one broken-down old remittance man.

But Sir George knew he had done well. The Guards should have won the Battle of Britannica in the first thirty seconds. But it seemed he had a sporting chance to turn a disaster into a victory. The Guardians were in trouble now.

"Pembroke here. Awaiting your reply. From what we're receiving on laser-link, I offer my congratulations, Captain."

"Thomas replying. Thank you. But it might be time for you to do your bit. We've split their fleet. There are twenty-six ships headed your way at one-gee. This will take some timing, but we are going to try forcing them to move faster—right into your gently grinning jaws, if we can manage. The twenty-sixth ship is their fuel ship, their ticket home. We think it can't *do* more than about one-gee. Knock that ship out, and our visitors can't get home. They won't have the fuel to run far, and we can hunt them down.

"Now let me be honest enough to tell you what you've already guessed. One very good reason that I left the rest of the fleet behind is all your commanding officers are dead. They were killed in the first moments. The junior officers commanding the ships I left behind are all we have. When we were facing an unknown enemy coming from an unknown direction at unknown strength, I could not risk His Majesty's ships in untried hands.

"The odds are better now. We've gotten a look at the Guard ships and what they can do, and I think if we use you properly, we can bounce the Guardian fleet to pieces. So far, to quote, 'We have scotched the snake, not killed it.'

"And I must ask you a question. The lives of your crew, the survival of the Britannic fleet—and the safety of Britannica itself—rely on your answer. *Can you young fellows handle those ships in battle, completely on your own?* I will not be able to help you. The *Impervious* will have her hands full. Say no, and whether you are wrong or right, the Britannic fleet will survive, and these Guard ships will escape, and possibly destroy a ship or two of ours. That will be a small price to pay for the survival of the fleet as a fighting force. Answer yes, and be wrong, and we face disaster. I order you to think before you answer, to confer with your fellow acting commanders, and consider well. Answer on your honor, not on your pride. That is all." Thomas cut the contact.

"And it's bloody well enough," he said half to the comm officer, half to himself. "But sometime you've got to trust in untried judgment, or you might as well pack up and go home. You need a little faith in people."

"Yes, sir." *You've proved that*, the comm officer thought. *I never would have risked my neck to your judgment if I had a choice. But it's sodden-drunk old Cap'n George that kept us alive*. A light glowed on the comm console. "Sir, we have a secure line to Albert Leader."

"To my headset, please. Thank you. Commander Larson. We have some tactics to discuss. . . ."

Ten minutes later *Mountbatten* sent a signal: " 'Let our just censures attend the true event, and we put on industrious soldiership.' "

Sir George grunted and said nothing for a moment when he heard it. Did Pembroke know his spacemanship as well as his *Macbeth*? Well, a sense of history never did anyone any harm, though Sir George felt, on the whole, he would have preferred a simple 'yes.' "

He transmitted his instructions to Pembroke, and decided to switch from tea to coffee. Black. Strong. He wished for a little something to brighten it up, but brandy wouldn't do at the moment.

The *Impervious*'s engines roared into life, bearing down on the thirteen Guard ships to starward. The Wombats and frigates turned to harry the Guardians as the *Imp* brought her firepower to bear on the enemy. *Mountbatten* lead the rest of the Britannic fleet in an all-out assault on the twenty-six inbound Guards, intent on blowing the tanker at all cost.

Sir George, still wearing a pressure suit over a much-wrinkled formal dress uniform, sat in his borrowed flag officer's chair in his backup Bridge, surrounded by half-trained junior officers doing their best. This was it. The Guards were in trouble, but either side could win. If the

Imp's lasers were powerful enough to thin the enemy ranks before the *Imp* was within their range—

They were. The lasers killed three of the Guards.

If the Wombat pilots weren't too shaken up and exhausted, if they had fuel and ammo enough to fight—

They did. They herded the Guard ships practically right into the *Imp*'s torpedo tubes, and accounted for a few more kills themselves.

If the *Imp* could hold together, survive inevitable battle damage—

She could. Commander Higgins reported only a few more hits, from fairly small and slow-moving armor-piercing missiles of an unknown type. Strangely, the missile warheads didn't explode. The things just bored into the ship, crashed through a few bulkheads, and came to rest. Sapper teams were taking a look at them.

And, the biggest *if*, if the *Mountbatten* and the other ships were skippered by *wunderkinden* and not cocky fools—

And oh, thank God, they were, they were. Pembroke led them in a classic interdiction maneuver, making masterful use of the bulk of Britannica to hide his ships, boring straight in for the fuel ship, ignoring all other targets until that one was gone, then chasing the attack fleet, fragmenting it. Two large Britannic ships and two more frigates lost. A few smaller ships reported hits by the same strange slow missiles.

It ended in a rout. Both Guardian formations were broken. Within eight hours, the Guards lost twenty-one more ships, including the last tanker. Ten Guardian ships were unaccounted for. Probably all or some of them managed to slip through the debris and confusion of battle away, get far enough out to jump to C^2. The remainder were chased down, pursued until they ran out of fuel, overtaken and destroyed. Several Guardian ships were invited to surrender. All refused. Not a single Guardian prisoner was taken.

As of that moment, the Britannic fleet lost one cruiser,

four corvettes, five frigates, eight Wombat fighters. Historians might call it a British victory, but both sides were bloodied, and the British had dead enough to mourn and holes enough torn in the chain of command. Fending off a raid is never a triumph.

But there was time to rest, and heal, and sleep, and patch up the ships. For the survivors, that was victory enough.

Aboard Impervious, Warsprite, *and* Mountbatten, *the sappers worked on the odd missiles and were baffled to find no warheads there to disarm. Only some odd off-white pellets of various sizes, packed in what seemed to be sawdust, that spilled out and floated around in zero-gee. Some of them were small enough to get sucked into air vents, others got caught in odd places, nooks and crannies of equipment.*

By the time they thought to x-ray the pellets, and found they were eggs, the first of them was hatching deep inside Impervious's *air system. The shell cracked and, in the darkness, a pale, frail, worm-like thing writhed and twisted mindlessly to get free. It crawled away from the egg, clinging to the wall of the air vent with hair-like cilia. It found a plastic coverplate over an airpump.*

It began to eat the coverplate.

It lay its first eggs two hours later, without pausing in its feeding.

It died shorting out the pump.

CHAPTER FIFTEEN

Survey Service HQ on Columbia, Kennedy's Natural Satellite.

Pete Gesseti opened the door to Mac's cabin without knocking, switched the light on, saw Mac in his bunk and tossed the oversized, bright red envelope marked *Secret* to him before Mac had time to do more than wake up.

Mac's reflexes snatched the envelope out of the air and he sat up in bed. "Pete, what the hell—"

"There are two reports in there, and they change everything. You're going to have two questions, so let me answer them before you can ask. Yes, Joslyn is safe so far as I can gather, and no, you didn't give the frigging Guards any ideas. They had to have planned the raid long before you said a single word."

Mac felt the bottom fall out of his stomach, and he ripped open the envelope. Two loose-leaf folders. *Naval Action Report: Guardian Attack on Britannic Fleet*, aka "*Battle of Britannica.*" And the second. *Report on the loss of His Majesty's Ships* Impervious, Mountbatten, *and* Warsprite. "Oh, my God," Mac said. He rubbed his face, trying to wipe the sleep out of it, swung his legs out from under the covers and sat on the edge of the bunk. "Oh my God, they got the *Imp.*"

"These two reports came in to State and the Navy Castle fifteen hours apart," Pete said, "and they wouldn't have gotten to Columbia until like next year, if they had gone through channels. But when they hit, all hell is going to break loose, and the big brass is going to need this base, and my boss put me on a high-gee shuttle to get these to Driscoll soonest so she could know what's coming. I sort of got two copies instead of one because I thought you'd want one. Shove that one under your blankets for now and read it later. Get dressed because I'm on my way to kick Captain Driscoll's door down now and I want you with me. Oh, as soon as my office saw these we put in a call to the Judge Advocate's office and it just so happens that your conviction was reversed and your permanent rank boomed up to captain about thirty-eight seconds after they knew we had heard about the *Imp*. They're going to look bad enough without you rotting away in a training job for warning them. The power of the threatened news leak."

It was too much. Still half asleep, Mac decided that when Pete Gesseti brought the word, the news was *always* too much. Shocked by the news, groggy and unshaved, relieved that his wife was all right, Mac changed into a work coverall, put on socks and shoes, and followed Pete out into the corridor.

"I always get lost in this underground maze of yours," Pete complained. "Lead the way."

Mac nodded and turned down the corridor. There were a hundred things he wanted to ask, but Pete talked on before he had a chance to say a word.

"Our Navy is going out of its tiny little *mind*. If this could happen to the Brits, we could be next," he said, following Mac through the corridors of Survey Service Base. "HMS *Impervious* and two other major combatant ships were eaten by *worms*. Not the steel hulls apparently, but every kind of plastic, pressure suit fabrics, graphite structural supports, insulation, you name it. Also any foodstuff—and corpses. They'd eat through something, and lay eggs, and the eggs would hatch and eat something, and lay eggs . . . one malfunction, then two malfs, then twenty, a hundred at once. And the cute little buggers excrete some kind of slime that reacts with oxygen and foams up. *That* eats up ship's air, so pretty soon there's none left to breath *and* the blobs of foam block air vents and feed pipes and what have you. There's some sort of poison gas, too, but no one is sure if the worms produce that directly or if it's a byproduct of the reaction that locks up the oxy in the foam. People dying because the worms ate through reinforced fabric and their pressure suits were swiss-cheesed. Ammo going up because the fucking worms ate through the *trigger safeties*. Airlocks shorting out and opening pressurized interiors to space. Fuel tanks rupturing. And the worms breed incredibly fast. It took about thirty-six hours for them to wreck the *Imp*. Captain Thomas—except he'll be an admiral by about next Tuesday because he's all they've got left, there were one hundred fifteen senior Brit officers killed, and some from other planets, too—Thomas finally realized it was hopeless and gave the order to abandon ship. They starting taking crew off and the worms got aboard the rescue ships before anyone figured out what the hell was going on."

Mac had been walking more and more slowly, listening to Pete's hurried words. Now he stopped dead and turned to look at the older man. All those people dead . . . and something popped into his mind. "Pete—wait a minute. It just registered. You didn't say Joz was okay. You said something like you *thought* she was okay."

Pete tried to look Mac in the eye, and couldn't. "Yeah. That's right. I *think* she's okay."

"Pete! What the hell does *that* mean?"

"Well—" he shrugged, "—the casualties were real bad, and survivors got shuffled to a half dozen places, a lot of them without ID and in bad shape, unconscious. They won't have a complete accounting of personnel for a while yet. But she's not on the casualty list, and there was a specific mention that three Wombat pilots were killed. I found three pilot names in the casualty list and Joz wasn't one of them. I dunno, Mac. That's the best I can tell you. Believe me, Mac, I tried. I tried like crazy. But she wasn't listed as dead, and that's all I could find."

Mac restrained an urge to grab at Pete, shake him, as if he could squeeze more information out of him. Mac felt a terrible emptiness open up inside him. Joslyn was supposed to be safe, at home, in the midst of a great fleet deep in friendly territory. And now she might be dead— and not a clean, clear report of exactly how, not when he was prepared for the news because he knew of the danger. No. She would be missing and feared dead, but the news never certain, an agonizing time when he dared not hope because he was an astronaut and he knew what the odds were, and yet could not help but hope because he loved her, but still not *knowing* until the last corpse had been accounted for. . . .

"Mac. Mac. Stop. This isn't the time. We have to see Driscoll. Now."

Mac looked up sharply, and suddenly realized he *had* grabbed at Pete, had his hands clenched around the diplomat's shoulders, gripping him hard enough that it must hurt. He let go his hold, and tried to breathe deeply, calm down. "So let's go. But for God's sake tell me everything you know."

Pete let out a deep sigh, and fell into step besides Mac. "Thomas got out okay, but there were hundreds dead. There's nothing alive aboard the *Imp* and the other ships but the foam worms. They wanted to tow the *Imp* out of orbit before the worms shorted out an engine control and maybe rammed her into the planet, but they're afraid to get near her for fear the eggs can survive vacuum and one egg might float into an airlock. For a while there was a rumor that the eggs could survive *re-entry*. Not true, but the people on-planet are going nuts for fear that the worms might get loose on the planet.

"And now the ROK Navy brass has to admit you were right, quit pushing papers around and get on with the war. Except that you were warning that a big ship could be killed just as dead as a little one by a nuke—substitute 'worm' for 'nuke' and you were dead on target. If a few frigates had been wormed, we'd have lost nine people per ship and a pretty smallish ship at that. Easily replaceable. We lost the *Imp*, and that's a significant fraction of the League's naval power and personnel wiped out. Now they *have* to go to smaller ships. But now there's not time to *build* smaller ships."

Mac grunted. "And all this time I hoping I was wrong."

"You weren't alone in hoping that, my friend. And here we are." They came upon the entrance to the captain's quarters, and were stopped by the ROK marine on duty. "Sorry, sir, the captain—"

"You'll tell me that the captain can't be disturbed," Gesseti said in a calm voice, speaking rapidly, "and then I wave my credentials and this pretty red package marked *Secret* at you and show you the sealed letter from the Kennedy Secretary of War and you'll let me in, right? Wrong. Instead of wasting five minutes on that little scene you'll let is in *now*."

"Ah, well, yessir, but the captain isn't in her quarters."

"It's three in the morning, local. Where the hell is she?"

"In her office, with two other gentlemen."

"Then we bust in on a private party. Lead the way."

"Sir, I can't leave my post."

"C'mon, Pete, I know the way without him." Mac turned and headed down the corridor.

The marine looked uncertain about what he should do, and stepped toward Mac as if to stop him. "Hey, wait just a second, ah, sir, she's not to be—"

Pete grinned evilly at the marine. "Stay put, soldier. You're not to leave your post, remember?" Mac and Pete headed down the hall to the captain's office.

Mac was thinking more clearly by this time, and there was an obvious and frightening question. "Pete, those worms can't possibly be some natural breed the Guards found growing under a rock. Not and eat shipboard plastics."

"No."

"And no one in the League can breed things like that."

"Nowhere near it. Been trying for a long time, too."

"And if the Guards can do that, what else can they do?"

"Don't make me think about it. I saw shots of the *Imp*'s interior and I'm already having nightmares." They arrived at Captain Driscoll's outer office door and went in, to find another marine sentry on duty, sitting behind a desk. "Good evening, Private," Pete said. "We need to see the Captain most urgently."

"But she's extremely—"

"Not any more, she's not." Pete said, neatly stepping around the desk and opening the door to the inner officer before the marine could react.

"Hey!"

"It's all right, Eldridge, let 'em through," Driscoll said, her voice coming from behind the door. "I know that voice, and when Gesseti wants in, he gets in. Law of nature, and we might as well cave in gracefully to it."

"Yes, ma'am."

Pete grinned at Mac. "Like I always told you—never hurts to have a reputation."

The two of them went in, and Mac forgot all military bearing when he saw who Driscoll's visitors were. "Randall! George!" He shouted, giving each of them a bear hug before they were out of their seats. At least some friends of his were safe and alive. His newborn fears for Joslyn made seeing old friends all the more pleasurable. "You guys are supposed to be on Bandwidth!"

"Yeah, Mac, but we *found* 'em!" Randall said. "I wanted to rouse you when we landed two hours ago, but George warned me you like your sleep—"

"You found 'em? The Guards? You found Capital?" Mac asked.

"Near enough," George said happily. "We got hold of an astronomer and the three of us doped out what sort of star system Capital had to be in—and we're here to hand Captain Driscoll a search list, all the possible systems."

"And the odds look damn good," Driscoll concluded, grinning. "You can salute me any time you're ready, Lieutenant Commander Larson."

"Uh? Oh, yes ma'am." Mac saluted and then caught the twinkle in Driscoll's eye. "Sorry about that. Ma'am." He liked Driscoll. She was a good officer, with a style of leadership that seemed wildly informal and ramrod straight at the same time. You were never quite sure where you stood with Driscoll, and that kept you on your toes. No doubt, that was what she had in mind. Captain Gillian Driscoll, United States Navy, was a short, stocky redhead, a gray hair or two beginning to show, still fighting to keep off the fat that desk work put on a person, but still trim, firm, and ready to bite anyone's head off, should the need arise.

"Forget it," she said. "Who can remember salutes at three in the morning?"

"Besides, we've got to break the boy of the habit," Pete said. "His conviction has been overturned and he's been bumped to captain his own self. That's the one piece of good news I've got. The rest is all . . ." Pete looked around and stopped talking.

Driscoll followed his glance. "Oh, yes, you might not know these gentlemen. Commander Randall Metcalf, U.S. Navy, and George Prigot . . ."

"Of no fixed address," George suggested. "No one has ever quite managed to figure out my status. Mac! A captain! Congratulations!"

"George Prigot. Yeah, Mac told me all about you," Pete replied slowly.

"Relax, Pete," Mac said. "They're family. Randall and George have security clearance for Secret, Top Secret, and Very Unlikely, even right up to Ridiculous. And they're in on this."

"Okay, so I bend a few more security rules," Pete said blandly. "But here's the report my boss wanted you to see, Captain," he said, handing the red envelope to Driscoll. As she opened it and started reading, he pulled a tape cartridge out of his pocket. "Is there a—"

"In the cabinet against the far wall," Mac said. "Here, I'll set it up." Mac took the cartridge, opened the cabinet, and switched on the playback unit. "I'll throw it on the big screen." He crossed back to Pete and handed him a remote control unit.

"What's on the tape?" Randall asked.

"Real bad news," Pete said flatly. "Captain Driscoll, have you read enough so you'll know what you're seeing?"

"Yeah. Jesus Christ. I've read enough so I don't want to see anything."

"I can't blame you. Okay, I'll start the tape." The lights went down and a meter-wide viewscreen on the side wall came on. After a warning that the contents were Top Secret, a line drawing of the *Impervious* came up on screen. "Okay, this is the way the *Imp* looked a week or so ago. Big cylinder. Here's a phantom view. Note the four hangar decks that take up the whole outer circumference amidships."

Suddenly, one of the hangar decks turned black, and a thick line of black bored straight through to the heart of the ship. "Blammo. A rock, launched from a linear accelerator that has since been captured, hits the *Imp* at extremely high velocity. A big rock, moving very fast. Hulls the hangar deck and keeps right on going, ripping deep into the ship, opens the bridge to vacuum and a lot of compartments in between. Kills people, wrecks equipment, tears up the ship's internal communication and life support. They lose more people before they can get backups going. And practically every Britannic line officer ranking captain or above was at a ball in that hangar. Plus many distinguished guests."

"Including my executive officer," Driscoll said grimly.

Pete Gesseti hung his head for a moment and sighed. So many losses. But there was no time to grieve them all. "I'm sorry. I didn't know. There were no survivors from

Hangar One. But by sheer chance, Captain Thomas and Commander Joslyn Larson, his chief fighter pilot, weren't in the hangar at that moment. Anyway." More lines of black bored into the image of the *Imp* on the screen. "More rock impacts. None of them do anywhere near the damage of the first. It seems like it was chance, not planning, that made the first strike so bad. The *Imp* wasn't even in her present orbit when the rocks were launched, weeks before. The Guards just threw a lot of rocks to soften up the Brit fleet and got lucky. Crippled the *Imp*. The damage control officer, a Commander Higgins, has been recommended for the Elizabeth Cross for his work in getting her back in shape to fight. A posthumous recommendation. With all his superiors dead, Captain Thomas, quite correctly, took command of the fleet and led a brilliant defense. The enemy ships only got in a dozen shots or so at the larger Brit ships before the Guards were destroyed or chased off. A long, complex battle. And Mac, the report makes clear that Joslyn was okay to this point. Afterwards, we just plain don't know. I'm sorry.

"As I was saying, the Guards only made a few shots at the Brits. But some of those shots impacted on target, and they carried these little wonders, or rather eggs, that hatched and grew into these bastards." The meter-wide screen was suddenly filled by the image of a foam worm. Its body was a glistening, sickly pinkish-gray, the color of meat that has begun to rot, covered with thousands of stubby hairs, cilia. It had no eyes, no apparent sense organs of any kind. "That nightmare is really only about four centimeters long. It can crawl. It has a toothless mouth that secretes God knows what, but it can dissolve practically anything. It has an anus that excretes nightmares. And it can lay eggs. God can it lay eggs. Asexual. It comes close to laying before it's finished hatching from its own egg. A generation about every two hours! No one can figure out how it can have that fast a metabolism without literally burning up. They sent a robot camera aboard the

Imp, and it radioed back these images. Before the worms ate the camera."

The scene shifted again. It was a zero-gravity charnel house, an abattoir, the signs of death all around, lit with the reddened gloom of emergency lighting. A blob of what might be machine oil, or blood, or something else, drifted into a wall and splattered there. Corpses and wreckage floated through the murky, poisoned air. The eye looked for signs of movement, life, in the bodies of the dead that drifted past the camera, and seemed to see it, strangely distorted, until suddenly it was clear *what* that movement was. Everything, everywhere, was covered with a writhing, twisting, mass of tiny gray-pink bodies that crawled and slithered and fed indiscriminately on human dead and plastic wallboard and clothing. The camera moved in on a swollen, horribly distended corpse—its skin roiling, knotting and unknotting, moving with the horrid mass of things that had eaten their way inside. The camera turned to look up at the overhead bulkhead. Blobs of the worms' foamed excrement had accumulated over and in an air vent, clogging it hopelessly. The camera found a junction box, and looked at it, its cover eaten away, the wiring inside sparking and melting, shorted out by the corpses of dozens of the worms. And live worms were feeding on the dead. One of the ghastly little destroyers lost its hold and drifted off the pile of its fellows, came floating straight at the lens, wriggling, struggling in midair to find a foothold, turning end over end, closer and closer, until it landed square on the lens, blacking out the scene—

The tape ended, the lights came up, and Pete suddenly was aware of a gagging noise coming from the office's head. George was crouched over the toilet, being hopelessly sick. Randall's skin had turned a greenish-white, and he looked close to joining George. Mac and Driscoll stared, grim-faced, at the blanked-out screen.

Pete retrieved the tape from the playback unit. "The camera lens was plastic, so the worm ate it." He shoved the tape in his pocket, turned, and faced the others. "Now imagine how happy and relaxed they are on Britannica right now. It might be an official secret, but try keeping *that* kind of disaster quiet. The Guard fleet didn't get within three quarters of a million kilometers of the planet itself, but suppose, just suppose, *one* missile with those things aboard was fired at the planet, or that *one* egg got out of the *Impervious* and re-entered somehow, or got aboard a ship that landed and came out on someone's clothing—how doesn't really matter, but suppose those nightmares got loose and started breeding on the planet. . . . Hysteria is barely the word for it. And the one piece of good news that makes that impossible is also the worst news. They've found out the things can't survive except in zero-gee. They caught some worms and put 'em in sealed glass containers to study in one of the orbital stations. As soon as they carried the worms into the spin section, they died. They've checked it other ways: The *eggs* can survive massive acceleration, but the worms die in anything but weightlessness."

"Why is that bad news?" Driscoll asked. "It means Britannica is safe."

"Because it makes it even more certain that these things are artificial."

"The Guards *bred* them?" she asked.

"Not bred," Mac said. "Manufactured. Invented. Jesus. Those aren't animals. They're *weapons*. Bioweapons? I don't know what the term would be. The old tired joke about designer genes. They decided what they wanted, drew up some blueprints, and either created a whole new creature or vastly modified an existing one. We can modify, say, a cow's genes enough so that it can digest Kennedy's indigineous plant life. That's about it. We managed to grow K-cows, but it strained our abilities to the limit—and killed a lot of cows before we got it right. Something like these worms is as far beyond what we can do as faster-than-light drive was beyond the Wright brothers. And if they can grow things that only live in zero-gee, they can grow things that endure gravity as well as we do—or breed an entirely different kind of creature that can attack us in a completely different way."

George rinsed out his mouth and staggered back from the head. "Artificial life is absolutely brand new, so far as I know," he said. "I never heard the slightest hint of any such thing. And if they had had those horror things a year or two ago, they'd have used them at New Finland."

"Pete. The genes of these things. Are they Earth-descended? DNA, RNA?" Mac asked.

"No. A completely unfamiliar genetic structure. Not Earth-based, or from any other planet we've ever got data from. Brand new. They got this far starting from scratch. Real smart guys."

"This is all obviously very important," Driscoll said. "But why the big rush to see that *I* knew about it?"

"I suspect the same reason that Commander Metcalf and Mr. Prigot are here," Pete said. "Some set of powers-that-be decided to hand the project of physically searching through Mr. Prigot's list of star systems to you. Another set is going to call you and tell you the League's combined fleet is going to be headquartered right here. Or at least, in this star system, with Base HQ right here on Columbia. They're going to pull in every ship they can. This raid scared the pants off the Brits, and they'll be able to sign up every government who gets a look at that tape. We're both here to warn you that company's coming."

Randall Metcalf stared at Pete. "You do good guessing. You must be a real smart guy yourself."

Mac grinned. "He is. Every once in a while I get the idea he's running the universe for his own personal convenience."

"Hey, somebody finally caught on," Pete said in mock surprise. "But seriously, Captain Driscoll. Columbia is a natural for an HQ. The reason for putting the search team here is obvious—you guys run the Survey Service already, and that's a lot like what the search team here will be doing. And there are good reasons to put the fleet here as well. It's near enough Kennedy so you've got an easy job supplying the place with foodstuffs and so on, there's an intact crew and base here and in orbit that knows how to handle ships—and your people are used to spacers from every planet and language wandering through—and here on the surface of Columbia is an atmosphere that's not only poisonous, it's unique. Unless the Guards breed something specifically intended for this moon's air, Columbia's own weird half-way terraformed air, the atmosphere would kill it."

"And if they breed something that *can* survive here, the air anywhere else would kill it, and the rest of the League is safe. It makes a grim kind of sense," Driscoll conceded. "Is this an official message to the effect that the combined League fleet will be here?"

"More sort of semi non-official. All the delegates back at Earth's moon will bicker and scream for a while, but the fix is in. The U.S., the Japanese, the British and the Brit Commonwealth nations are going to say *Columbia*—and Kennedy will agree, and all the other planets will be glad to stick someone else with it. Especially Earth. Who the hell would want to tempt the Guards into a raid on good old Mom Earth? You'll probably get the official orders cut for you in about two hundred hours.

"But why does Kennedy's government want the fleet right next door? The same dangers of drawing fire apply here as Earth," Randall asked.

"I think they figure we must be next on the list anyway, after Britannica," Pete said. "The Guards would probably hesitate about hitting Earth—the Yanks, the Brits, and the Japanese cut a deal with the Brazilians and the czar and linked all the space defense and detection systems—and that means coordinated listening posts on moons of all the outer planets, *and* in deep space. Their spotting is probably ten times as good as Britannica's, and you can bet there's lots of firepower to back it up. So if Earth is too scary for the Guards, Kennedy's the next juiciest military target. Couldn't hurt to have a great big combined fleet in the system."

"Uh huh. What about a commander?" Randall asked.

"You're going to love it. Politics again. The Brits insisted on naming one of their own as commander. They've been hit the hardest, except for the Finns, and the Finns don't have the pull—or the amount of hardware—the Brits do. The Brits are very concerned that the show be run the right way—their way. So they said, you want to play with our ships—and our battle data—fine, but we get to be team captain or we take our ball and go home."

"Wait a minute, Pete," Mac said, "you just got through telling us all their senior line officers were killed—"

"Except Captain, and soon to be Admiral, Sir George Wilfred Thomas. Right."

Randall's mouth fell open, he closed it, opened it, sputtered a bit and finally said, "*Thomas?* The man's a world-class drunk. You can't take a Brit into a U.S. Navy officer's club without someone telling a Thomas joke. And the man's nine thousand years old."

"He's only sixty-seven, Earthside. I'll grant you, the poop is they were going to put him out to pasture before all hell broke loose. But now he's all they got left. And he did damn well against the Guards in that raid."

"I notice he lost three major combatant ships."

Pete pulled out the tape he had shown and waved it in the air. "To the crawlies. He beat the Guard fleet. The worms took out the ships. So you tell me how he should have defended against them."

"Well, I don't have to like it," Randall said.

"No, just get used to it."

Mac glanced at his wristband. "It's so late it's about to become very early, and we've got a lot to work on. Can we keep talking in the officer's mess, and maybe throw some eggs in a pan and get some coffee? If I can't sleep, I want to eat."

Driscoll shrugged. "Why not? But if we want to talk we can't have the cooks around. We use my private galley. And Mac, since it's your idea, you do the cooking."

*   *   *

The informal rituals of morning—breakfast getting ready, coffee brewing, a brightly lit wardroom—cheered the group, relaxed and revived them, just as Mac had intended. And a change of scene from the room where they had seen the tape of the worms didn't hurt either. Everyone was surprised to find they had an appetite.

The breakfast table was more conducive to light banter and jokes than to political talk. Even Captain Driscoll relaxed a little. "You're not a captain yet," she said to Mac, "so I can still order you around. I'll take four eggs, over easy."

"Three eggs for me," Pete said. "Sunny-side up, and don't break the yokes."

"Two for me, soft-boiled," Randall put in.

"Civilians and everybody who doesn't outrank me will get scrambled eggs and like them," Mac said warningly. "The boss, I have to take care of. And you can all make your own toast." Mac enjoyed cooking, and he was good at it, or at least good at producing simple, hearty fare. His scrambled eggs turned out to be a huge omelet with half the contents of the refrigerator thrown into it, good enough to tempt Driscoll into changing her mind about taking her eggs over easy.

It was good to see old friends again, even in the midst of war and politics. No one wanted to mix business talk with the meal anyway, so Mac spent most of the meal catching up with Randall and George, hearing about Bandwidth and how they had figured out Capital's sky—and trying not to think about Joslyn. Randall wanted to hear about the court-martial, but Mac was quite firmly not interested in discussing it.

Finally the meal was over, the dishes cleared away, and the five of them sat and talked over one last cup of coffee. There was a lot of news, a lot to think on.

"Mac," Captain Driscoll said. "When your captain's bars come through, would you mind terribly hanging them up for a while? Very temporary, a brevet demotion?"

"What? *Now* what have I done?"

Driscoll smiled and shook her head. "Nothing like that. It's *my* problem. If we're going to have half the ships in space descending on us, this base has got to be run right. And Commander Ortega, my executive officer, got killed on the *Imp*. I want you in there as a brevet commander, my XO, until we can get things a bit sorted out. It's no time to bring in an officer who doesn't know the layout. You know the base, the way things run, who the right people are—and you're a name, and people will listen to you, respect you. I need you, at least until the fleet sails. Then you'll be wanted there, with the fleet. Will you do it?"

Mac sighed and stared at his coffee. He was just starting to get used to the idea of being a captain, the respect, the rank and privileges. And, though he had never been overly ambitious about rank, there wasn't a naval officer anywhere who could hear the word "captain" without thinking "admiral." It wasn't impossible. Well, yes, it nearly was, after the court-martial. Conviction overturned or no, it wasn't the sort of thing that impressed a promotion board. Still, being a captain was no bad thing in its own right. He was being paid as a lieutenant commander at the moment. A captaincy would practically double his current salary, for starters. The system owed him a little something, and the captaincy was a way to pay him back. And he was entitled, after all he had been through. Why settle for a commander's pay? No, wait, Driscoll had thought of that. She wanted him to take the permanent grade *before* the brevet move to commander—so Mac could draw pay at his new permanent rank, captain. But still, how would yet another brevet move look on his record? It seemed to Mac he never retained one rank long enough for the ink to be dry on the paperwork.

Ah, hell, his military career was a crazy hodge-podge already. One more cobbled-together assignment wasn't going to hurt. And besides, if the Navy owed him one, then he owed one to Driscoll. He knew damn well she had pulled strings to get him assigned back to the Survey base after he was convicted and demoted. Being in a place he knew, where he was a familiar face and not a face in the news—that had helped him a lot.

"Sure, Captain," he said at last, very slowly. "I'd be glad to."

"Thanks, Mac. I appreciate it."

Mac drank the last of his coffee. The dregs of the cup were bitter, and that seemed about right. Mac had never asked for reward or recognition for his part in the war. That was for others to offer, not his to demand. But he had always trusted people when they *had* offered. And somehow it was always snatched away; he was always asked to do one more thing he couldn't say no to, he was always shunted to one side for the very best of reasons. He was slowly starting to realize that the arrears would never be paid to him in full. And if the damnable war had killed Joslyn, they could never even begin to pay them.

CHAPTER SIXTEEN

Survey Service Base, Columbia

Mac might have found ways to worry himself to death over Joslyn, but there was work to do, a great deal of it. Suddenly everything had to be done at once, and there wasn't time to think of anything but work. Mac knew he wasn't the first—or last—man to hide from his fears in the exhaustion of overwork, but he was grateful for that exhaustion anyway.

There was the fleet's arrival to prepare for, the search for Capital to plan. Driscoll, concerned with the task of providing facilities for hundreds of ships, put Mac in charge of the search for Capital while she worried about everything else. There should have been a dozen officers, all kinds of specialists on call to plan the search, but there simply weren't enough warm bodies, or enough time, to allow such luxury. And Driscoll liked it that way—she was a great believer in lean, mean organizations. She wanted the search operations underway before the League brass could wander in and strangle it in months of studies on how to do it quickly.

Mac was, therefore, left with a bit of challenge.

George and Randall had arrived with a list of thirty-one star systems that were: distant binaries with rotation peri-

ods of at least seventy years; thus far unexplored; and
having at least one star of a brightness, age, and mass that
could support life. At first glance, the job was simple:
Send a ship to each system until one of them found
Capital. In practice, things were a lot trickier. Any attack
on Capital would benefit greatly from the element of
surprise, which meant the search ships could not risk
being detected themselves. If the Guards didn't know
they had been found, they might be less on the alert. It
made an optimistic sort of sense. Besides, the Guards
would be sure to go nuts trying to blow any search ship
they spotted. Of course, a ship that didn't come back
would tell the League something, but not as much as
they'd like to know. Mac wanted the ships to come back
with concrete information—and no doubt the ships' crews
would agree with that part of the plan.

But the Guards had shown just how good they were at
ship detection back at New Finland. So the search ships
had to look for signs of civilization from extreme distances
and, obviously, using only passive systems—monitoring
radio frequencies, telescopic observation, infrared checks,
neutrino detectors. No active radar. Fortunately, a world-
sized civilization was a lot easier to detect than a ship, or
even a fleet of ships. But not by so much. Oh, the planet
itself would be spotted instantly, but it could be tricky to
spot a civilization on it that wanted to hide.

It all depended on how hard the Guards worked on
camouflage. No search ship could possibly risk getting
close enough to observe a planet optically and, for example, detect the lights of cities. But there were other things
that could be spotted from fairly extreme range. Heat,
radio, neutrinos, fusion flames would all be giveaways.
The trouble was, the Guards could shield themselves pretty
effectively if they were willing to expend the effort. Power
sources could be disguised, all-but-impossible-to-detect laser communication and transmission over cable could be
substituted for radio broadcasts, neutrinos were tough to

stop but they could skip fusion power plants and use chemical rockets, as inconvenient and expensive as all those moves would be. There were lots of concealment techniques. But none of them could hide the planet itself, or long fool anyone observing with sensitive equipment, unless the Guards were willing to forego anything past 19th-century technology.

On the plus side, George was pretty definite the Guards *didn't* make extreme efforts at hiding, and trusted to isolation (and, until recently, the fact that no one knew they existed) to hide themselves. Another plus: The odds were against a given star system having a planet in its "ecosphere"—that range of distances from the star where a planet would get the right amount of light and heat from the star to support Earthlike life. On average, about one G-class star in twenty had a planet in the right place. That was the figure for single stars, and the odds were somewhat worse for binary star systems. So. If *any* of the target stars had a properly located planet, the odds were that it was *the* planet, Capital.

Mac, after considerable thought and a hard look at all the facts, concluded that the Guards would be best served if they hid themselves well enough to hide from a ship just happening by and taking a cursory look, but not well enough to hide from a ship deliberately arrived in the system and intent on a thoroughgoing search. Concealment of a whole civilization from someone who knew what they were looking for, someone who was determined to find—that would be impossible, or at least impossibly expensive. So the search was do-able, and could be done with off-the-shelf gear.

Thirty-one star systems, scattered far and wide. The closest: ninety light years out from Earth.

Driscoll had figured months ago that the Survey ships would be needed in the search for Capital, and had grounded the ships as they came in. Now she turned the Survey's small fleet over to Mac to deploy as he saw fit. It didn't leave him with much. Six of the Survey Service's ten fast frigates were in home port orbit around Columbia. The *Joslyn Marie* was still undergoing repairs in the New Finland system. She wouldn't be available for service anytime soon. *Spotter* was expected to return from a Survey mission around now—though you couldn't exactly set your watch by an exploration ship's arrival. The *Ismene Schell* had been launched just before Driscoll had shut down the Survey project for the duration, and *Vasco da Gama* was overdue and feared lost. Mac had the other six ships to count on, and possibly two more drifting in, someday. Maybe three, if *Vasco* showed up. He needed more. Unfortunately, the moment when the whole League was finally scared into mobilizing wasn't exactly the moment when there were a lot a lot of other ships available for duty.

He needed some sort of authority, some piece of paper to wave around that would convince people to loan him ships and crews. He asked Pete for help on that, and Pete said he'd see what he could do. Mac was sure that meant a fire would be lit under the right people, and fast.

In the meantime, the six ships in port needed to be cranked up for detection duty.

Spotting habitable worlds was the original prime task of the Survey, and the ships had been outfitted accordingly. Spotting an industrial civilization required somewhat different instrumentation. Optical and spectroscopic devices would still be handy, but Mac discovered his hidden skill as a scrounger, as he dug up neutrino spotters from New Harvard University, infrared sensors that could be patched into the fast frigate's telescopes from a mining company working the Kennedy's system outer planets, bits and pieces from all over.

Mac even beat Pete to the punch in scraping up more search ships. He spotted a brief article in *Aviation Week and Space Technology* that gave him ideas. The war scare had driven the Earth nations into close cooperation on intruder-detection, but the very act of merging the various systems had made some units redundant. The Brazilian stations were ideal for the Capital-search mission. They were designed to run at very low power, for long periods of time. And, since they were meant to be deployed quickly, they were fitted with C-squared generators and fusion engines. The Brazilians had an embassy on Kennedy, and Mac spent three days there, trying to wheedle five of the manned ship-detection stations out of them for the duration. The ambassador was willing to help, but it would take time to get word to his government.

In the meantime, Mac wanted to get his frigates out toward their first targets. He spent days studying the star charts, playing with a dozen variables in his head, trying to figure which were the most likely stars to harbor Capital. Distance from Earth, distance to suspected hijack points, the limits of space technology at the time the Guards had left Earth—he even dug up the specs on their colony ship, the *Oswald Mosley*.

And thinking about history brought up something he had almost dozed through in lecture, years before, a factor that hadn't been considered before: With the C-squared drive, it wasn't the distance between stars that mattered so much, but their *velocity*, relative to each other as they moved through space. A century before, with far less powerful and less efficient ship's engines, and with ships that tended to have much more mass than modern designs, that had mattered a great deal more than it did now. Crudely put, the *Mosley* couldn't go very fast, and so couldn't catch up with a star system that was moving more than about one hundred twenty kilometers a second, relative to Earth.

Mac had never actually believed that those History of Astronautics classes would have the slightest practical application, but he was beginning to appreciate the benefits of a well-rounded liberal education. He did the velocity calculations, which led him to throw out four of the target systems altogether—the *Mosley* couldn't possibly have matched velocity with them. However, it also pulled five new systems out of Randall and George's "lower probability" list and into the prime running. Now he had thirty-*two* target systems.

Finally, he had sifted the data and made as many hunches and badly-educated guesses as he could. It was time to send some ships out.

Three hundred fifty hours after Pete had brought news of the *Imp*, the first frigates headed out across the sky.

CHAPTER SEVENTEEN

Guardian Contact Base, Outpost

The forklift rolled another crate of rifles out of the cargo hold. Romero, watching from the viewport of his private office, smiled at the sight. Contact Camp was growing by leaps and bounds now. It was no longer a mere research station—it was a trading center, with warehouses and shipping clerks and inventory control. The Nihilists and the Guards were making lots of deals.

Romero had a letter in his tunic, tucked inside a pocket next to his heart, from Jules Jacquet himself, crediting Romero with the idea that had led to the destruction of three of the enemy's largest ships at Britannica. The foam worms had done their work. Romero smiled at the thought of the letter, and resisted the temptation to pull it out and read it again.

Promotion. Promotion was in the air for one Captain Lewis Romero. Things were breaking his way. That suicidal escape attempt by that half-breed Calder was the turning point. That had given Romero the excuse to yank that damned Gustav out of the Contact Camp and put *him* in charge of that dreary orbital station. Captain Lewis Romero was forced to take charge of the now all-important Contact Camp himself.

Across the camp were the labs that made it important, where the Nihilists brought their horrors to explain and demonstrate to the men of the Guardian Navy's new BioWeapons Command.

The Nihilists were smart—all of the bios they brought in were "ecologic engulfers," as the BioWeapons men called them—once the first generation hatched, that was it; the things would breed and breed and breed to the limits of the ecology's carrying capacity—and beyond, until the only things left were the bios, and the bios would starve, eat each other's dead bodies, and finally die in their own waste products. Nothing but death could halt the cycle.

The Nihilists showed the Guards how to trigger breeding, how to bring the horrors out of dormancy so they would hatch from their eggs or pods or whatever—but not how to stop it again. Once the things had started breeding, the only way the Guards could stop them was to kill them, wipe them out to the last. There was no way for the Guardians to set up controlled hatches or breeding groups independent of the Nihilists. They would always have to go back to their hosts for more.

The Guards, in their own way, played the same game. They practically gave away their rifles, their lasers, their heavy weapons—and then traded hard for ammo and power packs, once the 'Posters had seen the value of their new toys.

Romero had been worried a bit when he learned that the Nihilists already had projectile weapons—slug-throwing guns, cannon, and so on. But the native-built guns weren't as sophisticated or accurate as the Guards' stuff—and the native weapons barely had any range at all. From the largest to the smallest, they were made for stopping power, the ability to throw a round hard at short range, elephant guns in all calibres. All were intended for defense against animals, not warfare.

And it seemed the source of supply for native-built weapons was limited for a very good reason. The Outposters who made the gun would certainly stop trading with the Nihilists when the Nihilist started their attacks.

The Guards had more to sell than weapons. The 'Posters had fought among themselves in the past, but their tactics had never gotten much past the two sides slamming into each other for an all-out brawl. The Guardians taught them strategy, and military formations, and the concept of specialized troops.

Romero felt pleased with himself. Things couldn't be going any better. Except—

Except now there was a new element. Jacquet, in his letter, had instructed Romero to show the Guardians' gratitude to the Nihilists for their aid against the League. Romero was to modify the controls of a small passenger lander so Outposters could fly her. Romero was then to train a crew of 'Posters—and present the ship to the Nihilists. Jacquet made it very clear that the Outposters' ship was to be capable of no more than the roundtrip to Capital. No C^2 unit. No navigation system capable of plotting interstellar journeys. It was to be an embassy ship, a dramatic way to convey an invitation to the Outposters to visit their friends on Capital.

Romero had hesitated as long as he could before obeying the order. It worried him a bit to give the Nihilists the power of spaceflight. It might be wiser to keep them safely on Outpost without giving them ideas. Definitely it would be smarter. And safer. But Jacquet had ordered it, and Jacquet was backing Romero at the moment. It was no time to rock the boat.

He picked up his phone and asked the Camp's chief engineer to his office. He could find no good reason to delay any longer. The Nihilists would have their ship. What harm could one little inter-system lander do?

CHAPTER EIGHTEEN

Survey Service Base, Columbia

The ballistic shuttle settled down on its landing legs; the pilot throttled back thrust to zero and quickly set about securing the ship. Outside, the ground crew was already operating the remote equipment, rolling out an access tunnel, the autofueler wheeling itself into position.

Mac Larson stared out the port at the grounded ship, beside himself with excitement and anxiety. Why couldn't they hurry with that damn access tunnel? No, finally they were pressurizing it—all linked at both ends, it'd open any second.

But there was some unexplained delay, and the airlocks on the lander and the terminal building remained stubbornly shut. A small crowd shuffled around inside the terminal, held back by the rope barrier, patient for the moment but annoyed by the wait. Nothing happening. Mac rushed back to the viewport. The ship just sat there.

Was she even aboard? All the communique had said was that Admiral Thomas was arriving with staff. Mac had still gotten no certain word that she had survived the attack. Was this even Thomas's lander? This was supposed to be her, but schedules had been hashed up before. The *clunk, clunk thud* of a hatch opening came from behind him. He rushed back to the airlock, peered along the access tunnel as far as he could, until it curved away to hide the rest of its length.

There she—no, his imagination was playing tricks on his eyes. How could so many people fit on such a small lander—

And he was over the silly rope barrier and halfway down the access tunnel before his conscious mind registered that his eye had spotted her.

"Mac!" Joslyn dropped her bags and leaped up into his arms.

"Joslyn, you really are alive!"

"Mac, how did you know I was—"

"I didn't. I just hoped. Oh, thank God. Lord, you look good."

"Mac, I would have sent word, but they've gone absolutely potty with paranoia back home, not that I can blame them—" She looked up into his eyes, heedless of all the people coming past them from the lander, and the two of them were in a passionate embrace. Finally, almost reluctantly, they ended the kiss. She reached out and touched his face. "Oh, Mac. Let's get out of this tunnel and get home. With all these personnel coming in, it must be crowded here—"

"Swinging from the rafters."

"—But if we can't get nice, private married-couple quarters, I think I'll scream."

"Cancel the scream. I managed to wangle us our old stateroom and even the adjoining compartment. Just like before. Being XO has its advantages."

"You're Base XO?"

"Flying the second-biggest desk in the place. Privacy I had covered, but I wish I'd had some notice so I could have gotten some kind of meal—"

"Oh, Mac, I've got you, who needs food? But I wanted to send word. I'm sorry, I tried like mad to write and say that I was all right, that I was coming, but Uncle George ordered *everything* shut down. No mail, no nothing."

"Well, you can tell your dear old Admiral Uncle Sir George Wilfred Thomas that he's taken five years off my life worrying."

"No need," came a deep and cheery voice behind him. "He's heard already."

Mac let go of Joslyn, turned, and found the admiral grinning at him. He saluted and took the admiral's proferred hand. "I beg your pardon, sir, I—"

"Never mind. To offer a scandalous suggestion, if I was married to my great-niece here and some old duffer kept her away for this great length of time, I'd box his ears instead of saluting. Glad to meet you, Lieutenant Commander."

"Ah, actually, it's captain, sir, but currently serving as a commander. Full commander."

"Mac! Not again! You never could have just one rank!" Joslyn said happily.

"Congratulations, then. But let's get out of this mob. The regs say all these people have to salute me and this tunnel's not wide enough for all these flying elbows. Come along."

Mac was worried that his reunion with his wife would be interrupted by a nice visit with the admiral, but fortunately the admiral had his own reception committee decorously waiting at the roped barrier. Thomas's ship had arrived in orbit under tight security, not identified as his flagship, and the lander had come down with twenty minutes' notice. Captain Driscoll was tied up at the other side of base, but her aide had been able to get away and meet the admiral and see him to his quarters. Thomas was led away from the terminal and into the base proper, and Joslyn and Mac were left to their own devices for the first time in far too long.

For their sake, Thomas was glad to be steered clear of the reunited couple. If ever a pair of young people needed some private time together—and deserved it—they did. In any event, he had his own concerns. "Ensign—I think

I'd prefer to go straight to the situation room. I'd like to get right down to business."

"Certainly, sir."

The Survey Service base was a maze of corridors that looked like any base built on a tight budget. The situation room was behind an unmarked, double-locked door, guarded by a beefy marine who demanded Thomas's credentials before she let him through.

Inside, in holo tanks and displays and printouts, the story was told: The Combined League Fleet was slowly, quietly, with as much secrecy and misdirection as possible, drifting into Kennedy's star system. No large concentrations of ships this time—they were dispersed throughout the system, with small formations orbiting every planet in the system, and some ships in free orbit of Kennedy's sun. The neatly labelled spots of light moving in their displays hid no chaos, the calm of the situation room was reflected in the real world this time. No raiding fleet would be able to hit them all at once, worms or no worms.

The worms. The damned, horrible, nightmare worms. Thomas shivered, felt a twinge in the pit of his stomach. The worms would visit his dreams for the rest of his life. Even now, in the order of the situation room, the very thought of them raised his hackles. Worse than the worst delirium tremens he had ever had.

Wide disperal in space was vital in protecting against the vermin. They were not immune to vacuum and neither, as it turned out, were the eggs. The eggs could survive maybe thirty seconds in zero pressure. A raider, a saboteur, might get a few ships with the damn things, but the Combined Fleet itself would be safe. Even so simple a thing as rigging *Eagle* for flag ops had been a challenge. No one really liked the idea of using a carrier for a flag, not after Britannica, but the plain fact was that there was no other combatant ship that could carry all the specialized gear and equipment, to say nothing of billeting the specialists who would use that gear. No one really discussed the fact that the USS *Yorktown* had stayed behind in Earth orbit.

Combined League Fleet. In a more romantic age, it would have been called the Grand Fleet, perhaps—named by a sailor awestruck by its mighty size, and not by a bureaucratic technician who saw the numbers and not the ships.

Never had so many spacecraft, under so many flags, been joined together in one task. A procedure for coordinating their movements should have taken years to invent, but this was wartime, and those same soulless technicians had come up with the computer programming and the comm system in weeks. Practice at simply *talking* ship-to-ship, working through the Babylon of languages and the dozen standard radio frequencies, was the most important thing for these craft at the moment, and would be until the Search teams finally located the enemy.

You could hear the capital S in Search when people talked about it. Nothing was more important; and yet it had to be done by the tiny number of ships that could be equipped with the proper sensing devices. After over a month of round-the-clock effort by the Brazilians, their detection stations were just arriving at Columbia and would be heading out in a day or so. So far, only about fifteen target systems had been checked. Nothing so far.

Far Shore was still out there, and so were *Vasco da Gama* and *Jodrell Bank*. One of them might have succeeded. But for Sir George, it was time to do little more than wait.

Except for one project, and Sir George was following it closely. It was based on what some of the scientific johnnies had said about what was to be found at the barycenter of a binary star system.

It was a frightening idea, and a daring one. But try as he might, Admiral Thomas could think of no reason why it would not work. The research team had already come up with operational recommendations.

They gave it the code name Bannister. It seemed to

Thomas that the deadliest schemes always had innocuous code names.

Joslyn tried to let herself fall into the blissful mood of a happy, romantic reunion, and even succeeded to a certain extent. But there were too many things on her mind for her to manage it completely. Mac didn't seem to notice her worries, though, and she was very glad of that.

What about their new admiral, dear old Sir George? Their lives were in his hands now. She loved her great-uncle, but she worried. She knew him better than anyone else in the fleet, knew his strengths and weaknesses, and even *she* had no answer to the central question: *Was* he the man for such a command? If not for the foam worms, he would have had a major victory in his pocket at Britannica. Was that just luck, chance, or had old Sir George simply been given his first decent chance after a lifetime of being shunted aside?

And she worried about the drinking. She managed to keep his boozing under some control, but she couldn't be there all the time. How much worse would it make things?

But more than anything else, the death of the *Impervious* preyed on her mind. She resolved never to talk about it with her husband. Mac was already prepared to believe his words had cost them the *Imp*. It would be hard enough to convince him that wasn't so, that the Guards' plans must have been laid before he said anything. Joslyn was glad he hadn't seen that nightmare with his own eyes, glad that he couldn't know it was even worse than he imagined it being, or there would have been no convincing him.

And she herself had no desire to remember—though the disaster came into her thoughts, unbidden, time and time again. The nightmare trip from aux control to the emergency airlock, after the worms had done their worst and the *Imp* was dead, that was burned into her mind for all time. She could still hear the horrible shriek of the air roaring out the lock when they blew the outer door while the lock was full of air, because the pumps were dead. She could still see Ensign McCrae dying, strangling, screaming in silence before their eyes because the worms had eaten a hole in his suit somewhere. She could see the waiting cutter, framed by the worms that had gotten into the lock's vent system and so been sucked out with the air. The worms's ghastly, flaccid bodies bursting in the vacuum, and the cutter's lasers burning anything that even looked the size of a worm before it would allow them aboard.

And, the worst of it, somehow, the look on Sir George's face when they had half-dragged him out of the *Imp*'s lock and into the cutter. The *Imp* had been more than his ship for ten long years—she had been his life, his hope, his plan for salvaging something out of his life's work. Now she was scrap metal, the grisly grave for hundreds.

Had she, Joslyn, done the right thing then? Aboard the cutter, she had *handed* him the bottle of gin, and let him drink as much as he would. What the worms had done to Sir George's world was more than any man should be expected to face, and Joslyn could not begrudge him his means of escape. But should she have given him one more lesson in hiding from failure?

Was he the man?

If she had known about Bannister, she would have worried even more.

CHAPTER NINETEEN

Aboard *Far Shore*, En Route to Columbia

Girogi Koenig could think of nothing but a proper bath, a door thick enough to shut out noise and give some fellow some privacy, the sound of new voices, the sight of new faces. It was over, all over, and they were headed home, after hanging in space, lying doggo, careful not to betray their position, picking up every detail they could of the Guard solar system for far too long a time. And this damn crew would never be cooped up with each other again.

"C^2 drive in thirty seconds. Please stand by," Captain Toshiro announced. Even Lieutenant Pak was excited.

The *Far Shore* would be in Kennedy's star system in less than a minute. Girogi had the comm laser set for secure transmission already. It would take *Far Shore* long hours to get from her entry point to Columbia, but her news would reach there in a few minutes.

Survey Service Base Comm Center

The comm center had standing orders, but they were the sort of orders an ensign stuck with the lobster trick was hesitant to obey. But 0330 hours local or not, the admiral had said he wanted to be notified. Ensign Timility swallowed hard and picked up the phone. It rang twice, and then he heard the noise of curses as the admiral slapped at the answer button.

"What?"

"Ah, Admiral Thomas?"

"No, laddie, it's the Queen of Sheba. Who is this, and why the hell are you calling at this time of night?"

"Well, ah, sir, this is Timility in comm. We're—we're picking up something from a returning Search ship. *Far Shore.*"

"And?"

"It looks like they found it! We're getting a long text message now. I'll have a hard copy in five minutes."

"The devil you say. Jolly good! You did right to wake me, Tumulty. Let me jump into my pants and I'll be there straight away."

Sir George showed up in his pants, but not much else. He had thrown on a disreputable dressing gown, a long, threadbare thing of indeterminate color that might have looked smart twenty years ago. Sir George was bare-chested, and a sparse thatch of gray peeped through when the gown slipped a bit. Ensign Timility could smell the port on the admiral's breath, but Sir George seemed nothing if not sober and in control.

The admiral grabbed at the hard copy as it plopped out of the printer and riffled through the pages, growling to himself. "By damn, they've got it. Dimity, I want everyone in tactics and planning roused out of bed and to work on this *now*. I want enough copies of this report to paper every wall in the base. My God, they actually found it. This calls for a bit of celebrating." Sir George stuck the report under one arm, dug an enormous black cigar out of his dressing gown pocket, and bit the end off it. "I've been saving this for the right moment. Imported it straight from old Cuba." He fussed about, trying to light it for a minute before it began drawing properly, and then stood, puffing smoke like a dragon, reading the *Far Shore*'s report. He looked up and noticed that Timility hadn't moved a muscle. "Well, get on it, Dimity. Rouse 'em! We've finally got some work to do."

Timility started working the intercom system, bringing the experts in. It was going to be a long night.

Second Lieutenant George Prigot, Royal Britannic Navy (Naval Intelligence) got one of the first calls. George had never been much good after a sudden awakening, and it took him a while to get his bearings. The call, a rather peremptory call to the comm center without explanation, didn't help. For that matter, his bearing had been a little off ever since Admiral Thomas had breezed into the Survey base.

As usual, no one had figured out what to *do* with George at Survey base, and he was apologetically packed into some broom closet they called guest quarters. Then Admiral Thomas had noticed George Prigot's card going past, somehow—and that was that. The admiral didn't like anomalies, and Mr. Prigot was one. Lieutenant Prigot would not be one. The Royal Navy permitted non-British persons to enlist, and Naval Intelligence was an odd barrel of fish that wouldn't mind one more. Therefore . . . George had gone along with it. It would be nice to belong to something.

Intelligence. Why was it that every bureaucrat and brass hat in the League thought George Prigot belonged in Intelligence? He was an engineer, not a spy. Okay, so he was a native of Capital, and he knew which end of a Guardian screwdriver to hold. What good did that do them in Intelligence? George had used his brand-new clearance to peek at his own file, and the words there explained a lot about the cold shoulder he got from the rest of the Britannic Intelligence staff. All of them, right up and down, had urged that he was a bad security risk and should not be allowed to take up a commission. But Thomas had overruled them all. "There are times," the admiral's comment read, "when you have to have a little faith in people. Clearance approved."

George pulled on his brand-new uniform and staggered

his way down the corridor to the head. He automatically went through the motions of trying to make himself look presentable and made his way to the comm center. Comm was crowded and confused, and getting more so by the minute. There must have been a couple of dozen people jammed into the tiny room and more coming all the time. A harried rating handed George a copy of the printout from *Far Shore*, and he found a quiet corner to sit down and start reading it.

Before he could get a fair start, the section chief of the comm center ordered everyone to get the hell out of her radio room and move into the auditorium on the next level down. The section chief then grabbed Timility's arm and gave him a royal chewing out for taking the admiral's order too literally and mobbing her command with a lot of unauthorized personnel.

George followed the rest of the herd down to the auditorium and took a seat in the back row. There were about fifty pages to get through. Like any good engineer, he wanted to read all the specs and have all the data before he reached any conclusions.

Others around him were of a different opinion. By now, there were thirty or forty standing around in the aisle or perched in chairs, yammering on, arguing over what it all meant and what should be done about it.

Finally, Driscoll jumped up on the small stage, grabbed a mike and shouted into it. "PIPE DOWN OUT THERE."

The hubbub slowly died out.

"All right," Driscoll went on in a quieter voice. "Everyone take a seat and we'll go over this together."

The murmur of voices rose up again for a moment as people sat down. George spotted Mac and Joslyn sitting near the front of the house. He waved, and Joslyn waved back. Mac was too busy reading to notice anything else.

"TEN-SHUN!" Everybody got to their feet as Admiral Thomas came in a side door and took the three steps up to the stage. He had gone back to his quarters and taken his time to get into his uniform and shave, but he was still smoking that big Cuban cigar, and looked more cheerful and alert than anyone had a right to be at this hour.

"At ease, all of you. Take your seats and let's get on with it. As you have all seen, *Far Shore* has found the little spot our Guardian friends call home. The big surprise is that planets of *both* star systems seem to be inhabited. At least *Far Shore* picked up radio traffic from both sources. One of the two planets was definitely identified as Capital, and the other planet seemed to be called Outpost. *Far Shore* picked up numerous radio calls in clear referring to the planet names. Captain Toshiro and his crew did an excellent job—not only did they find our quarry, but they also managed to sift through the radio traffic and come up with some rough figures on numbers of ships and how and where they are based. Most of their Navy seems to be stationed in orbit about Outpost.

"Another bit of information. The anti-ship missile systems the Guards are so good at. There are no less than *three* of them in the system. One deployed around Nova Sol A, and so protecting Capital. A second deployed about Nova Sol B, shielding Outpost.

"And a third is being built around the barycenter. Toshiro's crew listened in on the chatter of the construction tugs, and Toshiro's best estimate is that the barycenter system is less than a third complete. Which sounds like an engraved invitation—though we haven't much time to exploit it.

"All this begs the question—what are we going to do? What is our plan? What are our war aims? Now we're all military here, and war aims are more properly a question for the politicians.

"So we drop the question of what to do in their laps. And when they come back with the answer we will be ready, because you lot here are going to break off into separate planning groups, each to plan for a different contingency. You will have your specific assignments within the hour, and some of you will stick with the jobs you have now and simply be expected to keep informed and assist.

"But we are going to plan for:

"A peaceful and open arrival—a show of strength that will scare the pants off the Central Guards and convince them to give up. Then I suppose we go around and hand out flowers to the people who attacked us without the barest hint of a provocation and then murdered our allies and friends using the most barbaric weapons imaginable, invaded our star systems and came bloody close to wiping out my fleet, and who have probably been kidnapping our kith and kin and enslaving them since before any of us were born. As you might have gathered, I rate the sweetness-and-light approach as not likely to work, and not bloody likely to be tried.

"Second, choosing among the various military options to find the one most likely to gain us a military victory with the greatest cost to the Guards and the least hurt to ourselves. In parallel with this, we will want to look at ways and means of rescuing any and all League-member citizens kidnapped by the Guards. I am certain that we *can* defeat the Guards, even in their home system, even against their loathsome bioweapons."

Admiral Thomas paused for a moment, and something in his ice-cold tone of voice horrified George Prigot before the new Intelligence officer understood what the admiral was saying. "The third option is simple. And since the Battle of Britannica, I must admit that it is more likely than it once was. Personally, I would oppose it strenuously. However: That third option is extermination. We wipe them out, down to the last. Bomb every city, every satellite, every ship, sterilize the planets of Nova Sol, and ensure that the damned worms are wiped out along with their masters.

"This, too, I am certain we could do."

CHAPTER TWENTY

Ariadne

Have they forgotten us?

No one asked that question anymore, at least not out loud. But all the CIs asked it of themselves, every time they saw the stars or thought of home. "Home" was gradually becoming a mythic place for each of them, an ideal that would never be seen again.

It had been a year and a half and more that they had been here, cooped up on *Ariadne*. The former members of the Survey Service's first class didn't think of themselves as being with the Survey or the League, or as citizens of their own nations anymore. It was a feat of selective memory, defense against pain. To forget what they had been helped resign them to what they were. But that made it easier for them to think of themselves as CIs—and Conscripted Immigrant was a polite term for slave. Yet that defense of forgetfulness, acceptance, surrender to the situation, was only skin deep. Every now and again, a certain look would pass across someone's face. The look of sorrow, the look of loss—the look of *being* lost. The outside universe thought they were dead, had given up on them. The CIs had lost hope.

Other things had been lost as well; the main strike fleet

had never been seen again. *Leviathan* had launched long months before. None of the ships had ever come back, and rumors swept the station that the Guards had suffered a grave defeat. That had helped morale for a while, and the CIs watched the screens and monitors, waiting for the great League fleet that would come to chase the Guards back to their home system.

But Sam Schiller, the CIs' best astronomer, had been pessimistic then, and he had been right. The League had to *find* the Guards first, and whatever else had happened with the main strike fleet, the Guardians at least had kept their home system hidden. No great League fleet ever appeared, and morale slumped lower than ever.

The CIs had no solid information about the outside world at all, beyond what they could see and hear for themselves, and what they picked up from the more talkative Guards as rumor. The CIs joked the time of day was a state secret, and Security was trying to track down who kept leaking the information.

At least there were the Outposters. Officially, they too were a secret. In reality, of course, everyone knew about them. Hiding their existence from the CIs was an obvious impossibility when it was the CIs themselves who manned the communications and traffic control consoles. Starting with Lucy's first trip to the surface, pictures and words had been bootlegged onto every screen and speaker in the station. Tremendous amounts of cargo and any number of personnel had moved through *Ariadne* en route to the Contact Camp. Everyone knew about the 'Posters, and everyone was fascinated by them.

And there was Lucy herself, and the strange truce that had developed between Gustav and the CIs. Only Cynthia Wu and Sam Schiller knew for certain that Lucy had escaped to the surface of Outpost—and even they had no idea why. Rumors swept the station, and it was hard to miss the connection between Lucy vanishing, a lander vanishing, a drugged doctor, one dead Guard and one badly wounded. But only Cynthia knew for certain that

Lucy was still alive, or at least that the beacon still moved. . . . On the time-honored principle that you can't tell what you don't know, Cynthia chose not to risk either the knowledge or her friends' safety by telling them what was going on, not even Sam. The two of them never discussed what had happened that night.

And Cynthia had yet to figure out Gustav's motives. Cynthia was ready to bet that Lucy and Gustav were up to something. What, why, and how she had no idea. Neither Gustav nor Lucy had told Cynthia anything, either. All she knew was that Lucy had to be made to disappear, and that she had a hunch that Gustav knew why. His arrival back at *Ariadne* just after her escape was too interesting a coincidence.

And so now the XO was running the show on *Ariadne*. He seemed to have his own ideas about what sort of game he wanted to play. Twenty hours after he got back aboard, Gremloid vanished from the computers without a trace. In fact, *every* supposedly covert computer operation went missing, without explanation, without reprimand or arrest. Gustav, the former Intelligence officer, must have known about the underground files long ago. For a time, it scared the CIs. They waited for the other shoe to drop. It never did. Gustav didn't touch them.

But diddling the computer was what the CIs did best, and a few of the bolder—and more bored—hackers couldn't resist the temptation. They went back to work, invading the computers again, this time hiding everything better, using more sophisticated locks and encryptions. They waited for detection, arrest, punishment—but nothing happened. As if Gustav had merely been telling them to cover their tracks better.

Disciplinary actions against the CIs all but came to a halt. Minor infractions went unpunished, and serious violations were met with proportionate responses, not Draconian punishment. Gustav stopped Romero's policy of unannounced searches and seizures, and instead posted a schedule of regular inspections of quarters and working spaces—almost as if he wanted the CIs to have time to hide what needed hiding. The inspections themselves took on an entirely new complexion. Instead of the old, crude, and rough searches for contraband goods and printouts, caches of food and information, the inspections came to resemble boot-camp checks for cleanliness and order—two things that had, Cynthia admitted to herself, come to be in short supply. The XO treated the CIs like a station crew, not a gang of imprisoned criminals.

Somehow, the CIs remembered at least a part of what they had been. After long months of using bare surnames, they came back to calling each other by their old ranks. Gradually, their captors picked up the habit. The Guardian troopers found themselves calling their prisoners "Sir," "Ma'am," "Lieutenant," and even started treating the CIs with the respect due officers.

Ensign Cynthia Wu thought she knew who to credit. By firm prodding and decent treatment, Gustav had brought the CIs back to pride and self respect in themselves, and self-respect breeds the respect of others. Slowly, grudgingly, morale, health, and efficiency all began to climb out of the murky bogs they had been in.

Gustav seemed to be working toward some purpose— and he seemed to be *waiting* for something. The mood spread to the CIs. There was only one thing worth waiting for in their minds, of course, and if Gustav was expecting it, then so would they.

And so, very slowly, the question changed. It was no longer *Have they forgotten us*, but *When will they get here?*

Sam Schiller finally knew where the Nova Sol system was—and where old Sol, the *real* Sol, Earth's sun, was. It had been a slow, maddeningly piecemeal job, but he had managed to get his bearings.

Strangely enough, it had been the Outposters that had led the way. The Guardian scientists working with the locals had wanted to find out just how much astronomy the 'Posters had, and requested several reference tapes on the subject—a trickier thing than it seemed, as all of astronomy was classified material to the Guards. The request had to go all the way up to Romero's office. Wu was working the comm board that relayed the order to Capital. She copied the message traffic and passed it to Schiller. He read it over, and found what looked like a series of library catalog numbers with no titles. He ran a search through the data files—and by God if they weren't astronomy texts that had been tucked deep inside *Ariadne*'s computer all that time. Schiller printed out copies of the textbooks, and found what he was after—precise spectra of several well known bright stars. Spectra were to stars what fingerprints or retina scans were to humans—infallible means of identification. Armed with them, he could scan the starfield, find some familiar stars, and triangulate back into Earth's position.

Even with the spectra in front of him, it took months of sneaking telescope time to find any of the stars in question—the chart hadn't given sky positions as seen from the Nova Sol system. But then he nailed Aldebaran, and that was the turning point. A week later he had Vega, and Deneb. With those three bright signposts in the sky precisely located, far more than half the battle was done. His doctorate was in astrocartography—he knew the relative positions of those three giants to Earth's sun as well as he knew the family farmyard back home. An hour or two of computer time and he had what should have been the sky position of Sol as seen from *Ariadne*.

And so, deep into a night shift, a tiny yellow dot of light, too dim to be seen by the naked eye, lay centered in the crosshairs of *Ariadne*'s largest 'scope. The sentries seemed to blunder past every ten minutes, and Schiller had to hide what he was doing, abort the job and start over a half dozen times. It took most of the shift to gather enough light to produce a spectrum.

But when the charge-coupled particle imager had finally accumulated enough photons, and a hard copy rolled out of the printer, Sam Schiller took that paper in his hands, looked over the slightly blurry pattern of dark lines, and wept. There was that dear old strong calcium line. He would know it anywhere, his professors had pointed that line out to him on the first spectrum he had ever made, a reading taken on the warm, friendly sunlight of a clear Cambridge spring day—but the light that formed *this* spectrum had left Sol decades before his professors were born. Those blurry lines were an indisputable portrait of the Sun. Home. Earth. The smell of honest dirt and the corn plants waving in the breeze and his mother sitting on the porch swing and the song of the barn swallows and the chirrup of the bats swooping through twilight, the harvest moon hanging low in the sky.

He should have burned that spectrum. It was evidence. It could get him shot. But he tucked it inside his pillow, and no one would ever know.

For what could they do? Radio for help? Even if the transmission was strong enough to be detected across the distance, Earth was one hundred fifty light years away—and none of the other populated worlds were much closer. A radio message would take a century and a half to get through. They couldn't wait on rescue that long.

There wasn't much better hope, in short term, of stealing a ship. Lucy had managed to swipe a lander, but the lander couldn't get them home. And security had been tightened up after Lucy's escapade. Even before her little adventure, nothing with a C-squared capability had been allowed to dock with the station.

Maybe, someday, at just the right moment, knowledge of where home was would do them good; but until then, what point in raising false hopes, why let frustration wreck morale, why risk endangering the knowledge itself if someone let slip the wrong chance remark? Why tempt someone besides Lucy into a fool stunt?

So Schiller slept with a portrait of Sol in his pillow, and dreamt of the cornfields.

But his search for home had been the thing that held

him together, gave some semblance of meaning to his life. With the hunt successfully concluded, both his time and his mind were far less occupied. He was left with little more to do than watch the radar screens, track the meaningless points of light on the screen—and think.

There seemed to be fewer of those points of light every day. *Ariadne*, with the job of supporting the Contact Camp, was a bustling and busy enterprise, but the other installations around Outpost were turning into ghost towns—or vanishing altogether, as the stations were towed up out of orbit to some other duty in space. Schiller watched, day by day, as the Guards pulled back from Outpost. A second attack fleet, this time made up of fifty small fast corvettes, was formed and launched. The fleet as such was never seen again. Long weeks later, fewer than ten of the corvettes straggled back into orbit of Outpost.

There were other things to be seen. The shield of anti-ship missiles around Outpost's sun had been completed, and the ships that had been involved with emplacing the missiles left. Then, there was suddenly a lot of radio traffic in the vicinity of the Nova Sol system's barycenter, encrypted in a way that seemed familiar. When Schiller trained his telescopes on the barycenter, he could detect the light of dozens of fusion engines.

So the Guards were building another anti-ship missile web around the barycenter. Not good news. It would further seal the Nova Sol system off from the outside universe, make it that much harder for the League to attack.

That was why Schiller kept his eye on the barycenter, tried to watch it through the scopes and the radio detectors.

And that was why he spotted the strange, far-off flickering lights in the center when they came.

CHAPTER TWENTY-ONE

On Outpost, Eight Hundred Kilometers North of Guardian Contact Camp

The Road had been long, and hard. Lucy's wagon rolled on, endlessly, it seemed. The Z'ensam kept to the Road, and the trade routes, forever going on. Lucy peered through the wagon's single small window and watched the landscape roll past. She estimated that the column was doing about forty kilometers an hour, a pretty good speed, all things considered. Some of the Z'ensam would get out of their carriers and gallop alongside the column for a while, easily keeping pace, just stretching their legs before climbing back aboard. Lucy knew damn well that was far beyond the abilities of a halfwalking monster from beyond the stars, such as herself.

She had to settle for being cooped up in her own specially built truck, or mobile home, or lorry, or wagon, whatever you wanted to call it. Wagon was close enough. It was airlocked and the Z'ensam had not only managed to keep the carbon dioxide down to a level she could stand, they had gotten the worst of the stench of Outpost out of the air. They provided food for her that hadn't poisoned or starved her yet, and she had a chance at a sponge bath every day or so. She was being as well cared for as she could expect to be, under the circumstances. And her wagon rolled along with the rest of them. It seemed to be running on some sort of liquid fuel that powered a smoothly purring engine beneath the floorboards. At least some sort of fluid was poured into a hole in the wagon every night. For all Lucy knew, that could be the feed for animals running on treadmills. She was never quite sure if machines were machines or some bizarre biological *thing* bred and grown for a tool. Her wagon didn't seem to have a driver. She assumed that some specially bred species of driving-beast sat in some tiny cab at the front of the thing, controlling it—but she couldn't be sure. They didn't tell her a lot. Aside from C'astille, the Z'ensam kept their distance.

Much of the transport was animal-powered, pulled by six-legged beasts, larger than elephants, that had speed and endurance far surpassing any draft horse on Earth. The Z'ensam were awesomely skilled in bio-engineering, and took their miracles for granted as easily as humans accepted light bulbs, or refrigeration, or star travel. The Road itself was a living thing, or at least the product of a living thing. C'astille had tried to explain, and had quickly run into language trouble. The best analogue Lucy had come up with was to think of the Road as a variety of dry-land coral plant (though if she remembered properly, coral was actually an animal), trained or bred or forced to grow in long, precise strips a half dozen meters wide and hundreds of kilometers long. Apparently, the Z'ensam road engineers did little more than sow road seed like a farmer planting a crop. The roadplant would grow, take root, dig down into the soil to form its own roadbed, and then produce a hard, porous carapace that formed the surface of the Road and provided excellent traction. The Z'ensam were able to control the roadplant's growth exactly; Lucy paced out the width of the Road again and again as it crossed forests and fields, mountains and plains, and never did its measure vary by more than half the length of her foot.

The column seemed to be stopping again. There came booming and thumping and roars. Lucy sighed and slumped back against the wall of the wagon. The Hungry Ones were at it again. Sometimes Lucy had thought the Outposters, the Z'ensam as they called themselves, *couldn't* wipe them out, other times she thought they simply chose not to.

The hungries had certainly lived up to their name in the long days before C'astille had found her lander and taken her to safety with her Group, which C'astille called the Refiners. (What they refined—sugar, ideas, oil, behavior in polite society, Lucy wasn't quite clear, though most of the Groups did tend to be bound by philosophical ideas.) In any event, several huge beasts had tried to *eat* the lander—and one had nearly succeeded. The Hungry Ones weren't any one species—any wild animal qualified as hungry—very, very hungry, and without the qualms of the Hungry Tiger in Oz. As far as Lucy could see, nature apparently didn't make much of a distinction between carnivore and herbivore on Outpost—anything would pretty much try to eat anything else. It was, however, the bigger species that gave the Z'ensam the worst time of it. On the other hand, Lucy had seen one species of pack-hunting animals, no bigger than mice, that didn't hesitate to attack the Z'ensam.

The sound of her landing must have scared off the animal life for a day or two, but when the great beasts returned, they were terrifying. Lucy had at first thought that she had chanced into an area full of particularly voracious carnivores for some reason, but when the Z'ensam came to rescue her, C'astille assured her that, if anything, things were a bit on the quiet side around her lander.

Riding in her specially built wagon, travelling with the Z'ensam, she had seen enough to convince her that was true. Compared to the violence, the liveliness, the voraciousness of life in the temperate-zones of Outpost, the lushest tropics of Earth were barren deserts. This world was far fuller of life. And, therefore, far fuller of death.

Now, as best Lucy could see through her window, the caravan was stopped by some pack of three-meter high, six-legged, befanged, warty, moss-colored, slavering horrors. The Z'ensam brought up their guns and weapons and calmly wiped the monsters out. There was a further delay while the massive corpses were shoved off the roadway, and then the caravan moved on.

Lucy had come to realize that the Nihilists must have been constantly patrolling the perimeter of the Guardian Contact Camp, killing or shooing away any and all animal life. Otherwise, the hungries would have wiped out the humans long ago. No doubt the need to cordon off the area around the landing zone had caused the delay between landing and First Contact. One little mystery cleared up.

There were certainly enough others to take its place. What drove the Z'ensam to venture out on the Road, to move from where they were to a town that might have been abandoned a week ago or a hundred years ago, to live there for a time, and then move on? They certainly had a high enough technology to settle down and build real cities and stay in one place. They didn't *have* to be no-mads. But when Lucy asked why they didn't settle down, C'astille couldn't understand why anyone would want to do that in the first place. Trade had something to do with the constant travel, but that seemed more a holdover from pre-technical times than out of any real need. The towns had started as trading posts, but the Z'ensam didn't need trading bazaars anymore. Their machine-powered and animal-powered transports could carry as much and as fast as modern rail or road-cargo handlers on Earth. Why move the entire population to the goods when it should have been easier to move the goods to the population?

Lucy gradually discovered that there *was* a small num-ber of settled folk, who lived pretty much permanently in a few larger cities. They seemed to be there to operate the manufacturing concerns too large to be made portable, to serve as brokers and to operate the communications centers, to use and operate the research libraries. All the permanently populated towns were such "company" towns or "college" towns. What slight central government there was emanated, more or less by default, from the cities, though no one much bothered with claiming territory or jurisdiction.

The settled Z'ensam had stepped off the Road and stayed in one place for much the same incentives that would tempt humans to accept hardship posts—wealth, power, the desire to escape from old ways, perhaps research into some subject. Some actually grew to like the settled life, but that was rare. Few accepted it for a lifetime. It would have been easy to form a comforting parallel with the settlement of Sumer, the birth of cities, primitive nomads inventing agriculture and settling down. Such had been the human dawn of civilization, but the simple nomads with which Lucy lived on the Road had radio, electricity and explosives far more powerful than gunpowder. They were skilled in chemistry, knowledgeable of astronomy and masters of bio-engineering. Lucy had learned nothing of their cultural lives, but there had to be such. Theirs was a mature, sophisticated civilization.

Lucy's wagon started up again with a slight jerk. She glared at its interior, tired of trading one prison for another. The Guards might have locked her up on the *Venera*, on *Ariadne*, kept her confined to base on Outpost, but at least they had never locked her in an small, utterly blank room on wheels with nothing to read, nothing to do, no one to talk to. After some wheedling, and a lot of drawing and explaining, she had managed to get a table and chair built. Neither quite fit her proportions, but it was a big improvement over squatting in a corner to eat, and made keeping her journal easier, too.

If only something worth reporting would happen. C'astille came sometimes, but not often enough to ease her boredom. The rest of the Z'ensam kept their distance. The higher-ups, the Guidance and the First Advice of this crowd didn't entirely trust her, didn't quite believe she had told C'astille the truth. Why believe there was to be a terrible war among humans, and the Nihilists were in an unholy alliance with M'Calder's enemies? There was no proof of that, yet. Until there was, the Refiners would harbor her, but they would keep their distance, and keep her existence a secret from outsiders. Potentially, she was of great value to the Refiners. But that potential had yet to be proved, and no one really liked looking at the weird little two-legged monster.

It seemed strange to be bored to tears while in the midst of a wholly alien culture travelling in an alien land— but Lucy was a prisoner again, able to do little more than stare out the window, and that got old mighty fast. There was nothing to do.

Her few possessions—a rather worn and dirty looking pressure suit, a sleeping bag, a toilet kit, a few pair of work overalls that served as changes of clothes, her laser pistols, some emergency rations, a first-aid kit—were neatly stacked up by the rear wall. There hadn't been much else in the lander worth the carrying—and lugging even that lot around while wearing a pressure suit hadn't been a picnic.

She worried about keeping sane. That was what the journal was about. Every day she carefully noted down everything that had happened, forcing her mind to focus on present reality, to keep track of the passage of time. She knew she'd be in real trouble if she ever lost track of how many days and hours it had been. So far it had been just over 3000 hours. About four months, Earthside.

It seemed like a lot longer than that. And she was just about out of pages in her journal.

Worst of all was the open-endedness of the situation. She had to wait it out here until the League arrived. The League would need her, because she could speak to the Z'ensam and supposedly knew their ways. But what she came to realize was that *she* needed the League. There was no return to the relative comfort of *Ariadne* for her, not if she wanted to live. There were less elaborate ways to suicide than flying back to the executioners. The League *ought* to come, logically. But Lucy could dream up a half dozen reasons why they never would. In which case she would live here, among the Z'ensam, and die among them. Perhaps she could survive a week longer, or a year, or a decade, or fifty years. She didn't know.

There was one bright spot—the Refiners were planning to move into a small crossroads village tonight. They expected to arrive at it toward evening, and settle in to live there for perhaps ten or twenty days while they repaired the wagons and waited for another Group that was headed toward the town from the opposite direction. The two Groups had struck a trade deal over the radio, and planned to carry out its provisions in the village.

For Lucy, it meant she would get a break from the endless days cooped up in her rolling cage. And perhaps these new Z'ensam would take more of an interest in her.

The kilometers rolled past, and Lucy returned to her window to watch the scenery. A huge bird zipped across her field of view. At least Lucy called them birds, because they flew. She had noted dozens of flying species. Like most of the life on this world, they were six-limbed, but with the middle pair of legs modified into wings. The flyers of Outpost didn't look quite as graceful as Earth's birds, but they were strong and agile on the wing. Air pressure here was about twenty percent higher than Earth sea level, which must have been a help.

There was one particular breed of flyer that Lucy especially liked. Things about the size of a big house cat, with gaudy, brightly colored wings that reminded her of giant butterflies. They were not the most graceful of flyers, and Lucy named them stumblebugs.

The Z'ensam seemed to keep them as pets, or at least the Z'ensam tolerated the stumblebugs and let them follow the Group from camp to camp.

The stumblebugs' front paws could serve for hands about as well as a squirrel's could, and Lucy enjoyed feeding them bits of food, getting them to swoop down and grab a morsel from her hand, or even land and waddle up to get a treat. They seemed to have the vocal skills of the comical parrots Lucy had kept when she was a kid, and she even managed to teach one or two of them to say a few words in English in exchange for a bite of food.

She named them and played with them, and, like many other lonely people, found pleasure and solace in the company of her pets. None of the Z'ensam seemed to approve of her spending time with the stumblebugs, but Lucy didn't let that bother her; she needed some pleasure to keep from going mad.

The line of wagons and lorries turned off the road into a small village. Good. They had arrived on schedule. Lucy was eager to get out and stretch her legs.

Suddenly, she heard a triple thump three times on the outer wall of the wagon. That was C'astille's signal that the hungries had been shooed off and it was safe to come out. Eagerly, Lucy climbed into her pressure suit and cycled through the lock. It was good to be out of that rolling prison, if only for a few hours, and if only in a shabby pressure suit.

It was a lovely evening, clear and still. As she hopped down from the airlock, Lucy was almost glad to be behind the glass of her suit's helmet—it kept out the overwhelming smell of mold and rotting plant life. Shielded from the stench, she could almost imagine it as a perfect night for a stroll back in Sydney—the air cool and clean, the stars shining brightly down, God up in heaven and everything in its place. A huge shape, hard to see in the twilight, shifted its stance and turned toward her.

"Hello, Lucy."

"Hello, C'astille. English tonight?"

"It is that you need less of the practice than I have need of."

"I don't know about that—but I certainly have more need of your language than you have of mine."

C'astille paused for a moment before answering, trying to sort out the difficult statements about knowledge and relative needs that Lucy had crammed into one sentence. C'astille could make herself understood in Human—no she must remember it was *English*, one of many Human tongues—but she could not yet manage the compression, the conciseness, with which Lucy spoke.

"I have less need now. There will be a time when my skills in Human talk will be of great value. So let me practice it tonight."

"Of course, my friend. I was only teasing you."

C'astille only grunted at that. Teasing wasn't a part of Z'ensam humor, or even a Z'ensam concept. What worried C'astille was that she had come to *understand* teasing. Was she beginning to think like a Human? How could she do that, when she couldn't even make *sense* of Humans?

Lucile Calder stepped away from her wagon and walked toward the center of the clearing. Around her, the bustle of unpacking and setting the village to rights went on. Light began to glow in the low one-story structures, and there were snatches of conversation—and of song.

A pack of Z'ensam children rushed past, chasing each other around the clearing in a game of tag that any human child would have recognized at once. The kids here had long ago gotten used to the halfwalker monster in the Group, and some would even gather round once in a while to hear stories about Earth and space. For the most part, though, they paid her as much mind as the adults did. Lucy barely realized how little she knew about Z'ensam family life.

All she really knew was that a child's name began with the prefix "O." C'astille was very proud of the fact that she had stopped being O'astille at a very early age.

Lucy looked through the scuffed plastic of her bubble helmet at the sky, the stars—Nova Sol A outshining all the rest, beaming down far more brightly than a full moon, casting crisp shadows. The night sky was lovely and clean, dark, studded with the glory of the stars.

She knew she belonged up there, and was but gradually coming to accept that she might be trapped where she was for all time. Strange to think that all humans, less than two centuries ago, were so trapped, and never realized that there were any other worlds, that they were in any sort of trap at all.

And strange to think that this was the first generation of Z'ensam which knew for certain that there was more than one world. But the Z'ensam didn't seem to have invented flying machines. Perhaps they weren't interested in getting off the ground.

"Would you travel there, C'astille? Would you be willing to go through the sky?"

Her friend moved closer to her, bumped her long, rough flank against the pressure suit, and placed a long, four-fingered arm on Lucy's shoulder. C'astille looked up at the darkness. "Willing? That is a weak word. The mightiest traveller of the Z'ensam, the heroes who have crossed every overland route, the seafarers who have spanned the globe—none of them has ever found a Road, a way, as long as your shortest journeys. I *yearn* to go that way, and see everything, everywhere, all the worlds the Humans have found and all the ones they have not."

"You'll get there."

"Yes. As passengers on your ships. But one day we will have our own ships, and grow our own star roads. But come. I must eat, and see to it that our chemists have grown enough of that dull stuff we force you to live on."

The two of them headed toward the mess wagons, the stars in their hearts.

Of all the Refiners, only L'awdasi, the lifemaker, was a stargazer. L'awdasi was in charge of caring for all the workbeasts of the Group, and she had campaigned hard before the Guidance allowed her to care for M'Calder as well. It gave her access to the halfwalker, and gave her the chance to talk with Lucy for hours about the sky. L'awdasi had a fine telescope, a rugged reflector of about thirty centimeters apeture, built by the craftworkers of a distant city. It had been well worth the journey there, and even worth enduring the company of the eccentric city-

dwellers, to obtain such a fine instrument. Recently, L'awdasi had a new goal to seek for among the stars. This halfwalker had spoken of a "barycenter," a place between the twin suns where matter would accrete. It was even possible that there was a small planet at the barycenter. The idea fired her imagination. A new world! L'awdasi searched each night, joyously engaged in the hopeless task of detecting a hypothetical dim and tiny dot of light, as distant from her as Neptune is from Earth.

And so only L'awdasi saw the faint, flickering lights, all but lost in the glare from Nova Sol A, that sparked and shone for a time about the barycenter. A strange phenomena. Tomorrow she would ask the halfwalker about it. After all, the halfwalker knew about barycenters.

CHAPTER TWENTY-TWO

Nova Sol System Barycenter

The skies flamed and flickered in the viewscreen, and the Republic of Kennedy Starship *Eagle*'s external radiation meters quivered, crawled a bit closer to the high end of the scale. All hell was breaking loose out there, exactly on schedule.

The *Eagle* and the rest of the League fleet stood well off from the barycenter of the Guardian/Outpost star system, and let the Snipe do their work.

All that wooing of the Bandwidthers had paid off. Admiral Thomas had sent them little more than a sketch on the back of a envelope, and they had responded a month later with five thousand custom-designed decoy drones. No other planet could have responded that quickly or effectively. Sir George was just glad the Bandwidthers were on the same side he was on.

The drones had gotten christened Snipe somewhere along the line (someone claimed the name stood for Special Nonexplosive Intrusive Probe Experiment, but obviously they had backed that acronym into the name). By any name, they were out there doing their job right now.

A Snipe was the size and shape of a standard torpedo, the smallest thing ever to get a C^2 generator crammed inside—and the Bandwidthers managed that mainly because the generators didn't have to be very precise, and because there was very little *else* that needed to go inside a Snipe. The big advantage to torpedo-size was that Snipe could be fired by practically any ship in the League fleet. At the moment, practically every ship in the fleet *was* firing them.

The League fleet stood off from the barycenter by about a twentieth of a light year, surrounding it in a vast ring, facing the 'center from every point of the compass. The ships themselves stayed well out of range of the defensive missiles, and the Snipe went in. Once fired from a torpedo tube, a Snipe would burst in and out of C^2 space in a millisecond or so, jumping from the fleet's encircling position to the vicinity of the barycenter, making as much radio noise and calling as much attention to itself as possible.

The Guards' automatic anti-ship missiles, designed to sense and home in on ships arriving from C^2, were drawn to the Snipe like lambs to the slaughter. A Guard missile would home on a Snipe and blow itself up—taking out the cheap, mass-produced drone instead of a warship, and there was suddenly one less Guard anti-ship missile to worry about. The real warships, the fleet, would wait until the anti-ship missiles stopped coming, until the skies about the barycenter were no longer lit by the fire of nuclear explosions.

Salvo after salvo of Snipe blipped into the barycenter and died, saturating the Guardian defenses before the main attack ever began. The Snipe were a rich man's weapon, a brute force solution to the problem of getting through the Guards' missiles.

But Admiral Sir George Thomas, watching from the battle information center of his flagship, the *Eagle*, had never much cared about subtlety for subtlety's sake. He would settle for the irony of bombing the hell out of the enemy's defenses with their own bombs.

Computer-controlled sensors, quite unconcerned by such things, counted and mapped the explosions, and monitored the "I'm-still-here" telemetry from the thousands of Snipe.

After long hours, the number of flashes in the darkness began to decline, and more and more Snipe survived longer and longer. Admiral Thomas, a guest on *Eagle*'s bridge, turned to *Eagle*'s master, Captain Josiah Robinson. "Well, Captain, either our friends have run out of missiles or they're shutting down the missile system until we run out of drones."

"Either way, Sir George, that leaves a nice hole in their defenses."

"My thoughts, exactly. What's say we keep sending in the Snipe and start slipping in some fighters among them? It's time that trigger-happy younger generation of ours had a chance."

Captain Robinson nodded to the comm officer, and the order was relayed to the appropriate units. This moment was planned for. Robinson, a short, middle-aged, dark-skinned black man with a peppery temper, rubbed his bald spot with the palm of his hand, noticed what he was doing, and stopped. Occasionally he wondered what he had done for a nervous gesture when he still had a full head of hair.

And there was plenty to be nervous about. *Eagle* was half the size of the *Imp*, but she still made a nice juicy target, not just for the worms and/or whatever other horrors the Guards had cooked up, but for a plain old-fashioned nuke. One of those pretty flashes of light would be enough to knock *Eagle* out of the game for good.

But that didn't happen. The fighters went in, and some of them died. The Guardian ships that deployed the anti-ship missiles were blown. Sir George sent in frigates and corvettes and resupply ships, gradually establishing coherent force around the tiny worldlet that sat right where the astrophysicists said it would, exactly at the barycenter. A few minor Guard warships fought hard, killed and were killed. Slowly, methodically, Sir George peeled back the barycenter's defenses. Finally the League fleet moved in, and found itself astride the centerpoint of the whole star system. No Guard ship could move between Outpost and Capital in normal space without battling its way through the League fleet. The League forces could also intercept and/or jam most radio and laser communications between the two worlds. Most important, they were in under the range of the anti-ship missile systems around Capital and Outpost. The missiles spotted ships coming out of C^2. As long as the League ships stayed in normal space, they could move against the two worlds without fear of the robot missiles. Of course, the Guards would see them coming, and the anti-ship missiles could probably be fired by remote control to go for ships in normal space. The fight wasn't over.

The planning for this attack had been hideously complex—the timing and communications problems mind-boggling. But it all paid off, with a clean, careful, methodical, smoothly run—and almost dull—operation. Captain Robinson liked it that way. So far, *Eagle* hadn't even had her paint job scratched.

Sir George was equally pleased, at the end of it. He had been in the task force control center seemingly every minute, always fresh and calm looking. It was time to put Bannister into operation. The specialists went down to the baryworld, and Thomas kept himself carefully appraised of their progress. Now it was time for him to wait again. Thomas didn't want to hack through the defenses of the two worlds. He wanted the Guards to come to him, force them to fight on his turf.

He intended to keep building up his power at the barycenter, bringing in an endless stream of supplies and ships. Sooner or later, the Guards would have to try and put a stop to it, or face the prospect of a huge and impregnable enemy fleet in their own back yard. He had to wait. But waiting was slow torture to Sir George—and he had spent a lifetime in that torture already.

One evening, Sir George invited Robinson to dinner in

the admiral's cabin. It wasn't until the mess steward had cleared the last of the dishes and left them to their port and cigars that Thomas really spoke. "We've managed to outflank ourselves, Captain Robinson," he said cheerfully. "We've hopped smack into the middle of it, and now the enemy has us surrounded without moving at all." He paused for a moment. "Things look good. We outgun them, we have more ships, we have the resources of every world in space to draw on. There are only two things to be afraid of. The unknown is the first. *Something* could happen; God knows what. And the second is the more dangerous, the more likely. If they have a genuis for a commander. A genius, a truly great admiral and not a tired-out old man like me, he could wipe us out more certainly than a planetload of worms and ten thousand nuclear weapons." He was silent for a long moment, and then slapped his hands together and spoke again, in a louder, more cheerful voice. "So—we prepare to defend ourselves once the Guards arrive, plan our next attack, and give praise for the rarity of genius."

Sir George reached for the port decanter again, a bit too eagerly, and filled his glass to the brim for the third time, while Robinson stared hard past him at nothing at all. How the hell do you keep an admiral dried out?

Aboard G.O.S. *Ariadne*

Schiller had waited twelve long hours before he had a chance to talk with Wu in private. Work schedules and sleep shifts had conspired to slow him down. Finally, he caught her as she was heading back on shift. He cornered her in a bend of the corridor and set her heart racing with two words.

"They're here."

Wu looked up at him sharply, her eyes opened wide. There was no point in asking who "they" were. That was in his tone of voice, the gleam in his eye. "Oh, Sam! Thank God." She grabbed his arm and looked up at him.

"When? How long ago? What are they doing? How do you know?"

"Quiet, calm. Take it easy. We're talking about how bad the coffee is here. Okay? Good. Now, I've been tracking the construction of the anti-ship missile system at the barycenter—and all of a sudden the center is full of flashes of light, fusion engine lights, the x-ray and gamma detectors start doing a dance—don't ask me who's winning, but there's a pitched battle going on out there. No other possible explanation."

"Who else knows?"

"I haven't told anyone, and I haven't made any records. We've got to let this out slowly, carefully, or else this crowd is going to mutiny and get itself killed to no purpose. You and I need to talk, figure out a plan of action. Once we decide what to do, then, when we spread the word, we're doing more than starting a riot."

"So why pick me to tell?"

"I need help with this from somebody. You've kept your lip zipped over that Lucy-and-the-lander bit, never mentioned it again. And besides this dull-witted Iowa farmboy, the lady from the inscrutable East seemed the most level-headed type left in the crowd."

Wu gave him the ghost of a smile, started to speak, but then he shushed her. "Meet me for a nice cup of bad coffee at your lunch break. Think on it all between now and then. So will I. Then we make a plan."

Cynthia Wu wasn't capable of much thought for a while. After so long, the League—their rescuers! She could dare to think of home again—family, friends. . . .

She went through the motions of powering up her console on automatic, not really thinking about the dull housekeeping chores that went with running the system. Check the power source, check the comm links, test antennae control, test beacon—

Beacon! It had almost ceased to have meaning for her,

the hidden beacon she bade the computer check every morning. At first, the signal had sat tight in one spot for a long time, and Cynthia had assumed that Lucy was in the lander, staying safe. At least Cynthia had been able to mark the lander's location. But then the beacon had started moving, and Cynthia couldn't make sense of what the beacon signal told her. Lucy was supposed to be on the other end of that link, and if she was, she was moving endlessly about the surface of Outpost, why and toward what Cynthia didn't know. It was perfectly possible that Lucy was dead, and the beacon was transmitting its signal from inside the belly of the beast that had eaten her. There was no way to know.

But if the League was here—then Lucy would be damned important. She knew more about the 'Posters than anyone. Cynthia would have to get a message to her somehow.

Cynthia called up the computer's tracking report of the beacon's movements, and got the second biggest shock of the day.

Lucy, or at least whoever had the beacon, had been moving at high speed straight for the lander for the last twelve hours.

Outpost, North of Contact Camp

A thing like a six-legged elephant with saber-toothed fangs blew up in a bloody pink fog, and the three wagons kept rolling down the Road at top speed, not even slowing as they ran over pulped carcass. The gunner on the lead wagon reloaded his cannon and got ready for the next one.

"Your lander is close now, Lucille M'Calder," C'astille said in her own tongue. "We will be with her in a few more hours." C'astille had grown more formal in her speech with Lucy, more careful to say the right thing. They were too close to what might be a last goodbye to risk hurting her friend with the wrong words. The two friends rode atop the second wagon, Lucy in her pressure suit, both of them too keyed up and excited to sit inside the wagon. The lead and rearward wagons were the Refiner versions of battle tanks, capable of killing anything that moved.

They might actually be used as battle tanks, soon. There were frightening reports that the Nihilists had begun their attack on other Groups.

C'astille hesitated for a moment, then spoke. "Still it is possible for me to be with you on this skyroad."

Lucy sighed deeply. "C'astille, it would make my job easier if you could come—they'd be forced to believe me. But you *can't* come along. There's no crash couch to fit you, and when I take off I'll be doing six-gees. You'd be crushed. And no offense, but you're just too damn big and heavy! I must travel as fast, as hard, as I can. I will throw everything I can off the lander, make her as light as possible, to let me go fast and save on fuel. I may not have the fuel for such a trip as it is—and with two along— besides, I have no food for you, no device to make our air breathable to you."

"All this can be solved—"

"*No!* Much as I want you to come, I can't risk failure, or everything has been for nothing. I'm sorry." She patted C'astille's muscular shoulder and stared down the road, straining for a view of the lander she knew perfectly well was out of sight. What sort of shape would it be in. Had some local hungry managed to take a bite out of it? Had some bug-eyed monster torn the hatch off and turned it into a nest?

If she managed a launch, would her luck go the wrong way? Would the Guards nail her, return her to Outpost very soon—as part of a cloud of radioactive isotopes? She prayed for Gustav. If *he* had survived, she might.

Lieutenant Johnson Gustav was alive, and he knew things. He was ex-Intelligence. It was his job, his profession skill, to know things. Wu was unaware of it, but Gustav also watched Lucy's beacon. Schiller didn't know it, but Gustav watched Schiller and monitored his use of the astronomical instruments. He knew when Schiller found Earth, and now, when Schiller found the League battle fleet as they cut the Guards' barycenter into pieces, Gustav knew that too.

And he knew that this was the day he had dreaded all along. It was time to pay the piper. It would be so easy to turn back. Push a few buttons, call in a few of the troopers, have Schiller and Wu and the rest of the schemers arrested. Call *Nike* Station and Lucy's lander would be dust settling into a crater an hour later. A soldier's job. None who lived would reproach him for fighting on his own side.

Easier still to do nothing, to let Lucy take her chances when she boosted and ran through the Guard ships around Outpost, heading for the barycenter and the League, to let the CIs on *Ariadne* stage some hopeless and bloody revolt to liberate the station once they knew their friends were here.

But then how many would die? How long could Jacquet and his thugs bleed the people of Capital white before they inevitably lost? How many dead? How many ships, factories, families smashed? What nightmare bioweapons were the Nihilists cooking up, and what horrible vengeance would the League exact for their use? The Guardians could not win. And the longer the Guardians fought, the more likely Capital was to be but a smoking ruin.

He had to act. But he had to act carefully. And privately.

It was toward the end of the morning. Cynthia hadn't had a chance to talk with Schiller yet, when she felt a tap on her shoulder.

She had almost gotten used to the sudden, bottomless fear at the pit of her stomach that came with any sudden, unwanted attention from the Guards. It had happened so many times before. When it did, you acted calmly, didn't turn around immediately, and innocently hit a few keys, so that whatever the hell you had been working on vanished off the screen. Then you turned around calmly and asked the sentry what was up. Usually it was nothing at all; the sentry wanted to borrow a book or a cigarette or wanted you to cover for him while he ducked down to the head. So this time, she casually cleared her screen, turned around—

—And there was Gustav himself. "Ensign Wu. Good day. I was just passing, and it occurred to me there were one or two questions about the comm schedule I wanted to talk with you about. Why don't you step down to my office with me?"

"Yes, of course, sir." Already her coverall was damp with sweat. She followed him through the corridors and into his office. He was very casual, calm; all was routine. It scared the hell out of Wu.

He went behind his desk and took his chair. "Sit down, Ensign. I need to tell you a few things. First, in case he hasn't told you, Schiller found Earth some time ago. *Did* he tell you? Or anyone, to your knowledge?"

Wu was too shocked to think up a lie. "No . . . he—he didn't."

"Good. I suspected he had good sense. That confirms it. Let me tell you some other things. I know you assisted in Lucille Calder's escape some time ago. But you should know that *I* helped too—in fact she and I plotted that escape together. At a guess, Schiller has told you that the League has taken the barycenter. Don't bother to answer, your face just did. Luc—Lieutenant Calder seems to have already discovered that fact for herself. She would have no other reason for heading for the lander. This saves us the trouble of trying to contact her. She too has a good deal of sense, so she won't try to make a run for it until both *Ariadne* and *Nike* are below her local horizon. The two stations are in fixed orbits; her lander's computers will know where they are. It's Guardian ships that are the danger. But you know how to check the orbits and figure out which will be where, when. Can you hit the lander with a tight radio beam on a frequency she'd be likely to listen on?"

Cynthia caught her breath and said, "Yes."

"Good. Note that I have given you no instructions as to what to do. You should know that you must assume normal surveillance of your activities, whatever they should be. If you are caught, you might be able to avoid implicating me under mild interrogation. If you are caught, I cannot try to defend you, or else I will be caught and shot as well. And if you fail, I can still try to help. But you are in a better position for covert acts. So be careful. I will say one more thing. *Ariadne* will be of much greater value in saving lives if it holds together. A revolt here, and more people—League and Guardian—die. You must try and keep the lid on things here. Now take a moment to calm yourself, then go."

Cynthia wasn't much use until the lunch break. When she carried her tray over and sat by Schiller in the mess hall, he immediately noticed something was wrong.

"Cynthia, have you got some kind of flu? This is one hell of a bad moment to get sick."

"No, no. Sam. Is there a word for—I don't quite know how to put it—for when the officers or the *captain* mutinies?"

"Yeah, it's called barratry. Any court of inquiry treats it as about twice as slimy and rotten as mutiny or treason. You won't even find it listed in the *Bluejacket's Manual*. The Navy leaves it out of the glossary with the other dirty words. Why?"

"It came up in a crossword puzzle."

"Oh. But let's get to the serious stuff then. What do we do about welcoming the new neighbors?"

"I think it would be wisest if we didn't do anything at all."

CHAPTER TWENTY-THREE

Outpost

The dear old lander was still there, God bless her, squatting in the middle of the field she had come down in. Tarnished and entangled in undergrowth, half hidden by vines and her once-gleaming hull begrimed and dull, but there—and whole. The Z'ensam from the lead and follower wagons started firing blank rounds to scare any squatters away from the lander. There was a brief stampede out from under the belly of the small ship, and the Z'ensam from the lead wagon got down and cautiously poked around the strange machine from the skies. Finally, they signalled all clear and Lucy climbed down from her own wagon.

"We'll need long knives or something to hack all this plant life back," Lucy said.

"That job is ours," C'astille replied. "You must be in that thing and see if it is ready to go."

Lucy walked up to the side of the stubby little ship and patted its hull affectionately. A ship, a ticket out, a way back to the clean skies and her proper life. "Aboard," she said to C'astille in English. "You don't say 'in,' you say 'aboard.' And never 'it'—this is a 'she.' "

"Someday I'll actually understand your pronouns," C'astille said. "That will be a great day."

Lucy grinned at her. "*This* is a great day. I'm getting back into space." The ladder to the personnel hatch was still extruded from the hull, and Lucy scrambled up it. *There* was a reason right there that C'astille couldn't come along. Maybe the descendants of apes and monkeys could climb that ladder, but the descendants of what must have been like six-legged horses certainly couldn't.

Even ten meters off the ground, thick creepers had grown up to ensnare the little ship, and one of them had grown straight over the personnel hatch. Lucy wrapped her arm around the top rung of the ladder and pulled her knife out of its belt sheath. It was a copy of the classic Bowie knife, forged of a steel that would never lose its edge, but Lucy didn't know that. She was just careful with its sharp point around her nearly decrepit pressure suit. She wouldn't need that suit much longer, but that would be no comfort if she ripped it and died of carbon dioxide poisoning three meters from breathable air.

The upper rung of the ladder was just to the left of the hatch itself, and the manual controls for the airlock were placed so they were right in front of Lucy's face as she stood at the top of the ladder. But vines blocked the hatch itself. Leaving her left foot on the ladder and hanging on to the top rung with her left hand, Lucy calmly swung over and hooked her right foot through a loop of vine that hung free of the ship, unaware of the fact that she was scaring the hell out of the distinctly non-arboreal Z'ensam below. Lucy got her leg around the vine and gave it a good yank. Enough of it came free so that she could get her knife underneath and saw through it. She resheathed the knife and peeled back the lower end of the vine from the lower lip of the hatch, then pulled the upper half off the hatch itself with one good tug.

Lucy got herself back onto the ladder, pulled the cover plate off the manual crank, unfolded the handle, and started cranking. Probably there was plenty of power aboard, but if some fluke had drained the batteries, she didn't want to find out she had wasted three ergs too many and so had three ergs less than she needed to start the generators.

Hanging onto the ladder, cranking the awkwardly placed handle, starting to work up more of a sweat than the worn-out suit could handle; peering through the world through the scuffed and dirty glass of her bubble helmet, breathing air that smelled of a mixture of unwashed Lucy and the moldy-bog aroma of Outpost, First Lieutenant Lucille Calder was happier than she had been since the *Venera* was peacefully cruising through space, two or three lifetimes ago. She was going home. The League was out there, past an obstacle or two.

And better still, there was an honest-to-God shower aboard the lander. A fresh pair of coveralls, and *coffee*. Even the Guardians' emergency field rations would taste better than the nutritious glop the Refiners gave her. You'd think an advanced culture might have invented cooking instead of eating raw what they foraged and hunted. But there was no accounting for taste.

The hatch, hinged at its base, slowly swung down from the vertical to form a platform she could step onto easily from the ladder. She hopped across, stepped into the airlock, and used the inner manual to crank the outer door shut.

From the base of the lander, the watching Z'ensam realized the acrobatics were over and got back to clearing the vines and undergrowth away from the lander.

C'astille, standing on guard against any Hungry Ones that might come for a visit, snorted, lashed her tail, and gripped her long-gun harder. She had forgotten the way humans climbed and jumped and scrambled to reach a height. They thought nothing of it all, seemed to have no fear of falling. It was a little thing, but it reminded them that Lucy M'Calder wasn't just a mutated Z'ensam with the back half missing. She was alien—a mystery so complete that she could never be solved.

And C'astille called her *friend,* and aided her cause against her own kind.

Something big growled at the edge of the clearing. C'astille fired a few rounds at it on general principles, and as the roaring boom of her gun faded she heard a heavy body slump over and collapse into the brush.

There was electric power. Plenty of it. The cryo-stable tanks had lived up to their name and held the liquid oxygen and hydrogen at temperature all this time. The air, which was probably a little musty in reality, was totally, blissfully odorless to Lucy's Outpost-acclimated nose. Lights came on at the flick of a switch, and Lucy had forgotten how *friendly* a warm yellow light could be, after so many days of Outpost's too-white sun.

So the lander had held together. The next jobs she could do better if she was clean. The shower. Clean clothes. Food.

Outside, C'astille wondered what was taking so long in there. In the excitement of being back on her own Road (she realized she was beginning to think a bit like a Z'ensam) Lucy forgot about her escort for quite a while. It wasn't until she had sat down in a real chair (well, a crash couch, but it was designed by and for a human), and had a cup of properly hot, fresh coffee that she remembered her escort. It took her a minute to find the external mikes and speakers on the unfamiliar comm control panel. She switched on the mike and spoke in English. "Can you hear me?"

"Very well, far too well," C'astille's voice replied a bit testily. "We all just bolted and ran half across the field out of reflex."

"Sorry. Let me turn it down. Is that quiet enough?"

"Much better. Now perhaps we won't attract every Hungry for a day's gallop around. What have you been doing? Night is coming on."

"Sorry, C'astille. I was just cleaning myself and getting some human food and drink. Things I even forgot I missed.

I lost track of the time. But if it's night, perhaps I'd better just sit tight here for the night. It would take a while to get into a suit and get out to the wagons."

"Very well, though you could have mentioned it sooner. We were getting nervous, and I had no way of contacting you. I thought the air might have gone bad in there and killed you."

"Thank you for worrying, C'astille, and I apologize for worrying you."

"No more will be said. Is your lander well?"

"She seems to be in very good shape, though it will take some hours more of work to get her powered up and operational. Tomorrow will be time enough. Rest well, and I'll see you in the morning. I'll leave the hearing and speaking devices on so you can call me."

C'astille, still a bit miffed, summed up the English exchange to her companions, and the Z'ensam retreated to the protection of the wagons.

If the truth be known, it wasn't the difficulty and delay of suiting up that kept Lucy inside the lander, but the comfort of being in human air, human light, with human food in her gut—and the thought of sleeping in a proper bed, even a collapsible mattress, was an overwhelming temptation.

She left the comm station on standby and beside the external pickups, she set the radio on scanner/receive without even thinking, unfamiliar board or not. That was standard operating procedure, one of a thousand things they bashed into a pilot's skull.

It was one of the thousand things that kept pilots alive.

Left to itself, the cabin air was lovely in its scentlessness. With the air-conditioning on, bringing the temperature down from the usual high thirties of Outpost to a sinfully cool eighteen degrees centigrade, it was paradise. Lucy dragged the fold-up mattress out into the center of the cabin deck and flopped it down. Sheets, top and bottom! A pillow! She felt that she truly appreciated civilization for the first time.

She dropped off to sleep the moment she had cuddled herself into a comfy position, the now-familiar growls and screams of an Outpost night coming through the external mikes to serve for a lullaby.

Half an hour after Lucy dozed off, the emergency alarm blared into life, and she was in front of the comm board before she was fully awake. Where was the bloody alarm cut-off? There. The yowling of the siren cut off in mid scream.

What the bloody hell was going on—a *text* message on channel 30? She shunted the message over to the computer screen:

URGENT YOU DEPART FOR BARYCENTER DURING TIME PERIOD STARTING IN ONE HOUR TWO MINUTES AND ENDING IN ONE HOUR NINETEEN MINUTES. MANY SHIPS IN ORBIT AND THIS WILL BE ONLY CLEAR WINDOW FOR SOME DAYS DEPENDING ON SHIP MOVEMENTS. GOOD LUCK FRIEND WU MAINTAIN RADIO SILENCE DO NOT REPLY WE'LL KNOW IF YOU GO. MESSAGE REPEATS: URGENT YOU—

Jesus! Lucy cleared the screen and rubbed her eyes. How the hell did Cynthia—of course, the beacon. Thank God for that.

A loud thumping noise came from the external pickups. Lucy kicked in the cameras. It was C'astille, pounding on the hull. Damn! That reminded Lucy that she had wanted to record some images of the Z'ensam, get some sort of proof they existed. She had planned to do it in the morning, but it was too late now. She twisted a few knobs and set the external cameras to record. "Yes, C'astille. What is it?"

"We heard a loud scream come from the talking device that comes from your ship. Are you all right?"

"Yes, thank you. It was an emergency message, from, from one of my Group who guessed I would be here. She tells me I must leave this place very soon, or not at all, because later the enemy will be where it can find me as I launch."

"You must leave now?"

"Yes." Lucy hesitated and shifted to Z'ensam. "You will sense me again. I will be here again, and we shall journey more. But there is a thing you must do. The device I called a beacon—the radio-direction finder. It is in the wagon. Keep it with you. It will show me the Road that leads to you, no matter where you are."

"It will be with me. Good luck." The last C'astille spoke in English. There was no way to say it in her own speech.

"Thank you. Now, bright lights will come on for a few minutes. My camera will get pictures of you for my Group to see, so they will have knowledge that you truly exist. My people still have never sensed you. The lights will stop before too many large night animals are attracted."

"Very well. There is no time for your descent from the machine for a true goodbye?"

"No." There wasn't much else she could say. "I wish there were time," she said, switching back to English. "But let me get your picture, and then you must all get quite far away, for the lander is dangerous to those outside."

"I have seen many landers fly. We will get well out of the way. When will you launch?"

"In about an hour. I'm sorry, I can't think well enough to convert that to your measures."

"I know what an hour is. We will be out of the way in time."

The floodlight blossomed on, blanketing the area around the lander in a harsh white light. C'astille shielded her eyes with her hand and waited for her eyes to adjust. She told herself to act intelligent, to convince this mysterious halfwalker Group of Lucy's that she wasn't just an animal. She wondered what, exactly, would constitute intelligent behavior.

Unsure of what to do, she did what billions in the same situation had done before. She waved at the camera.

*   *   *

Lucy would have smiled at that if she had been watching the monitors, but she was already over her head in calculations. How the hell to get off the planet without being converted into radioactive gases? If the Guards were in line-of-sight of her, they would spot the plume of her lander's fusion engines instantly. It would be impossible to miss. Having spotted her, they would know who it had to be, and where she had to be going. They would blow her out of the sky, and probably bomb her launch point just to be on the safe side.

She had to stay out of line of sight while firing her engine. Okay, fine. That meant a short boost at high thrust so she could get up to escape velocity and shut down the engine *fast*. She had to dive for southern skies, toward the barycenter, and that would help. She knew from running the radar on *Ariadne* that there was very little surveillance of that direction—and what there was was run from *Ariadne*—and if the Guards didn't breathe down their necks too hard, there were fair odds that the CIs could manage to look the other way. Cynthia Wu would make sure of that.

Then, a long run powered-down, to get far, far away before she relit her fusion engines for an extended burn that would get her to the barycenter, 7.65 billion kilometers away. The further from Outpost she was, the better a head start she would have on any pursuit. And if they couldn't backtrack her launch point, they couldn't identify her—and that meant that, with their hands full with an invading fleet, they wouldn't be likely to bother with her.

But she had to get this tub ticking along, bring her to life carefully after her months-long slumber. God only knew what systems had gummed themselves up without maintenance. Lucy had hoped to take at least a day or two to check things out, but it looked like it was time to have faith in the backups. Engine test cycle go. Fuel system at go. Fuel tanks at ninety percent—and she was going to need every drop of it. Food, water—there should be enough aboard for this trip, and if not she could stay alive on not much for a few days. No time to take an inventory now. Guidance. The computer seemed sane, and seemed to know where the sky was. She would have to trust it. No benchmark to test it against, and with forty-five minutes until her launch window opened, no time to calibrate against the sextant.

Damn! No time to toss the dead-weight mass out of the lander. Well, she'd have to deadhead it to escape velocity, then toss it through the airlock when she was running doggo, all engines powered down.

What about the hull? Did it still have integrity, or had some damned Outpost plant secreted some weird acid that had weakened it so it'd split a seam and start losing air under the stress of acceleration and vacuum? No time and no way to check. But she could take precautions. The second pressure suit. Lucy dug it out of the storage locker, and didn't realize she was buck naked until she started to put the suit on over bare skin. It had felt good to sleep in the nude, but time to get back into a damned monkey suit again. At least it was a clean one.

There was a rather awkward series of mechanisms on the suit that would take care of wastes, a sipping straw that would stave off death by dehydration, and even a little airlock gizmo that would let her pass food in toward the general direction of her mouth. If the hull leaked, she could stay alive in the suit long enough to get to the barycenter. But it wouldn't be fun.

She was on the clock and the minutes were dying. Back to the pilot's station. Fusion chamber pressure okay. Atmosphere engines cranked up and ready. She was tempted to skip them and boost on fusion, but C'astille and company might be too close. If the plume of fusion rocket exhaust brushed past them as she was on the way up, they'd never feel it before they died. Even if they were out of range, the actinic light of fusion could blind them.

No, she'd have to go up on the old liquid oxygen/liquid hydrogen engines. Half a tick. Why not ride the lox/l.h. as far as she could? It'd be the most efficient way to dump the mass of the liquid oxygen, and burning conventional propellant produced a much less noticable flame—oh, they would spot it if they knew to look—but more than likely they wouldn't be rigged to spot such an inefficient fuel combination.

Lucy knew that she might begrudge every gram of hydrogen wasted in the lox/l.h. burn later on, but she knew damn well there might not be a later on if she didn't take the gamble.

She wasn't the sort to look back once she made a decision. She'd use the lox/l.h. system. Eighteen minutes until the window—and when it opened she'd jump through it, with any sort of luck.

Luck. And there she was on a nameless lander. It wouldn't do. She did nothing but *think* of the name. That was enough to ward off bad luck. *Halfwalker*. C'astille was possibly the only person of any species who would appreciate the humor in that. Lucy resolved to stay alive long enough to tell her about it.

Working quickly and carefully, Lucy brought *Halfwalker* to life. The minutes died, all too fast. Too many systems were taken on faith, too much she just had to cross her fingers on.

Three minutes. She had a course, of sorts, laid in, a brute-force run into the south, and then she'd see what happened.

Two minutes; one; none. Show time. Power to take-off engines—

And a red light came on. Lucy's fingers rattled over the keyboard, demanding details on the malfunction, and her heart hammered in her chest. She had only seventeen minutes to solve it, fix it, or else—oh bloody hell, it was only the damn manual crank on the outer airlock. She had forgotten to fold the thing and close and cover on it. More than likely it would be sheared off by air resistance as she headed out of the atmosphere.

So be it. Lucy hit one last button, and *Halfwalker* grabbed for sky.

*   *   *

C'astille watched with a full heart as the pillar of flame clawed its way toward the stars, and the roar of the engines made the very ground shake. She had tried to describe this thing, *launch* the humans called it, to her companions. But words failed. To ride that pillar of flame, to race through a skyful of enemies to some sparkles of light in the night sky that you hoped was a mighty fleet— C'astille marvelled at her friend's courage and wondered if she herself had the nerve, the spirit, to do such a thing, to ride flame toward the risk of death.

But the stars. The stars lay at the end of that Road of fire.

C'astille watched the lander climb out of sight, leaving a ropy vapor trail behind that quickly dispersed into the wind. And she realized that she might be the first of all her kind to dream of flying without revulsion, for none of her kind had ever flown and kept a whole name.

CHAPTER TWENTY-FOUR

Outpost, Nihilist Encampment

D'etallis was a veteran of endless political infighting; she knew the value of good Intelligence. From a half dozen sources—Z'ensam who had befriended Guardians, from taps and listens-ins on radio traffic that the halfwalkers thought the Z'ensam didn't know about, through any number of little tricks—D'etallis knew the League had arrived at the barycenter.

She didn't know exactly what the League was, besides the fact that they were human and the enemies of the Guards. That was all she really needed to know. And the timing was just about perfect for her purposes.

D'etallis had made grand progress in her projects, but she discovered that her motives, her plans, her desires changed, even as she went from victory to victory.

She had seen Eltipa Divide. That was the turning point. Even after all the scheming, all the lies, all the manipulations, D'etallis had discovered that she still loved her old Guidance at that last, horrible moment. Too late to deny her the indignity of madness, idiocy, the loss of her name, D'etallis had killed her Guidance, and sworn that this would be the last generation that would suffer Division.

She would kill every Z'ensam who showed the slightest symptoms.

Her Guardian friends had helped bring that dream closer. With their weapons and tactics, D'etallis's followers, still half herd-mob and half army, would soon conquer or absorb every Group for an eight-day gallop in every direction. The Refiners still stayed ahead of her, stayed out of it, and a few others, but the day was not far off when she would have taken the entire heart of the continent.

And, under her direction, there were no Divisions. That was the main thing, or at least it should have been. D'etallis had found herself up against a paradox. An end to Division was merely a first step. The only absolutely certain way to ensure an end to Division was to ensure the end of the race. Which meant having a large enough base of power to support an army that could do the actual killing. Which, clearly enough, meant having a lot of live Z'ensam around. If there *weren't* enough Nihilist Z'ensam around, Nihilism would collapse. If it had gotten big enough first, it might manage to take some or all of the rest of Z'ensam civilization with it. But inevitably, some small number would have to survive, and Divide, and the species would continue, and repopulate the world.

Worse, there were some sub-Groups of Nihilists not at all interested in the great work of genocide. They had found the power in a rifle barrel, were living well, and weren't too keen to wipe out the Z'ensam that served them at gunpoint. They had lost the purity of their ideals to luxury. D'etallis was forced by her successes to realize that she was doomed to failure, if she went on the way she was.

But a good politician knows how to twist failure into victory, how to exploit advantages and chance opportunities while sidestepping problems.

D'etallis had worked it all out very clearly. First was the principle that *all* intelligent life was an abomination. There was equal merit in killing halfwalkers as in killing Z'ensam. More importantly, it should be easier to talk Z'ensam into killing ugly aliens—especially when the aliens had such interesting toys to serve as booty. The Guardians obviously had weapons far more powerful than what they gave to the Nihilists. Get her hands on those, and the job of wiping out the Z'ensam could be done. *Starsight* was another piece of the puzzle. The Guardians had made the formal presentation of the spacecraft a few days ago. D'etallis herself had christened the craft. The name was calculated to please and reassure the humans, and apparently it had.

Best of all was the news from the Nihilists' biological labs. They had carefully collected bits of human skin scraped from inside pressure suits; saliva from used drinking containers, even blood drawn from Captain Romero himself. The good captain had been strolling the grounds of the camp without a pressure suit, wearing a neck-sealed bubble helmet instead. C'ishcin had "accidentally" bumped into him and driven a tiny collection syringe into him and pulled it out before the fool halfwalker even had time to feel pain. It was perilously close to medicine, of course, but crimes had been committed in the service of a greater good before this. The biologists had burrowed in the human garbage dumps and latrines for samples. Discarded toenail clippings, mucus on a tissue, bacteria from human feces—all of it went into the labs for examination.

And now the biologists knew enough to build their plagues.

The Guards would be distracted by their war with the League. Presumably, they would try to keep it secret from the Nihilists. D'etallis knew how to take advantage of that, too.

The Guards had taught her a lot about strategy. It was time to strike.

CHAPTER TWENTY-FIVE

Barycenter

The whole fleet was on alert, thanks to one tiny ship. *Eagle*'s tracking had spotted her two days ago, coming toward the 'center from Outpost. It was the only response the Guards had made so far to the League's invasion.

It was easy to imagine a superweapon aboard, a bomb that could vaporize the entire barycenter, or a bioweapon that would make the foam worms seem benign by comparison.

But there were some strange things about that ship. She had started her boost from millions of kilometers this side of Outpost. And if she kept to the course and thrust she was using, about forty hours from now she would come to a halt, a hundred thousand kilometers away from the 'center. It was tempting to think that she wanted to stand off so as to not get too close and appear threatening. Or was she just trying to stay out of range of whatever she was going to lob at the fleet? Captain Robinson wanted to blast her out of space, but Admiral Thomas had some faint hope that she was a peace ship, negotiators aboard. If there was the slightest chance to limit the killing, he would take it. Besides, the League needed time to build up its supply and expand its beachhead in the barycenter.

They had pretty much shot their bolt, coming in with all guns blazing. (That matter-transmitter they had used on New Finland would have come in handy right about now, but apparently the damn thing was hideously expensive to run, and no one knew exactly why the one existing transmitter had spontaneously melted down a month after it was used to transmit the troops to New Finland.)

So supply ships shuttled in and out of the barycenter, bearing fuel and ammunition and food. The League fleet built up its strength, and waited. And with every day of waiting, Robinson noticed, Sir George was just a trifle later getting out of bed, and his cheeks were just a trifle rosier when he turned in.

Under the League's careful watch, the Guards likewise made no dramatic moves, but carefully reordered their forces. There were two large flotillas, each about a third the size of the League fleet, one orbiting Capital and the other about Outpost. Every day a ship or two launched away from Outpost and disappeared into C^2, only to reappear some time later on approach to Capital. Slowly, carefully, the Guards were shifting their strength to a direct defense of the home world. Presumably, in some computer simulator on Capital, they were planning the best way to dislodge the League. But an attack by hundreds of ships was not something to organize in an hour or two. It took time.

It could be weeks before either side was prepared for a major fleet movement.

In the meantime, there was that one tiny mystery ship, growing closer all the time. Robinson didn't like mysteries, especially this one. The *Eagle* stood ready to vaporize the visitor at a moment's notice. The comm crews tried to reach her over a hundred different frequencies, in a dozen languages. Since the Guards spoke English, it was hard to see the point of broadcasting to the visitor in Russian, but it kept the comm crews busy and happy, and that counted for something.

That was its only benefit; the visitor did not transmit a

syllable in response. Obviously, things would start happening after she had arrived and taken up her station a hundred thousand klicks out.

Robinson deployed a half dozen unmanned probes into the vicinity of space toward which the visitor seemed to be headed. One of these was the first to get a good visual on her when her engines finally cut off and the ship itself was no longer hidden in their glare. Robinson and Thomas were both on the bridge for the arrival, watching everything comm could pipe up to them. It was a lander, a rather weathered one, with Guard markings all right. No real shocker there, Robinson thought. Who else's ship would it be?

It was the first transmission from the lander that surprised him. It was a general broadcast in a woman's voice. "I have no directional radio gear. This is a wide broadcast transmission. Please jam this frequency for reception at Outpost and Capital. Do not respond until this is done."

Robinson hesitated a moment, then shrugged. He could play that sort of game. What harm could come from jamming the enemy's radio? He punched the intercom key and talked to the comm chief. "Comply with that, and give us a good overlap. Jam well above and below that frequency. Reply to our new friend when you've done it. And keep us patched in up here."

There was a few moments' pause as the comm station set up directionalized antennae and aimed them at the two planets. There was a increase in the background hiss as some of the signal leaked over, and then *Eagle*'s radio operator spoke again.

"*Eagle* to unidentified ship. Jamming commenced. Please identify yourself now."

There was another short pause. "This is Lieutenant Lucille Calder, Royal Australian Navy, on detached duty with the League of Planets Survey Service. I was last known by you to be aboard the *Venera*, and I suppose I'm listed as missing and presumed dead. I have a lot to tell you. I don't want the Guards to know I'm still alive. That's why the jamming. But I don't think I should broadcast my report, even so. Request permission to come aboard."

That started a hubbub. The *Venera!* She was more than a lost ship to spacers, she was a quick-born legend, a *Mary Celeste* or a *Flying Dutchman*, a mysterious story that had never had a proper end. The usual murmur of voices around the bridge rose to a dull roar until Robinson called out. "Put a lid on it! Admiral, your opinion?"

"Well, if it's some kind of trick, it's a damn clever one, and I can't quite see the point of it. If this Calder truly was with the Survey, Captain Larson and my niece can both identify her. I say let her aboard—with extreme precautions."

"I agree."

The decontamination boat launched from *Eagle* forty-five minutes later, Mac and Joslyn aboard. Mac could still not believe it. Calder, alive! Pete had been right all along— the *Venera* had been hijacked. Oh, it had all but been taken for granted after a while as a great theory, but here was *proof*. Joslyn and he had never known Calder all that well—she had been a smile in the mess hall, not a close friend. But if *she* lived. . . .

The decom boat was little more than a control panel, vacuum, engines, and fuel, cobbled together out of spare parts months ago in case the task force had to rescue anyone from a worm-ridden ship. Mac and Joslyn rode in crash couches welded to the midsection of the I-beam that made up the fuselage. At one end of the thirty-meter long beam were the engines, and at the other was a specially built personnel decom station. Midway between the bow and the pilot's station was a lethal-looking weapons pod, plus a disinfectant sprayer and other things to kill worms. Mac and Joslyn wore armored pressure suits. No exposed part of the ship or their suits was edible to the worms, so far as anyone knew. They had learned how to kill worms, and hoped they knew how to kill whatever else the Guards had dreamed up.

But how the hell did Calder get here?

Joslyn moved the decom boat at a stately one-gee toward Calder's lander, a careful, deliberate pace. It was easy to remember that any weapon not trained on Calder's ship was now trained on theirs. It was just over a four-hour run, accelerating for two hours, then turning the decom ship bow-to-stern and decelerating for another two hours.

"Mac, what can this mean?" Joslyn asked. "How the hell did she manage to steal a Guard lander? What's been going on out here?"

"Hey, kid, your imagination is as good as mine. Make up your own answers."

"Foo to you, oh captain mine. But the *Venera* alive! It makes a chill run down my spine."

"You're not alone. Just think of how Pete must feel. He was the only one who ever really dreamed that they weren't just a shipwreck."

"I'll bet he's glad he came along with the fleet."

"Watch your radar. We're coming up on her."

"Who's the pilot in this marriage?"

"Okay, so watch where we're goin—"

The engines stopped suddenly, and the decom ship was dead in space to Calder, not ten kilometers away from her. Calder had switched on the lander's navigation lights, and they could see them blinking across the darkness of the brilliant starfield.

Mac grinned and reached across to squeeze Joslyn's armored shoulder. "Very sweet, pilot. Very sweet."

"Shut up and open the secure channel, Cap'n."

"Aye, aye, ma'am." Mac told the computer to train a laser link back on the *Eagle*. "*Eagle*, this is Captain Larson speaking over a secure line. We are in position." Mac switched on the radio, and took a deep breath as he prepared to talk with a woman who had been a ghost to him. "Lucille, this is Mac Larson. Do you know me?"

The answer came back instantly, and there was delight and pleasure in the voice. "Mac! Dear Lord, what are you doing here?"

"I could ask you the same question. But, look, Lucille, the big shots want proof that you're you . . ."

"As well they should."

Joslyn plugged her suit into the radio. "Lucille! Who am I and who married me to Mac?"

"Joslyn! Hello! That dreadful Reverend Farnsworth Buxley. He put half the congregation to sleep."

Joslyn turned and grinned at Mac. "If you're not you, you do a great imitation. Now, we've got a whole decontamination rigamalore to get through. Did *Eagle* explain to you?"

"Yes they did. I'm in my suit and the ship is in vacuum. I have my personal stuff in a vacuum-sealed carrybag. Switching to suit radio. You might have to boost your gain, it's not a very powerful set."

"Yes, your signal just got a lot weaker."

"Okay, coming out the lock. Jumping free, toward you, and lordy it's a big first step."

"Don't worry, we'll get you."

"Oh, I'm glad to be here. I've been cooped up so long. The stars look so *lovely* and I don't care if I'm babbling—I'm free!"

The telephoto cameras showed a tiny human figure sliding away from the shabby-looking lander.

"Okay, Luce. Now listen. We're going to move in on you. If I come in too fast, let me know."

"Oh, don't treat me like a groundhog, Joslyn! This is more fun than I've had in ages!"

Joslyn played with the low-powered trim jets, and nudged the decom ship toward the suited figure. In spite of Lucille's urging, she moved the ship slowly, carefully, closing the distance from kilometers to meters to centimeters, until the suited figure reached out a hand and gently pulled herself onto the I-beam fuselage.

"Welcome aboard. And welcome to League territory." Mac watched with anxious eyes as Lucille swung herself around and waved.

"Thank you, thank you, thank you! Which way to the showers?"

"Straight toward the bow. Strip to skin in the airlock there. Once you're in the decom tank use the inside controls to open the outer lock and jettison the suit and everything else."

Lucy felt herself bubbling with delight. She had escaped! It didn't matter what happened next, didn't matter that the League would have to come down on her like a ton of bricks to get every bit of information on the Guards and the Outposters and *Ariadne*—well, that was the way it had to be. She owed that to Wu and Schiller and everyone else back on the station. And she owed Johnson Gustav.

She pulled herself along the I-beam toward the decom chamber. The outer hatch was open. She clambered into it, and shut the hatch behind her. The lock itself was a standard-issue aluminum and plastic box, little bigger than a closet. It didn't take long to pressurize. She wriggled out of the suit and her clothes and shoved them into a corner. She opened the inner hatch and tossed her carrybag into the decontamination tank. She followed the bag in and, working in the dark, dogged the inner hatch shut. She found a light switch and turned it on. Then she used the remotes to open the outer hatch with the lock still pressurized. There was a shower there, and several bottles of very strong, nasty-smelling soap. The paranoia about decontamination told her they had met with bioweapons already.

She didn't have to ask what the outcome had been.

Mac saw the outer lock open and the pressure suit and other clothes zip out into space, pulled along by the escaping air. He powered up the infrared laser in the weapons pod, aimed and fired as Joslyn played with the attitude jets to match velocity with the debris. The suit melted and then vaporized in the intense heat. Mac zapped the rest of the clothes, and then Joslyn moved the boat alongside the lander. Mac pulled a pair of heatflash grenades out of a satchel and tossed them through the open airlock into the lander's cabin.

"Pull her back, Joz."

The control jets flared, the boat pulled back, Mac hit the radio trigger, and the lander's interior flared with a sullen, killing heat. They headed for home.

Decontamination. Bioweapons. First Contact. The League still had no idea that they were mixed up in a First Contact. Sobering thoughts. There was so much to tell them, but how to start? Scrubbing herself, carefully drying herself and getting into fresh coveralls, Lucy pondered the question. In all her time of waiting, she had never considered *how* to tell them. Now she did, and resolved to say nothing until she was sure of her words, until the right people were there to listen. Lucy kept her silence on the journey back to *Eagle*, except to reassure Mac and Joslyn she was all right. She smiled and waved and said nothing of consequence to the small crowd that cheered her arrival in the hangar deck, smiled her way up into the conference room where the Intelligence staff was waiting.

She looked out across the faces, and thought of the Nihilists and lost her smile. And she knew how to begin. "You're fighting the wrong war," she said.

CHAPTER TWENTY-SIX

Aboard RKS *Eagle*

Lieutenant George Prigot sat there, silent and glad to be forgotten in the hubbub. The command staff and the Intelligence units had been in joint session for endless hours now, and the voices of argument swirled around him.

"We can't make First Contact in the middle of a war!"

"The bloody Guards made *First* Contact. We'll have to settle for second—and we don't have much choice about making Contact. How can we avoid it?"

"But in the middle of a war? How? Who? How can we get through the Guard ships around Outpost?"

Captain Robinson listened to it all for a while before banging his gavel and attempting to bring the talk back to the point. "Lieutenant Calder, I have seen the results of the attack on *Impervious*, and I am willing to grant that bioweapons are dangerous. I can't quite credit your claim that these Nihilists could or would wipe out the human race. For starters, how could they get to us? They have no starships, no spacecraft of any kind—

"But they *will* get them, Captain," Lucy said, with the weary voice of someone who has said the same thing many times before. "By trade or theft or by building their own, sooner or later they will have ships, now that they know such things exist. The Nihilists regard intelligent life as an abomination. Before anyone can ask me why, I'm not quite sure. The Nihilists want to keep growing in power— and they lose lots of friends if they start genocide against their own kind. Mostly, as I understand it, the Nihilists limit themselves to killing Outposters as they enter old age, which doesn't really seem to bother anyone. Again, don't ask me why, I don't know.

"But out of all this come some key points: They *can* kill us, and kill us by the millions. You have seen the results of weapons that can breed more weapons. They are, I assure you, actively seeking to get ships so they can get to us. That's opinion on my part, but every Outpost Refiner I've talked to agrees with that assumption. And *killing us has got to be politically healthier for them than killing other Z'ensam*—other Outposters. We are very ugly to the Z'ensam. Worse than ugly—mortifying to look on. The Guards are the only humans any Outposter has met, and they aren't the best ambassadors of good will. A lot of Z'ensam would stand back and let the Nihilists go after us—and if the Nihilists, say, take Capital, wipe out the population there, the weapons and the ships and the technology there would let them take over all of Outpost. And if they got starships, and they came hunting the rest of us—imagine, just for starters, a breed of those worms that *was* designed to attack a planet."

There was a long silence. Finally one of the New Finnish officers broke it. "Just once, right there at the end, did you mention Capital, the Guardians. *They* are our reason for being here. Your aliens are all very interesting, but we are here to fight the Guards! You know what those monsters did to my world. Why should we defend them against these Nihilists of yours? Let it happen. We would be well rid of the Guards. *Let* the Nihilists wipe them out. We of the League can handle the Nihilists afterwards. I would consent to that course of action, but even it would not satisfy me altogether. *I* say we must ignore these creatures

who don't even have spacecraft. *We* must flatten Capital.
We have waited in this dreary barycenter of yours long
enough, admiral. Enough of caution. We New Finns, at
least, came here to kill Guardians!"

George's blood turned cold. This crazy Finn was talking
genocide—and no one was disagreeing! They were concerned with the tactics of battle. No one raised the moral
issues against allowing the Nihilists to exterminate the
people of his planet. He wished Mac or Joslyn were in on
this meeting. They would have spoken up. George knew
damn well no one would listen to *him* on this subject.
Anything he could say would only make things worse.

Captain Robinson turned to Admiral Thomas, but the
admiral didn't seem to want to say anything. Robinson
looked to the Finnish contingent. "Gentlemen, we understand your feelings. But I don't think the situation is
simple enough for a simple answer. We are not properly
prepared to do it, we do not have the experts in xeno-
sociology and so on available, but nonetheless I think we
must establish some sort of relations with at least this
group of Outposters that Lieutenant Calder traveled with."

The Finns did not reply, but a murmur of agreement
came from the rest of the table. "So how do we do it?"
Robinson asked.

"Ah, Captain?" A nervous-looking young black woman,
an Intelligence lieutenant, spoke up timidly. "We *can* get
a team down there, with a minimum of risk. We just can't
get them back—at least not for a while. We have those
covert landers."

"Right! I'd clean forgotten about them. Thank you, Lieutenant Krebs."

"Wait a minute," came a voice from the rear. "What's a
covert lander—and what was that about not getting back?"

Krebs leaned in toward the center of the table so she
could be heard. "The coverts are one-shot landers designed to be transparent to radar and so on. We have a
number along so we could drop spies and saboteurs on
Capital. Each can carry six and some cargo. You can't get

back in one because they don't carry much fuel—and they land a little rough, too. A covert lander could follow that beacon down, we could get some people in there, and they'd have to sit tight until we could get them out. They'd have radios and so on, of course."

"Lovely," said the same voice from the rear.

Pete Gesseti sighed at *that* news, but such was life. He was along for this trip so the League could have some expendable diplomats on the scene to get negotiations started. The key word was expendable. You didn't send the dean of the diplomatic corps into a war zone. May as well get the volunteering over with. Pete rose. "Ah, Captain Robinson. I really hate to admit this, but it seems to me that I'm the logical one to send on this trip."

Robinson had given up looking to Thomas. The admiral was willing to just sit there and listen. "I'm afraid I had just come to the same conclusion. Talk with me afterwards and we'll put together a team. Obviously, Lieutenant Calder should be on it, if you feel up to it, lieutenant."

"I've been assuming that I'd go back. You'll need an interpreter, Mr. Gesseti."

I need a drink, Pete thought, but said nothing.

"Very well. Krebs, you get them organized after we're done here. But now we must move on to your other news about this Guardian officer, Gustav Johnson. Can he be trusted?"

Lucy opened her mouth to speak, shut it again, played with a pencil for a moment. "Johnson is a good and honorable man, but you must understand his viewpoint," she said finally. "He is a citizen of Capital, and his planet is at war with us. He makes a very clear distinction between the planet Capital and the political association called the Guardians. He hinted to me once or twice about an illegal opposition group called Settlers, but I don't know much about them. He doesn't want the League here. I don't think he actually *wants* the League to win. But he has concluded that those persons in power, the Central Guardians, have gotten Capital into a hopeless situation. Capital *will* lose. He sees that as inevitable. He wants to make that defeat as painless as possible. He believes that the use of bioweapons can only make the League more eager for revenge.

"I should emphasize that Johns—that Gustav—is in a very delicate situation. I have had no contact with him for months. He may be dead. He may have been drugged and tortured into revealing every plan he and I made. The CIs on *Ariadne* might be dead by now, or simply transferred to another posting. So the *situation* cannot be trusted. But, if he lives, Gustav Johnson *can* be. If we receive any transmissions from *Ariadne*, you must judge for yourself who is sending them."

"And at this range, we can't possibly be certain that a laser link would be secure," Robinson said thoughtfully. "We can't risk talking back to them. Somehow, this seems like a very new kind of war, and a very old kind, both at once.

"Meeting adjourned. We all have a lot to think about."

CHAPTER TWENTY-SEVEN

Eagle, Hangar Deck

"Lucy has a point," Joslyn said. "A ship needs a name."

Mac grunted and stared up at the thing. The covert lander was an ungainly arrowhead, a dingy gray aerodynamic lump. It looked like a blob of clay some giant had half formed into an airplane shape before he got bored and went away. She had been pulled in from her usual outside-of-hull docking to be checked out. Mac slapped his hand on the hull and it felt like crumbly concrete mixed with styrofoam. "How about the *Sick Moose*?"

"A real romantic, that's you, Mac," Lucy said. "A true sense of history. How's *Sick Moose* going in the books side by side with your name to the unborn generations?"

Joslyn laughed and twined her arm through her husband's. "I was on your side until you said that, Luce. Think of all the school kids that are going to have to write dull reports about the First Contact for history class. Let's make it *Sick Moose* and give them some comic relief."

Lucy shrugged, grinned, and kicked the lander's hull. "*Sick Moose* it is, then. I must say that I expected a little more sense of awe and wonder and fewer dumb jokes from you two on the subject of meeting aliens."

"I don't think either of us really quite believes it all yet,"

Mac said softly. "You've had a long, long time to get used to it. We found out an hour ago, when Pete said he had volunteered us to pilot this thing down to Outpost. I want to laugh and cry at the same time and then hurry there to meet C'astille. I'm scared to death—not just for me personally, but with the idea that *I'll* be the one to make the dreadful mistake that wrecks our relations with them for all time. And dumb jokes are the best cover we have for all that. But let's change the subject before we bog down for hours discussing the Wonder of It All. George, you're the only real engineer here. Is this thing really going to work? Can we get through without being spotted?"

George Prigot shrugged. "I'm not going along, so I don't have the same stake in the answer you do. But it should. Their radar isn't going to be geared to watch for an all-ceramic ship, and even if it was, it'd be hard to get a decent echo off it."

Joslyn snorted. "They won't be looking for it because no one has ever been enough of a damn fool to make a glass ship before."

"It's not glass," George objected. "It's more like a clay pot, though it should be a lot tougher."

" 'Should be' are the very words I'm worried about," Joslyn said. "And I say she's a glass ship because radar will see right through—and she'll shatter if you drop her hard. I'd love to know more about the propulsion system, though. Supposed to be some sort of cross between magneto-hydrodynamics and a linear accelerator. Extremely secret. She uses straight liquid oxygen for boost-mass. Not as efficient as fusion, but just try spotting the thrust plume."

George walked to the stern of the *Moose* and looked up into the engine bells. "Neat. It must jet the oxy at only a couple hundred degrees. Very hard to detect if you're watching for fusion plasmas."

"Neat it is. But I'd trade it for a hull you couldn't smash with a hammer."

Pete came through a hatch into the hangar bay and

wandered into earshot as Joslyn was speaking. "Say, you're just the sort of pilot that inspires confidence in a passenger."

"Hello, Peter," Joslyn said with a smile. "What's the situation?"

"Well, this is a top secret operation, so I only had to clear it with ten departments instead of twenty. They dug up a biologist, a South African kid by the name of Charles Sisulu. Civilian kid who knows a lot about bio-engineering. They brought him along to work on the bioweapons, so he might as well go straight to the source. So with Mac, Joz, Lucy, this Sisulu character and me, we have five and this crate can carry six. Any suggestions for the empty slot?"

"I've got one," Joslyn said. "Madeline Madsen. She's a Royal Britannic Navy second lieutenant, a pilot. I know she's checked out on the covert lander, and she's a big outdoorswoman."

Lucy sounded unconvinced. "She have any ground-combat training?"

"Standard RBN basic training, I guess. Why do we need combat for this trip?"

"Because Outpost is a very nasty place. Any animal that sees us is likely to try eating us. And Mr. Gesseti, with all due respect, we're going to be in armored pressure suits for that same reason, for long hours at a stretch. Are you up to that?"

"I dunno, but I'm sure as hell in better shape than the other diplomatic types along for the ride. I'm fifteen years younger than any of 'em. One reason I volunteered."

Lucy grunted. It was a motley crew, a hurry-up job, but maybe that was the best she dare hope for. "All right, Mr. Gesseti. That'll have to do. Any word about when we launch?"

"As soon as possible, they said, so I guess its in your hands. Mac, how soon can we be ready?"

Mac hesitated for a moment, figuring loading and check-outs and a little extra for glitches. "We'll go in eighteen hours."

*   *   *

Lucy was ready long before that. Aside from getting fitted for a pressure suit, there really wasn't much for her to do.

The *Eagle*'s purser put her up in a VIP cabin for her one night aboard. It was a kindly gesture, a welcome-back to the ex-prisoner who had to depart at once for a harsh and dangerous field assignment. A huge bed, plush carpeting on the deck, books she'd have no time to read, recorded music and films she'd have no chance to run—but still, it was good to at least be near such things again.

Lucy thought of C'astille and decided that she had to bring a gift back for her friend. Even as she had the idea of bringing a present, her eyes fell upon the perfect thing. A book, a great big, old-fashioned picture book lying on the coffee table of her stateroom. It was called *Works of Our Hands: Humans Shape the Solar System*. It was full of pictures of grand buildings and structures, old and new, and each was set against a glorious background. C'astille would love it.

Lucy felt only mildly guilty as she tucked it into her carrysack.

CHAPTER TWENTY-EIGHT

Aboard the *Sick Moose*

The long-range cameras tracked the great shape, brought it more frighteningly close than it truly was. "That's *Nike*," Lucy whispered. "She's big."

"That much we already knew," Mac replied in a whisper of his own. Logically, they could all be shouting at the top of their lungs and it wouldn't make any difference. But under the very nose of the huge military orbital command station, sneaking in past their radar, the desire to keep quiet went past the logical.

"Maddy, what can you see on passive detection?" Joslyn asked.

"Plenty enough," Madeline said, "and I've got everything cranked down to minimum power. But it looks to me that we should have *Nike* and *Ariadne* below our horizon when we hit the atmosphere."

"A bit of luck running our way," Joslyn said. "Even if this flying teapot is supposed to be invisible, I don't see any reason to experiment."

"Well, for what it's worth, we have now sailed through at least six different radars without being spotted."

"Mac, how are we, as far as the beacon signal?"

Mac was riding the comm station, which left him without much to do *besides* watch the beacon. He had gotten caught up on his reading this trip. "Right on the money. No change in its position since we picked it up. So do your bit and land us right on top of it."

The *Sick Moose*'s one small cabin was crowded with six people forced to sleep and eat in each other's pockets for several rather long and uneventful days, but the two civilians had managed to carve out a small corner for their own. Charles Sisulu had taken advantage of the long trip and methodically skinned Pete Gesseti's hide in four kinds of card games. Now Pete was grimly trying to win it all back in chess, fifty Kennedy dollars a game. Even with chess, his strong suit, Pete was just about holding his own. If he was even managing that, he thought, as he sadly watched his second bishop join its ancestors. "Charlie, isn't there any game you're not good at?"

Charlie grinned as he collected the bishop. He was a short, pudgy young man, perfect white teeth set off against his dark-skinned face. His hair was trimmed very short, and his rounded features and alert eyes suggested a quick and clever mind working behind the laughter and smiles. "If there was, why should I tell you? I figure you've paid for a month's vacation on Bandwidth already."

"And on what a diplomat makes. You should be ashamed of yourself. Seriously, though, how'd you get so good?"

"Easy. It's how I worked my way through college. My part of South Africa used to be one of those phony homelands. Technically not under South African law, which banned gambling among other things. The Afrikaaners'd come in to make a killing at roulette and we'd skin 'em alive. After the Rebellion, a hundred years ago, we got pulled back into the nation, but we had the smarts and the luck to hang onto our special exemption to the gambling laws. The marks might come in a different color but they still come, and we still clean 'em out and send 'em home. During the southern winter, that is the northern summer, I stayed home with the folks and played poker for a living. Or played anything. I'd just learn the odds and bet with them. When September rolled around I'd fly to America and live off my earnings while I studied at the University of California. If I got short of money, I spent a weekend at Las Vegas. Later on, when I started research at Wood's Hole, I'd go to Atlantic City."

"That's the last time I play with anyone before I check their resume," Pete said, pulling his queen back into what looked like a safer position. "So how do you like our odds here?"

Charlie shrugged. "No way to calculate them. But I'm a *biologist!* The stakes are so high. When they waved the foam worms at me, I signed every security agreement in sight—I *had* to work on that, top secret or no. And now I'll get to talk to someone who *designs* living things, from scratch! For a biologist, that's like a chat with God." Charlie moved in his own queen, took Pete's, and grinned. "Check. Mate in two moves. I'll take an IOU."

When they were about two hours from atmosphere, Mac called a meeting of all hands, which simply meant that everyone turned around in their chairs and faced the center of the tiny cabin. "All right," Mac said, "let me go over the situation one more time. So far the Guard radars haven't picked us up, but that could change at any time. This ship might be invisible to radar, but she's slow, she's hard to maneuver, and she's unarmed. And I don't care if she's made out of special-purpose ceramics or prune danish, when she hits the atmosphere, the light and heat of atmospheric entry are going to be detectable. We're going in on the daylight side, at a time when the bigger stations can't see our entry window. But we still might get spotted.

"Obviously, if we use our own radar, the Guards will spot us immediately, so that's out. But that means we're relying on inertial tracking and on visual. Those aren't really good enough for precise navigation in this situation. We don't have this system very well charted yet, we don't have maps of Outpost's surface, and we don't really know enough about the performance of this ship. There's some degree of uncertainty about where and when we'll hit air.

We've exhausted our fuel already, as you know. That was planned. In theory there's nothing to worry about. Once we do hit air, this thing is a glider, and it should be a good enough one to get us where we're going.

"The main point is that we're literally going in on a wing and a prayer. But while this will be a somewhat hairier landing than most, all of this was taken into account when we planned this flight. We *should* be all right. Mostly I want to tell this last to Pete and Mr. Sisulu, but it can't hurt for us rough-and-ready pilot types to be reminded too—when we go in, things might look worse than they really are. Relax and hang on, and the hottest pilot I know will pull this one off. Right, Joz?"

"Oh, sure. Mac's just trying to make it sound hard so when we come in you won't think it was too easy." Joslyn tried to sound chipper, and even brought it off, but she knew Mac had told it straight. Sometimes, though, the truth wasn't the best thing for a pilot to hear when she needed her confidence up.

Mac played it very conservatively. He had them all in pressure suits, strapped into crash couches and secured half an hour before they expected to hit air. He felt justified when the first faint quivering and thrumming sounded against the hull, fifteen minutes ahead of schedule. Now they were in Joslyn's hands. Mac had already watched Madeline enough to wish he were in the backup pilot's station. Maddy was good, but she wasn't seasoned, she didn't have that air of being calmly ready for disaster that combat pilots gained if they lived long enough. But it was too late for second guessing, and Mac couldn't think of anything that could take Joslyn out without killing the rest of them anyway.

Joslyn was trying to get the feel of the *Moose*. She seemed to be a pretty clumsy thing so far, and Joslyn was already worried about cross-ranges. Every second in atmosphere slowed them down, stole kilometers from the distance they could travel. There was enough fat in the landing program to cover the current situation, but just barely. She fought an impulse to tighten her grasp on the stick. This was her show, she had to keep calm and loose, ready for whatever the gods threw at her. She threw switches and let the computer handle the initial entry while she got a look around and tried to track that beacon. The planet's rotation had swung it out of their line-of-sight, but—hah! There she was, happily blinking away, and still within range of what the on-board computers were figuring was their likely glide-radius.

Then the *Moose* hit thicker air, and re-entry, and rode long minutes cut off from the outside world by a sheath of ionized air molecules and heat-shield ablation. This was the dangerous moment, when the *Moose* could not see, but was most easily seen. If there were any ships orbiting above them, and anyone aboard happened to look planet-ward, the *Moose* would be a blazing fire streaking across the dawn sky. No one aboard the *Moose* spoke as the computer dully went through its paces, maintaining ship's attitude at the right heading, keeping the shielding between the hull and disaster.

They went in, surrounded by a ball of flame that thundered through the skies of sunrise. The *Moose* shuddered and groaned, and the hull pinged and clicked as it absorbed the heat.

Slowly, the ball of fire guttered down, and the *Moose*, her hull still faintly glowing, coursed through the skies of Outpost. Joslyn pulled control back from the computer and took a look around. They were still nearly a hundred thousand meters up, still had line of sight on the beacon, though they might lose it as they glided lower. But they were in, and safe—

"Joslyn," Mac called. "I'm not up on reading Outpost weather, but it looks to me as if that beacon is right in the middle of one hell of a storm."

Joslyn's eye jumped from the beacon display to the pilot's window and back, mentally combining the two into one. "Damn! Mac, you're right. I wish to hell there had been time to put some decent viewing gear on this bird. I can't really get a good fix on where the beacon is, compared to the cloud cover."

"We've got the gear," Mac said, "it's just that we can't use it without giving our position away."

"Then I wish they had yanked it out so this thing'd be light enough to glide. We've got to go straight through that muck to get where we're going."

In the rear seats, Pete and Charlie Sisulu exchanged nervous glances. This might get to be too exciting a trip.

The *Moose* glided onward and down, Joslyn stretching every horizontal meter she could out of the clumsy craft. The storm clouds came up around them, engulfed them, the dark cobalt blue of the upper atmosphere vanishing into a witch's caldron of angry, writhing gray clouds that grabbed at the *Moose* and flung her to and fro. Lightning flashed about them, thunder exploded at deafeningly short range, and Joslyn wrapped both hands around the stick, braced her arms as best she could to retain control of the bucking, rearing ship. The interior lights flickered once, twice, and then came back on, and the hull rattled and clattered as hailstones and wind-driven rain slammed into it.

Joslyn knew the hull simply wasn't built to take this kind of abuse. Her every pilot's instinct was to get them down fast, now, anywhere, to wait out the storm. But the crew of the *Moose* was going to be stranded on Outpost, and their chances for survival rested with the Refiners. They had to hang on, travel as far as they could in the *Moose*. Joslyn held onto the stick and swore through clenched teeth as a hailstone smashed into the pilot's window, starring the viewpoint, making it that much harder to see.

"Maddy! Kick in the look-down radar and get me some hard numbers! If the Guards can spot our radar emissions through this bloody great storm, they *deserve* to win."

"Yes, ma'am." Maddy started flicking switches. "Give it a second to get some returns back—now! Airspeed, altitude, range and bearing to beacon and descent rate on your panel."

Damn! Those numbers weren't good. They were going to land a good fifty kilometers short of the beacon. Joslyn dragged back desperately on the stick, pulling the wallowing *Moose's* nose up as far as she could, risking a stall to try and drag some more range out of her. With no consciousness of what she was doing, Joslyn felt an updraft in the thrumming of the wings and the tricks of the wind. She grabbed at it, rode it as far as she could, felt the ship wallow back down into still air. The updraft might have bought them a kilometer, maybe two. Joslyn prayed for a tailwind, and got it, and then wished she didn't have it, a roaring, wailing banshee of a gust that almost knocked the *Moose* off her tail and into a fatal spin.

In the crash and the roar of the storm, Joslyn wrestled with the elements of air and wind and water, battling to keep her craft on course and in one piece.

They were getting lower now. They broke through the base of the cloud deck and looked upon the rain-soaked, wind-torn face of Outpost.

They were very low and too damn slow now—almost out of airspeed, headed for a stall. Joslyn swore and pushed the *Moose's* nose down, trading altitude she could ill afford for the airspeed she needed to keep her bird in the air. The ship seemed to wallow in the air, felt clumsier than ever, if that was possible. The damn porous ceramic hull must have soaked up the rainwater. And water was heavy. The added weight was dragging them down.

At least here, below the cloud deck, the winds had steadied down. No gusts or air pockets, just a hard, steady cross wind that did her no good, but no great harm, either. Joslyn turned into the wind and held her nose as close as she could to where it should be.

Now they were really coming down. Nothing fancy, just keep this thing in the air as long as it would stay there. Nothing but unbroken forest land below, no cozy meadow to set down in, just hope the local equivalent of trees had soft branches. How far from the beacon? Seventy kilometers. Sixty-five. Sixty. Still slowing. Come on! Fifty-five.

Fifty! And they were still a few klicks up in the air. Forty-five. Every klick was a gift from the gods of the air, now. Forty. There came the ground straight up for them. Thirty-five. What was that in miles? Never mind, figure it on the ground. They were only a thousand meters up now.

The wind came about to their nose, blowing them back against their course. Joslyn pulled the *Moose's* nose down and to port, trying to avoid a stall and maybe still make some headway. She kept it level, trying to pancake it down, spread the shock evenly—

—and the *Moose* ran out of sky.

She plowed into the treetops with terrible force, a roaring, screaming, keening crash of branches breaking and wings snapping off and shouts of frightened people and the horrible whistle of air screaming out of a broken hull. The *Moose* slammed on and on through the trees, far longer than seemed possible, tree limbs whipping past the cockpit windows, until finally a tree trunk stood its ground and the *Moose* shattered her nose square against it. The ruined ship tilted over to port and fell the last ten meters to the ground on its side.

Suddenly, the world, which had been so full of noise, was silent, or nearly so, with nothing but the creak of tree limbs, the patter of the rain, and the moans of people to be heard.

"Everyone still with us?" Mac called out, and got a ragged chorus of *yes*'s. "Good. That was some kind of flying, Joz."

Joslyn shook herself and forced her hands to peel themselves away from the stick. "Thanks, Mac. Though that has to be the least covert landing I've ever made." She felt herself trembling. Perhaps no one else would ever realize it, but *she* would always know just how close it had been.

Mac took a few minutes to check again that everyone was all right. They had all taken some bumps and bruises, but no one seemed much the worse for wear. All the pressure suits were behaving themselves, and that was a blessing. There was one spare aboard, but getting anyone into it with the *Moose*'s hull cracked and breached would have been a challenge, to say the least.

It was tempting to sit tight and wait for the rain to end, but Lucy warned them just how long the rains could last—there was nothing for it but to get moving. Within a half hour of landing, they had their carrypacks strapped on, rifles and other weapons at the ready, and the direction finder pointing twenty-nine kilometers *that* way to the beacon.

The six of them stepped from the wreckage of the *Sick Moose*, their hearts and spirits as gloomy as the dismal, rainswept forest that surrounded them. Lucy's helmet started to blur over with rain, and she switched on the wiper arm. The others followed her lead, turned to her. She was the only one who could guide them on this trek. She looked to Mac, and he nodded.

"You're our native guide, Lucy. We follow your commands on this leg."

"Right, then. Everyone make sure your external mikes are up, so you can hear them coming. You've seen what a Z'ensam—an Outposter looks like. If you see *anything* else move, kill it. I don't care if it looks like a sweet little baby fawn that only wants to nibble the grass. *Kill* it! There *are* no harmless wild animals on this planet. Any creature that spots us will try to eat us. So kill them, without hesitation. And make sure it stays dead. Don't worry about offending the locals either—it's the same way they deal with the wildlife. Is all that grimly clear?"

No one said anything.

"Mac, you take the rear. I'll lead. Lieutenant Madsen, you're behind me with the direction finder. Joslyn, you watch her back while she's watching our route. Mr. Sisulu, Mr. Gesseti, if you would follow Joslyn. Let's go."

CHAPTER TWENTY-NINE

Outpost

Charlie Sisulu didn't like the odds. He was sweating, not from exertion, but from fear. The forest was a grim, gloomy, wet and dismal place, claustrophobic—the vegetation shaded in livid greens that seemed horrid parodies of Earth's lovely plant life. His suit's external mikes picked up no birdsong, no musical calls of one beast to another, but instead an endless screaming, roaring challenge of defiance and death, set to the refrain of staccato, bone-rattling bursts of thunder. The rain came on and on, pouring down off his pressure suit, the wiper blade on his helmet barely able to keep his helmet halfway clear. And Charlie Sisulu had never been in a pressure suit before in his life. He felt trapped, sealed up, entombed in the clumsy suit.

This Lieutenant Lucy Calder led them on at a reckless speed, crashing through the thick underbrush, using a laser pistol or machete to hack down anything she couldn't get through. Twice she had dropped the laser, unholstered a heavy machine pistol and fired at *something* before Charlie had even seen whatever it was. Twice she had reholstered the heavy gun, scooped up the laser, and pressed on before whatever she had killed had finished falling to the ground. Twice he had stepped over shattered corpses that seemed nothing but teeth and claws.

And they had only gone about one kilometer.

He was scared, scared of drowning in the endless rain; scared of getting his foot mired in the ankle-deep mud they seemed to stumble into constantly; scared of some pocket-sized monster leaping out of the lurid greed fronds and weeds that hung down to brush against his suit with every step; scared of encountering some wild-living relative of the foam worm that might already be gnawing its way through some part of his suit where no one would notice it until it was too late; scared of his faceplate shattering; scared he might die of a carbon-dioxide reaction, his lungs hyperventilating, panic setting in—he forced himself not to think of such things. His breath was growing short, his heart was pounding. He felt himself close to vomiting, and *that* was a real nightmare in a pressure suit. Claustrophobia. Xenophobia. Did giving it names make it easier? He forced himself to look up, forced himself to watch more than the slogging feet and lumbering backpack of the figure ahead of him, forced himself to look around, told himself that this was a whole new world of life to explore, that his tutors in a new universe of biology, themselves a wonderous find, were just a few kilometers ahead.

It seemed to help. A little. It felt like his heart rate was down.

A rifle slug screamed past his helmet and splattered the muzzle of a brightly colored, fox-sized flying beast that was diving straight for him, keening for his blood in a high-pitched shriek. It fell out of the air and landed at his feet. That Captain Larson was a good man to have at your back.

Charlie had never seen a flying animal that size. It was a whole new taxonomy, a discovery of the first importance. Time for that when they were safe. He stepped on the ruined, lovely little body rather than break stride, and kept on.

At the rear of the column, Mac wasn't in much better shape. He devoutly wished for someone to be at *his* back. That fox-bat thing had gotten too damn close. He decided to shift to heavier firepower, unloaded the slugs from the rifle and slapped in a long clip of mini-rocket rounds with explosive warheads. Those should stop damn near anything.

He got the chance to find out almost immediately. A low-slung lizard with two cruel, grasping arms that reached up for Joslyn burst from the shadows and Mac blasted it into bloody confetti. Lucy didn't even look back, she just shouted "Come on!" over the suit radio and upped the pace to a dogtrot. Even for Mac, that wasn't easy in the armored suit, carrying equipment. It must be real hell on Pete, but the middle-aged diplomat made no protest.

They slogged on and on, not going a kilometer that some nightmare beast didn't burst out at them to die under their guns. It was a grueling, mind-numbing nightmare, Lucy setting an arrow-straight course toward the beacon, Maddy just behind her, dividing her attention between the direction finder and putting one foot after another. The relentless pace ground them down into automata, capable of nothing but marching on, and gunning down anything that moved. The rain never ended, the morbid forest never ended, the cacophony of animal cries never let up. All there was left to life was the simple act of marching on.

None of them knew it had happened until it was over, and of course Madeline Madsen never knew it happened at all. Or perhaps she did, because she threw the direction finder clear, unless the herd of whatever they were simply knocked it from her grasp as they plummeted past.

One moment they were alone in the forest, just stepping out onto an empty game trail, and the next, they were watching the backs of some tawny-colored, fleet-footed herd flashing back down the pathway, carrying Madeline's new-made corpse away.

They had moved so fast! Mac had seen just the slightest

flicker of movement, and then a single, moment frozen in his memory—a long, lanky body, its claws already raking open the armor of the pressure suit as if it weren't there, life's blood already gushing from her chest, her death scream cut short, and then hunter and prey alike were gone, followed by a small herd of the fleet killers, and Pete was down, the arm of his suit torn up, and he was bleeding.

Before Mac could bring his rifle up to fire, they had vanished into the forest. Too fast! The five remaining humans stood frozen to the ground in shock, and the fear grew in all of them. Mac shook his head, came to himself, and suddenly knew that, Pete injured or no, it was death to stay near that trail. He scooped up the older man over one shoulder, and shouted "Joslyn! The finder! Lucy! Go! Go—Maddy's dead, for God's sake—before they come back! Sisulu—get your gun out and stop playing tourist. Move it!"

Lucy took off again, full tilt, and they didn't stop again until they had another five klicks between themselves and Maddy's killers. Mac called the halt, and carefully set Pete down. The three military people surrounded Pete and Charlie and stood a frightened watch as the biologist tended the wound.

Charlie did the best he could for his patient. Pete was semi-conscious, and the injury itself was pretty ugly. The claws of one of those fiends had ripped clear through the armor of the suit and torn up Pete's arm. He was was bleeding, had already lost a lot of blood. Worse, Pete was already in carbon-dioxide shock, his face gray, his breath fast and shallow. Charlie used the chest panel on Pete's suit to up the oxygen flow and set up a positive pressure flow, flushing the CO_2 out of the suit through the torn-up sleeve. Charlie pulled the first-aid kit off his backpack, cut away as little of the suit arm as possible, slathered an antiseptic/local anesthetic on the wound, and bandaged it up as best he could.

He hesitated, then used the kit's jet hypodermic to give

Pete heady doses of anti-shock drugs and a stimulant. With the loss of blood, the drugs were risky, temptation to a heart attack. But if the group was to keep any sort of pace through this nightmare world, Pete would have to be on his feet. Mac was the only person big enough to carry Pete more than a few meters, and if Mac was crippled by exhaustion, that would put everyone else at greater risk.

The first-aid kit included pressure-suit patches, and Charlie slapped the largest one on the hole. Charlie worked the suit's chest panel again, backing off the pressure setting but keeping the oxy count high. Pete's color already looked better, and his breathing seemed easier. "That's all I can do," Charlie said carefully. "He should be all right if the blood loss wasn't too bad. Let him rest easy for just a few minutes before we go on. The patch on the suit needs to set."

Joslyn, watching the forest for whatever else was out there, felt a streak of moisture run down her cheek, and hoped it was a tear and not perspiration. She wanted to mourn Maddy Madsen, a bright young kid who had come a very long way to get killed, a fine young woman entrusted to Joslyn's care, who *died* in Joslyn's care. Joslyn wanted to feel guilt, wanted to feel sorrow, wanted to cherish Madeline's memory. But danger surrounded them still, and adrenalin coursed through her veins, and fear left no room for other emotion.

Groggy, shaky, Pete came back to himself and insisted he was strong enough to walk. He barely seemed aware of what had happened. Charlie helped him to his feet, grateful for the drugs that were holding the older man together.

They marched on.

CHAPTER THIRTY

Outpost, Refiner Camp

The far sentries to the south of the camp had reported the sound of a faint far-off crash in the midst of the storm, and then an occasional ripple of rapid explosions, like many guns going off at once, and animals came charging out of the south as if pursued by something terrifying. It all brought the damnable Nihilists quite rapidly to mind. Who else would crash through the underbrush, unannounced, traveling through the hazards of the woodland instead of the relative safety of the Road?

C'astille was the only one who thought of an alternate explanation, but she did not suggest it, for she hardly dared hope it was true. She volunteered to lead the team that would venture cross-country to investigate the disturbance. Ten of them set out on foot, heavily armed, not only against the hypothetical enemy, but against the forest beasts.

C'astille led them at a good pace, and soon heard the noise of rapid-fire guns for herself. Moving cautiously, the Z'ensam let their ears guide them toward the sound. It soon became clear that not only were they moving toward the sound, but the sound was moving toward them. C'astille, for no logical reason, became more and more convinced

310

that they were tracking something far more exciting than a band of marauding Nihilists, and urged her companions onward.

It was a miracle that humans and Z'ensam didn't open fire on each other when the two groups nearly tripped over each other toward midafternoon. But C'astille was the first to spot the humans, and fortunately had the good sense to call out "Lucy! Lucy!" instead of galloping blindly forward to greet her friend. If she had taken the latter course, unquestionably she would have gotten her head blown off.

As it was, the worst she had happen to her was near-strangulation, when Lucy ran to her and flung her arms around C'astille's long neck. "Oh, C'astille! Thank God! I don't know how much farther we could have gone."

C'astille returned her friend's embrace. "Lucy!" she said in English. "You did come back. Welcome!" C'astille stepped back from her friend and turned to the other humans, who looked just a trifle alarmed at being suddenly surrounded by natives bearing what were quite obviously weapons. And it occurred to C'astille that the Z'ensam must look rather large and threatening to a human. She hurriedly signaled her companions to holster their guns, and did the same herself.

She carefully addressed the other humans in English. "My name is C'astille. In the name of D'chimchaw, Guidance of the Refiners, I bid you welcome and offer our hospitality." She had rehearsed that speech a long time, waiting for the day Lucy would bring her friends back.

The largest of the humans—in fact the largest human C'astille had yet seen—came forward and bowed. The big human, indeed all the humans, seemed exhausted to the point of collapse. "My name is Terrance MacKenzie Larson. This is Joslyn Marie Cooper Larson, Charles Sisulu, and Peter William Gesseti. In the name of the League of Planets, we thank you for your welcome."

C'astille hesitated a moment, and then recalled a thing the Guards had done. She stepped forward and reached

ut her four-thumbed hand to Terranz Mac whatever-the-
ame-was. She could practice saying it later.

Mac seemed surprised by the gesture, but then he
ooked C'astille straight in her jet-black eyes and shook
er hand in the pouring rain of Outpost's woodlands.

The weary humans were relieved beyond measure to
ind themselves with an armed escort through the deadly
orest. There was something almost anticlimactic about
heir meeting with the natives. C'astille and Lucy walked
ide by side, chattering like two long-separated school
hums in a mixture of O-1 and English that no one else
:ould follow. The other Outposters seemed curious about
hese new and strange halfwalkers, but they were used to
seeing Lucy about and some of the novelty had worn off.
Besides, none of them could speak English.

Mac, Pete, Joslyn, and Charlie could do little but try not
:o stare at their hosts. But safety, and a pressurized wagon
where they could peel off their suits, lay ahead, and that
added a spring to their step. Even so, it was near nightfall
when they finally reached the Refiner's camp, and the
humans were just barely able to do more than stagger into
the wagon and collapse that night, Pete being half-carried
by Mac and Charlie. C'astille and Lucy agreed it would be
wise to wait until morning to meet with the Guidance.

Lucy re-entered her old pressurized wagon with mixed
feelings. She was glad to see C'astille, glad to be out of
that suit, but—all that effort, simply to return to her
mobile prison! Nothing had changed in the time she had
been gone. One table, one oddly-shaped chair, the possessions she had left behind neatly stacked in a corner, the
beacon whose signal they had followed so far carefully
hung on the wall. At least she wasn't alone anymore.

Pete was weakening, rapidly, his last burst of energy
barely enough to get him to the wagon. The humans
rushed him inside as quickly as possible. Pete fainted dead
away in the airlock. They got him into the main room and
stripped the pressure suit off.

Inside it, Pete was a bloody mess, and the stink of blood and sweat filled the wagon the moment they got his helmet off. The bandages must have worked themselves loose, and Pete had bled for a long time before the wound finally had clotted up. He was pale and weak. They got his clothes off. Lucy grabbed some washing sponges and soaked them at the wagon's water spigot. They washed him down as best they could and wrapped him in blankets to keep him warm, to try and ward off shock. Charlie peeled the old dressing off and took a look at the wound. Nasty, but not dangerous. "I think he'll be all right," Charlie said. "The wound seems to have just about closed, just oozing a little bit. His real problem now is loss of blood."

Charlie was just about to put a new dressing on when the airlock thunked and an Outposter came in. He stood up. With five humans and one Outposter the size of a house in it, the wagon's interior suddenly seemed quite crowded. And Charlie was just a bit nervous about their hosts.

Lucy recognized the newcomer. "You are sensed, L'awdasi," she said in O-1.

"As are you, M'Calder. Welcome."

"Who is this, Luce?" Joslyn asked.

"This is L'awdasi. She helped to care for me, growing food, controlling the air, when I was here. I'm going to introduce you all. When I gesture toward you, bow." Lucy shifted to O-1. "L'awdasi, here are Terrance Mac-Kenzie Larson, Joslyn Marie Cooper Larson, and Charles Sisulu. The one lying down is Peter Gesseti. He is unconscious. He was hurt by a beast in the forest, and we fear that he might not live. Another of our party was killed at the same time."

"Yes, C'astille told me of this, and I came to see for myself." L'awdasi stepped forward to get a look at Pete, and Lucy noticed the Outposter had a satchel slung over her neck. L'awdasi pointed at Pete's arm. "This is the wound? This is the danger?"

"Yes, though the wound itself should heal. But he has

lost much—a word I do not know. You see the red fluid oozing from the cut? It is called *blood*. It carries oxygen through our bodies and does other important things."

"Ah." Lucy was unaware of it, but perhaps the best description of L'awdasi's occupation might be veterinarian. L'awdasi was keenly interested in the halfwalker's biology, and had even secured a few samples of Lucy's skin, hair, and waste products. She had gotten the samples without telling anyone or asking permission, as she had the feeling someone was bound to disapprove.

But circulatory fluid was one thing she hadn't gotten. She had never seen a wound, never seen any part of the *insides* of a human. When she had heard of what had happened, she had scooped up her work satchel and come, not quite sure what she intended. She craned her neck down to get a better look at Pete's arm. The wound was still oozing . . . L'awdasi *had* to have a sample of that fluid—perhaps she could even do the halfwalkers some good. Hardly believing her own daring, she pulled a glass sample tube from her satchel, knelt, and filled the tube from the slow stream of red dribbling out of the wound.

Lucy looked on, astonished. None of the other humans dared to move. L'awdasi stoppered the sample tube, slipped it back in her work satchel. She looked around at the alien faces, staring at her with great intensity. She decided it would be wisest to retreat, offer them no chance to demand an explanation. "Departure is now," she said to Lucy, careful formality in her voice and bearing. Without another word, she left.

Charlie was dumbfounded. "What in the devil was *that* all about?"

Lucy shook her head, as baffled as the rest. "I don't know. I wish I did." It took moments like that to remind her just how little she knew about the Z'ensam. "Come on, let's get Mr. Gesseti as comfortable as we can and then get some rest. We all need it."

L'awdasi couldn't sleep that night. She was too excited.

For the first time, she had *living* samples, functioning cells, from a human being, from an entirely new and novel field of biology. She lumbered around her laboratory, examining the blood under microscopes, through filters, in a gaseous emissions tester, in a dozen devices. Human biochemists wouldn't recognize most of the machinery. If Charlie Sisulu knew what L'awdasi could do in her lab, he would have gladly traded off his soul for the chance to do a day's work there.

L'awdasi worked tirelessly. The clues she had gathered from Lucy's dead cells and waste-product bacteria were a great help. She understood everything she saw, almost *before* she saw it. She examined the various forms of white blood cells, and instantly realized these were the ancestors of some free-living form that had married itself to the bloodstream long, long ago, earning its keep by warding off less benign invaders. She admired the economy of the red blood cells. No nucleus, just the bare bones of hemoglobin transfer. But without a nucleus, the red cells could not reproduce themselves. Could they? She searched the red cells, and found no means by which they could breed themselves. But clearly the whites could and did reproduce themselves. She caught one in the very act of becoming two, and learned much. The gene structure was fantastic, clearly far more resistant to mutation than the Outposter equivalent of chromosomes. Then why was there such a great variation within the human population? L'awdasi had seen five humans with her own eyes, and pictures of many more—and *none* of them looked much alike. If the genes resisted mutation, everyone should look and be the same. Stranger still, there seemed to be no mechanism for transfer of acquired characteristic. The life of the human world must evolve with glacial slowness! But that same mutation resistance meant the human cell-stuff could be safely manipulated. And if the red cells were manufactured by some means external to themselves. . . . L'awdasi got what was a wild idea, even for her. The plasma would be trivial. But how to spawn the cells?

She dove into the problem with manic enthusiasm.

It was a long night, but perhaps the most exciting one of L'awdasi's life. The rain had stopped, and the sun was creeping up the eastern sky when she cantered back to the humans' wagon. She cycled through the airlock as quietly as she could, restraining a sneeze when the chill-smelling, lifeless air the humans breathed tickled her blowhole. The air mix would sicken her if she stayed too long, but L'awdasi thought she could work fast. The four healthy ones slept, wrapped up in blankets on the floor. They must have been exhausted, for she managed to move her bulky self without waking them, carrying her gear carefully to keep it from clattering and clacking.

The injured one, M'Gegetty Lucy had called him, lay still and pale on the floor, his skin cool, almost transparent. There was some sort of covering on the wound, no doubt to shield its ugliness from view for the humans.

There was one last challenge, the most trivial, and yet one that almost stymied her. But she understood circulatory systems. Working by guess, luck, logic, intuition and analogy, she found a vein and gently inserted the needle. But then she was stuck holding the bottle aloft by hand.

Thirteen hours after seeing human blood for the first time, L'awdasi had invented transfusion.

Charlie awoke with a start to see L'awdasi's rather ample hindquarters taking up his entire field of vision. Cautiously, he got up to see what she was doing—and let out a shout that woke everyone else and almost spooked L'awdasi into stampeding through the wall.

The damn fool 'Poster was doing sympathetic magic! Something red had come out, so it was putting something red in. Pete jerked his arm as he woke, his color better and his mind clear the moment he woke. He looked up into the face of a leather-skinned monster who was holding what looked like a three-liter bottle of blood in midair, and decided he was still hallucinating.

Joslyn, Mac, and Lucy jumped to their feet and saw an alarmed L'awdasi backing away from a spluttering, horrified Charlie. The biologist wanted to rip out the needle, but God knew what damage that could do. He reached in and pinched the feedline, cutting off the flow of blood, careful to stay as far from the Outposter as possible.

"Lieutenant Calder! Tell it to stop! Tell it to get that needle out of his arm!" The poor son of a bitch was probably as good as dead already, with red paint coursing through his veins, but there might still be hope if they stopped it in time.

"L'awdasi!" Lucy shouted in O-1. "What action is this? Do you seek M'Gesetti's death? That needle must come out at once!"

L'awdasi looked from one human to another, shocked, terrified. Her mad enthusiasm for the experiment vanished in a moment. These were not animals, these were thinking being! And she had dared to practice *medicine* on them. The enormity of the insult to them was beyond exaggeration.

Without a word, she pulled the needle, handed the transfusion bottle to Charlie, and left, leaving all her equipment behind.

There would a terrible reckoning for this. She had to speak with the Guidance, confess what she had done, before the damage was made worse.

If it *could* be made worse.

Charlie wasted not a moment. If he could identify the stuff L'awdasi had been pumping into Pete, maybe there was something in his portable field lab or the first-aid kit to counteract it. There was a sophisticated miniature automated analyzer in the lab. He got it out, gave it a sample from the 'Poster's bottle full of fluid, and set it running. He pulled his rugged field microscope from the lab kit, got a sample of the stuff onto a slide, and took a look at it.

And took another look. He squirted a little of the red liquid onto his fingertip and sniffed it. He hesitated a moment, then tasted it. That same salty flavor he got from a cut lip. The analyzer pinged and ejected a hard copy of its report. It had matched the sample with some substance stored in its memory. Charlie didn't really have to look at the read-out, but he examined it with great care anyway. It eased the shock, somehow, to see it in print like that.

"It's blood," he said, dumbfounded. "Perfectly normal whole human blood. Red cells, all the white cells, plasma, clotting factors, everything. Type A positive. The Outposter matched it from the sample she took last night."

Pete remembered that was *his* blood type, looked at the puncture mark where the needle had been, realized that this was no fever dream, and fainted dead away.

Lucy was the first of them to regain her wits. She ate a quick breakfast and hurried out in search of C'astille. She was gone a few hours, during which time the rest of the humans were left completely alone, and elected not to venture outside the wagon. When Pete awakened, looking much recovered and alert, all of them had a field-ration breakfast.

When Lucy returned, she seemed more baffled then when she left. "I had to wait on C'astille until after a meeting of the Guidance and all the other grand poohbahs," she said. "C'astille suggested that both sides agree that nothing ever happened," she said. "It sounded like the best idea to me. Apparently, L'awdasi went straight to the Guidance and confessed her terrible crime, and the whole controlling group nearly went bouncing off the wall that she would dare perform medicine on a thinking species. The way she put it, trying to save Pete's life was a deadly insult, a breach of a strong tabu like incest or cannibalism. They think *that's* why we got upset, not because L'awdasi blundered in here and treated him within explaining what she was doing. They were quite relieved that we weren't insulted enough to call in an air strike. I seriously think they were expecting us to react that harshly."

Lucy took a cup of tea and went on. "C'astille was

always a little cool toward L'awdasi when I was here before, and I think I've found out why. She's the camp veterinarian, more or less, and she was in charge of taking care of me. Veterinary medicine, I guess, is just barely socially acceptable. Don't ask me why being fed and cared for by the vet isn't an insult."

Charlie stared at her. "Wait a minute. Medicine is *tabu*? But these guys are the greatest bio-engineers anyone has ever seen!"

"Only with animals and plants. Not on themselves. Now that I come to think of it, I've never seen any Outposter treated for any illness, but on the other hand I never really noticed anyone who was taken sick, and their hides are tough enough to protect them against most natural enemies."

"But it doesn't make sense," Charlie insisted. "A really good strong tabu like incest or cannibalism always has some good strong practical reason behind it, even if people aren't aware of them. Commit incest and you get inbred, sickly babies. Commit cannibalism and you're liable to catch whatever killed the other guy—besides getting the diner's family very mad at you. What could drive a medicine tabu?"

Lucy shook her head. "I don't know."

Mac looked worried, and he had every good reason to be. "Lucy, I think we've got to think about the bug-out option."

"Already?" Lucy said. She thought for a moment, and sighed. "I suppose you're right. If we're into this much of a mess before breakfast, what could happen by dinner?"

Pete spoke. "Hold it. What's the bug-out option?"

Man started gathering up the litter of breakfast. "Lucy and I worked it out before we left the *Eagle*. We thought it might be possible that we would have to get the hell out of here before the League was in a position to come get us." He hesitated. "And if the League loses, God forbid, we still want a way out of here. We've got the beacon. The Guards, so far as we know, don't monitor that frequency—

which is why Lucy and Gustav picked it. But Cynthia Wu aboard *Ariadne* is watching it. It's just sending a steady tone now—but we can hook a mike into it, tell Wu to send to us on another frequency we've got the gear to listen on, and talk."

"And we tell *Ariadne* to send us a pick-up ship, something we can run like hell in if we have to. Some ship that can reach the barycenter or the League, and tell them what we have learned about the Outposters."

Pete was astonished. "Mac, we came down here knowing we were risking our lives. If we're going to cut and run the moment we're in danger, we shouldn't have bothered coming. And this Gustav character sounds like a valuable asset. Our side can't risk him just for our sakes."

Joslyn knew her husband, understood what he was thinking. "It's not us dying, it's the *knowledge* dying, or the knowledge going straight to the Guards and not to our people," she said. "With what we've found out today, already, we are the best-informed League personnel. It happens that the knowledge we've gained makes our hosts think they've insulted us. Suppose that runs the other way? Suppose some innocent bit of knowledge about us is a deadly insult to them? Suppose they kill us, and sign up with the Nihilists? We have to be ready to warn our side."

Lucy wanted to protest Joslyn's hypothetical case, but there was too much truth in it. She had lived among these people for months, and still was shocked by what she learned. "A little knowledge," she said, "is a dangerous thing."

CHAPTER THIRTY-ONE

Aboard *Ariadne*

"You're certain the signals were authentic?" Gustav asked.

"Absolutely," Cynthia Wu replied. "It was Lucille Calder, and she handed the mike to both Mac and Joslyn Larson. I recognized all three voices."

Gustav allowed himself to close his eyes and breath a sigh of relief. So far, she was still alive. But there were other considerations. He thought carefully, and stared up at the ceiling. He looked tired, drawn. "Okay. Two reports. One, Cynthia Wu shot trying to escape. Tonight. You vanish now. Two, loss of a ballistic lander two days from now. That's still putting the incidents too close together, but I don't know what else to do. I'll tell them a fusion system malfunction on the lander forced us to cut it loose and dump it into the planet's oceans by remote control before it blew. You stow away in the lander tonight—and don't touch the controls until the remote system is cut off. In the report, I try and distract them from my incompetence by complaining that this is the third fusion malf in two months, and that we were just lucky to get the first two under control. I ignore the fact that the previous complaints were phonies I sent in myself for versimillitude in case I needed a lander to vanish. I assume your people found the unaccounted for C^2 generator that wound up in the quartermaster's shop last week? It wasn't easy to arrange."

"Spotted it the day it arrived. The crate's already filled with scrap instead, and we have the C^2 unit hidden. Schiller will smuggle it aboard the lander tonight, and I can wait to do the actual installation once I'm on the planet."

"Good. Any questions?" Still, Gustav stared at the featureless ceiling. His fingers fussed anxiously with the buttons of his tunic.

"Two. First off, how sure can you be that they won't catch on?"

"They'll be too busy. In a few days' time the Guardians launch their counter-offensive. I don't know exactly when. No one in the fleet will have time to investigate a penny-ante engineering malf, and who ever cares about a CI to start with? I hope. And once that battle is over, no matter who wins, this little scheme won't really affect me one way or the other. If the Guards win, and have the leisure to investigate what's been going on around here—they can only shoot me once. If the League wins, I don't know and never have known what happens to me. What was the other question?"

"You want the war ended so it won't expand any more than it has. You want the killing to stop. I understand that. But this—it's not directly related. Why are you doing it? Why are you risking so much for this?"

For the first time, Gustav looked down, and stared straight at Cynthia. "Because," he said, "*she's* down there."

CHAPTER THIRTY-TWO

Outpost, Refiner Camp

Everything was a bit stuck until Pete got stronger. He was the only one of the League group empowered to discuss much of anything with any real authority. He was prepared to discuss technology trades, exchanges of ambassadors (or whatever the local equivalent was), and most importantly, a mutual assistance pact against the Guards and the Nihilists. But it would have to wait—and the flap over the transfusion made the situation that much more delicate.

All the humans were dumbfounded by the way L'awdasi, by all accounts a mere hobbyist in such things, had duplicated human blood overnight, but Charlie Sisulu was hit much harder by it than the rest. He knew better than the others just how complicated blood was. And if one amateur Outposter could do that overnight, what could a team of crack professionals do in a week, given the raw materials of a few human cells to work with? Clone a man? Clone an army of men? If they could make blood, surely they could make diseases, nightmare plagues. And none of them had even *seen* a human before last year. And with such biological power, what could they do to each *other*? With a biological science that powerful, Charlie could almost understand the medical tabu. Better the thousand natural shocks than the unnatural horrors a thousand L'awdasis might accidentally whip up any weekend.

And yet, it didn't quite play. Any element of human medicine could be abused, used to kill, from a scalpel used to slash a throat to an overdose of aspirin. Humankind had had the knowledge to unleash plagues at will for one hundred fifty years—but that didn't make anyone want to ban doctors.

Well, no percentage in playing until he understood the game. And Charlie did not yet know enough.

Lucy had mentioned to C'astille that Charlie was a biologist, and C'astille had instantly wanted to talk with him. There were a hundred questions she wanted to ask. Charlie, needless to say, was delighted with the chance himself. So, an hour or two after getting the message safely off to *Ariadne*, C'astille met the two humans by the entrance of their wagon and the three of them went for a walk. C'astille led them to a quiet corner of the clearing. The two humans sat down on the ground, a bit awkward in their pressure suits. C'astille folded her legs up beneath herself and curled her long tail around her body. Lucy thought the moment proper to offer her gift, the big picture book of Earth and the solar system. She pulled it out of her carrypack. "Here you go, C'astille," she said. "Take a look at this and you'll be all set to play tourist when you get there."

C'astille took the book eagerly, and spent a half hour with the humans, pointing to the pictures and asking endless questions. Lucy was pleased to have chosen a gift her friend enjoyed so much. It was good to get to safety, to the protection of the Refiners. The biggest part of her duty seemed to have been done. Charlie seemed far less relaxed. He found it very strange and incongruous to sit back in the grasslands, here on this world, with the sun shining, the sky blue, the area cleared of rapacious animals. To Charlie, Outpost would always be that deadly trek through the forest, and all the planet's other moods mere trickery and misdirection.

It was stranger still to sit with a six-limbed thinking creature nearly the size of a small horse, with a long reptilian tail, and big doll's eyes set in the front of that strange, egg-on-its-side-shaped skull—a creature who thought nothing of creating whole human blood from scratch overnight.

He found himself watching her hands most of all. Four long, slender fingers, all opposable to each other. Those were graceful, toolmakers' hands, strange to watch in their fluid motions that did what human hands did, but in a radically different way.

Finally, he got a bit tired of Lucy and the 'Poster oohing and aahing over pictures of Paris and the Outback and the space colonies. "C'astille," he said at last, in as cheerful a tone as he could manage. "We need to get started. I am so curious about you and your world! You said you wished to ask me questions, and I promise you I can match you, bafflement for bafflement. Time is short, so perhaps we might begin?"

C'astille nodded and regretfully closed the picture book. "You are right. The lovely pictures must wait until later. You have travelled far, at great risk, and the time might come quickly when we will need knowledge of each other."

"Good!" Charlie replied. "But let me say one more thing. Our peoples are quite strange to each other, and there is much we would know. Some questions might be delicate, but we have no way of knowing which ones. So if I speak rudely, I do not mean to, and I ask that you excuse me. Lucy and I will likewise not take offense, for we know none is meant."

"Thank you!" C'astille said. "I have been hunting the words to say that to you. I am glad you found them for me. And I'll test your promise about taking offense at once," she said with a cheerful tone. "L'awdasi, in the non-incident of this morning, noted something about your genes. Due to their structure, they are far less liable to mutation than our own. That would suggest that your species should look much more like one another than ours does—and yet just the opposite is true."

Charlie smiled thinly. He thought of a lot of people back home on Earth who would say otherwise—"they all look the same to me." Black, yellow, white, whatever, he had heard people of every color say that about people of every other color. "Let me save you some time, C'astille. You're leading up to asking why I in particular look so much more different than the other humans you have seen. Why is my skin so dark, why is my hair curly, why are my nose and lips wider?"

"Yes, I suppose that you're one example. But this Mac M'Larson must be twice the size of Lucy here, and she and Joslyn have quite different proportions than the rest of you."

Charlie found himself vaguely embarrassed. What could this extraterrestrial know of racial tension, of guilt and anger for deeds done a hundred, a thousand years before? She asked about variation in a population and he got his back up on the old prejudices. "Hmmm. Well, let me explain my case. Maybe that would help illustrate the others. Forgive me if I simplify a bit, but here is the basic explanation.

"All our people probably started out looking pretty much alike, when they all lived in one place, one climate. But our race, *homo sapiens*, humankind, had settled over pretty much all of our home world, Earth, by about forty thousand years ago, maybe a bit earlier. Some people lived in cold parts that didn't get much sun. Mac's ancestors came from such a place. Light-skinned people can absorb a lot of something in sunlight that humans need to stay healthy, because their skin is transparent enough to let in a large fraction of the light. My ancestors grew up in a place with very strong sunlight. Their skin needed to be dark to protect them from getting *too much* light.

"In Mac's part of the world, if your skin was too dark, you were likely to get sick and die from a lack of this special thing in sunlight. So mostly light-skinned people, with genes for light skin, survived to pass on their genes. In my part of the world, if you were too light-skinned the sun was so strong it could kill you. So only darker people, with genes for dark skin, survived. People in temperate climates survived best with a skin color somewhere in the middle. Once people had invented civilization, and could control their environments more, it didn't really matter what color you were, so there were no selection pressures for one shade over another and people moved about as they wished. The other differences between us have similar explanations. The people who survived in various spots on the globe and lived to have children were the ones who, by chance, had traits and genes for those traits that gave them a little edge over everyone else. Obviously, they passed their genes on to their children. But in terms of evolution, these differences are trivial. We are all one species, but with each individual still carrying around adaptations to whatever climate his or her ancestors lived in."

The explanation didn't seem to satisfy C'astille altogether. "I see. But while she was with us, Lucy's skin grew darker, and she explained this was a reaction to the sunlight. Suppose that she bore children while she was here and her skin was dark. Wouldn't those children start out darker, inheriting the tendency for darker skin?"

"No, no, of course not. That would be inheritance of acquired traits. Let's see. What would be a clearer example? Okay. There's an animal on Earth called a giraffe. It has a very long neck, perhaps two meters long, and the long neck helps it eat leaves at the tops of trees no other animal can reach.

"Long ago, it used to be thought that some short-necked proto-giraffe managed to stretch its neck through exercise, and passed that slightly longer neck along to its offspring, and the offspring did the same, and so on. The theory had

the physical shape of the body affecting the genes, and not
the other way around. That's the classic example of inheritance of acquired characteristics, or Lamarckism, after the
man who thought of it. But it doesn't work."

C'astille looked straight at Charlie, and pulled her head
in toward her body in surprise. "On Outpost, it *does*
work," she said, in a strange, querulous voice. "If I cut off
my finger, within a month the regulator cells of my body
will record the change and implant it in my ovaries. My
children, and their children, and theirs, will have a finger
missing. Or perhaps they will carry the gene for a missing
finger from one generation to the next, until it shows up
again, after skipping many generations."

Charlie stared back at her, astonished. Real, honest-to-
God Lamarckian biology? It was incredible, but it explained so much. He was tempted to contradict her, to say
that it must be a superstition, that she had to be wrong.
But these people were *master* biologists. They would *know*.
The implications went reeling through his head. It was a
revelation of the greatest importance. Lamarckism! It must
have shaped their skill in modifying and creating life forms.
It must have been easy to create a new and different
animal with simple surgery. They would have been past
masters at bio-engineering before they even invented the
microscope and learned to manipulate genes directly.

All of that shot through his mind in a moment. "That's
fantastic, C'astille," he almost shouted. "It's so unexpected,
so astonishing I don't know what to say. The implications—
my God, they're endless!"

Lucy looked from her human companion to the Outposter
and back. There was a strange sense in the air, a feeling of
being on the edge of a terrible truth. "Charlie—C'astille.
What's the big deal? You both look so shocked. So
Outposters and humans evolve in different ways. So what?"

"Lucy," C'astille said, speaking with a cautious precision. "Charlie and I have just stumbled across a fact that
explains many of the differences between our peoples. It
makes you more different from us than I had ever imag-

ined. We Z'ensam wondered at your lack of skill in shaping life. Now I understand. It must take a dozen generation to shape even the slightest modification of Earth life. Given the restraint you have worked under, I am amazed that you have learned as much as you have."

Charlie wasn't listening. A thousand new ideas were racing through his head. "Medicine!" he cried out, so wrapped up in his own amazement that he didn't consider the results of what he was saying. "Given Lamarckian biology, the tabu against medicine makes sense! A clumsy doctor's mistake could cripple not just one person, but all the generations unborn. An early experiment, say equivalent to boring a hole in the skull to let evil spirits out, could literally leave scars that would last forever. If the genes were recessive, old artificial genetic flaws like that lie dormant and could pop up anywhere, anytime, dozens of generations later!"

"They do 'pop up,'" C'astille said grimly, "to the present generation. We pay the price for the mischief the body-carvers made thousands of years ago. There are endless folktales of the too-proud fool who promised to 'solve' an illness and left a hideous wreck of a creature behind, one who would pass her deformities down through the genes of all her descendants." C'astille's powerful tail lashed angrily back and forth through the grass. She suddenly seemed much larger, much fiercer, more alien, more unknowable, more unreadable to Lucy than she ever had before. "Lucy, you must answer a most distasteful question. This Charlie has implied that medicine in *not* tabu among humans. Is this true? Does your kind willingly and shamelessly allow the body-carvers, the animal-healers, to play God with your bodies?"

Lucy was tempted to lie. There was nothing but trouble in an honest answer. But she thought of Peter Gesseti and his bandaged arm. It would be hard to hide that. Worse, C'astille counted Lucy as trustworthy, and being *worthy* of trust required that Lucy speak truly when the truth could but hurt her. She spoke at last, and spoke slowly, choosing each word. "There is no tabu against medicine. We call our body-carvers 'doctors' and hold their profession in the highest esteem. In its own way, the skill of our healers is as great as the skill of your bio-engineers. They have eliminated many diseases and causes of death. Our race has benefited greatly from medicine, and for creatures made as we are, there is no cause to ban the practice of healing."

To C'astille, it was as if Lucy had claimed there was no harm in being a child molester, or a murderer. "Revulsion is within me," the native said in her own tongue.

Lucy almost switched to O-1 as well to placate C'astille. But no, then Charlie would be left in the dark. And Lucy knew C'astille well enough to know that shifting away from English was a way of rejecting things human. She couldn't let her get away with that. Lucy replied in English. "C'astille! Judge not. My ways are not yours. Your culture and mine were shaped by our biology. I have heard time and time again about frequent, even routine, death by suicide and *murder* among your elderly. No words of this have been spoken between us, for one must not judge what one does not understand. *I* still have no understanding. Yet, among humans, such things would be grave crimes, sins of the darkest kind. Your complaints against the Nihilists are subdued, as if you mildly objected to some of their techniques. To me, they are merciless, amoral killers.

"The early would-be healers among the Z'ensam killed and maimed, and so you banned healing. So be it. Very well. It must be that your clinging to that tabu means your people die of infection and injury and illness, though with your current skill you could save them. But I will not judge.

"*Our* healers save our lives, and our children's lives, and do great good. I do not apologize for them, or for us."

C'astille grunted, a deep, guttural, non-committal noise, before she replied. "You say that you do not condone suicide and mercy killing for those humans near Division, 'elderly' as you say. You call it amoral. What honor, what morality, in letting them go their way to foolishness and idiocy?"

"You make my point for me. Foolishness and idiocy rarely come to an elder human. Some small number, yes. But the risk is small."

"Then humans remain sane after Division, after becoming implanters?" There was shocked surprise in C'astille's voice.

Lucy opened her mouth to reply, shut it, and stared at C'astille. It all fell into place. It was in that moment that Lucy finally understood. The cryptic remarks, the Outposter's confusion over pronouns, the obsession with "Division" made sense. Terrible, nightmare sense. She wished desperately for time to think, but there was none. *This* was the moment. "Charlie, I've just figured it out! C'astille, there is a horrible, ghastly misunderstanding here, and it's all my fault, because all the human understanding of your culture is based on *my* work, my initial translation of your language. And I made a terrible mistake. From the first time I heard the term 'Division' I assumed it was a euphemism, a prettied-up, polite word for 'death.' But that's wrong. It means something else, doesn't it?"

"Death!" C'astille said in amazement. "No! Division is—Division is the revenge Life takes on us for our intelligence. That is what the Nihilists, and all the other similar Groups of the past, have had as a starting point. To them, death is a welcome means of escape from Division. Our studiers of society say that our population has never been large enough to support a city-based culture *because* so many escape into death."

Lucy nodded emphatically. "This is all suddenly making sense in my mind. Let me ask you another question. The English terms 'male' and 'female,' 'man' and 'woman'—what do they mean to you?"

C'astille clenched and unclenched her fingers, the

Outposter equivalent of a shrug. "They refer to the two basic body shapes for humans. You are female, and Charlie is male. That much I understand. But you have always attached great importance to the concepts, and to using the proper pronoun for male and female. I've never quite understood why. Why do your pronouns focus on that minor a difference? Why not a pronoun-set based on height, or eye color? Such would make.as much sense."

"Did you ever get the idea that the reason might have something to do with—Jesus, Charlie, me and my bloody Baptist upbringing! I don't think I ever got around to explaining the words 'sex' or 'reproduction.' C'astille, did you ever get the idea 'male' and 'female' might refer to the way humans make more humans?"

"No, not really. Perhaps in the vaguest little way, some slight hint, but I did not wish to ask about such a distasteful thing."

"Ah."

Charlie couldn't contain himself anymore. "Excuse us a minute, C'astille. I think I just need to have Lucy bring me up to date." He pulled the phono jack from his suit and plugged it into the comm panel on Lucy's suit. Both of them cut their external mikes and radio. "Lucy, what's going on here?" he demanded. "How could they *not* have the concepts of male and female? I got a good look at C'astille and that L'awdasi. They were both obviously female. And I saw some little ones around the camp."

"Charlie. Take a look around at all the Z'ensam when we're back at camp. *All* of them look to be 'obviously female.' Until now I took it to mean that appearances were deceiving, or else they had some sort of divided society. I never figured it out. Until now. Shut up and listen. And for God's sake, if you have to talk, be careful what you say." Lucy pulled the connection, and switched her radio back on.

Lucy felt her heart pounding. She knew, somehow she *knew*, that she was at the crux of everything, at the threshold of the central fact of being an Outposter, a

Z'ensam. And she also *knew* that there was danger, terrible danger, in the knowledge. "Our apologies, C'astille. Charlie wasn't clear on why I was asking such things," she said in a gentle, quiet voice. "Tell me something. Tell me the life cycle of the Z'ensam. Tell me it as if I knew nothing. Tell me the way you'd explain it to a child."

C'astille stared at Lucy for a long moment. "There is a rhyme for young ones," she said at last. "Well, let me try and recite the sense of it in English for Charlie's benefit:

"First there are babies, to play and learn.
Then the adults, to bear young, reason, and teach.
Then the adult is taken by Division in the cocoon's fast
    womb.
At last, the implanter, more foolish than any child, is
    flown from its cocoon, reason having flown long ago.
Bewitched by the implanter, the adult makes children,
    and so the middle link joins end with beginning."

Lucy said "C'astille, I think I understand. But there must be no mistakes. The time has come when we must risk knowing each other, even if we don't like what we find. Tell me."

"You are right. That poem is so cryptic that I must say more. Especially to aliens. But, please, this is very difficult for me, for any Z'ensam, to speak of. Your medicine is polite conversation by comparison! So—each individual goes through the phases—child, born to adult. Adult, such as myself. There is no clear line between child and adult. One day it is recognized that a child has learned enough. It was a proud day when I was called C'astille and not O'astille, *O'* being the name-prefix of a child. The name prefixes are based on social status, by the way, not biological state. Someday, I will be M'astille, and then perhaps D'astille. I am still young, and there are perhaps thirty of your years before I must face the process of Division, the next biological phase. When Division comes, it takes only a few days. The first sign is a long red welt that forms down the length of the body.

"That is the sign for a Z'ensam to find a safe place. The body—collapses. The skin turns rock-hard to protect against predators. Internally, the body—I do not know a better English word—the body *digests* itself, reforms itself. Only a very small fraction of the body weight emerges from the body-cocoon, as an implanter.

"These implanters, then—when they find an adult who is ready to bear young, they—they *come* to that adult, join with the adult. They place within the adult their seed, which combines with the adult's seed, and grows into children, born some months later. When the implanter comes for you it is a terrible and debasing experience. It has only happened a few times to me, and as yet I have no children. But, when the implanter comes you are *compelled*, by feelings and sensations strong beyond imagining, to submit and cooperate. Nature would have it so, or else the Z'ensam would be no more. But be it unavoidable, be it beyond our control, be it necessary, we find it shameful to be taken so by the mindless implanters, and mortifying to know we will one day be like them. So we do not fault the Nihilists overmuch for offering escape.

"That is our way. I have gradually realized your way is different. Now you must explain it."

A thousand thoughts flashed through Lucy's mind, and she wished desperately for a chance to talk with Charlie privately. But C'astille was already suspicious; another humans-only chat would make it seem as if they were lying, trying to make up a story.

But no wonder the 'Posters didn't understand the male/female dichotomy. Each 'Poster was first sentient female—adult—and later non-sentient male—implanter—in turn. Whether or not you had a mind was more important in defining yourself than what shape your genitals were. Female/male was submerged under thinking/nonthinking. Lucy knew how careful she would have to be in her answer. "It is quite different. One is born either an immature adult or immature implanter. In either case, one grows up, lives and dies as one or the other. The two kinds come together, as you two kinds do, and the adults bear the children, usually only one at a time."

There was a strange, half envious, half-astonished tone to C'astille's voice when she responded. "You—you adults. You never lose the power of thought? You remain sane and wise all your lives?"

"The vast majority do. But as the body ages and wears out, occasionally the brain, the seat of the mind, wears out as well, and in such cases the mind weakens with the brain. But this is much rarer than it once was." The moment Lucy had finished the last sentence, she wished she had withheld it.

" 'Less often' thanks to your wonderful medicine, no doubt," C'astille said bitterly. She shook her head, a human mannerism she had picked up. "Whatever god formed your kind was kindlier than our creators. My life, my culture, my people, are formed, warped, distorted by the certainty that madness and idiocy will overtake any who do not choose to flee the world by suicide. To have the foreknowledge that I would stay sane . . ."

"C'astille." Charlie spoke, for the first time in a long time. Philosophy was all very well, but they needed more hard facts. Where the hell were the males? "I would like to ask for something, a favor. It might not be possible for you to do it, or it might be painful or distasteful for you. If so, I withdraw the request. But I would like to see one of your kind in the implanter phase."

The skin on the Outposter's head wrinkled up in humorless amusement. "Then you have seen them and not known it. Did you not know what they were, Lucy? Did you not wonder why we kept them around? Come, I will show you." Abruptly, she got to her feet and trotted off into the underbrush, forcing the humans to scramble after to keep up. "Let me ask you another two words I never quite learned, Lucy." C'astille stared straight ahead, not looking back at her companions, and there was a brittle sharpness to her voice. "The adult who gave birth to me, what is the English for that? And what would you call the responsible implanter."

Lucy ran to catch up, drew up alongside C'astille's head. In a low, hushed, voice, Lucy said "Mother. The English is mother. And the implanter who joined with her to form you—that would be your father."

"Ah. I see. Thank you." C'astille slowed her pace slightly. "We'll be there in a few minutes."

Lucy trudged along in her armored pressure-suit cocoon, shielded from the stench and the dangers of Outpost, only the visual beauty of the day able to penetrate to her. She felt tired, ashamed, guilty, appalled. Madness! Madness, idiocy, and the *foreknowledge* of coming madness and idiocy the common lot of *every person.* Nature, Earth's kindly Mother Nature, had shielded her children far better. Could humans have built a culture if their biological heritage had been as cruel as the Z'ensams'? The caravans, the fledgling cities, the tiny population that wouldn't—no, she realized, *couldn't* control the rapacious Hungry Ones. Those were accomplishments to rival anything humans had done, in the face of such a mocking, demeaning life cycle.

C'astille led them into a tiny glade. "They like this place, when we camp here. It is near us, and yet they can play undisturbed. They will be nearby." C'astille raised her head and let out a strange, high-pitched keening.

It took Lucy a second or two to recognize that call. That was the sound they used to call the—

And there they were. Stumblebugs. Wings flapping, coming from all around them, fluttering down to landings in the grass. The laughing, giggling comedians, the silly pets the Z'ensam kept, the pretty, multi-colored, cat-sized flying beasts that Lucy had loved to play with, the cute little things that knew a word or two of O-1. Lucy had even taught a few of them a word or two of English.

She recognized one of them. The most foolish of them

all, the one she had named Zipper for the way he flew so fast.

Zipper spotted Lucy, and let out a cheerful squeak. He hopped over to her, swished his tail back and forth, and chirped "Cookie? Cookie?"

In a voice near to breaking, C'astille said "Lucy M'Calder. Charlie M'Sisulu. Allow me to present Ameser, whom you call Zipper. Allow me to present my father."

"Cookie?"

Lucy tried to speak, but the tears welled up in eyes, ran down her cheek. Her voice choked up, and she let out a strangled sob. She raised her hands to her face, tried to wipe away the tears, but the helmet stopped her hands. She sobbed uncontrollably.

Charlie felt his bile rising, felt the urge to run home to Earth, to claw his way up the sky to a place where the rules of life were not so brutish. These were civilized people, but their creator was a barbarian.

"Cookie?"

Slowly, all too slowly, Lucy forced herself to be calm. She tried to think coldly, to analyze. The irony of it! For she could see at once that culture-making, intelligence itself, were lethal mutations here. From the point of view of a reproductive strategy, from the viewpoint of evolution, the transition of each individual from female to male made good sense. The ancestors of the Z'ensam, who had not yet evolved intelligence, must have been served well by the pattern of their lives. It was the females, the mothers, that needed the smarts, the big brains, the brawn, to shelter and protect the children. And child rearing would be a shared duty in a herd species. The herds, ancestors of the Groups, would have cooperated in raising young. And the males, the flying males, would have been capable of travelling great distances, keeping the gene pool well mixed in the small, widely dispersed population. They could spread any advantageous mutation rapidly, and also ensure that the species stayed genetically cohesive. And each individual had a double chance to spread her/his genes around.

Only when the females developed true sentience, only when they developed the ability to reason and remember and communicate, would the strategy backfire. A thinking creature would *know* she was the offspring of a mindless animal, fated to mate with an animal, fated to *become* an animal.

How many humans, suffering brain damage or disease, confronted with the prospect of madness, had killed themselves rather than degenerate? And that happened to *all* the Z'ensam!

No wonder it was impossible for them to maintain a stable population. No wonder it was easy to find empty camps, the building left by some group of Z'ensam that had just given up. . . .

Lucy thought of her own mother, still strong and sturdy, warm-hearted and sharp-witted, if a bit grayed and tired. Senility, at worst a faint and far-off danger, was nowadays largely preventable. And her father. Her strong, happy, laughing, clever, kindly father, full of wisdom and understanding when his children needed him.

What would she, Lucy, be like, what bitterness would every human child carry inside, if they knew their fathers were mindless brutes?

"Well, then," C'astille said. She looked down at the pathetic, bewildered Zipper, the little fool wondering why his friends were all so sad. "You have seen my future. A gibbering fool who can be trained, with great effort, to ask for a cookie. And this will not happen to you, and that will scar the relations of our species for the rest of time. That saddens me.

"But, I must confess some curiosity. Something I have wondered about, and never dared to ask. But you have seen ours, and turnabout is fair play. You didn't bring them along, of course. But tell me about them. Describe your implanters to me."

Charlie looked sharply at Lucy. *My God*, he thought, *Lucy's little description of our life cycle*—she left out that males had minds! C'astille still thinks I'm a female! He caught Lucy's eye, and she nodded. The truth was going to be bad news, probably disastrous. But they owed C'astille the truth, and lying would only make the inevitable discovery of the truth even worse later on. "We did bring 'em along," he said. "Our name for an adult is 'female.' Our name for an implanter is 'male.' You're talking to one of each."

CHAPTER THIRTY-THREE

Aboard *Reunion*, En Route from Outpost Orbit to Refiner Camp

The ocean waters exploded into a raging cloud of superheated steam and molecules disassociated into component atoms, heated by the lander *Reunion*'s roaring fusion engine. The very air flamed as superheated oxygen and hydrogen cooled enough to recombine, setting a halo of faint blue fire around the lander. The lander actually *submerged* below sea level before rising again and settling to a steady hover. But the heat of fusion and the pulse of expanding air and steam forced the water back, and the lander stayed dry.

Cynthia Wu was glad for small favors. It had been a hell of a ride. Gustav was trying to convince anyone who watched on radar that *Reunion* was being ditched, crashed into the ocean before she blew. It had been a hard entry. The autopilot had run an unpowered punch through the atmosphere, relying on air drag for braking, not lighting the fusion engines until *Reunion* was a bare five kilometers up—wavetop level for a spacecraft. The flare of the fusion engines and the roaring cloud of steam should look plenty enough like an explosion and impact for anyone watching from orbit.

More importantly, the ion sheath formed by the burning should foul up their radar. Cynthia took the control, checked her location against the last ground-track of the beacon, had the computer spit out a minimum-burn ballistic jump to the beacon, and throttled up the engines.

Reunion pogoed back up into the air, and instantly cut her engines. With any luck, no one was watching but if they were, they might not be able to spot *Reunion*, even so.

Reunion skittered up through the sky, headed north, then turned tail, and fell back toward the planet. The beacon signal came back over the horizon, Cynthia tweaked up her course to head for it and rode on it.

It would be good to see Lucy and Mac and Joslyn again. Cynthia had named *Reunion* with this meeting in mind. She could hardly wait. She kicked in the chemical landing rockets and looked for a place to put her down.

Reunion landed without incident about five kilometers from the Refiner sight. Cynthia was still buttoning up the craft when the line of pressure-suited figures came into sight of the external cameras. There was Mac, all right, gigantic in his pressure suit. And Joslyn! After God knows how long without seeing them, they still looked the same. Cynthia smiled and laughed out loud with the sheer joy of seeing people from home.

But something was wrong out there. She could see it in their tense, nervous movements. She hurried through the airlock and down the ladder to the ground. Mac crossed the ground scorched by the lander engines and hugged her.

"Cynthia. Damn, are we glad you're here," he said.

"Oh, Mac. It's good to see you." She looked at him, his face half-hidden behind the faceplate. And she inhaled sharply. She saw something she had never seen before. Mac was *scared*.

"Cynthia, let's get aboard and make sure that lander is cranked up and ready to go when we need her. We're going to camp aboard her instead of with the Refiners. Things have gone very wrong. Not just for us here. The Refiners might not help us against the Guards and Nihilsts. Lucy is scared they might *help* the Nihilists get rid of us. We might have to get out of here fast, carrying a warning."

Ariadne

Commander Richard Sprunt, commander of *Nike* Station's radar room, opened the door to Gustav's office and walked in without knocking or announcement. "You have some explaining to do, Gustav. And you'd better do it now."

Gustav calmly signed his name, put down his pen, tossed the paperwork into his out box, and leaned back in his chair. "Have a seat, Commander."

Sprunt pulled off his hat and sat down heavily. He was a pale-faced, sandy-haired man, medium height, with angry pale gray eyes and sharp, abrupt mannerisms. "Twice now, Lieutenant Gustav, CIs have vanished from this station, and twice landers have been lost. The official reports from this station say the CIs are dead and the landers crashed. Once I could buy, but not twice. Escapes, Gustav. Those were escapes. I saw both of them go down personally on *Nike*'s radar, and the visual evidence could go either way—*if* it had happened once. Not twice. I'm here to do you a favor. I'm using a perfectly good three-day pass to come over from *Nike* to tell you, man-to-man, quietly, that you can't go covering up escapes. I knew your father, and he was a good officer. You owe it to him to straighten up, fly right, investigate these incidents properly, and take your lumps like a man."

"I've been expecting you, Commander Sprunt, though I admit it's a bonus that you came on liberty. Obviously, you haven't filed a report, and no one will have to know where you were for three days."

"*What*? Just what the hell are you saying?" Sprunt roared, his eyes almost popping out of his head.

"Your crew must be pretty good, I admit that," Gustav said. "But not great. They missed the first lander launching toward the barycenter a week or two ago. And they

missed the covert glider/lander that went in a few days
ago. And they never had wit enough to do a frequency
sweep-check and spot the Refiner's beacon. Of course, the
Outposters have radio. Maybe they thought that was just
one of the Refiner's normal signals, so I can't really fault
them there. But my CIs didn't miss anything, not even
the covert. Schiller nailed that, just barely. A very tough
target. I can't blame you for missing that one either."

"Gustav, you bloody traitor—" Sprunt rose half out of
his chair at Gustav, and froze. A laser pistol had appeared
in Gustav's hand, pointed right at Sprunt's chest.

"Sit down again, Commander. Let me tell you a version
of the truth. You know I'm ex-Intelligence. Suppose I told
you that I was working desperately, taking enormous risks,
playing the most daring games with the enemy, to prevent
what I believe is a possible attack on Capital that could
wipe out our nation?"

"I'd say that you were a bloody traitor with paranoid
delusions of grandeur," Sprunt said.

Gustav realized his visitor was angry, not scared. Give
Sprunt that much credit. "In a few days' time, Commander, I doubt it will matter very much what you think.
But right now it might matter, and in blindly doing what I
grant is your duty, you could doom millions. So I will put
you under extremely quiet arrest. I think I might lie to the
computer and put you on a flight down to the Contact Camp,
a tourist going to see the aliens. There are already cases
of men wandering off into the woodlands and vanishing.
Sometimes the sear-chers find the torn-up remains of pressure suits. The native life is vicious. I grant you that would be
a dangerous game, too. But know that I am prepared to kill
you and cover it up as best I can if you force me to it.

"But I'll make you a promise. If I fail in what I'm trying
to do, I'll hand you this gun and surrender to you. Let you
take me to justice, arrange a court-martial.

"But if I fail, I doubt you or I or any other human in this
star system will survive long enough for a court-martial to
convene in the first place."

CHAPTER THIRTY-FOUR

Guardian Contact Base

Captain Lewis Romero was scared to death. With the distinct and uncomfortable feeling of entering a trap, Romero walked up the broad gangplank to board *Starsight*, the intersystem ship the Guards had given to the Nihilists.

D'etallis clumped solidly up the ramp behind him, followed by the Outposter pilot and co-pilot, L'anijmeb and L'etmlich.

Starsight had been up and down into orbit a few times, shakedown cruises. The last two flights had been made solo by the Outposter pilots. But this was the first trip that would actually take the ship anywhere. D'etallis had requested a chance to visit Capital, and the response had been a warm and eager invitation from Jules Jacquet himself. For the sake of wartime security, the flight itself would be a closely held secret, but once on Capital, the Outposters were sure to be a grand center of attention. The Central Guardians were understandably curious to get a look at their new allies—and Romero had been ordered to accompany them. Career-wise, it was a splendid moment for Romero, but this was one honor he would have been willing to forego. He had no faith in the

Outposter pilots, no faith that the *Starsight* could stay out of trouble in the midst of interstellar war.

Romero had wit enough about him to read the reports and figure out what was up. Odds were a major battle would shape up while the Nihilists were away from home. Supposedly, the *Starsight* and those aboard would never know. The ship's course was laid in by Guard astrogators under orders to keep their guests the hell away from the war zone. *Starsight*'s detection and communications equipment were deliberately not very powerful, and the odds against accidentally blundering into some patrol ship in the vastness of space were nil. Especially since the course laid in for *Starsight* arced far out of the plane of mutual orbit for the two stars. She would never get within five hundred million kilometers of the barycenter. There was enough natural debris and sky junk in the vicinity of the baryworld that such precautions would have been prudent even if the enemy fleet hadn't been anywhere near the place.

But flying through a war wasn't smart. Lewis Romero could understand putting the best face on things for the Nihilists, but he knew there was trouble in the future.

What he didn't know was that the *Starsight* was carrying it.

D'etallis genuinely enjoyed the bustle and fuss of getting strapped in and ready for a voyage into space. And she was genuinely looking forward to the great adventure of travel on the longest Road any Z'ensam had ever travelled. It would be a leisurely journey of some days, and there would be great delight in seeing the stars, in seeing Outpost from space. But this was no pleasure trip.

Romero would have fainted dead away if he had realized just how much the Nihilists knew about the military situation. The Nihilist's radio gear was good, as was their skill at opening burn bags, examining the contents, and resealing the bags before anyone noticed. D'etallis knew what was going on in space, and knew that a time of turmoil, with the Guards occupied elsewhere, was the time to strike.

Starsight might have been headed for Capital at the Guards' bidding, but the Nihilists had their own plans upon arrival. Once she was there, once she had landed, D'etallis would take a Guardian-provided mortar from the hold, set it up on the landing field, and fire the specially modified rounds. The rounds were set to fire straight up and explode in midair, releasing an air-borne plague. Within days, every human on Capital would be dead. The Nihilists' plague was deadly to humans, and not to Z'ensam— several of the Guards thought to have wandered off from Contact Base had actually been kidnapped by the Nihilists and exposed to the plague virus. They had died quickly and nastily—and the corpses proved to be highly contagious. With the humans of Capital dead, *Starsight* would begin shuttling back and forth between Capital and Outpost, bringing in more Nihilists, the heirs of the Guardians' industrial base. There would be much to learn there.

In a stroke, the Nihilists would have shipyards, the plans for the human stardrive, star charts that could lead them to the other human worlds.

Within the year there would many other emptied worlds, full of gleaming machines and vast stores of knowledge, waiting for their Nihilist inheritors.

The Z'ensam radio did not offer anything like a news service; the closest thing to reporting of events was what amounted to the neighbors gossiping over the back fence— one radio operator chatting with unseen friends in other Groups. But that sufficed; word travelled.

The launch of *Starsight* was a secret among humans but to the Z'ensam it was a most public event, and the Nihilists made no secret of it—though they made no mention of the real purpose of the mission, either. They announced it and described it as an embassy mission.

That didn't fool C'astille. She heard the news as she came out of the Guidance's house. The Guidance and all the leadership had, of course, been appalled by the news that humans had committed so grave an insult as to send implanters, 'males,' to negotiate. The adult, 'female' humans were the ones to blame, of course. That was too repellent to think about. No one was to have any further contact with the humans. Shun them, ignore them, allow them to leave, be done with them.

But *Starsight*. C'astille knew the Nihilists well, knew their plans and schemes, and how what they did compared to what they said. She *knew*, instantly, that the *Starsight* was intent on a bio-attack. And she knew how hopelessly unprepared the humans, Guards or League, would be to defend against that.

The humans. Lucy had seemed a *friend*, and C'astille felt dirtied by the thoughtless, unmeant betrayal. Medicine. Supposedly "intelligent" implanters. Treating implanters as equals, and tricking all the Z'ensam into doing the same.

Disgusting, half formed creatures, with their shameless ways, their perversities unpunished. C'astille knew, somehow, that it took no trick of hormones, no sublimation of conscious will, that forced the human females to mate with the males. They would go to it willingly, perhaps even eagerly, rutting like filthy, mindless beasts.

To hear the humans say it, their kind was never dragged down to the level of animals. But C'astille knew better. The humans never, once in their life-cycle, rose *above* the animals.

She wished the Nihilists and *Starsight* well.

Let the humans die. All of them.

CHAPTER THIRTY-FIVE

RKS *Eagle*

The first thing Chief Petty Officer Nyguen Chi Prihn noticed was the slight wear on the status panel's hold-down screws; the Phillips-heads were slightly chewed up. Someone had overtightened the screws, or perhaps used the wrong-sized screwdriver. In any event, the screws were damaged, and *that* was something to bear down on the maintenance techs about. It was just the sort of minor sloppiness that could lead to disaster. If those screwheads got much more chewed up, it might suddenly get very difficult to unscrew the screws to lift that panel and repair the innards in a hurry, in the midst of battle. And that panel reported on flight status of some very important birds. If the status panel went out, it could incapacitate the whole port side launch ops bay.

Who had done the last work on this panel? He or she needed a good bawling out. Prihn signed on to a computer terminal and pulled up the maintenance log for the status panel. He studied it for a moment, then let out a string of curses that could be traced right back to old Saigon. He, Prihn, was listed as the last person to work on that panel, over one thousand hours ago. And Prihn would bet his life that those screws hadn't been damaged two day ago.

Someone was going to be lucky to be alive after Prihn got through with him. Doing repairs without logging them! But wait a second. Prihn knew his spacers well. All of them knew, and believed, that lives, the fortunes of battle, the tide of history itself, could easily depend on how well they did their work. Overtightening a screw was one thing, that might happen accidentally, but none of his kids would screw around with logging procedure. Writing up a careful description of what they had done was second nature to all of them. They knew that not doing so was one of the quickest shortcuts to catastrophic failure. Prihn chewed on his finger for a moment, then ran a beefy hand over his prefectly combed, well brillantined head of hair. Something was seriously wrong here.

He pulled a tool kit out of the cabinet, grabbed a screwdriver, and opened up the panel. And there was no string of curses suitable for what he saw. Someone had rewired the panel lights to give phony readings. Sabotage. Clear cut, unmistakable sabotage. It took him a moment to trace the reworked wiring. The telltale lights on the number three Rapid-Deployment Docking Port had been shorted out so as to show green on all counts no matter what the real situation was. *Covert Lander Two* was supposed to be hanging there.

The external cameras. One after another, he punched up the cams that should have shown RDDP-3. All of them were dead. He switched in the intercom. "Comm room, this is CPO Prihn at port side launch control. Emergency Priority. Request any ships at close station-keeping distance with *Eagle* to feed us a visual of our hull in the area of the port side Rapid Deployment Docking Ports. Pipe the feed to me."

"Stand by, Port Side Launch. One moment. We have a feed from *Bismarck*."

The video screen came to life, showing nothing but space. Then the camera panned over and locked in on the huge cylinder that was *Eagle*, dimly lit by the distant suns. Then *Bismarck* powered up her searchlights, and the big ship seemed to shine against the darkness of space, proud and stately in her rotation about her long axis. *Bismarck*'s camera zoomed in toward the RDDP ports, but they slipped out of view with *Eagle*'s spin before Prihn could get a good look. The camera pitched up slightly to catch the docking ports as they came about again. There should have been four covert landers docked to the external hull.

There were only three.

Prihn swore again, and felt a cold knot of fear and anxiety twisting together in his stomach. "Comm. Prihn again. Emergency Priority. Get me the captain. We've got trouble."

Zeus Orbital Command Station, Circling the Planet Capital

The radio signal came out of nowhere. Long-range interferometry placed the source very close, only thirty thousand kilometers away, but radar hadn't detected anything and still couldn't. The radio source, whatever it was, was requesting permission to rendezvous and dock with *Zeus* Station, but the commodore would have none of that. He didn't want any ship that radar couldn't see getting too near his command. It could be a sneak attack, a trick bomb. He deployed a squad of fighters and ordered them to home in on the radio signal, pick up any crew or passengers, and then leave the ship, or whatever it was, in a stable orbit far from any Guardian installation.

Not only *Zeus*, but the entire ring of bases and ships around Capital went on alert. There might be more of these invisible ships out there.

The fighters made the personnel pick-up without incident, reporting that there was only one person aboard the strange ship. The fighters hurried home, and their passenger was taken aboard *Zeus* and hustled straight into the Intelligence section. Captain Phillips himself decided to interrogate this one. There was only one place that ship could have come from. And to get a voluntary defection, flying such an advanced ship—it could be the sort of

Intelligence bonanza that changed the course of a war. Captain Phillips took a look at his visitor—tired, frightened, worried. He decided this one required gentle handling.

"All right, son. You gave us a quite a start there for a moment, but now here you are. Who are you, and why did you come here?"

"I came to warn you of the Nihilists' plans," the visitor said. "They'll betray you. They're going to launch a plague attack that could wipe out every person on Capital. My name is George Prigot, and I'm a native of Capital."

After a four-hour interrogation, Phillips was forced to conclude that he had a credible witness. A check with Central Military Records matched this fellow's fingerprints and retinal patterns with one George Prigot, listed as Missing and Presumed Dead on New Finland. And this Prigot knew too many things, his story fit together too well.

"You realize, Mr. Prigot, that by coming here, you place yourself in grave danger. Whatever your reasons for coming here, by your own admission you are a deserter from the Guardian Army, and by your own admission, you have repeatedly committed acts of high treason against Capital. When your case is brought before the proper authorities, the only question left open to debate would be whether to shoot you as a spy or hang you as a traitor."

"I realize all that, sir," George said, his voice steady, only his eyes betraying his agitation. "But whatever my feelings about the government of Capital, I couldn't just sit back and allow the Nihilists to wipe out every human being on the planet. I decided I couldn't live with myself if I didn't try to stop them."

"And you are convinced that the Nihilists mean to turn on us?"

"Yes sir."

"But your only reason for so thinking is the report of this Calder woman, who in turn based her conclusions on what one single Outposter, a member of a Group that opposes the Nihilists, had to say."

"Sir. I don't have to tell you that the truth isn't determined by majority rule. The truth is just as true if *no one* believes it. And that's *not* my only reason for distrusting the Nihilists. I saw the tapes of what their foam worms did to the *Impervious*. Whoever invented *those* had no love for humanity. And why should they care about us? Their philosophy says intelligent life is an abomination. Alien intelligent life must be a double abomination. They kill their own kind. Why not us, too? And if they wipe us out, they get Capital. A whole world, and all our technology. Think of all the power that would represent, and tell me that wouldn't tempt them.

"Hang me as a traitor if you like, but listen to me first. *Stop the Nihilists*, before it's too late."

It was not until this George Prigot character had been led off to a fairly comfortable cell, not until Captain Phillips had befouled the station's air conditioning system with two pipefuls of the most hideously expensive and malodorous out-system tobacco, not until Phillips had sat there in thought for a solid hour, that the Intelligence chief came to the conclusion that he believed Prigot. Not only that, Prigot was telling a story and voicing a warning that he, Prigot, thought was honest. Phillips decided that the story and the warning themselves were legitimate. The Nihilists *were* going to attack Capital. He had never really trusted them in the first place. The bioweapons deal had been too rushed, too rashly and hurriedly considered.

But Mr. George Prigot, late of both the Britannic and the Guardian armed forces, had sent other messages by coming here, though such had not been his intention.

With Prigot flown the coop, the League forces would be forced to assume that all their plans had been exposed, all their schemes revealed, all their traps turned around. That meant they would be forced to change their plans.

And that meant the enemy would lose time, would be somewhat more vulnerable for a while.

Even though he had not brought a scrap of tactical planning material with him, Prigot, by his very presence, had wrecked all the League's schemes and forced them to start over. Captain Phillips could see the advantages in that great but fleeting advantages. He powered up his terminal, and rattled off a priority preliminary assessment to flag HQ.

But there was another point, a more private one. Prigot had never mentioned the name, never mentioned any Guardian Navy officer involved in the plans that had gotten Calder to the League fleet. But there had to have been one. Phillips *knew* that. Johnson Gustav, Phillip's former aide in Naval Intelligence, was assigned to *Ariadne* station. Gustav had dealt with Calder; Phillips had seen action summaries written by Gustav that mentioned her by name.

The connections were tenuous enough, but Phillips knew Gustav, knew what he would do in a given situation. And Phillips had read the report that Gustav had written so long ago. The one that had flatly stated that Capital would lose the war, suffering greater and greater loss of life and political freedom the longer the war was allowed to drag on. The report that had cost Gustav a step in rank, gotten him thrown out of the Intelligence Service, and nearly gotten him shot.

Yes, Gustav's fingerprints were all over the place. He was mixed up in this scheme.

There was only one last important fact that Phillips had kept secret from everyone until now. But now, at last, it was time to act on. For the fact was, Phillips had agreed with every word of that report.

It was time to contact Gustav, privately, over a secure channel. Phillips had a lot to talk about with him.

CHAPTER THIRTY-SIX

Captain's Cabin, Aboard the *Eagle*

Captain Robinson poured himself another cup of coffee and shoved his untouched-and-now-cold breakfast away. Hot, black, strong coffee—his morning repast was down to that. He was losing weight, he knew that without getting on a scale. He always stopped eating properly when he was nervous, on edge. Tension made his appetite vanish. Robinson had never been more tense and on edge than he was now.

He thought of his wife, Mildred, back home on Kennedy, and knew how she would worry if she saw him now. She knew the danger signs, the tiny twitches and microscopically small nervous gestures that warned things were not good.

And they weren't. For the first time, Robinson was seriously entertaining the thought that he might not get home to Mildred. He raised the cup to his mouth, sipped at the coffee, and burned his tongue. Too hot.

Prigot. Prigot was the last damn straw. They had mustered the ship's complement the moment *Covert Lander Two* turned up missing, of course. Prigot was the only person unaccounted for. The bloody twice-told traitor. He was competent enough to crack into any data file aboard and make a copy. It had to be assumed the Guards knew exactly where every ship had been—and so all of them had to be moved, or else be sitting ducks. Every plan, every disposition of forces had to be thrown out and reworked, and that was a crippling blow; the League forced into its second-best plans. Time, energy, and fuel chewed up.

Well, maybe not *time* lost due to Prigot. They had been wasting that right along, without any help from traitors. The League forces had simply been sitting astride the barycenter for weeks now, not attacking, not being attacked. Admiral Thomas seemed quite content to wait the Guards out. He did nothing all day, every day, but putter around the bridge, watching this report, talking to that ship's captain. The only thing Thomas really seemed interested in was the exploratory team going over the lump of rock called the baryworld. Robinson couldn't see any great value to a roughly spherical lump of skyrock barely one hundred kilometers across. Certainly nothing to merit such close attention from the Commander-in-Chief. He vanished into his stateroom each night, and early each morning the mess steward brought out an empty bottle of port. Hours later the admiral himself would emerge, looking very bright and chipper, his skin flushed, a twinkle in his eye. He *had* to be constantly drunk, putting away that much booze day after day. But it never showed. He was always sharp, always alert, always in control. But Robinson knew about drinkers and false fronts. Sooner or later the facade would crack, unless something was done.

His great-niece, Joslyn Larson, she seemed to have some effect on him, some ability to keep him from drinking. But she was on Outpost, chatting with the natives. There wasn't even any real way to know that the League's tiny, improvised First Contact crew was still alive. With Guard stations and spacecraft orbiting Outpost, reporting via radio would have been suicide. No, dealing with the company of the *Sick Moose* would have to wait upon the outcome of battle.

There might be some way to contact *Ariadne* Station and Johnson Gustav, but to what point? What could they say to each other that would be worth the risk of communicating?

Robinson's coffee had gotten cold as he sat there, worrying. He drank it down anyway, throwing his head back and downing it in one swallow. He winced at the taste and his stomach kicked up a fuss, but it was time to go to work. In ten minutes the long-range scanning team would be ready with the morning report on the disposition of the Guard fleet.

Robinson didn't know it yet, but that report was going to be badly in need of updating by the time he got it. Outpost and Capital were both many light hours away from the barycenter. The information gathered by the telescopes and other sensors watching from the barycenter was hours old by the time the photons carrying the news were collected by League technicians. The telescopes were limited by the speed of light, but the Guard ships weren't.

Guardian Orbital Command Station *Nike*

George Prigot wasn't sure about why he had been brought into the Intelligence section again, but he didn't like being there. He was brought from his cell straight to Phillip's office.

"Prigot," Captain Phillips said. "I thought you'd like to know. Thanks to your arrival, our attack on the barycenter was brought forward by fifty hours. The first craft are already launching. If we move quickly, we should catch the League while it's still repositioning its forces, while their ships are at their most vulnerable. The change in plans should allow us to do a great deal of damage."

"But why are they repositioning their forces? What's that got to do with me?"

"Didn't you work that out when you risked this trip of yours? The League will be forced to assume you betrayed every bit of information you had access to. Every battle plan. Any other assumption on their part would be risking suicide."

"But I didn't betray any League battle plans. I never *knew* them!"

"But they are forced to assume otherwise. Didn't you realize that? Tell me, Prigot, having betrayed both of them, which side *do* you want to win?"

But George Prigot was too stunned to answer.

Eagle

"Jesus H. Christ! Bridge, this is Detection! Bogie contacts all of a sudden, all over the place! Repeat, many contacts, presumed bandits and closing fast! Bridge, do you copy?"

"Captain here, on the bridge. We've got 'em on the repeater here, too, son. Don't go shouting and bouncing off walls. Get us numbers and vectors."

"Ah, yessir. Still more blips coming in—tactical plot shows they're all popping out of C^2 on trajectories that track back to Capital—

"Oh, my God. A whole new family of 'em—at least fifty *more* targets, with track-back at Outpost."

"Damn good break-out pattern," Robinson said. His voice was calm, but his stomach was suddenly twisted into a monstrous knot. "Comm, call battle stations and relay all our information to the fleet. Then call the admiral and inform him that we are under attack."

Klaxons hooted, the usual murmur of background noise on the bridge grew louder as relief crews and specialists rushed in from their quarters. Normally, only a third of the consoles were occupied. Within four minutes, they all were. Within five minutes, every combat station had reported in.

Except one. Robinson shouted out without turning his head. "Comm! Where the hell is Admiral Thomas?"

"No answer in his cabin, sir. It might be an intercom malfunction. I've dispatched a runner already."

"Thank you, Ensign." They both knew damn well it wasn't the intercom. Robinson was ready to bet that the admiral was passed-out dead drunk.

Comm Technician Third Class Carl Lieber was already pounding at the admiral's door by that time. He cursed as the spin-down alert was called, and the *Eagle* abruptly cut her rotation with her altitude jets. Lieber could do nothing but hold on to a stanchion for forty-five long seconds—during which time the admiral still hadn't responded. Lieber hesitated only a moment longer before he pulled out the pass key he had been carrying for a week now. Commander Wendell, the head of the comm section, had given it to him after the rumors of the old man's drinking had gotten as far as the comm department. Wendell wanted to make sure that no drunk could lock a door and keep his men from their duties. Lieber used the key and entered the cabin.

Admiral Sir George Wilfred Thomas was peacefully asleep, drifting in midair over the bed.

Lieber tried shouting, but Thomas slept on. Lieber shoved himself off the deck and grabbed Thomas by the shoulder. He gave the older man a good shaking, but nothing came of it. Lieber could smell the port on the admiral's breath. The spacer knew the next thing to try in waking a drunk, and decided this was enough of an emergency to risk it. Mentally kissing his rating and career goodbye, he towed Thomas into the head, shoved him into the shower, and twisted the nozzle over to *cold*.

Thomas awoke, spluttering, infuriated, and woozy. "What—what the devil is the meaning of this? Who the hell are you?"

"Sir. Spacer Lieber. The Guards have launched their attack on us and you're wanted at the Task Force Command Center."

Thomas stopped his spluttering on the instant and reached to shut off the shower. Suddenly he looked and felt more alert that he had for a long time. "The devil you say! Finally decided that they'd kept me waiting long enough,

I suppose. Well . . . well get out of my way and let an old man get dressed."

Thomas launched himself from the shower and made his way into his stateroom, leaving a trail of water blobs quivering in the air behind him. He peeled off his soaking wet pajamas, and Spacer Lieber found himself in the presence of a naked—and rather scrawny looking—admiral. Thomas tossed his pajamas aside and they splattered flat against the overhead. He quickly ran a towel over his body, then pulled undershorts and socks out of a bureau, uniform out of the closet, and was dressed in seconds. He bounced back into the head for a moment, shaved quickly, returned, jammed his hat down on his head to keep it on securely in zero-gee, and left Lieber behind in the stateroom completely forgotten, as he headed for the Task Force Command Center.

His combat staff was already in place, pulling in data from the *Eagle*'s sensors and from other ships. None of the TFCC crew so much as looked up as he arrived. Good enough. Pomp and circumstance could wait until they had all lived through this.

"This is TFCC Comm to Bridge. Admiral Thomas has arrived."

Thomas caught his comm officer's eye and gestured for a direct patch through to the *Eagle*'s bridge. "Good morning, Captain. This is where you and I earn our pay. What can you say about their disposition of forces?"

"Well sir, it's a pretty classic enfolding maneuver, in fact so far it's a lot—"

"A lot like the one we performed against them," Thomas agreed cheerfully. "You are quite right. I have been hoping against hope that they'd come after us. The half-built barycenter defenses were tough enough. I wouldn't want to try cracking through their completed missile screens around Outpost and Capital. Now they've saved us the trouble."

"An optimistic viewpoint, Admiral."

"True, captain. But I believe you will see it borne out.

Task Force Command Center out." Thomas turned and studied his screens, feeling good, feeling useful. Yes, an enfolding attack, from both sides. And that after the slow, cautious shifting of forces that was supposed to look like preparations for an assault from Capital alone. Either the whole force-shifting had been a feint all along, or else this Prigot person's defection had led the Guards to shift their plans. It didn't matter. None of it mattered. Thomas's plan, the real plan, had been kept too close a secret to be endangered by anything Prigot could have known. Thomas smiled to himself and busily worked through all the reports and data coming at him. There was a fear underlying his chipper enthusiasm, and he knew it. Now was not the time to analyze it, or acknowledge it, but there it was, the same old fear that had dogged him—and overwhelmed him—so often throughout his life. Not fear of death. He was an old man, quite pleased that he was still alive, but having long since accepted his own mortality.

No, he feared failure, disaster. Fear of finding out that the bottle had stolen his soul, his ability to think and feel, even as it deadened his capacity for fear, his loneliness and frustration at the endless waiting. He had told himself that work, and battle, and necessity would conquer the bottle when the time came. Now he would find out.

"Comm, order the fleet to prepare a phased fighting withdrawal away from the Capital fleet bringing us toward the Outpost fleet. All personnel off the baryworld *now*, and I want all League ships at least one million kilometers away from the baryworld, headed toward the Outpost fleet. Only once pull-back has *commenced*, drop anti-radar chaff and begin radar jamming. I want them to know we're moving, but not to where."

Aboard GSS *Adversary*, the Guardian Fleet Flagship

Admiral Bernard Strickland, Guardian Navy, was pleased by the performance of his ships and men. The breakout into the space around the barycenter had been performed with impressive skill and precision. It had taken endless maneuvering, constant stops and starts of the engines for every ship in the fleet, in order to jockey everyone into position.

But they had come in on the League at exceedingly close range. The baryworld was a rather small lump of rock and there was no other large mass in the area to speak of—the two Guardian fleets had been able to drop back into normal space almost right on top of the League forces. The lead ships of the Capital fleet would be within range of the enemy in minutes. The Outpost fleet, which was flying practically as an autonomous unit, was smaller and moving not quite as crisply, but they'd pass muster. So far all was going well. No cat-and-mouse sneak attack as at Britannica this time—the Guard forces were staging an all-out frontal attack from two directions at once.

The League ships were maneuvering, pulling back away from the baryworld. Suddenly his tactical display scrambled, blanked out, and restarted, showing only empty space. For a wild half second, Strickland thought the entire League force had entered C-squared space *en masse*. But no, that was ridiculous. The tactical display started to show a few League ships again, very faintly. Obviously they were using some sort of jamming equipment to cover their pullback. "Tactics officer! Clear the real-time display and give me projections based on tracks up until jamming commenced. Detection. Punch through that jamming somehow! Weapons! How long until we are in effective range?"

"Allowing for our best guess at enemy maneuvers, they'll be within engagement range of the Outpost fleet in twenty minutes, sir."

"So they take their first crack at the smaller fleet. Very well. Let's see how they do," Strickland said.

TFCC, *Eagle*

Admiral Thomas watched his screens intently. In the vastness of space, even the high-speed maneuvers of the two fleets seemed to move in slow motion. But slowly, gradually, the League fleet was pulling away from the baryworld. Left behind on its surface was a collection of sophisticated sensing equipment, even now relaying information to the Task Force Command Center. The baryworld sensors would be destroyed in hours, but by then they would have done their job. But now it was time to look forward instead of back. Their retreat from the Capital fleet was moving them straight for the smaller Outpost fleet. "Comm, give me all-ships relay."

"You have the relay, admiral."

"This is Admiral Sir George Wilfred Thomas to all ships. All ships without specialized assignments are to attack the smaller enemy fleet coming from Outpost." There *was* only one ship with a "specialized" assignment—*Sapper*—but never mind that now. "Their ships and ours should be in range of each other's weapons in a few minutes. Should your ship be hit by any sort of missile, I need hardly emphasize the need for the strictest decontamination procedures. We must assume that any and all Guard weapons include a biological component. I want a moving attack, not a stationary defense. I want to pass *through* their fleet. Good luck."

The two fleets moved toward each other at a pace that was almost leisurely by the standards of modern spaceflight. Thomas watched his screens intently. This was it, the make-or-break movement.

"Admiral, Captain Robinson wishes to speak with you," the comm officer said.

"Thank you, I'll take it on the private channel." It was just about time for Robinson to get a little nervous. Thomas couldn't blame him for that—if he was as much in the dark as the master of the *Eagle* was, he'd be a little on edge, too. Especially since he was dealing with an alcoholic commander-in-chief. . . .

Thomas slipped on a headset and punched up the private channel. "Yes, captain."

"Admiral, with all due respect, you're aware that by

passing *through* the Outpost fleet, you're leaving nothing between them and the Capital fleet. The two of them can form up into a larger combined force."

"I am aware of that, Captain. That is in fact my intention in ordering the maneuver."

"Sir? Could you elaborate?"

"Captain, I *am* sorry, but no. We have had a very serious breach of security already. That Prigot might have put some sort of tap on our internal communications. I may have said too much already. But I assure you that the situation is under control. Thomas out." *At least I bloody well hope the situation is under control,* Sir George thought. If Bannister worked as advertised, all would be well. A quick drink would have gone down very well just then, but Sir George shook his head to clear his mind of *that* idea, and concentrated on the evolution of the battle.

The League and Outpost fleets drifted into each other, pretty colors on the screen. A dot of League-green light labeled *Bismarck* took the first hit, flared into incandescence and nothingness. But a pair of fast frigates revenged *Bismarck*, their lasers tearing open her killer's hull from stem to stern. Thomas gripped the armrests of his crash couch hard, and tried to think of dots of light and not ruined young bodies.

Elsewhere aboard the *Eagle*, Captain Robinson sweated out the battle far more personally as the flagship went into harm's way. This was his ship, the lives aboard were in his care, and he was following the orders of a man he no longer had faith in. At least his fighters were staying close to home, assigned to protecting the flag rather than forward attack. After what one torpedo full of foam worm eggs had done to *Britannica*, no one wanted to risk a Capital ship in the fore of the action. If the *Eagle* hadn't been the only operational combatant large enough to carry a planning staff, a full tactical system, bio specialists, a clutch of diplomats and so on, she would have stayed behind in orbit of Kennedy. At the moment, that sounded just fine to Josiah Robinson.

A Guard destroyer got entirely too close to the *Eagle*, barely a thousand kilometers away, and let off a salvo of torps. The fighters got all the torps, but the enemy ship got away. Robinson considered dispatching a flight of fighters after her, but instead he let her go. *Eagle* was to defend herself, nothing more. No grand attacks. The most powerful ship in either fleet, and they didn't dare risk her.

Score one for Mac Larson.

CHAPTER THIRTY-SEVEN

Barycenter Battle Zone

Both the Guards and the Nihilists had improved their deployment techniques for the bioweapons since Britannica. The Nihilists had developed ways to delivery adult animals instead of eggs, and techniques to hold the beasts in a kind of suspended animation using a special gas mixture. The Guards had abandoned torpedoes that crashed through hulls and opened compartments to vacuum. Now they used limpet mines that attached themselves to the hull and carefully bored a hole through it. A torpedo could carry a stack of six limpets, and release them when it got close enough to the target ship. The limpets would slap themselves onto the ship, the hull-borers would do their jobs, the bioweapons would be awakened by the fresh air aboard the ship, climb, slither, or crawl aboard, and go to their deadly work.

And there were new types of bios, each of which could wreck a ship in its own way.

The USS *Benjamin Franklin* was killed by a swarm of beetle-like things the size of a man's thumb. Each beetle, as it crawled, excreted a chain-molecule monofilament thread too thin to be seen by the unaided eye, and dragged the thread behind itself. The tail end of the thread was adhesive, and stuck firmly to the first spot of hull the beetle landed on. Two limpets successfully attached to *Franklin*, one amidships and one near the engine compartment. The limpets cut their holes through the hull and the beetles wandered off. Almost immediately, one of them sliced through a hydrogen feed line, and the explosive gas was injected into the cabin air mixture. Fifteen minutes later, another beetle caused a spark as its thread cut a high-voltage cable. The ship blew up.

Europa pride of that planet's fleet, was wrecked by a cloud of air-borne micro-organisms that metabolized atmospheric nitrogen and oxygen with most sorts of plastic, and left hydrochloric acid and poison gases behind as waste products.

Maxwell, a supersophisticated heavy cruiser from Bandwidth, was attacked not only by the foam worms, but by a species of spider-things bred to eat human flesh. The latter murdered the crew before the former could wreck the ship.

Conventional armament spread its more familiar sort of horror as well; lasers, torpedoes, exploding limpets—all did their work and League ships died.

Thomas tried to ignore the death, the destruction, and concentrate on the battle itself, the progress of the opposing forces.

It was working, as well it should be. The Guard's Outpost fleet was passing through the League's fleet to link up with the Capital fleet around the baryworld. The Combined Guard fleet was eagerly taking the chance to form into one fighting force. And the Guard fleet seemed to be significantly larger than anyone expected, with any number of smaller and slower ships deployed. After their losses at New Finland and Britannica, it was incredible that they could field that many ships. But then, this battle was for all the chips. If they lost here, they lost altogether. No point in holding reserves. They must have stripped their docking ports clean, must have taken along every space tug and broken-down old rustbucket.

The elderly admiral watched the screens. Yes, the Guards were forming up nicely about the baryworld. It was almost time. "Comm. Raise HMS *Sapper* if you please."

"*Sapper* is standing by, laser link ready."

"Very good." Suddenly, the admiral's voice shifted and he spoke in a stern, abrupt tone of voice. "*Sapper*, this is Admiral Sir George Wilfred Thomas. I hereby instruct you to proceed with Procedure A1A in exactly ten minutes from my mark—3,2,1, mark."

"Order received and acknowledged, admiral," said an efficient sounding voice from *Sapper*. "Activation codes to be transmitted in nine minutes, fifty-five seconds. Allowing for speed-of-light delays, you should detect first results in ten minutes, thirty-eight seconds."

"Thank you, *Sapper*. Good luck." Thomas swung around to face the comm officer, and spoke with the same crisp severity in his voice. "Send to all ships. Emergency Priority. Break off any and all engagements with the enemy and proceed at full thrust away from the baryworld. You must be underway within nine minutes. That is an Emergency Priority order. Send it *now*. Clear the tactical view off the main screen and get me the highest magnification you can on the baryworld. Those of you here in this room are about to find out about the closest held secret of the war. Officially, it's called Bannister."

The moment he had given the Bannister orders, Thomas wanted to countermand them. There *had* to be another way. But it was already too late for that by the time *Eagle*'s own engines lit, for *Sapper* had sent the start codes, and nothing could bring them back.

The main screen shifted to the view from a long-range camera that was already zooming in on the dark, barren, cold lump of rock. Here and there, tiny sparkles of white flame could be seen as Guard ships maneuvered and lit their engines.

"It will start in a moment," Thomas said quietly. "Unofficially, everyone called it WorldBomb."

The viewscreen was filled by the rough, worn old face of

the unnamed baryworld, formed by the slowest and most tedious process of gradual accretion over billions of years. It was a very old, very tired-looking sort of world. Suddenly, there was a bright lance of fire, and then another, and another, across its scarred and cratered face, and then it seemed as if the entire surface of the tiny world was afire.

"Implosion phase," Thomas said. "Hundreds of small explosions, from shaped nuclear explosives placed all over the surface of the planetoid. The bombs shatter the rock, and force shockwaves in toward its core to concentrate the explosion—smashing the structure of the world."

From equally spaced points around its surface, a dozen huge and terrible tongues of blood-red fire shot out from the baryworld, reaching out far into space, casting a horrible ochre tint across the universe.

"There go the larger nukes, the deep bombs. The flame is jetting back up the tunnels we dug to place them."

And then, in a blast of pure white radiance, the baryworld itself swelled up, expanded, exploded—the little planet shattering into a billion bits of shrapnel that were flung out into space at terrible velocity.

Ninety percent of the Guard fleet was within fifty thousand kilometers of the baryworld when the WorldBomb was detonated. None of them had a chance. A huge pulse of electromagnetic energy, born of the nuclear explosions, flashed through the Guard fleet, scrambling computer banks, throwing circuit breakers, forcing arcs and shorts in electronic equipment. The Guards ships were instantly blinded and crippled. Hard on the heels of the electromagnetic pulse came a virtually solid wall of rock fragments, from mountain-sized boulders down to grains of dust and molecules, all moving at incredible speed. All of it rushed out from the world that was no more, slamming into ships, ripping through their hulls, tumbling ships end-for-end, crashing one ship into another. A large fraction of the baryworld's mass had been vaporized altogether, and expanded out into vacuum as a shock wave of terrible force, popping hulls and ports and hatches that were meant to hold pressure *in*, not keep it out.

The problem with explosive weapons in space has always been the lack of an atmosphere to carry the shock wave, the absence of debris to be thrown. In short, in a vacuum, an explosion has no mass to throw around. By destroying a small world, the League had solved these problems.

The command center crew watched the screen in stunned silence. Then the comm officer let out a low-pitched wail, and Thomas could hear the sound of quiet sobbing. "That's horrible, that's horrible," a voice whispered over and over, so quietly that at first Thomas thought the chanting was inside his own head. But no, it was the detection officer, his face ashen-white, unable to tear his eyes from the screen as the cloud of dust and debris that was once a tiny world and a proud fleet of ships expanded out into space.

"Even though that is a terrible, terrible end," Thomas said, "at least it *is* an end. And I shall ask myself if I truly had to do this for the rest of my days. But the war is over."

But Admiral Sir George Wilfred Thomas didn't know about *Starsight*.

CHAPTER THIRTY-EIGHT

Starsight

Captain Romero happened to be watching the monitors when the flaring light that was the baryworld's death blossomed across the dark of space. It took him a moment to realize where and what that terrible light had to be, and he was suddenly afraid. Who had done that, Guard or League? The great battle had begun, and he was here, still days out from Capital, cooped up with aliens he had grown to distrust.

D'etallis was irritated by the human's bothersome nervousness, and once again toyed with the idea of killing Romero immediately. But no, they might need a human face to parade in front of the cameras later on. She could endure Romero's company a while longer. He could die with lots of company, on Capital.

Ariadne

Perhaps there was no practical, rational need for caution anymore. Any fool who could count the number of ships left knew the days of the Guardians were over. After the barycenter disaster, there was nothing much left to oppose the League forces *with*. But Gustav knew warriors were not always practical or rational in defeat. Even *he* burned with a white-hot anger, a new hatred of the League that had smashed so many ships, killed so many young men, humiliated his planet and his nation. Johnson Gustav, who knew the Guards had started this war, who had known all along that the Guards must lose, even Johnson Gustav, who still might be executed as a traitor—even *he* thirsted for mindless revenge against the League for what they had done.

And *Nike* Station was still there in orbit, bristling with weapons that could leave a smoking crater where *Reunion* was. No, there were still plenty of reasons to be careful when talking to the League Contact party and *Reunion*. He waited until *Nike* was below the horizon, and then Gustav went to the comm room and set up the link himself.

He didn't know that *Nike* had deployed snooper buoys in orbit.

Reunion

Reunion's radio crackled and came to life. "Gustav to *Reunion*. Come in please."

Cynthia looked up from her work at the computer. She hit the right buttons and said, "This is *Reunion*. Wu speaking. Stand by a moment." She shut off the mike for a second and shouted down to the lower deck. "Message coming through from Gustav!" As the others scrambled up the ladder, she kicked the mike back on. "Go ahead, Lieutenant."

"There's some news you ought to know—the League has just plain destroyed the Guard fleet. We pulled every ship we *had* into the fight, and they were all virtually wiped out. It's all over but tidying up the details. The war is over, and—and your side won, in spite of the data that Prigot fellow seems to have given us." Gustav couldn't resist that dig into League sensibilities.

"Prigot fellow!" Mac cried out. "What the hell are you talking about?"

Gustav had assumed that the League people would have heard of Prigot through channels, but he hadn't expected to get that much of a rise out of them. "According to a report I've gotten, a man claiming to be a citizen of Capital, calling himself George Prigot, slipped through both the League and Guard detection systems, and got to a station orbiting Capital. I just got a very brief description of what he had to say, but apparently his information had a lot to do with the timing of the Guard attack on the League—for whatever good it did us."

There was a pause, and then Gustav's voice went on. "In any event, I'm not clear if Prigot claimed to have been a prisoner of the League or if he was pretending to cooperate with you. But he crossed the line the first moment he could, so obviously he was a double agent. I don't know all of what he told us. One thing he *did* say was that the Nihilists would betray us. No one seems to be taking him seriously on that. I take it you've heard of this Prigot?"

Mac felt suddenly sick inside. George a turncoat? A double agent? No, it was impossible. It couldn't be. The two of them had risked their lives for each other a dozen times on New Finland, and George had again and again provided information vital to the League war effort. Gustav had to be lying, there was no other explanation. But how the hell could he have known who George was, or that he was with the League fleet? What motive would Gustav have for lying?

And George had changed sides once before. . . .

Joslyn took her husband by the arm, tried to comfort him with a quiet touch. She knew how much George meant to Mac, how responsible her husband felt for his friend.

Mac shook his head and tried to collect his thoughts. "Yes, I've heard of Prigot," he said angrily. "But that's to one side. Lucy has told me time and time again that you want to cut this war short, end it before too many die. It seems to me that this is the time for you to move."

"I quite agree," Gustav's voice replied over *Reunion's*

speakers. "I called asking for your advice in how best to proceed. The same person who told me about Prigot was primarily interested in getting contact with your side to start some very quiet talks. I believe you have a League diplomat along with you. Is he available?"

"Right here, lieutenant," Pete called out. "My name is Gesseti, Peter Gesseti. Exactly what would the topic of those quiet talks be?"

"Very simply, Mr. Gesseti, we want to kno—"

The speaker went dead.

Nike *Station, Orbiting Outpost*

Nike's comm center had been jumpy ever since Sprunt had vanished. They were the ones who finally picked up the chatter *Ariadne* was broadcasting, though they weren't able to locate the receiving station or locate the answering frequency. They only heard Gustav's side of it, but that was enough.

Laser Gunner's Mate Henderson didn't get told what was behind his orders, but he could guess. The damned CIs. They must have taken over *Ariadne* altogether. For Henderson's money, he wished they had ordered him to blow the place up, except there were probably still loyal Guards alive on her, prisoners. If there had been any ships at all left docked to the station, or orbiting the planet for that matter, they could have sent someone to arrest them all, but there weren't any ships. Which left things to Henderson. He powered up his cannon, tweaked up its long-range aiming unit, waited for the next close pass, and sliced every aerial and antennae clear off *Ariadne*. That would shut them up. And if a comm station was silenced, it couldn't do any harm.

Reunion

Cynthia worked the comm controls frantically. "They're gone! Nothing, no carrier. Not just our signal, but everything that should be coming off *Ariadne* is gone. Oh, my God."

"No!" Lucy cried out, grabbing at the microphone. "Johnson! Damn it, come in!" Suddenly tears welled up in Lucy's eyes, the first tears she had allowed herself in a long, long time. "Cyn, shut the radio off," Mac ordered. "Before they can trace us, too. I'm sorry, Luce."

Thousands of kilometers away, Johnson Gustav closed his eyes, sighed, and felt defeat. The game was up. They had caught him. He thought of all the things he had never be able to tell Lucy, and cursed the universe that had brought them together only to tear them away from each other.

Task Force Command Center, *Eagle*

Thomas felt drained, used up. He knew the reasons all those ships had had to die, but he didn't have to like it, or feel good about killing them. No man or woman goes into space without falling in love with spacecraft—with all spacecraft—with the very *idea* of those splendid miracles of metal and glass and plastic that spanned the dark between the planets.

And the WorldBomb had smashed hundreds of those wondrous machines, killed thousands of people who had no greater flaw than being born on the wrong side of the line.

But he had a job to do now, still. He ordered prize crews to pick up survivors, and then turned his attention to the next task.

Unless the Guards saw sense and surrendered, he was going to have to bleed his fleet white trying to break through Capital's defense screen.

CHAPTER THIRTY-NINE

Aboard *Starsight*

L'anijmeb performed the navigation check slowly, carefully, and then ran the whole test over again. All was well. They were on course—and no human group, League or Guardian, seemed to have spotted them yet. No human but the Guard's first Guidance, Jacquet, and a very few Guard officers, knew they were coming—and now that the Nihilists had changed the ship's course, the humans would have no idea where or when *Starsight* would arrive. There was some danger that the humans would realize what was happening and attempt to stop *Starsight*, but that was of no matter. If L'anijmeb could even get *Starsight* into the atmosphere for a few moments, that would suffice. Like most Nihilists, L'anijmeb didn't much care are about dying. She glanced across the cabin at the pathetic little halfwalker.

"You'll want knowledge, M'Romero," L'anijmeb said in her slow English. "We should be landed in just over twenty-six of your hours." *And you, little halfwalker, will be dead in twenty-seven,* she thought.

Aboard *Reunion* **on Outpost**

Mac stuck his head up through the opening in the deck

plates and shouted through the overhead hatch. "Okay, Cynthia, run the phase-three calibration." Mac ducked back into the underdeck and watched the test meters hook up to the C^2 generator. The displays flickered briefly and settled down to satisfactory settings. Joslyn nodded at the figures. "That's it. It ought to work. Only way to be surer than we are now is to try it." She started unplugging the test gear.

A strange sense of calm had come over the *Reunion*. It was all over now. All they had to do was sit tight and wait for some word from the League. Suddenly, there was time on their hands.

Charlie watched as Mac and Joslyn climbed out of the underdeck. "I still don't see why you're bothering to hook that thing up anyway," he said. "Or even why Cynthia swiped it off *Ariadne* in the first place."

"In case we needed to get the hell out of this star system on our own," Cynthia said, climbing down from the control room.

"Yeah, but the League *won*," Charlie objected. "We won't need it. The League can come get us or we can fly out to the barycenter and meet them. Why hook it up now?"

"*Could* be we won't need it," Mac said. "If so, we've kept ourselves busy, instead of just sitting around doing nothing. And let me put it this way: If we *do* need a C^2 generator for some reason, we'll *really* need it. They just blew up their own comm station to silence Gustav. If they track *us* down, and come for us, we're going to want to be able to run and run fast."

Pete Gesseti applauded, and winced slightly as he did. He arm was still pretty sore. "Spoken like a true paranoid pioneer. Take a lesson or two from Mac, Charlie. He's gotten out of *plenty* of nasty situations. And you do that by being sure you can use any advantage you've got, and thinking of all the unpleasant possibilities. If we keep that mind, we might up the odds on getting out of here alive.

But I sure as hell wish I knew what Gustav was going to say. Poor guy."

"Poor Lucy," Joslyn said. "It didn't take much imagination to see there was something there. Where did she go, anyway?"

Charlie shrugged. "Out. Just put on her suit and left without a word while you guys were in the underdeck hooking that thing up."

"What's she up to?" Joslyn asked. "Do you think she was going to try and patch things up with the Outposters?"

"Joslyn, you weren't there when C'astille and Lucy and I dropped our little bombshells on each other," Charlie said. "I doubt very much that *any* Outposters will even *talk* to her."

Joslyn shook her head sadly. "I still can't get over it all. The poor, poor Outposters. To have your sex drives force you into sex with mindless animals, the bloody *stumble-bugs*—it amounts to bestiality. And to *know* your whole life long that you're *sure* to turn into a dribbling idiot."

"You know, they can't possible have any notion of an afterlife or a soul," Pete said thoughtfully. "They know for *sure* there is no life after death—they see death *in* life every time a stumblebug flutters past. They see the death of mind *during* life. They see life as *detached* from mind. Our life cycle allows us what are probably comfortable illusions about the soul and the afterlife."

"The poor Outposters," Joslyn said again. "Their whole lives warped by their reproductive cycle."

Charlie snorted. "And ours *aren't*? Then what's marriage? Where did divorce come from? Why the very, very large importance we place on the male/female dicotomy? Think about child custody. Pornography. Incest tabus. Monogamy. Polygamy. Polylandry. Rules and traditions that encourage marriage with someone from outside the tribe. Homosexuality. Age of legal consent and statutory rape. Family reunions. Teen-age dances that are rehearsals for courtship. Royal lineages. Inheritance laws. Dowries. Adoption. Illegitimacy. Keeping women at home—the way the Guards and a lot of other cultures do. Prostitution. Birth control. Population pressures and immigration. Hell, any shrink will tell you *gambling* is related to sexual impulses, and a lot of them will tell you starships are the ultimate phallic symbol. You could make a pretty good argument for just about every human activity being affected by our reproductive urges.

"Practically all of the things I just mentioned, and a thousand more that are basic to human society, must not only be unheard of for the Z'ensam, they must be impossible. And all of them are tied up, directly or indirectly, in the way we make babies, or avoid making babies, or decide who should make a baby when, and who stands in what relation to the child. We define so much of ourselves, and our culture, sexually. And all of that is right out the window with the Z'ensam.

"*Every* human culture invents marriage and marriage rituals. It's so ingrained into us, we don't notice it. But can you imagine a human culture where there were no marriages—for anyone, anytime, throughout all of history? Can you imagine there being a dicotomy more important than male/female for humans? Our lives are every bit as warped by biology and reproductive strategy. But human and Z'ensam are used to being the way they are."

Cynthia squatted down on the decking and stared at the gunmetal gray of the cabin bulkhead. Her mind's eye saw the murky, dismal green fields and forests beyond. "I don't envy them their way one little bit," she whispered.

For the hundredth time, C'astille resisted the urge to fling her picture book into the pond and be done with it. But she *couldn't*. She was so angry with the humans, so infuriated with all they did and built. They were *blessed* by their perversities. Without foreknowledge of doom, with intelligence lasting to the end of life, they had apparently invented the bizarre idea of the mind actually *outliving* the body—if she was inferring from the captions of the pictures properly. Their self-confidence, their incurable optimism, their huge monuments to themselves, all stemming from the crazy idea that they would live forever. And that live-forever idea stemmed directly from their weird, disgusting sexual practices! Practices that they probably saw as natural and right.

C'astille flipped through the pictures. Paris. The Moon colonies. The great bridges. The space stations and the huge starships. The observatory in the rings of Saturn, the lab nestled in among the craters of Mercury, the towers of New York, the Kremlin, Ulan Bator, the Taj Mahal, Machu Picchu, the Great Wall, the Washington Monument, the Pyramids, the Parthenon, Kennedy Space Center. All of them so *big*, so *grand*. And the Roads! Grand highways that made the widest Road on Outpost look like a rough-and-tumble game path. How had these puny halfwalkers done it all?

Their self-confidence, their lifelong intelligence, and their foul, foul medicine that extended lives, were the difference between humans building future glories, and Z'ensam, at best barely holding onto their modest present; between huge cities suffering from *overpopulation*, of all things, and a tiny Z'ensam populace that wasn't big or organized *enough* to build proper cities.

Their perversions had not been punished, they had been rewarded. Their vile ways had been their Road to the stars!

She wanted so much to hate them. Her jealousy was so strong, her anger at being accidentally deceived so great, her pride so wounded by talking to *implanters* all these months. She tried to hate them, tried to keep her anger alive. All she had to do was keep silent, offer no warning of the *Starsight*, and the humans would soon be no more.

But the picture book, and the grand works of the human hand—she wanted to *see* those things. Could she really let the Nihilists inherit them through murder? And Lucy was her friend. Lucy could not help being what she was.

With a sudden burst of understanding, C'astille realized something more—the worst, the absolute worst. The *humans* would feel *sorry* for the Z'ensam, would pity them. But she remembered their shock and fear at L'awdasi's simple trick of making their blood, and their fear of the Nihilist bioweapons. The humans would have some fear and respect, as well. Perhaps that would be enough. But perhaps not. She turned the pages of the book, and stared hard at a picture of Earth as seen from orbit. She wanted to see that! Her very soul was knotted in anger and confusion.

Lucy had been walking in the clearing for hours; at first with no clearer aim in mind than getting away from people, being out by herself, but after awhile, she found herself looking for C'astille. The other Z'ensam gave her a wide berth. They didn't want to interfere with her and meet with the revenge of her people in return—but they certainly wanted nothing to do with her. Lucy knew she couldn't rely on non-interference for long; she had the very definite sense of being surrounded by tolerance that was near its end.

When she spotted C'astille lying on folded-up legs by the pond, looking at her book, Lucy was almost afraid to approach. So much accidental damage had been done—but she suddenly wanted someone to talk to, a friend to be with. She walked slowly toward the pond. And C'astille was looking at the book. That was a good sign. Perhaps there was still a chance some of the damage could be undone. For the moment, at least, Lucy managed to forget her own troubles and worry about someone else's.

C'astille saw Lucy approaching but did not acknowledge her in any way. Instead, she pretended to be fascinated by her book. Lucy hesitated a few meters off, and then came to sit alongside her friend. Neither of them spoke for a long time.

It was Lucy who broke the silence. "I'm sorry, C'astille."

No response. Lucy tried again. "C'astille, I wish there was some way to make it all right, some way that your people and mine could see each other, know the way each other lived, and not be horrified." Still no response, but at least she was listening. "Because you are good people. I like you, I like most of the Z'ensam. And the Z'ensam who can stand the way we humans look seem to like us. Even if it means I die here and now, I wouldn't regret having known you and your people. I would never give up that experience. But you must accept the way we are, perversions and all. We must accept you, and not be afraid of your great bio-skills, and try not to blame all Z'ensam for what the Nihilists do."

"Mmmmph," C'astille grunted. "I *know*. I *know* all that. But it will take time for my anger and my disgust to die."

C'astille said nothing for a long moment and closed her book, her prize possession that catalogued the great works of humanity.

"There is at least one piece of good news. My Group has defeated the Guardians in a great battle. That will put an end to the Guards and their Nihilist bioweapons. I suppose the League will try to ban such things. A treaty like the ones banning germ warfare," Lucy said absently.

"What is germ warfare?" C'astille asked.

"Mmmm. I suppose you might call it war medicine. Medicine deliberately used to kill instead of cure."

C'astille sat bolt upright. War medicine! The term translated well into her language, as one of the worst obscenities, one of the gravest sins possible. The Nihilists had stooped that low, and C'astille *knew* about it, knew what *Starsight* had to be intending, and had *done nothing*, as if the humans were pests that needed elimination. C'astille looked down again at the picture book, the gift Lucy had impulsively filched from the VIP stateroom of the *Eagle*, and thought again of the fine and mighty things these humans could do. Weird star-mutants or not, these halfwalkers were thinking, talking *people*, not animals, not Hungry Ones to be killed off if they became inconvenient.

And this was war medicine to be committed against *Lucy*! Sooner or later her people would die—her family, her Group. Wiping out the faceless Guardians was too huge and impersonal an assault to engage C'astille's imagination. But the Nihilists wanted to kill *Lucy* along with the rest of humanity. Lucy, the human sitting next to her now, the adult—no, the *female* who had risked so much for the sake of others. A strange creature, but as brave and civilized as any Z'ensam. It had taken Lucy, an alien pervert, to remind C'astille of the horrible wrongness in what the *Starsight* was up to. "Lucy, there is something you must know. . . ."

Lucy broke all records getting across the clearing to *Reunion*. She tried using the suit radio to get word back that much quicker, but she was breathing too hard and the radio's range was too short for that.

She rushed through the airlock and collapsed in a corner, panting hard. She wrenched off her helmet, and the others gathered round.

She took a big gulp of air. "C'astille said that the damn Guards were fool enough to give the Nihilists a spacecraft. The Nihilists named her *Starsight* and launched her on a course that should have her on Capital later *today*—and C'astille is pretty damn sure *Starsight* is carrying a shipload of plague virus, and anything they'd develop would make the black death look like a bad cold. It'll wipe out every human on Capital—and let the Nihilists take over there."

All of them stood in shock for a moment. Mac was the first to respond. "How sure of this is she? How does she know?"

"The only hard fact she has is that *Starsight* launched. But she knows the way the Nihilists think, what their plans are. And why the hell else would they risk a flight in the middle of a war?"

Mac thought hard for a minute. "Cynthia, can you raise the League fleet at the barycenter, warn them, so maybe they can shoot her down?"

Cynthia shook her head. "Not with this ship's gear. Not

in a million years. All the frequencies are preset, and there's a scrambler built into the system. The only reason we could talk to Gustav was that we had the beacon modified for voice. And the portable radio we used to talk back to him just doesn't have the range."

"Can you get a beam strong enough and tight enough to hit Capital? Can we call one of their stations and warn them, let their ships do the job?"

"I think so."

"Mac! Wait a second," Pete said. "Gustav told us they had thrown every ship into the barycenter battle. And the way he talked, I think he meant *every* ship. Certainly, every *combatant* went. There may be nothing besides a few unarmed tugs left around Capital."

"Hold it," Mac said. "Let me get this all clear in my head: We can't contact *Ariadne* because it isn't there any more. We don't dare contact *Nike* Station. They just blew *Ariadne*—if we radio to them, they'll drop a bomb on us the moment they track the signal. And you can bet they won't listen to what we have to say. We can't contact the League. We *can* contact the Guard orbital stations, but they won't have any ships.

"Which boils down to the fact that this is the *only* ship in the whole double star system with any sort of chance of stopping *Starsight*."

CHAPTER FORTY

Reunion, Surface of Outpost

"Mac, yes, *Reunion* can make it," Joslyn said. "With the C^2 generator installed, we could be in the Capital system four hours after launch—but we don't have the codes or the signalling equipment that will let us through the anti-ship missile system *around* Capital. That system is still intact, don't forget."

"Won't it stop the Nihilist ship as well?" Charlie asked hopefully.

"No, the anti-ship missiles use a sensor that detects a ship's arrival from C^2 space," Mac said. "There's a very specific burst of radiation given off. They can probably control the missiles manually to attack a target moving through normal space, but *Starsight* is an invited guest. She had clearance, and she's probably inside the defense shell already, where the missiles can't get to her. And once she's inside the defense shell, they probably will have trouble tracking her. She could change course and vanish from their screens."

"Can we radio them, tell them to shut off the system, and then go in?" Pete asked.

"Who'd listen to us? Who'd believe us?" Cynthia asked. " 'Hey guys, let down your last line of defenses just after we've smashed your fleet so we can rescue you. Honest, it's not a trick.' "

"I can think of one guy who'd believe us," Mac said quietly. "Or at least believe *me*."

"Mac!" Joslyn said. "Not George. He's somewhere around Capital, yes, but he's there because he *betrayed* us!"

"I don't believe that," Mac said firmly. "No offense, but I know George. Gustav must have gotten it wrong. And even if it's true, that means he betrayed the *League*, not me. He's my friend, he'll know I wouldn't lie."

"But how could we know he'd hear it? How do we know he could convince anyone else?" Joslyn asked.

"We don't. But do you have any better ideas? And if the Nihilists get Capital, they'll have ships and material and technology and starmaps—they'll be able to drop plagues onto League worlds two weeks from now. Unless someone else has an idea, we've got no choice but to try it."

No one said anything for a while.

"I guess we have to chance it, Mac," Charlie said quietly.

Ten minutes later, Cynthia, Mac, Joslyn, and Lucy were at work in the control room.

"There's a big problem," Mac said. "We have to give the radio signal time to cross from here to Capital. We're twelve billion kilometers away—it'll be nearly twelve hours until they get the message. If we wait for a reply, confirming that the way is open, that's at least *another* twelve hours—and we can't afford to wait. The damn Nihilists will be there by then."

"So we send the signal," Joslyn said, "then wait twelve hours—plus, say two—to give them time to think about it and shut down the system, and then launch. No, wait half a tick—we'll have to boost well away from Outpost before we're far off enough to use C^2. We can subtract about four hours. So we launch ten hours after we send the signal."

"That's a hell of a big risk," Cynthia said.

Lucy shrugged. "We're taking a lot of risks already. And by rights all of us should be dead twenty ways each by now. I don't see we have any choice. Do it. We send the message, figure our course, and *go*."

"Okay, I guess I'm the one to do the talking," Mac said. "I want to send an audio message rather than text, so George can recognize my voice."

"Let me set up the recorder," Cynthia said. "Okay, everyone else keep quiet. Mac—go."

He took a deep breath and thought before he began. What to say? What words were strong enough to convince George, strong enough to convince anyone else who happened to hear it if he didn't?

"This is Terrance MacKenzie Larson, calling George Prigot or anyone else in the Capital star system. George: I trust you. I don't know why you are where you are, but I have faith in you. I know you would never deliberately do anything to harm me, or any other person. I ask you to trust me, as you have many times in the past.

"There is a Nihilist ship coming toward you. She intends to land on Capital and release a deadly plague into the ecosystem. The plague will kill everyone on the planet. You should know by now the Nihilists are willing and able to do such things. If you have ships that can find her and stop her, use them, do it—stop her, whatever it costs.

"But I know your fleet has been wrecked in the war, and probably left you without combat pilots or ships. I cannot contact the League fleet and get them to stop the Nihilists. The ship I am in, *Reunion*, might just be able to do the job. But it can't get through your anti-ship defenses. I ask you to shut down those defenses two hours after this message arrives. We will have no way of knowing if you have shut down the defenses. *Reunion* will launch toward you in any event, and those of us aboard will simply have to trust that you have opened the way. If you haven't, the missiles will get us, a quick and painless death.

"But if *Starsight* isn't stopped, everyone on Capital will die. And they will not die pleasantly.

"I trust you. I beg of you to trust me. The war between

us is over. Please let us help you. For God's sake, shut down the missile screen and let us in!"

Some hours later, C'astille watched the pillar of flame that was *Reunion* roar into the sky. They were gone. They might die. But her world, she herself, would never be the same. Change was like the Nihilist plague—infectious.

"Good luck, my odd little halfwalkers," she whispered.

CHAPTER FORTY-ONE

Zeus **Station, Orbiting Capital**

Phillips shut off the recorder and stared across his desk at George. "That came in fifteen minutes ago. We have about another fifteen minutes left until we have to send the shut-down signal, since the actual anti-ship missiles are about ninety light minutes away. So. Ignoring the question of how he knows you're here, ignoring the fact that Larson somehow knew the top-secret fact that *Starsight* was enroute, and has been since before the battle began, ignoring the fact that *Starsight* is overdue, ignoring a hundred other things my suspicious Intelligence officer's mind thinks of, *do you trust and believe this Larson?*"

George squirmed in the visitor's chair and felt the cold sweat of fear pouring out of his body. He was just a dumb engineer who liked playing with gadgets and didn't like to see people get hurt. Now he was mixed up in the fate of worlds. And, intentionally or not, he *had* betrayed Mac and the League. George *knew*, deep down in his gut, that League people had died because of his run for Capital. Who could blame Mac if he did scheme for revenge, if this was all an elaborate plot to get the Capital defenses down so the League fleet could pour through and bomb the planet down to radioactive cinders? The League had just demonstrated they could and would blow up a planet. If George wrongly trusted Mac, Capital was a corpse of a world.

But this was *Mac*. And if George wrongly *dis*trusted Mac, Capital was just as doomed by the Nihilist plague. George was plenty ready to believe they could invent a disease that could wipe everyone out. The risks were equally balanced.

And then, suddenly, in the middle of his knot of fear and turmoil, George found his answer. George could kill millions if he answered either way and was wrong. He had no control over that. But he, and only he, had control over whether he had faith in people. And if Mac was telling the truth, then Mac was deliberately putting his life in George's hands.

George decided he could live with himself, somehow, if millions died because he made an honest mistake. But he couldn't live with himself if he let a friend down. You had to have a little faith in people. Admiral Thomas had scrawled that across the bottom of George's Britannic Navy commission papers. Well, if he had betrayed the admiral's trust, here was the time to make amends.

"I trust Mac Larson," George said in a strong, firm voice that was nonetheless near tears. "I would, and do, trust Terrance MacKenzie Larson with my life and the life of every human being on this planet."

Phillips stared hard at George, and realized the fifty-fifty odds, the head-or-tails gamble with the fate of Capital was now in his hands.

Then Phillips remembered that he trusted George Prigot. Trust was trust—there was no middle ground to it, no way to water it down and have it be any use to anyone. He reached out and picked up the intercom phone. "Get me the defense control room," he said.

Both men felt a great burden rise off their shoulders. It was up to others now.

Aboard *Reunion*, En Route from Outpost to Capital

Lucy had *seen* it, seen it with her own eyes through the computer-aimed long-range camera, as *Reunion* headed for deep space. *Ariadne* was still there in orbit, nothing but the bloody comm antennae gone! She spent the long hours of boost celebrating that, deep in her heart, Johnson Gustav was alive!

Joslyn snuck another quick peek at Lucy, and smiled. Joz was pretty good at reading expressions, and true love was an easy one to spot. And it did tend to crop up in the oddest times and places.

But there was other work now. They were well clear of Outpost, far enough from her gravity well to make the jump. When Joslyn hit one last button, the computer would take over and fling them across C^2, to whatever awaited them. "Mac," she said, "it's now or never. We go?"

Mac's face was stern and solemn, and he was an honest enough man to let a little fear show through as well. But he looked at his lovely wife and grinned—a brave, open smile, because living with love and courage and faith was the only worthwhile way *to* live. "We go. I love you, Joz."

"And I love you, Mac. Always." She had to blink away the tears as she hit the button.

The bootleg C^2 box beneath the lower deck grabbed at space around *Reunion*, carried the ship for an incredibly brief moment, and dropped them down deep inside the Capital system.

Mac shushed the cheer that came from Charlie and Pete in the lower cabin. "Hold the applause down there!" he shouted. "We've got at least ten minutes before we're sure the missiles aren't coming."

"Screw that, Mac," Pete's voice came back. "If the missiles come for me, they'll catch me while I'm glad I'm alive!"

Joslyn powered up the radar. The Guards knew right where they were anyway, and trying to hide wouldn't exactly inspire confidence. "Space is clear as best I can tell, Pete. Go ahead and cheer."

"Cynthia," Mac called, "use the radio and tell the Guards

to kick in the defense screen again, just to prove we're sincere."

"Will do, Mac."

Mac turned to the two hot pilots, Joslyn and Lucy, trying to be cool, calm, rational. There was far too much at stake to for him to get excited and make a wrong move. "Okay, here we are. And since we're not a radioactive cloud, we must be doing something right. So, how do we find *Starsight*?"

"And, short of ramming, how do we stop them?" Joslyn asked. "We have lasers if we get within range for them, but no torps or any other sort of weapons."

"I was afraid you'd bring that up," Mac said, in what he hoped was a cheerful sounding voice. "But one thing at a time—we've gotta find them first. Lucy. Try and think like a Nihilist. Never been in space before, probably getting your plots from a Guard astrogator who knows the straight-line route takes you right though the barycenter and the battle zone. Where do you go? What's your flight path?"

Lucy shut her eyes and concentrated. "I'd say they'd tend to a very simple and conservative route, and also assume they'd change course somewhere along the line. That way, if the Guards got wind of them, they'd still have a chance to avoid interception. But they can't have any very sophisticated ideas about how to hide in space. Which makes waiting until the Guards are busy elsewhere very smart. If the Guards were in any shape to fly, the Nihilists wouldn't have a chance." Lucy powered up the tactical display and fiddled with a joy stick to sketch things in as Mac and Joslyn watched on their repeaters. "I'd say put us *here*. I figure they'd head in *this* way, looping back to come in straight over the southern hemisphere. It brings them in right over the populated areas to give the plague a chance, and they don't approach the planet straight from Outpost. But that's a long-odds guess, Mac. No guarantees."

"But it makes sense, and we've been on the long end of the odds for quite a piece now. Do it. Put us there, and we watch and wait."

Starsight

The long journey down the space Road was nearly at an end. The lovely globe of Capital grew in the viewscreen. It was time to slow the ship. L'etmlich swung the ship around and fired the fusion engine.

Reunion

"Fusion light!" Cynthia cried, after hours of watching a screen that showed nothing. It had been a long and wearing wait. "Lucy, go in for xenopsychology—they're headed almost right down the path you figured."

"Range and rate!" Joslyn demanded.

"Stand by, still tracking. But they lit awfully close. Hang on, getting a doppler. Okay, here come the numbers to your screen, Joslyn. Call it about seventy thousand kilometers from the planet and closing at five hundred klicks a second. If they hold course, they'll pass about twenty thousand klicks in front of us. Heavy gee-load, but I'll need a better track to give any good figures."

"Are our movements shielded by their fusion plume?"

"No way. We're in plain sight. But I don't get any active radar from them. I doubt they'll spot us unless we advertise. They're nearly in decent laser range."

Mac thought fast. If the lasers didn't work, the Nihilists would still be out there—and they'd know someone was gunning for them. But if they could take *Starsight* out here and now—"Lasers," he said, with more confidence than he felt. There were times he hated being a commanding officer.

Starsight

L'anijmeb shouted in surprise. The image of Capital in the viewscreen turned a bright, horrid red, and then the screen died altogether.

Romero would have jumped straight out of his crash couch, but for the safety harness. "Laser attack!" he cried. That terrible flash in the barycenter—that was the *League*.

They had won, and now they had taken over the skies of Capital itself. "Put the ship in a slow roll, spread the heat evenly! And pitch us around, run for the planet! Drop and get out of here!"

D'etallis almost told the human to shut up, but then she remembered who aboard knew the most about space, fool or not. "L'anijmeb. Do what it says. And kindly use the radar to find our attacker."

Reunion

"Damn it!" Cynthia cried. "Real even heat pattern. I think they're rolling the ship. Fusion light gone, radar on, they'll have spotted us for sure now. Whoa! Fusion light, right down our nose! Now they're running. Diving for the planet—accelerating instead of braking."

"Chase 'em, Joslyn!" Mac yelled. "Lucy! Crank up the damn lasers right into their fusion flame. Try to overheat them!"

Joslyn powered up *Reunion*'s own engines and quickly brought them up to full thrust. Slowly, they started to gain on the Nihilist ship. She watched the fusion light ahead of her on the scopes. She pitched up and back—hard, suddenly. *Starsight* had come about, trying to fry *Reunion* in her exhaust.

"Skin temps high and going up!" Cynthia shouted.

An alarm sounded, and Lucy slapped the cut-off. "Mac, we've lost the laser. I think we caught the edge of their fusion plume and that overheated it."

"Mac, how the hell do we play this one?" Joslyn yelled over the roar of the engines.

Sweet Jesus. Mac stared hard at the screen, and felt his heart hammering in his chest. Damn it, there was only one chance, no time to fiddle with this tactic or that. He had to call it right the first time. A stern chase was no good, not with these short ranges. All the advantages were with the pursued. But how to outguess an alien pilot? And they had to get that ship in space. If they chased her into the atmosphere, blowing *Starsight* up would probably serve to throw the plague germs into the atmosphere.

The planet was coming up fast now. Okay. Cool, calm, collected thought. Those were unexperienced pilots up ahead. Someone with lots of entry practice could take a ship down with all ship stresses shoved right up to the limit, but could a green jockey? "Run a hot-box on them, Joslyn. Put their backs to the wall on entry. Back off, then jump down their goddamned throats. Try and force them to dive too hot."

Starsight

L'anijmeb was scared. The planet as getting close, very close. They had to start braking *now* if they were to survive. D'anijmeb swung the ship around and started into the braking pattern. *Starsight* slowed her headlong rush. Gradually, all too gradually, she decreased her madcap speed to a sane level. Behind her, her pursuer matched her maneuver for maneuver, but hanging far back.

Now, *Starsight* was a bare one thousand kilometers above the cloud tops, and her pursuer was far above, no longer interfering. L'anijmeb didn't even know exactly how long a kilometer was, but that almost didn't matter. She just had to follow the meters, keep within the tolerance the Guards had taught her. Now nine hundred klicks. Eight hundred. She snorted nervously through her blowhole and wished endlessly that someone else could do this job. Seven hundred, six hundred klicks; five hundred, four hundred fifty, four hundred. Very close now, and maybe they had slowed enough.

Reunion

Mac watched the meters, the screens, the planet rising up around them. They were headed straight in. The Nihilists would have to keep braking if they were to survive.

But the same was true of *Reunion*.

"Do it, Joz," he said. "Rush 'em. Give it everything you have."

Starsight

D'etallis's face crinkled in pleasure. They had outrun them. They were nearly there. No point in even bothering to land. Three hundred klicks. They could fire the plague shell out the airlock while they were hovering. More effective, and probably safer all around—

That loathsome Romero screamed again, and pointed at the radar screen.

D'etallis's jaw dropped in horror.

The chase ship had reversed thrust again, and was diving, accelerating, straight for *Starsight*.

Reunion

Eight-gees. For a brief moment, nine. Watching her space-track and *Starsight* and her attitude and her skin temps all at once, Joslyn dove nose first for her enemy. The two ships closed at a terrifying rate, dead for each other. Split seconds from a crash, Joslyn spun ship one last time. There was no radar to guide her; she aimed her fusion flame by luck and feel.

And *Starsight*'s hull was clawed open by the heat of a sun's core. The tongues of starflame sliced through to the hydrogen tanks, bursting their pressure seals—the escaping hydrogen flaring into fusion itself. A tenth of a second later, what was left of the Nihilist ship exploded.

Reunion shook from stem to stern as she dove through the cloud of debris. Tiny fragments of the enemy ship bounced off her hull with terrifying reports, and suddenly *Reunion* was in the midst of atmospheric entry, pointed in the wrong attitude, moving at far too high a speed.

Joslyn held the engines to eight-gees, and felt their speed begin to die. Slowly, painfully, *Reunion* clawed its way back up into the dark of space, and scrabbled into a stable orbit. Joslyn cut the engines and started breathing again, staring at a status board with more red lights than green on it.

That was as close to ramming another ship as she ever wanted to get.

CHAPTER FORTY-TWO

Eagle

It was a week later when Pete Gesseti set off down the corridors of *Eagle*'s officer country, intent on barging into Admiral Thomas's stateroom. And it had been a *hell* of a week. Peace so far had been anything but peaceful. At least the trip back from Capital had been less nerve-racking than the trip out. The impromptu cease-fire that Thomas had ordered was holding, but negotiations were just about under way. Another three days and they'd settle on the shape of the table.

The Guards still had their defense screens around Outpost and Capital, but the League had the only intact fleet around and a decisive victory in its pocket. Conditions were right for cutting a deal. Pete had a hunch the Settlers, whoever exactly they were, were delaying things until this Jules Jacquet could be neatly deposed with the rest of the Central Guardians and they could move in.

Lucy Calder was champing at the bit to fly the rescue ship that would pick up the Survey Service CIs from *Ariadne*, and just incidentally reunite her with Johnson Gustav, once the anti-ship defense screens were down.

Pete was hoping and betting and expecting that Mac and Joslyn would call it quits from the military and settle

396

back to have some kids and name one of them Peter. But knowing the two of them, they'd probably outfit their own ship and have their kids out in space on the flip-side of nowhere.

George Prigot was probably going to end up as hero and villain to boot, for history books written by both sides. No one ever *had* known what to do with him. Another loose end. At the moment, it seemed that he was drawing pay from the Britannic Navy and the Guard Army at the same time. It would get worked out. That was what diplomats were used for after a war—to come in and tidy up the mess, somehow.

The Guards still held stocks of bioweapons. Pete had a feeling that they wouldn't last long. Pete had made it very clear to the officials on *Zeus* that the League would have two absolutely unnegotiable demands: repatriation of all Conscripted Immigrants (and any of their descendents who choose to leave), and the verified destruction of the bios. After what the *Starsight* had nearly done, the Guards didn't seem likely to argue.

When Thomas allowed an unarmed Guard lander (with a New Finn officer aboard to keep everyone honest) to make the transit from Capital to Outpost, they found every human soul at the Guardian Contact Camp was dead and rotting, massacred. The Nihilists themselves were nowhere to be found. They were out there on the planet somewhere, with their Guard-provided combat weapons. *They* would have to be dealt with.

And no one knew exactly what to do with the Outposters— no, the Z'ensam—in general. Pete was doing his best to learn the one known Outposter language quickly. Someone would have to negotiate with them. He hadn't made much progress there on his first trip to the planet, but the second time round he expected a more dignified journey than a crashlanding, a forced march, plus getting a chunk of his arm taken off and artificial blood put in. Pete, however, didn't want to be in *charge* of deals with the natives. Too much paperwork. No, he'd need a boss to take the flack and do all the dull ceremonial work.

And Pete knew himself well enough to know he'd need a boss of wisdom and experience, someone who might be able to understand the Z'ensam.

Which brought him to the point of his present visit. He arrived at Thomas's cabin.

Pete had gotten a key from somewhere and used it to walk in uninvited and unannounced. As expected, he found Thomas quietly pouring a good strong spine stiffener. As planned, Pete calmly walked up and knocked bottle and glass out of the admiral's hands and onto the deck.

"You not only just went on the wagon, you just decided to retire," Pete announced cheerfully.

"Mr. Gesset! How dare you barge in li—"

"How do I dare? Easy." Pete took the visitor's chair and settled back comfortably. "Work it out, admiral. It's time you hung up your gold braid. Oh, if you harrumph loud and long enough, they'd let you stay on. But to do what?"

"I hadn't quite had time to think about—"

"But I have. I'll tell you what I think. *I* think you're going to be the first League diplomatic representative to the Z'ensam. No one knows what the legal ramifications of diplomacy with aliens are. No one has had any time to make any up. But you and I are on the scene, so *we* get to make them up."

"Diplomatic representative?"

"Sort of an over-ambassador, is how I see the post. It'd be damn sloppy to have God knows how many League signatories each with their own ambassador, each following an uncoordinated policy. And on the other side, Lucy Calder estimates there are at least one hundred twenty major Groups to deal with. We'll need some centralized organization. And I like you for top man."

Thomas was trying hard to be angry at this cheeky upstart, but it was hard. "I see. And why should I fill this post?"

For the first time, Pete hesitated a moment. "I could

say because your grand victory here puts you in the public eye, would give you the prestige to do what has to be done. I could say you deserve it for the way you've fought this war. But though that would be true, it's only part of the reason. With all due respect, admiral, you should have this job because this job *demands* a tired, cynical, embittered old man."

Sir George almost lunged across the desk to bash Pete's face in, but Pete raised his hand, very gently, very slightly, and gestured for Sir George to sit down. There was something in Pete's tone and manner that forced the admiral to listen. Pete started to speak again, in a far more gentle voice. "By virtue of your unhappy life, you're the best qualified to understand the Z'ensam, admiral. Your until-recently undistinguished career, your rather advanced age, your fear of failure, your obvious search after oblivion in your heavy drinking. And think of what you've seen—the bioweapons, ships wrecked, an entire small world literally destroyed. You know what power, their kind and ours, can do when it goes rogue. You know we can avoid destroying ourselves and each other only if we make a conscious decision not to destroy. Both humans and Z'ensam must control *themselves*, for so much that we both do can escape our control.

"You've seen all that. And you see grand victories through eyes that have seen a lifetime of defeat and humiliation.

"And you've seen death. You understand how final death is, far better than any sleek young career diplomat could.

"Perhaps most importantly, admiral, only someone who has chased oblivion so hard and so long through the bottle could understand the Z'ensam's fear of losing themselves in Division.

"All that tempers your great successes here, gives you a sense of proportion. But here's a frightening fact: Failure is impossible now, admiral, because you've already won. I'd bet my life you've dreamed for generations about what you could do, given half the chance. Now you have the chance. Grab at it with both hands.

"Admiral, it's time to climb out of the bottle full time and take hold of the long hard work that your victories have won for you."

Thomas spluttered and felt himself ready to explode in anger, when the smell of the spilled liquor wafted its way to his nose. Suddenly he wanted, no, he *needed*, a little something. A soother, just a drop that would calm him and help him avoid this argument—

And at that moment, in that instant, for the first time, he really caught himself. For the first time, he didn't wave off his problem, or ignore it—he admitted it. Everything this snide young fellow was saying was true. Damn him. He ought to chase the little sod out, slam the door and get some peace and quiet, so he could—

—So he could what? Sir George looked at the broken bottle on the floor and knew how he had intended to complete that thought.

Damn the fellow for being right! The truth hurt. But—if Gesseti actually thought he could maneuver Thomas into that super-ambassadorship. . . . A post like that, with real work, a hundred lifetimes' work to keep him busy, keep him occupied, a job with endless challenges. . . . Thomas decided he didn't want that drink after all. Oh, of course Gesseti's schemes were all pie in the sky, one-in-a-thousand shots of coming off, but Sir George knew he'd gain more in trying and failing than he ever would in not trying at all.

"Mr. Gesseti," he said at last. "You are a very rude person, and I look forward to working with you. I am forced to admit I see your point. I must further admit that the job sounds a lot better than collecting dust in a corner office until I keel over stone dead from boredom. You will have my most energetic—and sober—cooperation.

"But you are taking a grave chance, Mr. Gesseti. You and I both know that. You just got through saying I'm a drunken old fool, who might just have finished his streak of luck. Granted, you might have read me right—there might just still be enough marbles clattering around upstairs for me to do the job. But you can't know that. No matter how much my background qualifies me, it also damns me as a likely flop. Why are you taking that risk with such important work?"

Pete grinned. Mission accomplished. The last of the war's tension went away, and he gladly said goodbye to the endless worrying and fear that had started when the *Venera* had vanished. Things were in six kinds of a mess around here, but that was the normal human condition. It was all going to be all right. " 'Why,' admiral? Because I have a real gut feeling you're the man for it. I really believe that. And there's another thing.

"When *Reunion* docked with *Zeus* Station and we were getting the first cease-fire worked out, I asked George Prigot why the *hell* he had trusted Mac with the fate of George's whole planet."

Pete stood up and got ready to go. The admiral rose from behind his desk. Pete offered his hand. The admiral took it, and asked "But what *did* Mr. Prigot say?"

Pete laughed out loud, shook the admiral's hand again, and opened the door to the corridor. "He said, if I might quote him, that 'You've got to have a little faith in people.' I wonder where he heard that?"

AUTHOR'S NOTE

As a second-generation novelist, I learned the great traditions of the publishing business at my father's knee. I watched as manuscript pages vanished, checks failed to materialize, and editors came and went faster than the seasons.

I saw editors extend to writers the same courtesy one might expect prison-camp guards to offer the inmates. I found that publishers had as great a willingness to provide information as the KGB. I saw decisions made and actions taken at a pace so leisurely that it could not be dignified with the term "glacial", for that word at least implies movement.

It is clear that Baen Books has no respect for tradition. This unknown writer has been treated with great kindness and patience; all my business dealing with Baen have been handled efficiently and promptly; and all schedules (except the ones that call for me to deliver manuscripts on time) have been kept. This is not only notable in publishing—it is almost scandalous: When my father heard that Baen refused to be bumbling, incompetent, and late, he muttered, "They'll never make it in this business." I am pleased to report that they are doing just fine.

There is another great publishing tradition that needs to be broken: the one that says fiction editors aren't credited.

Despite all the work a good editor puts into her writers' novels, her name is never seen inside the books she brings into creation. *My* editor deserves more credit than I can give her—for giving an unknown writer a chance, for being patient with an endless stream of letters that probably toted up to be longer than my books; for making exactly the right suggestions at exactly the right times; for the aforementioned promptness and courtesy; for decoding my typos; for generally giving me the pokes and the prods and the encouragement that make it possible to write. And, most importantly, for starting out as a business associate and ending up a friend.

So let me break that tradition here and now: This book, I am proud to say, was edited by Elizabeth Mitchell.

Thanks, Betsy.

RMA
August, 1985
Washington, D.C.

Here is an excerpt from Roger MacBride Allen's next novel, THURSDAY'S CHILD, *coming in 1987 from Baen Books:*

Dr. Jeffery Grossington, Associate Secretary for Anthropology at the National Museum of Natural History and Man, Smithsonian Institution, Washington, D.C., was a man well suited to a position with such a long and ponderous title. He had the character traits a man engaged in the study of the long-dead past needed: slow, deliberate, careful thought processes; the patient willingness to sift through minute bits of evidence and fragile shards of bone for one tiny fragment of meaning; the capacity to build knowledge out of mystery; the imagination and vision to understand what the rare, tiny clues scrabbled out of the earth could tell of human ancestry. But of all his skills, virtues, and talents, Jeffery Grossington was certain that the greatest of them all was patience.

Students of other scientific disciplines might feel compelled to compete in a race against time, against constrained budgets, against colleagues who might be hot on the trail of the same discovery, but not Grossington. That sort of nonsense (he believed) didn't have any place in paleoanthropology (though many of his fellows would have disagreed). After all, the persons of interest to Grossington's studies had all died thousands or millions of years ago; their bones could wait a day or a year or a decade more before revealing their secrets. Rush made for errors; cautious deliberation and painstaking care were the hallmarks of his work. There was simply no *need* for a good paleoanthropologist to scurry manically toward conclusions.

Indeed, he strongly disapproved of rush, or commotion, or *any* sort of urgency—and suspected that most hurry was not only unneeded, but quite often detrimental. Outright frantic activity infuriated him.

Fortunately, he was also slow to anger, or else when Barbara burst that morning into his office there would have been hell to pay.

She all but bounded into the room, grinning ear to

desk, her whole face shining with enthusiasm. "The end, Jeffery. The end of so many searches. *That's* what in there. Maybe even the collapse of every existing theory of human evolution. *Open* it."

Grossington swallowed hard and undid the cord. He lifted the worn black-lacquer top off the octagonal box and set it aside. There was a layer of shredded bits of foam rubber hiding the contents proper, and Grossington removed the bits of padding carefully, one by one. Years of field work had made slow and careful work a matter of reflex action for him. He wanted to make sure there was no danger of his damaging whatever-it-was by moving too fast.

Gradually, as he dug it out from under the bits of padding, he could *see* what it was: a skull, a human skull, a fully intact cranium and mandible, all the teeth intact, every detail fully present and preserved.

And then he looked again, and saw more, and his eyes widened in shock: hominid, yes—but it was not human.

Grossington could feel his heart starting to pound, the sweat coming out on his forehead as he carefully, oh so carefully, removed the prize from the hatbox.

The prominent sagittal crest, the huge, flat molars, the human-like canine teeth, the box-shaped dental arcade, the obvious positioning of the skull's balance point to allow for an erect, bipedal gait. The prominent, exaggerated brow ridges—a dozen, a hundred things that spoke, even shouted, the impossible. This was an *Australopithicine*, a member of a hominid species that had died out a million years ago.

But this was no fossil. This was *bone*, not the mineralized shadow of bone; none of the once-living material of this skull had leached away to be replaced by other matter. What he held in his hands was the actual, true, once-living matter, browned and leached and stained and weakened by time, but still formerly living bone—and of recent vintage. Not so long ago, these bones had been as alive as Grossington himself.

Grossington stared at the grinning skull, mesmerized, for a long time. Finally he spoke. "When and where, ear, and charged straight toward his desk. He should have immediately given her a good tongue-lashing, but she had the element of surprise working for her. No one in the history of Grossington's tenure had ever dreamed of barging into his office like that. Dr. Grossington opened his mouth to offer an infuriated rebuke, but he never got the chance. Before he could react to the intrusion, Barbara compounded her offense by scooping up his coffee tray and placed it none too carefully on a sidetable, sweeping all the papers from the center of his desk, and vanishing back out into the hall, only to return a moment later carrying, of all things, an old-fashioned wooden hatbox.

Suddenly moving with great care and deliberation, she set the box down most gently on the exact center of his desk blotter, and stepped back to stand in front of his desk, like a student waiting for the teacher to examine her science project.

"Dr. Marchando, what the devil is the—" But Dr. Jeffery Grossington stopped himself in mid-outburst and took a good hard look at Barbara. She was flushed, excited, and her dark brown face was alight, exhilarated. Her eyes gleamed, her hair was dishevelled, her makeup was blurred and smeared, her clothes, which she normally kept up so carefully, were wrinkled, mussed-up, and looked as if they had been slept in for a day or two. All of which was totally out of character for the prim, careful Dr. Marchando.

"Well, open it, Dr. Grossington," she said. "Aren't you going to open it?" she asked breathlessly. "I've been travelling all last night and the whole day before— bus, train, plane, taxi—to get it to you. *Open* it!"

He looked at her curiously, and his big, callused, well-manicured hands moved involuntarily toward the cord that held the lid of the box. He hesitated, much unnerved, and looked hard at the hatbox, as if he feared it might contain a bomb. Then he looked to Barbara. He had a nasty feeling things in his world were about to turn upside down. "Barbara, what's *in* here?"

She grinned, almost wild-eyed, and leaned over the

Dr. Marchando," he managed to say at last, very quietly. "How old is this, and where in heaven's name does it come from?"

"Sir, that skull—and the well-preserved *complete* skeleton found with it—were buried—deliberately, ritualistically buried—140 years ago. In Alabama, U.S.A."

Grossington sat there, stunned. "How? How could that possibly *be*?"

"I don't know, sir, I honestly don't know. But I have a very strong hunch—and some evidence—that our friend here has some living relatives still around, if we knew where to look." For the first time, the excitement went out of Barbara's voice, to be replaced by something else, something mixed of awe, and fear, and wonder. She reached out and touched the face of the musty skull. "After finding this, I no longer think we're the only hominid species currently living on this planet."

BAEN BOOK CLUB ANNOUNCES THE ADVANCE PLAN

The Very Best in Science Fiction and Fantasy
at Super Savings

BUILD A LIBRARY OF THE NEWEST AND MOST EXCITING SCIENCE FICTION & FANTASY PUBLISHED

Having trouble finding *good* science fiction and fantasy? Want to build up your library without tearing down your bank account? Sign up for Baen Book Club's Advance Plan and enjoy super savings on the world's finest selection of science fiction and fantasy.

NEW BOOKS, HIGH QUALITY, LOW PRICE

With the Advance Plan, you'll receive 6 to 8 *new* paperback books every two months—the very best from your favorite science fiction and fantasy writers—*as they are published*. All books are new, original publisher's editions, and you pay only half the cover price (paperback cover prices range from $2.95 to $3.95). There are no additional costs—no postage or handling fees.

SAVE EVEN MORE ON HARDCOVER EDITIONS

To increase your savings, you may choose to receive all hardcovers published by Baen Books, at the same half price deal. With this option, you receive all paperbacks and hardcovers. (Hardcovers are published six to eight times per year, at cover prices ranging from $14.95 to $18.95.)

Sign up today. Complete the coupon below and get ready for the biggest and brightest in science fiction and fantasy.

Yes, I wish to take advantage of the Baen Book Club Advance Plan. I understand that I will receive new science fiction and fantasy titles published in paperback by Baen Books every two months (6 to 8 new books). I will be charged only one-half the cover price for books shipped, with no additional postage or handling charges. Charges will be billed to my credit card account. I may opt to receive hardcover as well as paperback releases by checking the box below. I may cancel at any time.

If you wish to receive hardcover releases as well as paperback books, please check here: [ ]

Name   (Please Print)

Address

City

State   Zip Code

Signature

VISA/MasterCard Number   Expiration Date

MAIL TO:
Baen Book Club
260 Fifth Avenue, Suite 3-S
New York, NY 10001

Please allow three to six weeks for your first order.